D0042041

THE
GATEKEEP

THE
GATEKEEPERS

JEN LANCASTER

ISBN-13: 978-0-373-21261-3

The Gatekeepers

HARLEQUIN®TEEN
www.HarlequinTEEN.com

Printed in U.S.A.

For Officer Bob Heelan of the LFPD–
thank you for your thirty years of service to this community

THE
GATEKEEPERS

AYSO Youth Sports, North Shore.

OBITUARIES

Paul "Paulie" Barat, age 17, a North Shore High School junior and cherished son of Henry Barat and Merle Sloan-Barat, died suddenly on Saturday, May 28, in North Shore. He's survived by his parents and his younger sister, Anna. A gifted actor, Paulie participated in NSHS's musical theater productions, senior one-act plays, and variety shows, and won the Illinois State speech team titles in both Humorous Interpretation and Original Comedy. His joyful personality and captivating laugh will be eternally missed. Visitation will be held from 5 to 9 p.m. Monday, May 30th, at the Good Shepherd Methodist Church at 191 Oakley Road in North Shore. The funeral service will be held at 11 a.m. Tuesday, May 31, at Good Shepherd, with interment to immediately follow at North Shore Memorial Gardens, South Quadrant. In lieu of flowers, the family requests that donations in honor of Paulie be made to the Paul Barat Memorial Fund, c/o North Shore Thespians.

the Paul Barat Memorial Fund.

OBITUARIES

Macey Lund, age 18, of North Shore, passed away on July 17th. Loving daughter of Therese and Geoffrey; sweet sister of Knox and Langley. A seasoned athlete, Macey led the Lady Knights to capture the Illinois Division I Soccer Championship and was blessed to perform her beloved Irish dance on three continents, including special presentations for Pope Francis and Queen Elizabeth. Memorial Service to be held Wednesday, July 20th, 3:15 p.m. at the Church of Christ, 212 West Wisconsin Ave., North Shore. Info: Harper and Horvath Funeral Home, North Shore. Interment will be private. In lieu of flowers, the family requests donations in her name to AYSO Youth Sports, North Shore.

1

―――

MALLORY
GOODMAN

SEVENTY-ONE, SEVENTY-TWO, SEVENTY-THREE.
Harder.
Faster.
You can do it, I tell myself. *You have to do it.*
Seventy-four, seventy-five.
*Stop being the kind of lard-ass who let her boyfriend pressure her
into scarfing down onion rings.* "They're *so* good," he'd insisted.
"Extra salty, really crispy. They're the perfect balance of light
batter and onion, like tempura. The chef brought his A-game
to the deep fryer. You'll be sorry if you don't at least try one."

Whenever our squad wants to meet for dinner, I suggest a
place with a salad bar. I always eat the same thing—a blend
of arugula and romaine, shredded carrots, red cabbage, diced
peppers, and celery sticks, tossed in lemon juice, with a side
of fat-free ranch dressing. If I've been good, I grab a grape-
fruit or an apple for dessert at home.

Obviously, I wasn't good last night.

Liam wouldn't let it go, though. He leaned across the table,
doing that baby-feeding, airplane-in-the-hangar move with

the onion ring, complete with sound effects. Everyone in the whole restaurant started looking at us. Sure, they're always looking at us, because Liam's kind of our school's Golden Boy, but last night they were seriously staring. The easiest thing was to open up and just eat the stupid, greasy thing. So I chewed and smiled when all I wanted to do was to spit it into my napkin—but I'd never hear the end of it if I did that.

I swear Jasper Gates was ready to search inside my mouth afterward to make sure I'd actually swallowed, like on those cheesy survival game shows where the host verifies contestants downed the whole worm. Jasper was the one who demanded I eat another, because the first one was "too small." Sitting there, all kicked back and smarmy in his obnoxious plaid shorts and Ray-Bans, I wanted to smack him. Who wears sunglasses inside at night? We're in Illinois, not LA. And my diet is Jasper's business *how exactly*? Do I get on him for the stupid loafers he insists on wearing without socks, even when it's snowing?

Can you believe he actually *wonders* why I call him the JasHole?

Ugh, I hate Liam's friends.

Seventy-six, seventy-seven.

I dig in my heels and try to spring up even more quickly as I run the stadium steps for the third time. My pulse quickens inside my chest.

Okay.

That's more like it.

My brother Theo and his best friend, Braden, turned me on to running the stairs, something their football coach makes them do first thing in the morning during the season. That way they can spend the afternoon drilling on the field or weight training for their two-a-days. Kids at other schools can't believe how much our teams practice. They always say this *after* we've beaten them, so you tell me who's got it right.

One twenty-one. One twenty-two.

Well, *most* of us believe in all the practice.

Ahem, *Liam.*

First, he makes me ingest a fatty carb bomb and then he doesn't even show to run the stairs with me this morning? He claimed he hurt his knee playing ultimate Frisbee after soccer practice yesterday. Last night, the JasHole was all, "You should give it a rest, brah. Don't want to be a gimp when the season starts. Take it easy."

Well, guess what, Liam?

Winners *walk it off.*

Winners play through the pain, *brah.*

Winners make time to run the stairs, each day, every day, even those days when they know they'll be up until 2:00 a.m. writing their final AP Italian theme on *Il pendolo di Foucault.*

I keep going.

I mean, my calves feel like they're on fire right now, like they're being poked with burning hot knives, but the discomfort's just spurring me on.

Go. Run faster.

I make it to the top and sprint back down the steps double-time. I don't count the stairs on the way down; that's considered rest.

Rest is for the weak.

Three hundred. Three hundred and one. Three hundred and two.

Move it, Calorie Mallory. Get your fat ass up those steps. Knees up. Knees up to the chest. More. Do more.

I ask myself, *Do you think the New Trier Trevians ate onion rings last night? Hell, no. Did the Lake Forest Scouts wolf down fro-yo last week? Doubtful.*

Hustle. Now.

I glance at my iWatch. All right, I'm in the zone. I'm at 95 percent of my target heart rate. I'm a finely tuned machine, burning off serious blubber. *Keep it up.*

Five hundred forty-nine. Five hundred fifty. Five fifty-one.

I'm sweating now, but that's good because sweat is fat crying for mercy.

I mean, why would Liam slam on the brakes now? Why would he look for an excuse to slack? Our senior year starts Monday.

This is the time to go balls-out.

We haven't reached the summit. There's no time to coast. We're coming up on the hardest part of our twelve-year academic climb—applying to college.

Now is when we show the world what we're made of.

Now is when we prove we have the right stuff for Princeton's early decision.

Now is when we lay the groundwork for our senior year.

Liam and I spent the past couple of months honing our skills at our camps, getting in our volunteer hours, and doing our extra coursework so that we'll to be ready to kill our exams and nab our respective state championships when classes start. Winning those matching Homecoming King and Queen crowns come October wouldn't hurt, either, because that would show that we're social as well as athletic and academic.

We're the full package. We're hashtag *BarbieandKen.*

Which is why we have to push ourselves harder *right now.*

I don't want to give up. Quitting? Not an option. I remember what happened over the summer with Paulie and Macey, and I feel like I've swallowed glass, like I'm all slashed up inside. They had everything…until they decided they didn't, so

14

they gave up. Stopped fighting. Braden speculates that maybe they both burned so brightly, flaming out was inevitable.

I refuse to accept that.

So I need to be strong. I need to be hard. That's why I'm not even allowing myself a drink of water until I hit my first one thousand steps.

I give myself a gut-check. *Are you tired, Mallory? Do you want to surrender? Yeah? That's because you're not reaching your full potential. You're at a B-minus of effort right now, and that's an unweighted grade, non-honors track. Your performance doesn't even merit a state school, let alone Ivy League early decision. What are you going to do, end up somewhere mortifying like the University of Iowa, with all the slackers? NO. You've sacrificed for this. You've earned this. Claim what's yours.*

I step it up.

I push and pump my arms.

Explode. Off. Each. Step.

I won't give up.

I can't flame out.

I harness the energy inside of me.

I go harder and higher.

Senior year starts in three days.

And I will be ready.

2

STEPHEN
CHO

"SO THIS IS your homerun swing?"

I don't reply.

Kent persists. "Walking back and forth in front of the new girl's house in the broiling sun 'til she notices you?"

The beads of sweat dotting his upper lip give him the illusion of having a mustache.

Yeah, he *wishes*.

"Trust in the process," I assure him. As we approach her house, I slow my pace so drastically, it's like we're suddenly a couple of senior citizens mincing along behind our walkers.

"I *trusted* in the process an hour ago, back before my Chucks were melting into the asphalt." He points at his black Converse. "Now I just want to strip down to my underwear and lie on an air conditioning vent. I wanna mainline a pony keg of Gatorade."

I attempt to explain my rationale again. "She's gonna notice us out here. She's gonna notice us and then she's gonna invite us in, at which point we're gonna be charming and shit and it'll all happen from there," I say. "My plan is foolproof."

Kent tugs at his vintage Run-D.M.C. Adidas T-shirt, which is now drenched in perspiration and clinging to his narrow frame like a second skin.

"Please. Your 'plan' is the opposite of foolproof." Kent makes air quotes with his fingertips when he says the word *plan*. "This is the worst 'plan' in the history of 'plans.' If this 'plan' were in World War II, this would be your Stalingrad. PS, you're the Germans losing 330,000 men in this scenario, *not* the Soviet resistance. Pretty sure MENSA's revoking your membership over said 'plan.'"

Kent's probably right, but I refuse to admit it. See, I'm so desperate to meet this girl that I don't even care. While it sounds premature, I have a good feeling about her and I can already tell she's different in all the right ways. (I'm not psychic. My mom had the 411 long before the first moving truck arrived. She's not only on the Homeowners' Association but she's also the Realtor who listed the house.)

I've been thinking about this girl ever since I heard she existed. Scoop is, the family's here from London and the mom's writing some book about the suburbs. Maybe one of those coffee-table books, wide and thick, with as many pictures as words? North Shore makes total sense because nowhere is more suburban than here.

I'm serious—we should be listed in Wikipedia under "suburbs" because this town elevates the suburbs game to a whole new level. Peace and quiet? Check. Amazing school system? Check. Lots of natural beauty and green space? Check. Nonexistent crime stats? Check.

Beyond that, North Shore sets rules on how things should look. Image is everything up here. For example, like every other suburban town, we have a McDonald's. However, there are no golden arches out front of ours, 'cause someone decided that would be tacky. Instead, there's a small, tasteful wooden sign posted amid a bunch of wild roses. Also, the restaurant's housed in a big green Shaker-style barn, with columns and white-paned windows.

It's weird.

The town's as strict with home standards as it is with businesses. Like, no one's allowed to chop down trees on their own property without a permit, so every home is surrounded by lots of old-growth oaks. Most of the houses, especially those close to the lake like ours, sit on two or three acres. (Ask me how much this sucked when we used to trick or treat. We wanted *candy*, not cardio.)

Basically, North Shore's nothing but big ol' houses on huge green lawns, yogurt shops, and fancy, useless designer boutiques. I hate having go all the way up to Gurnee or Libertyville to buy comic books, yet there's three places downtown to pick up a two-hundred-dollar sweater for your purse dog. I'd be all, *Who wants that stuff?*

Except I know at least ten people who would.

Anyway, the new family bought the Barat house, which is why I feel conflicted about being excited that they're here. I hadn't talked to Paulie much since junior high, or hung out with him since grade school, but it's still really sad. My mom, who's usually totally in the know, isn't 100 percent sure where the Barats went. Their attorneys handled the sale because the family hauled ass out of North Shore ASAFP.

I can't blame them.

The new girl's dad is this world-famous, super-eccentric British artist with a man-bun. I looked up a lot of his stuff online. He's always doing these avant-garde art installations, often so bizarre they end up on the news. I read a listicle on BuzzFeed about him. The piece that stuck out most was his exhibit in Burundi, a country where something like 75 percent of all the residents are undernourished. The guy built a replica of McDonald's golden arches out of bags of liposuctioned fat as a statement about global inequality.

What did that even smell like once the sun hit it?

(FYI, his piece was not shaped like a Shaker-style barn.)

My point is, no one's like that here in North Shore; no one has that kind of social conscience.

No one's super-eccentric.

No dads have man-buns, that's for damn sure.

The girl's name is Simone and she's my age and on her Instagram, she's smokin' hot, but not in a fake, plastic-y way like everyone else in this town. Maybe that's because her mom was a famous model. Simone's got this long, coffee-colored wavy hair that's shaved on one side and she kind of dresses like a vocalist from a '70s rock group. The times I've spied her from the street, she's been wearing lots of scarves and bangles and other cool stuff that definitely does not come from J. Crew.

Simone has a casual elegance, like a Disney princess who doesn't know what she is because an evil queen gave her amnesia and forced her to live in the forest. She strikes me as worldly and wise and chill, deep and interesting in a way that all the brittle future sorority girls in my school are not. She definitely doesn't seem like the type of girl who'd eviscerate you for the cardinal sin of asking her to a middle school mixer, leaving you shamefaced and speechless in the middle of the cafeteria, too terrified to ever try again.

Kent says no one could have possibly have drawn these opinions, nobody could have come up with all these positive character traits by simply *walking past her house.*

I maintain that *he* couldn't because he has no imagination;

20

he's too linear in his thinking. That's also why I always beat him at chess.

I wouldn't expect him to understand my fascination with Simone. He's been obsessed with this generic blonde goddess named Mallory since grade school. I bet Mallory wouldn't even bother to spit on him if he were on fire, but I keep that to myself. Kent soldiers on in his relentless pursuit, hope springing eternal. He kind of reminds me of a dog chasing a car when it comes to Mallory—he's never going to catch the vehicle and he'd have no clue what to do with it if he did, but damned if he ever stops running behind it.

While he might whine about stalking Simone, he's helping me anyway.

"There's no fluid left in me—I sweated it all out. I'm literally leeching salt at this point," Kent complains. He swipes his forehead and rubs his fingers against his palm. I hear the grit when he scrapes his hand against itself but pretend I don't.

He says, "Seriously, bro, there's a crust on my brow. Come on, Stephen… It's over. Give it up. Let's head to the beach. I wanna go walk directly into the lake, like, shoes and all, I don't even care."

I need to admit defeat.

And yet…

"One more pass?" I want this to sound like a command, a marching order, but my words come out more plaintive than planned.

He narrows his eyes and stares me down for a solid thirty seconds. "You suck."

I guess plaintive worked.

We turn at the corner for our final walk-by when we see her garage door opening in the distance. Like Botticelli's *Birth of Venus*, Simone comes into focus from the darkness of the garage, her form slowly revealed as the door inches upward, only instead of being surrounded by angels while naked astride a clamshell (my preference), she's standing in front of a mountain of cardboard, buttressed by recycling bins.

She is the embodiment of divine love, august gold, wreathed and beautiful, clad in the heavenly raiment of a baggy, tie-dyed overall dress.

Oh, yes. She will be mine.

"You said that out loud, dude," Kent tells me. "You may want to work on keeping your internal monologue, you know, *internal.*"

Simone spots us and waves.

"Check it out, she's waving!" Kent says, shielding his eyes with his hand as he squints down the long, curved, sun-drenched driveway. Every house in our 'hood is set back from the curb no less than one-tenth of a mile. (Again, this *blew* at Halloween. Batman shouldn't have to wear gym shoes.)

Kent continues, "No, that's not a wave. She's gesturing for us to come up to her garage. Yes! *Score!* You know, I doubted you, Cho. I did. Thought we were wasting our time, but you proved me wrong. Get up there and claim your woman. 'Bout time something *good* happened around here." He gives me a small push in her direction.

"Walk faster," I hiss, my heart beginning to race like a hamster on a wheel. "Actually, *run.*"

Kent comes to a dead stop. "Aw, *hell* no. Not this again. I am not walking faster and I'm sure as shit not running. I did not just sweat out half my body weight going back and forth for you to wuss out when you finally get your chance to talk to her. You wanted her to see you? Mission accomplished. Get your ass up there and *have a conversation.* 'Cause I'm done here. We have less than a week left before school starts and the last thing I wanna do is stand in the blazing hot street for one more second. Now, I'm going for a swim and you're gonna go work your magic. Text you later."

He walks toward the wooded path that leads to the residents-only beach on Lake Michigan a couple of blocks away while I stand frozen by her mailbox.

I want to talk to her. I do.

I want to work my magic.

I want to so badly…but I just can't.

Maybe Kent's not the dog who's caught the car. Maybe it's me.

I open my mouth to try to explain but the words won't come out.

Kent's a whole house away when he glances over his shoulder. He sees that I haven't moved. He looks at a bemused Simone—she's still midwave—and then at me. With a small shake of his head, he jogs back over. He's out of breath by the time he reaches me.

Grudgingly, Kent says, "I could probably be your wingman for a few more minutes." Relief washes over me and I'm able to move again. We start walking up the drive together.

He asks, "How is it that you're both the smartest *and* the dumbest guy in our school?"

I shrug.

If I knew, then I'd tell him.

3

———

KENT
MATHERS

"YOU ARE COMING across as a fucking lunatic right now, you hear me?"

Stephen won't look at me.

I tell him, "You don't seem like someone walking up to introduce himself to a girl he's been crushing on, oh, no. You look like someone who wants to make an ottoman out of her skin. Take a deep breath and chill."

I'm trying to not sound as frustrated as I feel...and totally failing.

I don't know how Stephen always ropes me into his schemes, but here we are. A-fucking-gain. All I want to do is go to the beach and catch some sun so that I don't look like I spent the summer walking to and from the dorms at Physics Camp (which I did). I mean, I can live with being short and I've made peace with the fact that I'm still carded for PG-13 movies, but I draw the line at a farmer's tan. One good afternoon on the sand; that's all I need.

Yet am I chillin' on the shores of Lake Michigan gettin' my bronze on?

No.

Instead, I'm on another one of Mr. Cho's Wild Rides and I'm *over it*.

Stephen's always all about this false bravado, Mr. I Have a Plan and Mr. I Will Make It So. He's such a nerd that he actually *draws* what he envisions. I mean, he storyboards out the whole damn thing. Because he's so good at picturing himself Making It So with the Plan He Has, we reach the point where everything clicks and he actually could achieve his goal but then he chickens out and blows everything.

He had one job today, which was to go up and say hey to the new girl, and he can't even do that on his own.

I want to help him, I do, but being his keeper is getting old. We've been locked in this wingman dance since we met in preschool. This is his pattern. Today reminds me of when we used to go to the waterpark in the Wisconsin Dells as kids. The whole school year, he'd boast about jumping off the high dive and all the flips and somersaults he'd do, comparing himself to Sammy Lee, the first Asian American to win Olympic gold in platform diving. How he'd be a better diver than anyone else at the pool because he understood aerodynamics and would use that to his benefit. I have no doubt that's true. Stephen's getting early acceptance to MIT, count on that. Dude's got a brain the size of Montana.

But then he'd climb up, tiptoe to the edge of the board, look at the water and *freak the fuck out*. Everyone would have to scramble off the ladder so that he could climb down. He'd talk a huge game but couldn't follow through, could never commit. He didn't dive off the big board, not once. He had zero confidence in his execution, regardless of having it perfect on paper.

His problem is, he builds all this stuff up in his head.

25

Thinking about whatever he wants to do ends up being so much scarier than the act itself that it cripples him. The only reason he ever made it down the giant slide at the park is that I went in tandem with him.

I can only say, "Just do it" so many times.

I mean, I'm not a goddamned Nike T-shirt.

Don't get me wrong, he's great at what he knows. He's the strongest competitor on our Physics Olympics team. But the second there's not a set answer to a question or he encounters an untrodden path, he falls apart.

The bitch of it is, I bet he has a chance with this girl. At a cursory glance—and given the full, rich backstory Stephen's already assigned Simone, provided it's true—she could be a match. I mean, I spend all day, every day with him, so I know he's interesting. He has to be, for me to put up with all his bullshit. He can fascinate me and I'm not easily entertained. When he feels comfortable, he'll talk at length about any subject, and he's not like those boring-ass meatheads at school who are *All Sports, 24/7.*

At the very least, Stephen could be the first guy to ask her out here in North Shore. They don't have to fall in love; maybe they could be great buds. Maybe no end zone, just friend zone? At least he'd have tried to score, you know? But if I weren't here walking him down the long-ass driveway, telling him to not look like a *goddamned serial killer,* even *that* would have no chance of happening.

I don't want to be all, *He holds me back!* because that's a shitty thing to say about my best friend. Although sometimes I think about where I'd be if we hadn't met, if my parents had bought that smaller house in Kenilworth and not the one a few miles up the road in North Shore. Then he'd be my archrival at the Physics Olympics and not my closest companion.

Would that be so bad, I wonder?

Would we push each other toward greatness, his Tesla to my Edison?

Guess we'll never know.

The closer we come to the garage, the more Stephen slows, and I feel like I'm dragging a reluctant mule to market.

Ridiculous.

On second thought, I wonder if Stephen's just freaked out about this being the Barats' old house. Didn't happen here, but there's still kind of a bad vibe, you know? We hung out with Paulie all the time when we were little. But Stephen and I stopped running around with Paulie around the time that friendships solidify more because of shared interests and less due to geographical proximity.

Neither of us ever fought with Paulie, never had a falling-out or anything. We just went in different directions. It happens, you know? God, though, I felt so bad for everyone in his family, especially his little sister, Anna. How do you even *deal* when you're twelve?

Stephen took it extrahard. He was fixated on the whole thing, to the point that I was secretly kinda glad about going to a different camp than him over the summer.

I thought he was moving on, but what if he's not? Maybe that's why he's suddenly panicky about his plan working. Maybe he's freaked out about seeing the inside of Paulie's house again.

When we're about ten feet away from Simone, I get my first good look at her. Beyond her mountain of dark hair, I notice her eyes, which are a warm amber color. Through Stephen's extensive social media stalking, he found out that her grandfather's from India. But for being part Indian, her skin's surprisingly pale and she's covered in freckles. She's cute in a

27

messy, hipster way, except she doesn't give off a pretentious vibe. She strikes me as the kind of girl who'd forget she'd stuck a paintbrush behind her ear.

While she may not be my type, I see what intrigues Stephen. She's about the first girl up here who doesn't come across as a miniature version of all our mothers, with sculpted triceps, blown-straight hair, and a splashy floral tank dress.

(Is it weird/kind of oedipal that I find that combination oddly erotic? Wait, don't answer that.)

"Cheers!" she says. I don't hear much of a British accent. Huh. Thought she was from England? "We have a right mess going here. Look at this rubbish—we're practically drowning in it! Can you please tell me when and how they collect the wheelie bins?"

I can't help it, I start laughing at her turn of phrase while Stephen shoots me a murderous look, I mean, really full of poison. I get a hold of myself, explaining, "Sorry. That sounded exactly like something Mary Poppins would say. By the way, hi, I'm Kent Mathers."

She holds out her hand. "Pleasure to meet you. I'm Mary P."

Stephen bleats, "I thought you were Simone!"

I want to face-palm out of secondhand embarrassment but I quickly interject with a subject change to afford him some dignity. "So, the garbage cans and recycling bins are picked up on our street on Tuesdays and Fridays. Just leave them by your garage and a guy from Streets and Sanitation will pull up to the side of your house in a little golf cart."

"That's brilliant!" she exclaims.

"Nothing but the best for North Shore," I say.

"A bit fancy here, isn't it?" she replies, which is an understatement in the same way that saying that the ocean's fairly

28

sizable or a Maserati's kind of a zippy ride. The average home around here has six bedrooms and just as many baths. And everyone renovates their kitchen every five years. God forbid we keep our almond milk in a fridge from 2010.

Simone tells us, "My friend Cordelia says my strategy for America should be finding the biggest bitch in school and immediately taking her down. Is she right?"

"Hmm," I reply, pretending to muse. "That's less 'high school' and more 'prison.' You should probably Netflix *Glee* and also *Orange Is the New Black.*"

"I shall make a mental note. I already feel you're both full of helpful advice, *you* possibly more than *him*," she says with a grin in Stephen's direction, "so I insist you come inside for something cold to drink before you melt on the spot."

Even though she's teasing, I can see Stephen blanch and yet again I feel like I've gotta rescue him.

"Okay, very important to discuss before we come in and definitely will determine if we're gonna be friends," I say, referencing the one subject that will absolutely, positively draw Stephen out of his shell and into the conversation. "Are you Biggie or are you Tupac?"

She tilts her head to the side. "As in…Smalls and Shakur?"

"Uh-huh. As in the most violent and hotly contested rap rivalry from the mid '90s."

She crosses her arms over her chest and looks thoughtful. "When my parents were our age, they said they could immediately identify kindred spirits by scanning their vinyl/cassette/CD collections, but now that music's digital, it's impossible to walk into someone's home and assess their tastes. Kind of a shame, really."

"You're dodging the question," I say.

"Not a dodge, just providing context. Honestly, my musical proclivities are profoundly eclectic. I listen to everything from opera to Swedish death metal depending on my mood."

I raise an eyebrow. "There you go, dodging again. This gonna be a *thing* with you?"

She makes an X mark over her heart. "No, promise, won't be a *thing*."

"Then what's your answer? Or did you need to step into your car first to collect your thoughts?" She seems confused as I peer around the four-car garage. I clarify, "You do drive a *Dodge*, right?"

Simone holds up her hands in the universal *stop* symbol and I notice she's wearing dozens of funky bracelets. Do they get in the way in the bathroom?

(Is that a strange thing to wonder?)

"Okay, okay. Point taken. Hmm… Who do I prefer? Well, both artists had such an influence on modern hip-hop that to choose one over the other would be like deciding between peanut butter and chocolate. Both are perfect, for different reasons."

My suddenly mute friend Stephen avoids eye contact and traces circles on the floor with the tip of his sneaker. Some days it's like I want to take video of him so he can see how he comes across. Bro, give me *something* to work with here.

(I should storyboard that shit out for him.)

I persist, "Oh, you must be into baseball because clearly you root for the *Dodgers*. Listen, anyone who's familiar with the genre has an opinion. Can you like them both? Absolutely. But you have to *prefer* one over the other. So who's it gonna be—Biggie or Tupac?"

"I feel like there's a lot of hidden weight in this question," she says, tucking a wild strand of dark hair back into her scruffy topknot.

"There is," I reply. In my peripheral vision, I see Stephen sizing up all the cardboard. Ten bucks says he's mentally drawing himself inside a fort made of boxes.

Simone tucks her thumbs into her dress pockets and leans back on her heels. "You understand my reticence, what with being new and all."

"I do."

"I clearly run the risk of alienating one of you, potentially both."

I nod. "Distinct possibility."

"One that I fear."

"Right now, your choice is the Schrödinger's cat of opinions. At this moment, you *say* you prefer both Biggie and Tupac but that can't be. It's simply not the natural state. You have to be one or the other. We need to open this box and find out for sure."

I like her.

I don't *like her* like her but she seems fun, seems like she'd be a fine addition to our crew. Let's be honest, it's a fairly exclusive crew, as Stephen and I aren't exactly the most popular kids in school. We're not hated, we're just not even…considered, you know? Adding an interesting person to our social circle could only make our senior year better. We used to be friends with everyone growing up, but people started to splinter four or five years ago, forming their own cliques, and now Stephen and I are way too insular. We're a party of two, which is kind of depressing.

Maybe if we tried a little harder, we'd be invited to stuff. We'd be welcomed back into the fold, reintroduced into NSHS's social scene. (People are always crying about all the drinking and the drug use among high school students up here, but I'll be damned if I've ever even seen any.)

31

However, Simone's not going to want to be around me and my fascinating friend Stephen if he can't find a way to *open his goddamned mouth* and interact.

"Then, my answer is… *Me Against the World*," she says, naming off a Tupac album.

Stephen breaks into a massive smile and fist bumps Simone, the thrill of this unexpected victory infusing him with a turbocharge of confidence. "I'm Stephen, Stephen Cho. Welcome to the neighborhood."

I exhale.

He may just be okay after all.

30 likes

MalloryGood 2m
Ready for day 1 senior year. Love this
fishtail braid look. #firstdayhaironpoint

View all 5 comments

NShoreKnightBraden Nice one, Mal.
EliseALot #senioryeargoals
YesTHATJasper thirsty much?
SupaFlySpencer 🖤 ✌️ 😈
MidfieldNoell you slay!!

4

MALLORY

YOU PROBABLY WISH you were me.

I don't actually say this out loud. Not an appropriate topic for our campus tour, and also super bitchy, even though that's not my intention. Still, I can tell by the way the new girl sizes me up that she believes I have it all, that I check off all the right boxes. How could she not when I've got:

natural blond hair, super long and straight but not stringy, never stringy, *check.*

a British SUV, *check.*

a twenty-six-inch waist, *check.*

a cute, popular, universally *beloved* boyfriend, *check.*

a limitless future, *double-freaking-check.*

My Balenciaga backpack's full of credit cards in my name, yet I'm not even legal to buy cigarettes. That is, if anyone smoked, because, *no.*

I wonder if this Simone person partakes, though? She seems super European with her bizarre felt clogs and layers of scarves. They LOVE smoking over there. When the Italian Club went to Venice last summer, I noticed every high school–aged kid puffing away, as though lung cancer weren't even a thing.

At the time, my girlfriends were, like, "The Venetian boys are sooooo hot! We won't tell if you cheat on Liam!" However, (a) I'm faithful, and (b) every single guy I met was five-foot-three. I was a head taller than all of them. Again, *no*.

Anyway, my wrist is stacked with Cartier Love bracelets, and not the weird, breakfast cereal–type jewelry this girl has piled on, like she's wearing a bunch of Cheerios on a string or something. She seems the type to own four T-shirts that she washes in the sink at a youth hostel, whereas my walk-in closet's the size of a studio apartment. Even clad in my team uniform—a North Shore first day tradition—I have better style.

If I had to describe myself/my life, I'd say I'm kind of a suburban version of Kendall Jenner, except I have two brothers and no sisters. Also, I'm not forced to spend holidays with Kanye West. Can you imagine how annoying *that* must be, enduring a festive meal while trapped at the table with him? Oh, those poor things! I'm sure he's always all, "I'm the greatest artist who ever lived!" And poor Kendall is, like, "Bible, Yeezus, but I asked you to please pass the yams."

Anyway, when this girl looks at me, she probably can't see past the symmetrical face or enviable accessories, but there's more to me than that. I'm not just the queen of last year's Junior Prom and not just the girl the guys want to get with and girls want to be.

I also have a 3.96 GPA from the most competitive high school in the country.

Baccalaureate, baby. Beauty *and* brains? Yeah, I'm the full package.

Which is why she might secretly aspire to be me.

But if I could offer her a bit of advice?

It's way easier to just be you.

5

SIMONE CHASTAIN

"WE BREED EXCELLENCE here at North Shore High School."

I nod instead of saying anything, because how do I even respond to a statement like that?

I also nodded when Vice Principal Torres said the same thing as he welcomed me to the school. He clasped my hand and nearly crushed it in a crippling shake. Then my guidance counselor, Mr. Gorton, went for the conversational trifecta. WTF? Are they all working from the same script?

And how does one *breed* excellence here, anyway?

In a lab? In a test tube? Or is it more like in a barn?

What does she even mean?

The *she* in this case is Mallory Goodman, the stick-thin girl in a field hockey uniform who interprets my silence as complicity. While I'm not naturally quiet, she's been plowing over me like a conversational bulldozer, razing everything in its path.

Is it that I make her nervous?

No, impossible. She's tall and trim and bloody perfect and

I am none of those things. I'm small and arty and far more likely to pick up a sketchpad than a piece of sporting equipment. I can only catch cold and can only throw shade. (Really, not even great at that.)

Feels like every answer I've given her has been wrong, like when she asked where I live. Told her we'd bought our house from the Barat family. She gave me the oddest look, and that's when she really launched into her monologue.

Mallory's the president of the NSHS *Novus Orsa* Club ("Latin for *new beginnings*," she explained) so she's showing me the campus, even though I'd begged off an escort, explained I could make due because of my fine sense of direction. Last year, when my mum and dad were delayed getting to Art Week, I explored Berlin for two days on my own before they finally arrived and I didn't know a lick of German. Got by on pointing, smiling, and Google Translator, although most people I met spoke brilliant English anyway.

However, Mr. Gorton insisted I have a guide, so here we are, Mallory and me…breeding excellence. Together.

I needed guidance only while dressing, apparently. Picked out my favorite tee and scarf and skirted leggings, figuring I couldn't go wrong with such basics.

Wrong.

Every girl not in a team uniform is clad in small shorts or a flippy dress with bare shoulders, tottering around on sandals with sky-scraping wedge heels. I'm overdressed and pale and out of place. If there were a book on how to blend in here, *that's* what I could have used. I suddenly miss my hateful old school uniform.

Truth is, I'm overwhelmed.

This place is huge to the point of ridiculous, spread across twenty acres with a dozen outbuildings. Nothing prepared me for this. Yes, I'm a US citizen (technically, I hold dual passports), but my only experience with American high schools comes from this week's binge watch of old episodes of *Glee*. Trust me, William McKinley bears zero resemblance. With all the French Renaissance–style red brick and white stone facings enveloping vast squares of tidy green lawns, NSHS looks a lot more like Lady Margaret Hall, a college at Oxford.

Mallory continues, pressing a hand against her chest like she's pledging allegiance. Her identical gold bracelets slide down her narrow wrist and clank together musically. "In this school, and let's be honest, in this town, being good isn't sufficient."

Suspect Mallory takes herself awfully seriously.

She goes on like this, but I'm distracted from her monologue when I spot my neighbor Owen Foley-Feinstein strolling across the quad. He looks like he's listening to a jam band, grooving down the path despite not wearing any earbuds. Some people are just naturally fluid like that. He has a languid grace, all loose-limbed. Reminds me of the jungle cats we fed at that sanctuary in South Africa. He flashes me a big grin and holds up a peace sign when I wave.

Owen and I met while I was out walking Warhol, our new rescue puppy. He lives on the corner of my new street. He thought my dog was awesome, laughing at the pup's underbite, which I so adore. Warhol's teeth cause his bottom lip to jut out in a way that perpetually makes me want to kiss his sweet face. Owen mentioned passing us the number to a good canine orthodontist and it took me a moment to understand he was joking. (Teeth are a *very* serious business in this country.)

As we chatted, Owen complimented my stack of bracelets, piled up and down my wrists in a profusion of beads and hammered silver and leather. He was impressed when he learned that I'd made them. I told him I fancied his dread-locks and he seemed genuinely pleased. I get the feeling he doesn't hear much positive feedback about them. (Suspect there's little room for nonconformity at NSHS, what with the bred excellence and all.)

Seeing Owen reminds me I have a handful of Hindu prayer stones he might want. I drilled the holes too wide in these longish, tubular beads and now they don't lie right when strung. But they'd be perfect to weave into his hair. I make a mental note to drop them off at his place sometime soon.

Mallory frowns as she follows my line of sight to Owen. She clears her throat and continues, "*As I was saying*, we're the best in whatever we do. Always. Our parents expect nothing less."

I try to digest this concept, and… Christ on a bike, that sounds *exhausting*.

Mallory's words do make me think, though. What do my parents expect of *me*, I wonder? With their track record, I'd say they expect me to:

embrace life.

find beauty in unexpected places.

seek out what makes me happy.

experience the world with an open heart and mind.

That's what they did at my age and it worked brilliantly for them. Hell, Mum didn't even finish high school before she left New York, running off to Europe. People had been telling her she should be a model since she was nine years old—at seventeen, she went for it. For a ten-year period, you couldn't open a magazine without seeing a million shots of Fiona Whitley Suri, known to the world simply as *Fi*.

Once she tired of being in front of the camera, she stepped behind it. While Dad made it into university in his native Northern England, he quickly realized he couldn't sit still in a classroom and took off for the Big Smoke (London) before his second term. They like to tell me that if they hadn't followed their hearts, they'd have never met and I wouldn't be here today.

Looking at Mallory, I'd wager our parental units have trod different paths. For one, hers are probably legitimately married to each other and not just common-law. Suspect her dad did not become world-renowned by sculpting a fetus out of crystal meth, either. (Said piece is still on display at Tate Modern, if you're so inclined.)

After Owen passes by, a boy built like a wall comes up behind Mallory, yanking her ponytail with a blindingly white, toothy grin on his face. He's wearing a football jersey. She flushes bright red, but I can't tell if that's from embarrassment or pleasure. She shoos him off without introducing me.

"Your boyfriend?" I ask.

"Oh, honey, *no.*" She wrinkles her nose, as though the idea of dating this boy is simply *too* distasteful. "That's Braden, my brother's friend."

"Lucky you! I *wish* I had a brother with attractive friends. Total convenience, right?"

"Please. Braden's practically family and hooking up with him would be creepy. Like, unimaginable."

I persist, "He's awfully cute if you fancy that massive, Channing Tatum sort of thing. You've really never considered—"

Mallory clears her throat and shuts me down, conversation over. "*As I was saying,* for us, it's not enough to be, say, decent equestrians or quick speed skaters. Riders will be going to the next summer games. The school allows them to do half days to accommodate training."

"Wait, the Olympics? To compete?" I ask. I clarify because she says it so casually, as though earning a spot on the USA

41

roster were no more difficult or unusual than watching a show on Hulu.

She furrows her perfect brow. "Obvi. And the skaters have cadres of—" she looks up at the brilliant blue late summer sky as she begins to tick off the experts on her neatly manicured fingertips "—coaches, managers, sports agents, trainers, nutritionists, branding experts, publicists, attorneys, and social media gurus to help them reach their personal bests on and off the ice. There are six North Shore Knights with an eye toward 2018 and 2020. Like I said, we breed excellence."

I stifle a laugh—both my folks are legitimately famous in their fields and their "cadres" consist of one agent apiece and a financial guy who stops them from blowing all their money on impulse purchases, à la Michael Jackson. It's only because of Mr. Hochberg that we don't own fifteen capuchin monkeys or every Aston Martin ever used in a James Bond film, I'm sure of it.

I realize that I'm drifting, which is rude.

Time to focus. I fight my instincts, which trend toward sitting in the back of the classroom, tuning out whatever the teacher's saying while I daydream about what piece of jewelry I could make next. Often, when I'm introduced to someone new, I create a piece for them in my head. Like when I met Mr. Gorton today? I envisioned a thin, gold tie bar, very simple and tidy, perhaps engraved with his initials on the end in a nice font. With serifs, I think. For Owen, I pictured an etched shark's tooth, strung on braided leather cord.

For Mallory?

I imagine she'd appreciate a gift certificate for Tiffany & Co. instead.

Mallory leans in, all conspiratorially, as though she's about to share the secrets of the universe. Her breath is overpoweringly minty, but with a faint trace of ammonia behind it. Wish I'd thought to stock up on tubes of Ultrawhite before we left England. I don't care for the scent of American tooth polish. I should have Cordy ship me some.

"Here's what you need to understand about this place. We're winners. Hashtag *champions*." She forms a pound sign with the first two bony fingers on both hands when she says this. "All of us. Like, if music is our jam, we *expect* admission to Juilliard. If we're actors, we're *so* getting in to the Yale School of Drama. And for the rest of us, *hello*, top-tier college of our choice."

Her confidence takes my non-mint-and-ammonia-scented breath away. What would it be like to have such self-assurance? To be so convinced of my own abilities?

I do appreciate having inherited the family's artistic perspective, though. We view situations through the eyes of an artist and see something entirely different than a casual observer would. So, when everyone else looks into a forest and spots nothing but trees, we three are endlessly fascinated by how the faint rays of crepuscular sunlight filter down through leaves and branches like spotlights, illuminating carpets of moss and tiny mushrooms and woodland creatures.

Although, let's be honest—I bet a lot of their artistic vision is due to the metric shit-ton of drugs they took twenty years ago.

Mallory notices I'm losing focus. Mum says my face is easier to read than a Dr. Seuss book, so I should never play strip poker...unless I'm looking to experiment and then I should relax, tune in to my body, and enjoy myself.

Mallory explains, "While it sounds like we're arrogant, as the old saying goes, 'It ain't bragging if it's true.' You've seen our stats, right? 156 Illinois State Scholars? A 27.4 ACT composite? 97 percent of us score 3+ on AP exams? I mean, we have thirty-five interscholastic teams that have won more state championships than any other school in Illinois history."

Should I respond that my old school was next to Soho's number one falafel stand?

Mallory hustles us to the main building, where the walls are covered with a century's worth of ivy. I'm loving the gravitas of this campus. I assumed everything in this part of the United States would be like a shiny-new strip mall, just constructed last week, so I'm pleasantly surprised to see buildings with history. I love anything with a past.

Mallory sprints up the steps and bids me to follow. I'm mesmerized watching her legs pump as she leaps from one wide stone riser to the next. Every rock-hard muscle contracts and contorts, each fiber working to propel her forward. Lot of power in those skinny legs. Does the tan help? Zip, zip, zip, like a mountain goat on a vertical face.

Yes, the tan must help.

Once we step inside, the hallway's less *Glee* and more Hogwarts or perhaps *Downton Abbey*, with grand, dark oak-paneled walls and wide staircases illuminated by two stories' worth of stained-glass walls.

Mallory isn't interested in sharing the *Architectural Digest* details, though. Instead, she leads me to the trophy case, spanning from one end of the timber-beam-ceilinged hallway to the other. She practically levitates as she names the various championships the Knights have won over the years. The pitch of her voice rises as she prattles on about achievements both athletic and academic.

I should be impressed by all the bred excellence, but she's giving off a peculiar vibe. Her energy is Rumpelstiltskinfrenetic, as though all the gold in the world still isn't enough, she just needs to spin more, more, more.

I'm uncomfortable.

Suspect Mallory and I won't be friends. I can tell I'm too mellow for her liking. Not focused enough. Too bohemian. I had the inkling we weren't destined to be pals when she noticed the shaved patch over my right ear. Guess she didn't spot that part at first because the rest of my hair's pretty shaggy. When she did, she caught her breath and asked if I'd had skull surgery.

Um, no, I'd replied, *just personal choice*.

Then she shuddered.

Now she says, "I could not be more proud of everything the senior class has achieved thus far. Do you realize we have 211 AP scholars?"

I do not; that's largely because I have no clue what it means.

"Last year, 98 percent of the graduating class went on to college, at 176 colleges and universities." Her cerulean eyes practically brim with tears as she recounts this triumph.

Then she pauses and stares at me.

What in the bloody hell is she waiting for? Applause? Back slaps? Tips? A biscuit? Actually, a biscuit may be the best option. Her manic behavior could be due to low blood sugar.

"Um…everything sounds fab?" This comes out more as a question than a statement.

"Awesome. So, do you have any questions so far?"

"Um…yes," I say, thinking about the one big question mark I keep encountering since moving here. "Why's everyone so uptight when I mention we bought the Barats' house?"

Her face clouds over. "Long story."

I glance at the clock on my phone. "I have time."

"I don't," she replies, shutting me down yet again. She appears to take a moment to center herself.

Once righted, she tosses her braid. "*Anyway,* we're going to hit the athletic fields and then the math campus, followed by the activities hall, and then I'll get you to your Good and Evil in Literature first-period class. If we hustle, we can grab an espresso at the coffee cart in the quad before then."

She smiles at me expectantly.

Maybe she *is* expecting a tip. Mum says Americans tip more than Europeans and I should be prepared, so I'm keeping dollar bills in my pocket at all times. When Kent and Stephen saw my wad of cash, they laughed, asking me if I was planning to hit up a strip club.

Still, a tip can't be appropriate here… Can it?

While I internally try to calculate how much 15 percent of a campus tour is worth, I reply, "Thanks for such a thorough introduction. I appreciate it." Yet what I'd like to say is that I've been at this school for only half an hour and already I'm exhausted.

At first glance, Mallory seems the sort to have it all. Lovely and bright and tons of energy. Girls defer to her in the halls as though she's important, like she owns the place, and boys eye her pretty hair and lean, tan legs. Teachers nod at her in a way that makes me suspect she's a worthy adversary. But given her reaction to a simple question about the Barats, I wonder if there isn't something going on beneath the surface.

Also?

If she's spent twelve years running at this frenzied pace, then I'm so very glad to *not* be her.

6

MALLORY

OKAY, A FEW more stops and this stupid tour will be over.

Have I mentioned how much I *loathe* being the campus cruise director?

Nothing personal with Simone. She seems nice enough, albeit seriously clueless. At one point, I thought she was going to *tip* me. (Who does that?) My issue is that now I'm going to be *responsible* for her, which is the last thing I want. That's what they don't tell you about this club. *Novus Orsa* isn't just about giving tours; it's about taking new students under your wing for however long they need guidance.

Ain't nobody got time for that.

When I told Liam that I was appointed as the leader of *Novus Orsa*, he didn't ask why. One of the reasons we get along is that he recognizes a command performance when he sees it. Hell, he lives it, too.

"Step it up, Mallory," my mother had said last spring, giving me the side-eye over her nth glass of wine. To myself, I was all, *Glad you don't let the daylight stop you from getting your drink on.*

I stood there in the kitchen, bracing myself for another one of her Your Brother Theo Is Perfect and You, Mallory, Are Sadly Lacking lectures. (At least she never compares me to our older brother, Holden, anymore.) So I stood and waited for her to describe what unspeakable crime had I committed this time.

In what way was I not reflecting proper glory on her now?

She sat there in the breakfast solarium, posing on the padded bench like it was her throne. I knew that she'd jump all over my shit about posture if I didn't hold my chin up and keep my shoulder blades pressed together, so I stood extra tall. *Stop curling up like a shrimp in a sauté pan*, she'd hiss when I was kid, until standing up straight became as second-nature as breathing. I stiffened even more under her penetrating gaze.

She took a long pull from her glass and then said, "Your father tells me you were asked to lead *Novus Orsa* and you declined."

"I did."

Dad agreed with my decision when we spoke about *Novus Orsa*. Said he worried I was spreading myself too thin—ironic coming from the guy who puts in seventy-plus hours a week at his law firm. But maybe his schedule feels like he's slacking—before he made partner, it was more like one hundred hours per week. For a couple of years during elementary school, weeks would pass without my seeing him, even though we lived under the same roof.

"Why's that?" She said this more to her glass than to me, as though I weren't even worthwhile enough to demand her full attention while being addressed. Wouldn't it be something if she ever looked at me with the kind of affection she happily bestows upon Theo—especially when his team is winning—or bottles of Sauvignon Blanc or her Facebook timeline?

48

"I'm already slammed," I explained. "I've got peer counseling, the Social Service Board, the Italian club, and Student Alliance." I spun through my mental checklist. There was so much, I felt woozy even thinking about it all. But I was missing something... What else? "Oh, yeah, there's my *a cappella* singing group, and next fall I'm captain of the field hockey team. There's literally no more room on my plate."

Whenever I list everything I have going on like that, I feel spent, like I can't be on my feet another second, so I sank into one of the big wrought-iron chairs bordering the breakfast bar. No slouching, though. We don't *do* that in the Goodman house.

What I couldn't understand is why she'd be so invested in whether I took on one more extracurricular. Like she could be bothered to attend my games or performances. She didn't need to *be there* to be able to brag about my wins on the field.

Anyway, I was suspicious of her concern and had a good idea where this conversation was headed. She perpetually has ulterior motives; I just wish she were more adept at disguising them.

My mother got up and dug into her bottle-green suede Chloé purse on the counter, pulling out a set of keys before returning to the bench. "Give up peer counseling. That's the one activity that won't get you anywhere."

Right. Peer counseling's the one activity I *like*.

I decided to appeal to her sense of reason. "I feel like I do nothing but walk back and forth to school fifteen times a day."

"You can use the exercise."

So reason was out. And only in my mother's world was a size two *fat*.

"All the walking is cutting into my study time." That'd get her attention, tapping into her FUDs—Fear, Uncertainty, and Dread. If my grades were to slip so that I didn't get into Princeton on early decision, she could never show her face at The Daily Om again.

"Easily fixed. Here, take Holden's Land Rover." She bought this vehicle as a bribe to induce him into coming home. As her plan had yet to work, she'd sometimes drive it herself when her purchases wouldn't fit in the Jag's trunk.

She slid the LR4's key fob across the table to me the way TV bartenders send shots of whiskey to regular patrons. I didn't stop the keys as they flew past me. We both watched as the set dropped to the floor with a metallic clang. Any other kid would be overjoyed at the prospect of a free luxury vehicle, but the whole conversation made me mad. "I don't *want* my own car, I *want* more than four hours of sleep a night," I argued.

She sat back on the padded bench and folded her arms across her surgically enhanced chest. *A full C, never a D, Mallory, unless you're looking to work the pole*, AKA the sum total of wisdom she's ever imparted.

"Car's yours, that's nonnegotiable. But you will need to lead the newcomer's club. Can't take much time—I mean, how often does anyone your age move here?"

Actually…she was probably right; I wouldn't have to do much. If anyone relocates to North Shore with children, they're in elementary school, or early junior high. By the time high school rolls around, newcomers are a rarity. Generally, if someone winds up at NSHS, they grew up here and have enrolled only after being kicked out of boarding school. (That happens quite a bit.)

"The activity would look great on my college applications," I conceded, too tired to continue the debate, ready to cut my losses. Here's the thing—I always argue and I never win; you'd think I'd be smart enough to not start.

She sipped her wine and nodded, victorious.

Like that wasn't a given.

Then, almost as an afterthought she said, "Did you know that Kimberlee's daughter Elise tried to join *Novus Orsa* and she wasn't accepted? Guess she's not what the school wants to offer by way of first impression."

Ah, there it is, I thought, mentally snapping my fingers. Like she'd ever suggest something that was truly in *my* best interests. You see, Kimberlee is my mother's frenemy. They've been pitting Elise and me against each other since we were in diapers, in a never-ending competition of who could walk and talk and use the potty like a big girl first.

In my mother's head, Elise is my sworn rival. IRL, we're totally cool. We text all the time. We hate being used as pawns in our mothers' twisted quests for social media dominance. Elise is braver than me, though. She dyed her hair black, pierced her nose, and gained thirty pounds. I thought her acts of defiance would make life easier on me, but that's not the case. Now my mother's even more vigilant about what I eat, hoping to keep up the disparity in our waistlines.

Which, again, *exhausting.*

Before I could say anything else, my brother Theo clattered in with Braden, two bulls in the proverbial china shop. Although the kitchen's something like five hundred square feet and opens into the solarium and massive great room, the whole space feels cramped when the boys enter. They're both built like brick shithouses. While Theo's pretty big, Braden dwarfs him. He's a younger version of The Rock, with all his muscles and toothy, white smile, but minus the shaved head.

"Hey, Ma, these your keys on the floor?" Theo scoops up the Tiffany key ring and tries to hand it to her.

"Nope, those are your sister's now. I gave her the LR4."

"Badass!" Theo exclaimed, holding up his hand for a high-five I did not return. "Will you start driving to school in the fall? Can you give me rides? I'm over this bike business. It's bullshit that only seniors can park on campus."

Were I to swear in front of our mother, she'd go apoplectic. But Theo cursing? Doesn't register. For that matter, Holden could sacrifice a virgin on the wooden butcher block part of the kitchen island and she wouldn't even blink.

"You know what?" she said. "It's unfair that Mallory gets a car and you don't, Theo. Let's fix that. We can go to the dealership this afternoon and you pick out whatever you'd like."

Hopefully Theo drives, I thought, eyeing the empty bottle of wine.

"Fuckin' A! Can I get a convertible Beetle?" he asked.

"Sure, if that's what you want," she replied, glancing at me with an indulgent smile that didn't quite reach her eyes.

"Bro, you can't get a little VW, you'll look like bear driving one of those Shriner's cars," Braden said. "Think truck or jeep or something more manly. Can't be cruising around in a Barbie car."

I noticed my mother rolling her eyes. She's not a huge fan of Braden, thinks he's a useless, good-time party guy, even though he does well in his classes and has been nothing but amazing to Theo. She's always telling me how much better Liam is compared to Braden, more focused, more disciplined, more destined for success, like she somehow needs to sell me on *my* boyfriend's finer points. She acts like she's worried I'm trying to choose between them, which is so untrue.

Theo nodded. "That does make sense, now that you mention it. Hey, Ma, let's go into Dad's office and look at vehicle pics on the big iMac," he suggested.

They exited, leaving Braden and me alone in the kitchen. He turned to me and said, "Now make sure you clean all the ashes out of that fireplace, Cinderella."

"Right?" I replied. "Like I need my bird and squirrel friends to help me, too."

I sighed and slumped in my seat. I felt all my bones turn to jelly as soon as she left the room. Staying upright was sapping me of my remaining energy, so I propped my elbow on the counter and rested my head in my hand.

Why was I so overwhelmingly tired?

"You understand she's a bitch like that because she's jealous of you, right?" Braden said.

Maybe *that's* why she's never liked Braden; he sees right through her.

Liam isn't snowed by her either, but he's a lot better at hiding it. Liam's perpetually polite, deferential, even pretends to flirt with her, which she completely eats up. In a lot of ways, Liam's like my dad, defaulting to smiling and gritting his teeth when it comes to dealing with her because that's the path of least resistance.

No wonder Dad puts in fourteen-hour days.

Braden, on the other hand, has no interest in trying to charm her.

I looked over at him and we locked glances. Were his eyes always flecked with bits of gold leaf? Seems like I'd have noticed that before.

"Why would *she* be jealous of *me*?" I asked.

He shrugged and then hopped onto the chair closest to me. I felt heat radiating from him, warming up this room that's perpetually chilly due to all the glass in the solarium.

53

"'Cause you're awesome," he told me. The corners of my mouth began to tug upward. "'Cause you'll always be younger and hotter and smarter than her. 'Cause she'll feel better about herself if she's able to make you feel small. Take your pick." That made me think of the time Braden warned me to never accept an apple from my mother—said she gave him Evil Queen from *Snow White* flashbacks.

He put his arm around me and brought me in for a side hug, and I was enveloped by the scent of clean cotton and ocean breezes and the wintergreen Tic Tacs he perpetually chews. (His running joke is that he has a two-pack-a-day habit.)

This gesture—or maybe it was his words—made my insides twist. I had this overwhelming urge to bury my face into his neck and inhale. Something about Braden always made me want to melt into him, to seek him out like a sheltered harbor in a tempestuous sea.

But I stopped myself because that seemed wrong.

I felt like sharing this moment of intimacy or discussing my problems made me somehow unfaithful to Liam. I know it sounds weird, but Liam's supposed to be the one I talk to about my issues with Mom. *He's* my ride or die, not Braden. Plus, I worry that Theo would be upset if he saw Braden and me this close. We're all great friends but if I were to inadvertently cross a line, Theo would be upset.

I jumped up and out of Braden's grasp.

"Gotta go," I said.

Braden looked hurt and his fallen expression weighed on my heart, which only served to confuse me more.

"I do something wrong, Mal?"

I'm always surprised at how easily Braden can express himself. He perpetually cuts right to the chase and isn't afraid to say what he feels. He's probably the sweetest person I've ever met; I'm astounded that he doesn't have a serious girlfriend.

"What? No. No, not at all," I stammered, trying to tamp down the butterflies in my perpetually empty stomach. "I remembered I have to give Mr. Gorton a call. I'll be heading up *Novus Orsa* next fall and I need to get on that."

"A'ight," he said, lapsing into the bro-speak he normally reserves for conversations with teammates. "That sounds like it could be tight."

"Yeah," I agreed, while lying my ass off. "So tight."

I collected my things and skittered away but when I got to the doorway leading to the back staircase, I glanced at Braden over my shoulder.

He was watching me walk away from him.

Like I always do.

Like I always fucking do.

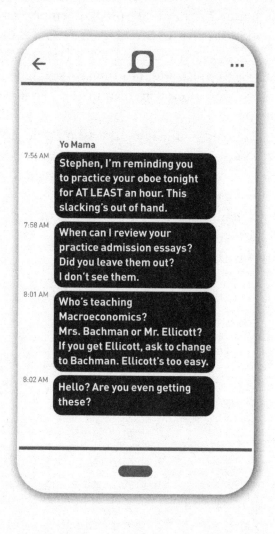

Yo Mama

7:56 AM
Stephen, I'm reminding you to practice your oboe tonight for AT LEAST an hour. This slacking's out of hand.

7:58 AM
When can I review your practice admission essays? Did you leave them out? I don't see them.

8:01 AM
Who's teaching Macroeconomics? Mrs. Bachman or Mr. Ellicott? If you get Ellicott, ask to change to Bachman. Ellicott's too easy.

8:02 AM
Hello? Are you even getting these?

7

KENT

"WE'RE GONNA BE US, only a better version."

"Uh-huh," I reply with zero enthusiasm.

Stephen insists, "No, Kent and Stephen, 2.0. I mean it, man. This is it. This is our year."

The whole walk to school, Stephen's been sharing his plan for World Domination. I've smiled and nodded, but I'm not putting much stock in his words.

I hear this speech every first day of school, like clockwork.

While Stephen actually believes himself, he perpetually forgets that the second something goes the tiniest bit awry—like we have to play dodgeball in gym class or the cafeteria runs out of Sloppy Joes or he gets an A—instead of an A+—that's it, game over. His whole demeanor changes and he slips into a funk that's so *not* commensurate with whatever tiny disappointment it is he's suffered.

Don't get me wrong; I'd love for this to be our year. I'm all about World Domination and I would rock *Kent and Stephen 2.0*. But I can't be Mr. Hells, Yeah, Bro! because I have to straddle a fine line between supporting him and managing his expectations. If I'm too enthusiastic, then I'm the one who deals with the inevitable fallout when situations don't turn out exactly like he'd built up in his fantasies.

Maybe having Simone in the mix will help. At least I won't be solely responsible for keeping him on an even keel.

"Yo, check it out, our *girlfriends* are at the coffee cart together," Stephen says, poking me in the ribcage.

"Wait, what?" I reply.

"Cheers!" Simone calls from across the quad. That's when I notice that she's in line next to Mallory.

My Mallory.

My stomach clenches in fear and anticipation before the caveman portion of my brain takes over. Then I stand as straight as I can, chest up, shoulders back, chin down, wishing desperately I'd done a set of pushups this morning to get my swole on. Granted, I'd have to do "girl" pushups, which is a total misnomer, considering I've seen Mallory do the full military press kind in gym class. Would not be surprised if she could even go one-handed.

(Mental note: start doing pushups.)

My current unimpressive stature isn't going to capture my future girlfriend's attention, so I decide to aim for charisma. We make a beeline over to them. I will never be the biggest or the baddest or the best player on the field, but I can be clever. I can be delightfully idiosyncratic. Hell, Stephen Hawking can land ladies—they've even made movies about it.

This is not an insurmountable challenge.

And as soon as Mallory stops terrifying me?

I'm golden.

"Oy, guv'nah!" I reply, with my best terrible English accent. "Top o' the mornin' to ya."

Mallory winces.

Yeah, might have overshot the charming mark.

"Pip, pip, cheerio." Stephen follows my lead, pretending to doff an imaginary top hat. His black, spiky hair doesn't move when he bows.

(Mental note: he and I need to have a conversation about his rampant gel abuse.)

"That stopped being funny, like, three days ago," Simone says with a big grin. Stephen is vibrating with excitement, just being in her presence.

I like what she brings out in him. I'll say it again—she's good for us.

"What's that all about?" Mallory asks Simone, as though we're not standing here. How rude is that? I would hate her if I weren't desperately in love/profoundly afraid of her. She narrows her eyes. "And why don't you sound more British? I only hear it here and there."

Simone smiles at all of us, making it clear that she considers this is a four-way conversation. "Because I was born in the US and we've lived all over. Plus, my mom's an American and she never really picked up the accent."

Mallory waves a slim hand at us. "Then what's their problem?"

Acknowledged!

Yeah, I realize that as someone who scored a perfect 36 on the ACTs, I should be smarter than this, I should expect more for myself, I should not consider *terror* analogous to *erogenous*. And yet when she raises her arm to wave it dismissively at us, her field hockey uniform reveals a sliver of golden side-boob, so you can see my dilemma.

Simone says, "They're mocking me because of my expressions." Mallory looks confused, so Simone clarifies. "I use a lot of British idioms and those two crack up over them. They keep accusing me of secretly being Mary Poppins."

59

Mallory rolls her eyes. "They're such nerds."

"*They're* standing right here," Stephen says with great indignity, shooting me an incredulous look, like, *Can you believe this bitch?*

It's awkward.

Yet I maintain this interchange is less awkward than when we first talked to Simone on Wheelie Bin Day. Plus, that turned out well, especially after we met her parents. Her dad's kind of a trip—he tried to give us beer! Her mom was all, "Let's not ply minors with alcohol, Angus."

I didn't even want one, but was psyched that someone finally, *finally* put the beer option on the table.

Simone insisted on giving us a tour of her place, which wasn't new to us. I remembered everything about the house—from the two-story Christmas tree in the entry hall every December to the powder room where Mrs. Barat perpetually burned cinnamon candles to the screening room in the basement where we'd watch the movie *Cars* again and again. As I looked around, I noticed not a single thing had changed, not even the paint colors. So I mentioned that we'd been in her house before, but I didn't explain the context. Figured that was the easiest thing to do.

Once we went upstairs, I was glad to see she'd picked Anna's room and not Paulie's, because that would have been too weird for us. I wouldn't know how to tell her that once upon a time, we'd logged a million hours lying on the floor of her new room, playing "PaRappa the Rapper" on our PSPs with our old friend. So I was glad we could avoid that conversation.

Sometimes it's easier to gloss over what's happened around here.

Anyway, Simone was way proud of her jewelry-making setup, and, really, she should have been. She owns more tools than either of us and we build robots! She explained, "I have this habit of imagining jewelry designs for people when I meet them."

"Yeah? What do you see for us?" Stephen prompted.

Personally, I'm not a jewelry guy, but I was so thrilled that he was being himself that I wanted to let out a goddamned cheer. I'd assumed that Paulie's house would throw him off his (practically nonexistent) game. I'd gladly go the full Liberace if it meant Happy Stephen and not Crappy Stephen.

She grabbed a pad and a pencil and with a few graceful strokes, sketched out a design. "Here. Look at this. I envision you in silver Tuareg crosses, looped with a leather tie." She gestured toward a couple of wide circles with arrow points on the end. "You see? They're quite masculine. The Tuareg tribesmen believed these amulets possessed magical powers and wore them as talismans."

While we were looking at her design, this blur of tan-and-white muscle came bursting into the room, underbite on full display. Took me a second to figure out what was even happening.

"Hold up, you have a *pit bull*? In North Shore?" I couldn't help it, I started laughing all over again, even though I'd never met a pit bull before and I was worried he would eat my face before I ever had a chance to grow a beard, which would suck.

"No, he's a Staffordshire Terrier," she replied. "Do you not have them here? They're everywhere in the UK."

Her puppy Warhol bounded from person to person, unsure which one of us to lick first. He was so friendly! I appreciated that when he wagged his tail, his whole body got involved, from the top of his square head to the tip of his fat butt. He seemed too cute to maul me.

"They're the same breed, basically. Staffys are actually pit bulls and they're everywhere here, too," I said, trying—and failing—to avoid being French-kissed by Warhol. (How sad is it that *that* was the most action I'd seen all summer?) "Just not in North Shore. People here have fancy dogs with AKC-registered papers, like Labs and poodles and springer spaniels. Not us, because both our moms think any pets are filthy, but everyone else."

Stephen ran a palm over his crunchy hair and said, "I'm sorry in advance when my mom gives you shit. Not only is she the self-appointed neighborhood watchperson, she's a Realtor. That means she's, like, obsessed with property values in our hood. Goes full-on, banana-sandwich anytime anything poses a threat to them. Remember when the Bernardis wouldn't re-blacktop their driveway? We thought she was gonna *send some guys*. She's gonna be *furious* to see a pit bull."

"Staffy," she corrected.

"Again, same difference," Stephen said.

I added, "She's *especially* gonna hate him because she's convinced any dog that weighs over twelve pounds is dangerous. Let's just say she's not a fan of danger."

We glanced at Warhol, who had since left my side to chew on one of Simone's clogs.

"Warhol, release," Simone said, snapping her fingers.

The dog not only immediately let go of the shoe, but also rolled over on his back. I suspect if he had thumbs and the ability to spell, he'd have written a heartfelt apology note. I rubbed my new BFF's belly while he squirmed in my lap, his tail thumping so hard, it would likely leave a mark. "Who's a neighborhood terror, huh? Who's a big, scary brute?"

Anyway, how is it that I can be fearless upon making out with a strange pit bull but I don't have the balls to defend myself when Mallory's just insulted me?

Especially when I know that showing courage and confidence is absolutely attractive to the opposite sex?

I swear I'm as bad as Stephen sometimes. Maybe worse. He's had his act together lately.

(Mental note: work on confidence/courage.)

"Mallory, have you been properly introduced to my good friends Kent and Stephen?" Simone asks.

Before Mallory can say anything, her phone pings, so she steps away to answer a text without even looking at us.

"*Imma* take that as a *no*," Stephen snorts.

Stephen and I keep Simone company as she places her order. "Mallory... Um, she seems like a very busy person," Simone says.

"That's probably the nicest thing anyone's ever said about her," Stephen replies. "By the way, our boy here's in love with her."

"Really?" Simone says. "You're into...frenetic?"

I shrug and try to play off my embarrassment at this private crush being made public. "Don't hate the player, hate the game."

(Mental note: kick Stephen's weenie-ass later.)

(Again, metaphorically.)

Before I even realize what he's doing, Stephen treats us both to my favorite coffee cart offering—triple shot cappuccinos with extra Splenda and a side of almond croissants. Then I feel bad about ragging on him.

He and I tear into our pastries, leaving a trail of powdered sugar and stray slivers of nuts as we move over to the open bench next to the cart. I had a massive plate of bacon and eggs and half a cantaloupe at home less than an hour ago, but somehow I'm still famished. My mom says this is because I have a growth spurt coming on. God, I hope so. I don't want to spend the rest of my life being barred from the big rollercoasters because I'm not as tall as the frigging alligator at the entrance.

Simone sips her coffee thoughtfully. "Mallory's tour was exceptionally thorough. Yet I'm surprised to have held her attention for so long. Suspect she'd benefit from some mindfulness."

Stephen laughs, which sends little flakes flying. "Mindful, please, this is 'Murrica. Bitch needs ADHD meds."

Mallory returns and Simone hands her a cup and a brown paper bag. "Here you go."

"What's this?" Mallory asks.

"A tip," Simone replies.

"What?"

"Kidding, sort of. This is a white chocolate mocha and a banana nut muffin to say thanks for your time."

Mallory waves her off. "Totally unnecessary. Keep them."

Simone gently presses the cup and bag into Mallory's hands. "Come on, I can't manage two mochas and two muffins, and the boys have already eaten. Please enjoy them. Cheers and thanks again!"

Mallory stalks off without a word—so rude, yet so hot—and Simone returns her attention to us.

"Have a great first day of class, Mallory!" Stephen says, his voice oozing with sarcasm. He *hates* Mallory. Which would prove awkward if we got married and he was my best man. We have time to figure that out, though.

Simone says, "Explain this to me—is initial gift refusal another American thing?"

"I don't follow," I say, brushing thousands of tiny crumbs off my shirt. Croissants don't crumble; they detonate.

She replies, "What is and isn't culturally appropriate here? I truly don't want to offend. What I mean is, every country has its small proclivities. Like when we visit Mum's extended family in India, we don't wave 'hello' because to them, the gesture means 'no' or 'go away.' So I didn't know if here you say no to a gift before you say yes."

"Like how you're not supposed to write in red ink in Korea because it's considered a bad omen?" I ask.

"My mother always throws away my red pens. I have to hide them, like they're part of a porn stash or something," Stephen says. "Otherwise, we have, like, *zero* ties to our culture. We're the least Asian people you'll meet in North Shore. The only time she ever pulls the South Korean card is with my stupid school supplies."

"Yeah, the pen thing is not weird *at all*," I say. Every time I think my mother is a challenge with her relentless nagging and endless micromanagement, I remember Mrs. Cho and I feel better. For all her opinions, at least my mom keeps her paws off my writing utensils. Fortunately, my dad's pretty normal. But, like all the other fathers in the consulting business up here, he's away on assignment all week, every week, so he's not here to be the day-to-day buffer. Stephen's in the same boat as his dad's a road warrior, too.

"That's really sad," Simone says.

"Eh, it's just pens." Stephen shrugs.

"No, that you guys don't connect with your Korean heritage. I mean, I'm only a quarter Indian and I can't get enough. I love every aspect, from wearing saris to cooking chapattis, and, my God, an Indian wedding? You've never seen anything like it."

After she tells us the story of some distant cousin's wedding in Mumbai—with elephants and everything!—the first bell rings.

"Do we go now?" she asks.

65

"No, that's the initial warning. We have ten minutes," Stephen says.

"Anyway, are you ready for today?" I ask Simone.

She knits her brow. "Hmm, well, I'm worried that my courses might be difficult. I mean, I have Forensic Science, 3D Animation, 9/11 and Its Impact on the Modern Middle East, just to name a few. Honestly, I didn't know classes like this existed outside of university."

"You don't have to worry," Stephen says, with great reassurance in his voice.

Simone brightens. "Because they won't be terribly hard?"

Without a whit of sarcasm, he replies, "Oh, no, they'll be hard as shit. Frigging killer. You'll be doing homework six hours a night and you'll barely keep your head above water. But now you *know*, so at least you don't have to worry."

I shake my head. Here I was thinking that *I* had zero game.

The five-minute bell rings, so Simone and Stephen head off toward the liberal arts building and I make my way over to the science hall.

Right before I open the heavy wooden door, I take one more look at Mallory on the other side of all that neatly clipped grass. She's been standing there talking to Braden, who's totally making sausage eyes at her. Her face is all relaxed and radiant, like he's the sun shining down on her. She's not blatantly flirting with him, but their chemistry's obvious. I can practically smell their pheromones from here.

Great, *him*, too?

Like Perfect Mr. Soccer Star Liam isn't already enough competition. Yeah, let's *definitely* add the funniest, nicest, handsomest guy to her list of admirers. I can't even legit hate on him, because he's such a good dude.

They say a couple more things to each other and he takes off, but I notice he keeps glancing back at her until he's swallowed up by the crowd going into the math and science building.

Now that she's alone, she dives into the paper bag Simone gave her.

Mallory holds up the muffin and takes a deep whiff, burying her nose in its still-warm center. The bakery that stocks the coffee cart is here in town, so everything's always right from the oven. She practically gets to second base with it before stuffing it back into the sack.

How pathetic is it that I'm jealous of a fucking carbohydrate right now?

She repeats the process with the mocha, removing the lid and taking in the milky steam from the chocolate brew. She leans in so close to the surface of the cup when she inhales that a small dot of whipped cream ends up on the tip of her nose.

(To confirm—it's inappropriate to run over there and lick it off her?)

As she wipes at the foam with the back of her hand, she smiles a quiet, private smile. The whole sniffing ritual seems oddly personal, like I'm witnessing something not meant for my eyes.

But she doesn't eat anything.

No bites, no sips.

Instead, she glances over both of her shoulders before she dumps everything in the trash. Then she stands there and stares into the garbage can for a minute, all wistfully, almost like she's about to cry.

It's disconcerting.

Watching Mallory makes me wonder if maybe we're all struggling with something around here, only some of us are better at hiding it than others.

8

OWEN
FOLEY-FEINSTEIN

RISE UP...

I open one eye and consider my options: rise with the morning sun like Stephen Marley and Jason Bentley suggest or hit the snooze button?

Ha, like that's even a consideration.

Seven minutes later, the "Three Little Birds" remix comes through loud and clear on my iPod clock/dock again. Their lyrics tell me I shouldn't be stressed about anything, rationalizing that every little thing is gonna be just fine. I believe 'em, so I hit snooze again, and then again, and again.

At some point, I glance at the clock and realize if I were still playing lacrosse, I'd have been at morning practice for an hour at this point.

Pfft, enjoy your sunrise, suckers.

See, I used to play because lacrosse made me feel connected to the Native Americans who invented the sport. They'd totally get into it, prepping for the games like they were going to battle, putting on their war paint and decorating their sticks. These rituals were spiritual to them, like, real ceremonial.

That's why I was so pissed when Coach demanded I chop off my dreds. I feel like the Native Americans would have been, all, "Dreds? Those make you look like a badass—hell, yeah!" So I made a stand and I quit. Felt good about it, too.

I snooze so many times that showering's no longer an option if I want to make it to school on time. I raise my arm and take a whiff. Please, totally fine. I went swimming yesterday, I'm still plenty clean. People are way hung up on hygiene around here. When you shower too often, you kill all your skin's good bacteria. Plus, it's wasteful. I mean, California's in a drought right now. We're obligated to conserve. Yeah, this is Illinois and we're right next to a big lake, but every drop still counts. Butterfly effect and all.

I grab a polo from its spot on the floor between my acoustic guitar and my film edit bay. My mom ordered a bunch of expensive stuff for me for back to school. I was copacetic with what I had already, didn't need to consume anything more. Said if she was insisting on shelling out the duckies, I could use a new boom mike. She countered, telling me I could have whatever movie-making gear I wanted, but I still needed some outfits that looked "respectable."

Whatever that means.

The shirt I pick up has two crocodiles on it. (I ripped one scaly li'l bastard off a similar shirt and superglued it onto the first one's back, and now it's like they're making alligator *amore*.) I crack up when I see myself in the mirror. Yes, sir, I sure do look like everyone else in my golf shirt. Nothing subversive about that.

I pull on some cargo shorts and old-school checkered Vans and I'm ready, so I strap on my GoPro to capture all the going-to-school realness. I slide down the banister, careful to hop off before I hit the newel post. (You make that mistake only once, trust me here.)

I call, "What's up, party people?" and my voice echoes through the two-story foyer. Nobody returns my greeting. Guess the 'rents already left for work without saying goodbye. There's a shocker. Not. The way the old man rushes to the office at the ass-crack of dawn, you'd think he was headed for a day of nothing but titties and beer. I always tell him, "You own the joint, Pops, you can get in whenever," but he never listens. My mom's the same way. Kind of a toss-up as to which of their jobs I'd hate more—running an executive search firm or being a VP of Ethics and Compliance (WTF even is that?) at a giant pharmaceutical company.

The idea of putting on a suit every day, being cooped up in some high-rise, baking under all the fluorescent lights (kind of like a hot dog on those rollers at the 7-Eleven), and talking about spreadsheets or bottom lines makes my skin crawl.

Not Interested, party of one.

I take off the camera. *Nothing to see here.* Last year, I was all about short, fictional films—I even have a screening coming up in a few weeks for a class project. Now I'm thinking more along the lines of documentary. Reality's the ultimate rush, right? I just need a good angle. I figure the inspiration will come, so I don't push it.

I check out the fridge and settle on a cold slice of pizza. Breakfast of champions! Before Seamless, we kept a whole folder of takeout menus next to the landline. Every place had my mom's credit card number on file, so I could call and ask for whatever I wanted. Now I just order from my phone. It's easier.

My bros are always, like, "You're so lucky that you never have to do family dinners," and they're probably right. I'm kind of a Ninja Turtle with all the pizza I eat and if we took our meals together, I'm sure they'd be all up my ass about it, especially because my mom's on a gluten-free kick right now. I feel like gluten-free pizza is a legit crime against humanity.

I eat my slice over the sink and then wipe off my face with a dishtowel, making sure there aren't any crumbs in my scruff. Earthy is good, dirty not so much. A quick trip to the restroom (yellow, not brown, no need to flush it down), and I'm ready to locomote. I grab my backpack and set the alarm on my way out the door.

If I have a challenging day ahead, like if I've got to give a speech or have a big test or something, I'll rip a few bong hits in the a.m. or I'll stop under the railroad trestle with my pipe. Honestly, I don't make weed *too* much of a habit. People think I smoke way more than I do because I'm generally so relaxed as-is.

Socrates used to say, "Everything in moderation and nothing to excess." I'm into Socrates. He was all about a life of simplicity, which is how I think it should be. Or, in the words of Bob Marley, "Every little thing's gonna be all right." I wonder if those two are kicking it together on the Other Side. I feel like they'd be buds. I bet Carl Sagan's hanging out with them, too, just, like, blowing their minds about the universe. That's a party I'd like to attend.

I'm barely down my drive when I hear, "Cheers, Owen!"

The new girl, Simone, jogs over and falls into step beside me. She's pretty chill. "What's up? You livin' the dream?"

She gestures towards her bulging backpack. "Hardly. This thing weighs a metric shit-ton with all the books I've brought home. Will they lighten up on us with all the homework? We haven't been in school for a week yet! It's madness!"

71

"You wanna hear the truth or do you want to hear what's gonna make you feel better?" I reply.

She considers her options. "Definitely lie to me."

Poor Simone's in for a real treat when midterms roll around, if she thinks this is a lot of work, but I'm not into scaring her or encouraging her to become one of the other grade-obsessed automatons up here. Seriously, I don't get all the fuss about academics. For me, when I receive Bs on my tests? I'm stoked, I'm celebrating. Anywhere else in the world, Bs are pretty good.

I tell her, "Then you can expect smooth sailing over calm seas."

"Outstanding," she replies.

"Trick is, you've gotta pace yourself," I explain. "Everyone gets so bunged up about their classes that they never take time to, I don't know, give themselves a minute. Smell the roses. Just *be*. Like Ferris Bueller says, 'Life moves pretty fast. If you don't stop and look around once in a while, you could miss it.'"

I love John Hughes's movies. He's my favorite director, even above Kurosawa or Scorsese. He doesn't always get the respect he deserves in my film classes, so I just smile and nod when the instructors dismiss his work. The man defined my parents' generation, you know? The film-snob teachers can't take that away from him.

I tell Simone, "Way I see it, we're never going to be seventeen again. We're never going to have less responsibility. I say we milk it."

Simone looks at me like I'm a unicorn or something. "You don't have your entire future mapped out with every single thing you're going to *do* and *be* between now and age sixty-five?"

I don't get that compulsion, either. Why would I pre-plan the next seventy years *right now*? I'm sure I have something that I'm meant to do, but I'm under no obligation to figure it out right this second.

Even if I did know my purpose, who's to say I wouldn't be into entirely different stuff in the future? I mean, around my bar mitzvah, I went through a phase where I kept Kosher because I wanted to be a rabbi. Another time, I was on a huge burrito kick, and now I barely eat them anymore. I was all about fiction last year and now I want real life in my movies. I'm not about to lock in the GPS coordinates until I'm sure of where I'm headed.

I say, "Definitely not. Like, some days I want to move to Colorado and be a whitewater rafting guide or maybe live in the Caribbean, scraping together a few bucks by tending bar and playing guitar. And sometimes I want to go to college and major in philosophy. I'm all about the examined life, you know? Thing is, I have time to decide. If I want, I can do everything. As for right now, *girl*, I don't even know what I'm doing for lunch."

Probably not burritos, though.

She glances at me from under a sheaf of hair that's the same color as Buckeye, this big ol' seal-brown stallion I used to ride when I was into show jumping. "That's an extraordinarily refreshing perspective."

I shrug. "I'm an extraordinarily refreshing kinda guy."

"How come you're hoofing it to school, too? Can't seniors drive?"

I have my own car and a Vespa, too, I just don't use 'em much. "Why burn fossil fuel when these work perfectly well?" I point to my feet.

"You remind me so much of my friends at home," she says.

I raise an eyebrow at her. "That a good thing?"

"Absolutely." Her cheeks get all pink when she says this. I can't tell if she's flirting with me. If so, cool. If not, that's cool, too. I'll hang with her however it shakes out.

She twists a piece of her hair and then becomes real interested in looking at her cuticles. "Owen…" she starts, before hesitating. I give her the space to find her words. I'm in no rush. "Um…would you ever want to get together to study or something?"

"That would be badass," I reply, nodding. "Just gotta know when and where."

She tucks her chin into her neck, but I can still see her grinning under all her hair. "Then it's a date!"

With her happy aura, she looks like she's making me feel. I get real good vibes coming from Simone and I kind of wonder if she means it's a date or it's a *date*.

Either way, I can't say that I'm worried about a thing.

9

STEPHEN

I FEEL LIKE I've been punched in the gut.

I thought I was making inroads with Simone, like she was starting to consider me as more than just a friend. I've been my best self. I've put it all on the line. I've been wittier and more outgoing than ever before. I've stretched, I've left my comfort zone, I've taken chances.

I let her see who I really am.

Thought that was good enough, that *I'd* finally be good enough.

She hugs me way more often than Kent and she's always finding reasons to touch my hair. She says it's because it's so spiky and that she's amazed at how immobile it is. She's always trying to mess it up.

In my mind, my sad, mistaken, pitiful mind, I figured this was her way of signaling she might be open to something else.

Nope. Not even close.

At lunch today, she asked Kent about Owen. Was trying to find out if he had a girlfriend. Admitted she might "fancy" him.

I wanted to throw up my fish sticks and Tater Tots.

I can't tell you what happened in my afternoon classes; they went by in a blur. Like it was Charlie Brown's teachers up there lecturing, all *"Waun waun waun waun waun."*

I felt my pulse throbbing in my head, and each beat of my heart pounded out the question *WHY?*, every thump increasing the pressure until my brain was going to explode. Was like a black cloud blew in and took away the color from every part of my life.

I didn't even go to my Robotics Club meeting, normally my favorite part of the week. I came straight home.

I need to decompress so I put on my black Compton hat with the white Gothic lettering, turn up the speakers on my computer, and play the one song that can always make me feel better, that soothes my soul.

Before Tupac can even get to the chorus about laying him down in a bed of roses and sinking him in the river at dawn, my mother busts into my room. She says knocking's a consideration for people who pay the mortgage.

"Ugh, no, this is *the worst*," my mother says. On the outside, she looks like all the other women in the neighborhood, her statement jewelry and sleeveless dresses and hundred-dollar yoga pants. She's always going to Pilates and playing tennis and drinking wine with her girls. But unlike a lot of the absentee parents up here, she's totally a Helicopter Mom.

"Sorry, Ma, I'll use my headphones." I grab my Beats by Dr. Dre and go to plug them into my laptop, but she stops me.

She glowers at my computer, as though it's personally insulted her. "How about not playing it at all? This music has a *terrible* message. No one says you have to go all Taylor Swift, but this stuff is garbage."

I don't argue with her.

Because I really can't.

My mother's family came to California from South Korea when she was in junior high. Her folks had nothing when they got here, but they worked their asses off, building a small grocery story in the Koreatown portion of LA, pouring all the profits into my mother's schooling. They were so proud to be in America, the land of opportunity, where education could literally take you anywhere.

In the early '90s, my parents were already married and Caitlyn—my sister—was a toddler. While my dad was taking classes towards his MBA at USC, my mom sometimes helped at my grandparents' store. She was working there during the LA riots when the store was looted, ransacked, and finally burned to the ground.

The Korean community in LA refer to the riots as their *sa-i-gu*, meaning 4/29, which is the same kind of shorthand the rest of this country uses to describe 9/11. My mother never talks about what she witnessed over that six-day period. I think she just wants to forget the whole thing, which is probably why there's very little Korean American about us.

Of course, I feel like the worst son in the world when she hears me listening to classic hip-hop, because it's possible the music's a trigger for her. She never says it is, but who really knows?

The problem is that these songs are what keep me sane, which is my dilemma.

I turn it off anyway.

My mother lingers in my doorway, as she's clearly not done with me. "So, I called the Chalet. I asked them to drop off a brochure and price list at the Chastains'. I also touched base with Landscapes by Mariani and Greenworks. I figured they'd want to compare services to make an educated deci-

77

sion. Has Simone mentioned it to you? Given you any idea of their plans? I'm happy to make more helpful suggestions."

Any compassion I feel for my mother dissipates. Her "helpful suggestions" are why Kent's mom no longer calls her to play tennis.

"What the Chastains do with their lawn is none of my business, Ma. It's none of yours, either."

She clucks her tongue. "Stephen, property values are everyone's business. *They* aren't fulfilling the social contract. What, we're supposed to be okay with our home's asking price plummeting because they can't call a yard crew?"

I grit my teeth. It's *grass*, not a social contract.

My mother's upset about Simone's lawn, which is now unkempt, at least compared to the twenty other immaculately manicured homes on our street, one tidy green oasis lined up after the other. I just imagine Simone's parents have better things to do than to chase after landscapers with a ruler, making sure the fescue hybrid is clipped to a uniform one point five inches.

Oh, yeah.

The crew that comes here *loves* Mrs. Cho.

"Ma, they'll get their yard in shape when they're done settling in. They've only been here a few weeks."

"I just don't want potential buyers to assume this town's full of crack houses."

Considering starter homes in our neighborhood go for one point five million and a bunch of Chicago Bears live here (along with tons of Fortune 500 CEOs and hedge fund managers), no one's mistaking North Shore for Skid Row. And we're not even in one of the "good" neighborhoods. Three blocks away, next to the lake, places start at four mil.

"Ma, is there anything else?" I ask, anxious to put on my headphones and start properly feeling sorry for myself.

"Shouldn't you be at your meeting?"

I say, "I didn't feel well," because that seems easier than telling her I'm heartsick, that I'm enveloped in blackness, that I keep punching myself in the thigh just to see if I can *feel* anything.

"Stephen, please. If you're okay to listen to music, then you're certainly healthy enough to study. Seriously. Your father and I will be mortified if you fail any more classes."

Fail. Right.

She's referring to the C that I got last semester in my speech class, a requisite for all students, and one that I put off as long as I could. Most kids take it when they're freshmen. For everyone else, the class was our school's only easy A, but it was rough for me. I killed it first semester when we were allowed to write out everything and work from a script. The extemporaneous speeches of second semester are what slayed me. I couldn't get the hang of speaking off the cuff in front of a group on topics outside of my wheelhouse. I'd freeze up and break into flop sweat. My teacher giving me a C was generous.

For anyone else, one C would not a be a big deal, but speech class took me out of the running for valedictorian, thus ending the Cho legacy of being first in the class, which included my sister, brother, mother, and father.

They're all so proud. Or they were.

The bitch of it is, I'd probably have given a kickass commencement speech, because I'd have been allowed to write that shit down first.

Speech class is what started me resenting Owen, too. I kinda liked him when we were kids. We even hung out sometimes because we lived two houses apart. But now he's this useless stoner, this complete wastoid. How was he able to get up to the podium and ramble with perfect ease and at length about anything in speech? Like he could be a politician or something. I resented his confidence, his conviction in what he had to say. He made everyone in class look bad, particularly me.

Now he's using that golden tongue to win over Simone. FML.

My mother studies me as I'm stretched out. "You are not lying down to study, (a) you'll be asleep in two minutes, and (b) you're going to mess up your back. Use your desk."

Then she exits, knowing I'll be powerless to refuse.

I do what she tells me to, relocating across the room. I drop into my chair and roll over to the center of the desk, resigned. The "back" argument is one I'll never win. She's been oddly relentless about our spinal cords my whole life. Apparently she never got over it when that actor Christopher Reeve became paralyzed in a horseback riding incident. I guess she was obsessed with him, as she learned English watching *Superman* again and again. Due to her age or maybe the language gap, some part of her must have thought the movie was real. So, when he was hurt, she was traumatized.

I swear her obsessive overprotection is why I was never able to take the leap off the big diving board. I'd get to the edge and then I'd hear her in my head, talking about how she didn't want to have to feed me through a tube, then I'd wuss out.

I'm sure my trajectory, my social standing, my whole damn life would be different if I'd have been allowed to play soccer. I spent the summer before seventh grade practicing on my own because I'd never been permitted to join a peewee league and I was tired of feeling left out. Plus, my sixth grade gym teacher had noticed my potential as a foreword and he'd encouraged me to try, even though starting in junior high is pretty late when you consider that a lot of kids had been playing AYSO since pre-K.

I memorized the rules and then I spent endless hours drilling, doing ball work like toe taps and inside-to-outside touches. Plus I worked on my sprinting skills.

I was respectable.

Maybe I wasn't great, but I was skillful and quick and determined. I understood angles and trajectory and velocity so I could always get the ball to exactly where it needed to go. More than anything, I was motivated. Kent was always right there, helping me. I don't know which of us was more jazzed when I was chosen for the team.

I made it through two practices before my mom found out and yanked me—literally *yanked me*—off the pitch. I was so humiliated. Such is my shame remembering that day, I still turn my head when we drive past the middle school soccer fields. Every single kid out there was laughing at me, except for Macey Lund. She was the only one who had any compassion. I'll never forget her mouthing *I'm so sorry* as my mother frog-marched me to her waiting SUV.

Figures that now I'll never have the opportunity to thank the one person who was cool to me back then.

Anyway, my mom said if I was so desperate to play sports, she'd pick one for me.

Now I bowl. I'm a frigging *bowler.*

Turns out, I'm a great bowler because the geometric portion of this game also comes easy to me. Aces. Owen was a star on the lacrosse team until he quit because he didn't feel like playing anymore. He just threw away an opportunity I would die for. Such bullshit.

As for me, I participate in a sport where you can be fat,

where you can drink, smoke, and eat pizza in the middle of a game. I excel at a sport where the median player age is, what, *fifty*?

How do I even have to wonder why Simone isn't into me? How could she like me?

I don't like me.

I mean, I try to give myself positive self-talk, try to display a confidence I don't feel. Like, if I say I'll be successful, then I'll manifest it into being, all Tony Robbins–like. I work to psych myself up by doing stuff like boasting about all my wins, calling my shot like Babe Ruth used to when he'd come up to bat and point at where his homerun was headed. I visualize. I storyboard out the exact outcome I want.

But every time I do, I feel like I'm destining myself to fail.

Then when I inevitably screw up, it feels worse than the time before and it's harder to bounce back. The cloud of failure and desperation just gets bigger and blacker, thicker and more all-encompassing.

Am I ever going to get anything right? Then, if by some miracle I were to succeed, would what I accomplished be good enough for my family?

Probably not.

Sometimes I wonder why I even bother trying.

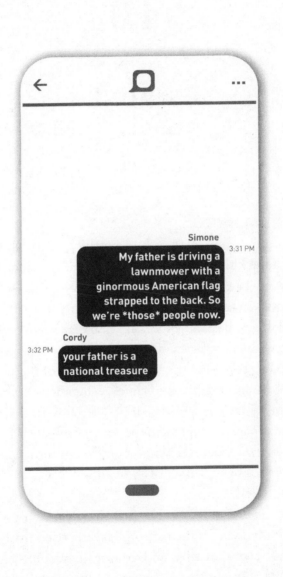

10

SIMONE

"MUM, I'M HERE."

My satchel lands with a thud on the granite island in the center of the kitchen. I rub my right shoulder, which bears the brunt of my bag's weight. Owen says everyone orders a second set of books so that they don't have to lug theirs back and forth.

I'm going to be a hunchback if I don't take care of that soon.

Even with an extra set of books, I still don't know how I'm supposed to complete the five to six hours of nightly homework. Who has that kind of time? When does everyone else hang out with their families or play fetch with their dogs or just take a nap? I simply can't focus that much. My strategy is to prioritize whatever assignments seem most urgent, and whatever doesn't get done? Oh, well.

Has worked so far.

My courses feel like I'm at uni already, except there's no beer or casual sex for distraction. Haven't tried the latter, but my best friend, Cordelia, enthusiastically recommends both, and in large quantities. Cordy's at University of Leeds, in the Institute for Medieval Studies. No idea what she might do with that professionally, but for now, she likes the idea of banging around old castles. (Tremendous fan of banging in all respects, then.)

Anyway, when I'm not prepared for class, no one notices. My teachers don't seek me out, what with all the hands thrust in the air. Most students are begging to be called upon, desperate to show off every nuance they memorized about Julius Caesar's fatal flaws in my Ancient Roman History class. Personally, I don't need a textbook to tell me who Caesar was. Standing in the ruins of the Roman Forum, imagining every surface covered in shining white marble, I could easily envision the conflict between his genius and hubris.

My mother enters from her darkroom off the kitchen, converted from a walk-in pantry. As always, Warhol's at her heels. Even though her hair's held in place by about six pencils haphazardly stuck in her bun and her skin's bare, she's as gorgeous now as she was when she prowled the catwalks with Cindy, Linda, Naomi, and all the other first-name-only supermodels two decades ago.

Everyone used to know who Fi was, no surname required. The few who couldn't place her name recognized that curtain of black hair from her Indian father and her unique eyes, inherited from my Norwegian grandmother. They're liquid gold, reminiscent of a wolf, or a sexy vampire from a terrible young adult novel. With her every feature ideally placed and perfectly symmetrical, we're told that lots of ladies still take her photo to plastic surgeons, saying, "*This*. Make me *this*."

Figures I'd inherit most of my dad's features, so even though I have mum's hair, I'm short with pasty English skin and constellations of freckles. On the bright side, at least I have a chance of growing some boobs. Not a secret—he's always bitching "My tits are bigger than Mum's."

"Hello, Simba." No one in the family uses my proper name. Threw me off here for the first couple of days to hear "Simone"—I kept tensing up, assuming I was being scolded.

"Did you see what Dad's doing out there?" I ask.

She claps her palms over her eyes and shakes her head. "Yes, the stubborn *arsehole*," she says, but without contempt. "He won't listen to me so I called Mr. Hochberg and I'm waiting to hear back. He's going to invalidate the insurance rider! Did you see him touching the blade with his bare hands? Claims he didn't but he's a bloody liar."

I nod. "Yes, *and* I have witnesses, too."

I'm referring to Kent and Stephen. We walk home together on Tuesdays because it's the only day they don't stay late on campus. They're both student tutors and members of the Robotics Club, as well as delegates in the Model UN. Presently, they're ramping up for competitions with the Physics Olympics. Poor Stephen's been particularly stressed because he's the team's leader. For the two of them, their ultimate goal, other than winning the gold, is early admission to MIT. But on Tuesdays, their intramural bowling matches don't start until early evening so we get to hang out a bit, which is always good for a laugh.

The lack of free time is what's so bizarre about this school, beyond the blatant displays of wealth. I know loads of rich kids back in the UK, even some in line for the throne, but none of them live as large as my current classmates. The student parking lot is basically a Mercedes dealership. And the size of the homes up here? My God! Some of my mates have country estates, but those places are all cold and damp and threadbare, shot through with mice and quietly decaying. You have to sleep with a hot water bottle because nothing is properly heated. Plus, those castles have been in the family for hundreds of years—no one's forking over a five-figure monthly mortgage on one that's brand new and ready-made with a proper HVAC system.

Even more than the wealth, I'm dismayed by how little time there is to be idle, to just *kick back*. Most of the fun's orchestrated and school-sanctioned, for the sole purpose of shining on a college application. Behind the scenes, I suspect there's a fair amount of alcohol and drug use. No judgment, though—who wouldn't want an escape from the unrelenting pressure of being conveyed from activity to activity 24/7? When do people sleep? I'm exhausted every day and I've yet to tackle more than half of my homework.

Anyway, the three of us were coming home when we spotted a man on a fancy riding lawnmower in front of my house.

"Someone's clipping our grass!" I exclaimed.

"Oh, thank God," Stephen said, letting out a mass expanse of breath. As we walked earlier, I noticed he'd been clutching his backpack with both fists. Very tense, that one. "My mother's been sending angry emails to the neighborhood association every day, trying to call an emergency board meeting."

"I'm so sorry, I had no idea," I admitted.

Kent added, "Yeah, and if Mrs. Cho ain't happy, ain't nobody happy."

I expected to see Stephen's trademark grin at Kent's quip, or perhaps hear something equally cutting in response. They both have challenging, tiger-type mums who henpeck them to oblivion, inspiring their epic sessions telling "yo mama" jokes. But instead of smiling, Stephen nodded in grim agreement.

Stephen wasn't playing today.

Huh.

As for the lawn situation, it had truly gotten out of control and absolutely was our own fault. In our defense, we'd never owned a suburban home before, just city flats. We planned to be in North

Shore only for the year or so it'll take Mum to photograph and write her book, so we planned to rent a condo, but Mr. Hochberg insisted we not "set money on fire." Then this house came on the market, mostly furnished, and it seemed like kismet.

So, now we have this place where the sheer amount of space feels almost absurd after all the eighty-square-meter rabbit hutches we've lived in across Europe. My father spent the whole first week ignoring his studio and walking around the joint, peeking in walk-in closets and exclaiming about how marvelously *beige* everything was, how delightfully *bland*, like a cup of milky tea.

We didn't know what to do with the grass, so we did… nothing. Then last night we temporarily lost Warhol in the jungle that had become the backyard. He bayed mournfully until we hunted him down (heartbreaking!) and that's when it dawned on us that we should address the lawn.

Mum and I assumed Dad would hire someone to do the job. Never assume.

Now he's out there, cutting the grass himself on the lavish tractor mower just delivered from Home Depot, singing along badly to Johnny Cash, chuffed to bits about the whole enterprise. He offered to take us on rides around the yard. (We declined.)

As for him reaching under the chassis and clearing the blade? Well, that's plain ludicrous. His hands are so valuable that they're insured by Lloyd's of London. Trust me, the first time Mr. Hochberg hears about Dad's Great Landscape Adventure will be the last time.

"How are the boys?" Mum asks.

"Good." I stop myself, thinking about Stephen's taciturn presence. "No, scratch that. Stephen's out of sorts. Kent says he can be moody, but this is the first I've seen of it. He's not himself. He has the best grin in the world and he's not smiling. I'm worried."

Mum knits her brow and places a finger to her lips while she ponders. Finally, she says, "It *is* September."

"That's significant?" I ask.

She nods and one of her pencils comes loose. She tucks it back in, along with a stray tendril of hair. "Can be. In September, the days shorten rather quickly and the nights get longer. That can trigger Seasonal Affective Disorder—SAD. People often become depressed due to the lack of sunlight. You know, he can counter this with one of those light boxes that replicate sunshine. Lots of people at home have them."

"Do they work?"

"Dunno. Never needed one. Just know that the autumnal equinox can be tough."

I nod.

She wraps her arm around my shoulder. "Simba, if you're worried about him, talk to him."

I shrug. "We're not tight enough for me to ask him about his inner feelings. Plus, I'm half British and we're terrible at that sort of thing."

She smiles as she runs her hands through the unshorn portions of my hair. (I've dip-dyed my bangs an indigo blue this week; they're amazing!) "You forget you're technically half American. You'll be fine."

Without needing to ask if I want tea, Mum pulls out a package of Jammie Dodger biscuits and plugs in the kettle. Our house came with a boiling water tap, but Mum doesn't trust it to heat the water properly. In some ways, she acts more British than my Dad, who's embraced all things American since we've been here. Case in point, the size of the telly he bought—we could land a plane on its surface.

"Let me guess—Dad did nothing in his studio today?" Galleries perpetually scramble to book my father's next installation, long before he even brings his ideas to light. As he has unlimited free time and ample workspace here, we thought he'd be prolific, but that's yet to happen.

"Let's just say *one* of us has been productive. Interested to see what I just developed?"

With my mouth crammed full, I reply, "Absolutely!" Bits of crumbled cookie fall onto the floor but Warhol makes quick work of cleanup.

She comes out of her darkroom with a stack of slightly damp, chemical-smelling eight-by-tens. The pungent, sour scent of the fresh photos is as familiar as her gardenia and neroli perfume. She prefers film to digital because she loves the element of surprise film affords, and the delayed gratification, really, the whole scientific process. She claims anyone can "spray and pray;" film separates artist from amateur.

I thumb through the black-and-white photos. There's shot after shot of enormous sport utility vehicles, all queued up, one after another.

"Was the vice president in town?"

"Nope. Keep looking."

The vehicles snake into what appears to be a never-ending line, each one dark and shiny and sober, so many, it's like they're tracing the curve of the earth.

"A military funeral?"

"Here's a clue."

She taps a photo. In this one, an SUV door is ajar and a set of tiny legs appears in the frame, clad in opaque tights, capped with a pair of shiny patent leather Mary Janes, festooned with matching tulle pom-poms.

"Was a royal family visiting?"

Mum laughs and tells me, "Nope. You won't believe it. This is the drop-off line at the elementary school a few blocks over!"

"No!" I'm a bit astounded.

"Yes!" she laughs. "Ran across the scene while I was out with Warhol. So glad I had my camera bag with me. It's insanity, right? These children were practically escorted by the Queen's Guard. Who needs that much protection around *one child*? When you were little, your father would fly through the streets of Paris in a tiny Citroën. I held you on my lap and you were *fine*. Christ, why not just house the kids in Plexiglas?"

"This whole place is kind of surreal, right?" I ask.

Her saffron eyes wide, she nods. Everything about the suburbs is brand new to her, too, as she was born the wealthy daughter of jet-set parents on the Upper East Side. That's why she was so excited to work on this book. My grandfather was from Mumbai and my grandmother from Oslo. They met at the United Nations while serving in their respective countries' diplomatic corps. It's funny that, while my mother embraces all cultures, the only place that's alien to her is her nation of origin.

Dad comes clattering into the kitchen from the garage, reeking of sweat and chlorophyll and gasoline. He offers a "cheers, ladies" as a greeting before he reaches into the giant stainless Sub-Zero and pulls out a Budweiser, then selects a bag of Cool Ranch Doritos. He washes his hands—thankfully no worse for the wear—before joining us at the island.

He takes a long draw on his beer before he picks up one of the photos. "Hmm," he says, inspecting the shot. "Beautiful shot, Fi. Fine perspective. Economic use of negative space. I like how... Whoa, blimey, that's a *huge* car. A beast! It's massive! Ooh, I'd look right smart in a vehicle like that, wouldn't I?"

11

OWEN

"MAGIC HOUR."

I kick back and close my eyes, letting the sun shine on my face. Feels real good after being cooped up inside for so many hours. Sometimes the recirculated air blowing down on me is, like, so oppressive that I can't catch my breath. That's why I don't use the underground tunnels that connect the whole campus, even during blizzards. There's never enough outdoor time in my day; I'm always jonesing for more. Like Ralph Waldo Emerson said, "Live in the sunshine, swim in the sea, drink the wild air." Transcendentalism for the win!

Simone's beside me and we're hanging out on the stadium bleachers. This is my favorite spot around school because it borders the woods. I like all the old oak trees, with their gnarly trunks, some of them real scarred and beat up, as though they've seen some shit in their time. The trees are out there, like, *Son, we've been here for hundreds of years before you and we'll be here for just as long after you*. Bet they will, too. This town goes ballistic if you chop anything down without about a million village permits, so these bad boys aren't going anywhere.

Simone and I planned to study together, but we've yet to crack a book. Fine by me. What's the hurry, right? Like Shakespeare said, "Wisely and slow. They stumble that run fast." In a month, it's gonna be forty degrees and raining sideways and then I'll be the only idiot venturing outside. I figure we should enjoy the weather together while we can. *Game of Thrones* called it—winter is *always* coming here.

"Magic hour?" Simone asks. She opens a Coke and takes a huge sip. The bubbles cause her to burp. Her eyes get real wide, like she's surprised herself, and then she laughs. "Pardon me!"

I appreciate that she's not mortified, like it's not a big deal, so I don't even acknowledge it, instead explaining, "Magic hour's a cinematography term. Means the time after dawn or before sunset when the whole sky turns a real smooth, soft orange because of the angle of the sun. Directors go apeshit for it. Sometimes they blow their budgets just to capture it on film, 'cause it's worth it. At this time of day, the sun's rays are still bright but less intense, you know? All dissipated and everything has, like, an ethereal glow. Picture every Nancy Meyers movie your mom has ever watched—boom, magic hour."

Simone's face lights up with recognition. "Oh, yeah, 'course. Mum calls it 'golden hour.' This time of day always inspires her to take out her own camera. Reminds me of Rome, really. The whole country's practically swimming in gilded light, just so diffused and gorgeous, but Rome takes it to a whole new level. During the magic hour, the sky becomes a burnt sienna wash, covering everything with its brilliance. The Tiber River always looks like it's on fire."

"Sounds badass."

Her voice takes on a dreamy quality. "More like *magnifi-*

cent. Then, as the sun sets, the sky turns from copper then to rose pink before morphing into lavender. All the colors are gradient and they reflect off the pale old alabaster buildings. The whole thing is almost too beautiful to comprehend, like a box of Crayons that's melted together." She stretches like a cat and sighs contentedly before adding, "Rome's one of my most favorite places. Ever been?"

"To Italy?" I clarify.

Simone nods and her indigo bangs fall in her face. I sorta want to brush them back.

"Nah. We've made plans before, but one of the 'rents always has to cancel at the last minute. Work stuff."

"Damn shame, eh?"

I shrug. "Tell me about it."

We had to bail on our most recent European vacay because my mom's company was hit with a class-action suit and everyone in her department bitch-panicked. My parents felt bad and I got a boss Vespa out of it, but I'd rather have just rented one and been with them while we navigated the continent as a fam.

She puts a tentative hand on my shoulder and gives it a little squeeze. "No worries, you'll get there."

I feel good when I'm with Simone, like I have a buzz, even though I'm stone sober today. She *gets* me. Don't consider myself a big player or anything, but more than a few girls have been into me, especially back when I was on the lacrosse team. Was real flattering. I'd hook up with one of them and we'd vibe and it would be cool for a couple of weeks. But, like, every time, whatever girl it was would eventually start in with the pointed suggestions, all, "Maybe lose the cargo shorts?" or "The dreds are super cute, but you would look *sooooo* much more like Ryan Lewis with a haircut."

Then that would be it for me.

Done.

I'm not a fixer-upper, you know? Like one of those ranch houses people snap up on the cheap, slap on some paint, and then sell at a huge profit? If someone genuinely digs me, then they don't think I should change to fit into some random societal construct. Not cool to suggest it, either. I'd rather be alone.

That's when I notice Simone's staring at my dreds. Aw, man, she's not going to try to tweak me, too? Almost subconsciously, I raise my hands to my hair, like I'm trying to protect it.

"I brought something for you. Have you ever considered..." She pauses as if to gather her thoughts, or maybe courage.

Well, Simone, I think, *this was fun while it lasted.*

She says, "This might be weird and you're welcome to say no, but I've been carrying around these Hindu prayer beads that I think would look amazing strung on the tips of your hair. Wanna look at them?"

Pretty sure my smile in response is more golden than magic hour.

"I could have a brilliant career ahead of me in the hairdressing arts," Simone says, all pleased with the job she's done.

I nod, then turn my head right and left, feeling the weight of the beads. Makes me happy that they're special to her and that they came from the other side of the world. She said she'd picked them up in an open-air market in sub-Saharan Africa and everyone would travel from miles around to shop there. Vendors would set up their stalls on the dirt, stacking up their wares, the market's air thick with the smoke of cooking fires, which helped repel the flies, and the African moms would do everything with their babies strapped to their backs with brightly colored strips of cloth. She described the scene so vividly that I itched to capture it on film.

Bottom line, I'm inspired when I'm with Simone. And I liked the warmth that radiated to my back from her legs while I leaned into her as she sat on the riser behind me, stringing my beads while telling stories about her travels. Felt real natural. Comfortable as an old habit, but still exciting.

These beads are more than just an accessory; they're proof that she sees me as I see myself. I'm not afraid she's gonna show up at my house next week with a package from Vineyard Vines, saying how "totes adorbs" some pink collared shirt might look on me.

She likes me for me.

"These are the best," I say, pinching one between my thumb and forefinger before letting it fall. I scoot back up onto the riser to sit beside her.

"Right?" she agrees, beaming.

"You're the best," I add.

At this, she leans in closer, like she's feeling my vibe. I'm stoked at how she doesn't find me wanting, not a renovation project, not a Before picture. I was taking my time with her, afraid of, I don't know, maybe the inevitable disappointment? But I trust her now and I'm ready to make a move. Like Rousseau says, "Patience is bitter, but its fruit is sweet."

Let's do this.

I angle in for the kiss, quiet and deliberate-like because our eye contact is so intense. I move in excruciatingly slow, building anticipation. If our lives were a feature film, this is when the score would swell as our faces come together. I wanted the moment to be right and it finally is. Her breath is sweet from the Coke, mingling with mine as we exhale at the same time. But right before our lips come in for a landing, the riser we're sitting on shakes briefly but violently.

"What the bloody hell?" Simone says, her head snapping up, the moment broken. We look over to see Mallory Goodman barreling up the bleachers.

Figures.

I say, "Mallory's always out here."

"You know her?"

I nod, delighting in how the beads clack with the motion, like my own personal castanets. Every time they bang together, I'll think of Simone and this, the beginning of the beginning. "Sure," I say. "I've known Mal forever."

"Mal…" Simone rolls the nickname around on her tongue, like she's trying to determine if she enjoys the flavor, then finds it wanting. "You're friends, then?"

She almost sounds jealous, but we were never like that and I'm quick to convince her. "Back when we were kids."

Simone's shoulders, which had inched up around her ears, ease down. Her reaction is confirmation that we're feeling the same thing. This gives me a surge of dopamine, a better high than any street narcotic.

I explain, "Our parents all grew up in North Shore and they went to school together so everyone's known everyone forever. Our folks used to hang out so I spent a lot of time with her family. Her brother Holden's a real Zen dude."

"The footballer?"

"That's Theo. He's okay, even if he's kind of a meathead, which is way less interesting. He's pretty much *eat, sleep, football, repeat.* Holden's my favorite. He's older, out of college. When I was a kid, he'd talk about 'escaping the Matrix,' and he's in the Peace Corps now, so I guess he did."

Holden used to say this place wasn't reality, but he didn't

start to hate North Shore until one of his friends shot himself with his father's hunting rifle. His buddy was wait-listed by Brown and figured since his life was over anyway...

God, that was sad.

I was just a kid, but I remember it clearly, maybe because it marked the beginning of a real bad trend around here. Used to think I was so far removed from suicide, because it happened only with kids who were way older. But after Paul this summer, and then Macey Lund, I realize that *we're* the older kids now.

I wish that I hadn't grown apart from Paul when we hit junior high, but we didn't have much in common outside of a similar address. But everyone in this 'hood splintered. With Paul, he dug being onstage and I was into science and sports. Our interests didn't overlap at all. Still, I have to wonder...if we'd stayed close, would things have been different?

Holden was messed up for a long while after his friend died. I get that; I do. Didn't really pull himself together until he decided the best way to honor his friend's life was through service to others. I wonder if he wasn't on the right track.

"Are your families all still tight?" Simone asks, snapping me out of my reverie.

"Nope, they had a falling-out."

Her eyes twinkle. "Ooh, that sounds rather gossipy. Do tell."

I wave her off. "You'd assume it was standard old people stuff, like someone shaved a few too many strokes off their short game. But what really happened was a big fight about academic standards. There was some scandal about test scores or something and part of the town believed one thing, and the other part felt a different way. What started off as a conversation got ugly fast one night over dinner and then that was it. *Finito*."

What's twisted is, I always assumed that being grown up meant you didn't get bogged down in petty high school bullshit. Don't think that's true, though. Our folks were buds, then they weren't. They didn't grow apart, they were just done all of a sudden, like, game over. My mom was pissed, but I never caught the whole story. End result is, we don't do holidays with the Goodmans anymore, which is a bummer. Then again, Holden doesn't come home so I'm probably not missing much. What's weird is that for most of my life they were my extended family, until they weren't.

Simone begins fiddling with her bracelets. "Was Mallory..." She grasps for the right word to end her sentence, but I get what she means.

"Was Mallory always like *that*?" I volunteer, watching her pound up the bleachers a few meters away from us, her face set in deep concentration, the muscles of her legs cut like the Kenyan guy who won the Chicago marathon last year. "Like, intense and hardcore and—"

"Hungry?" she offers.

"Ha. Negative. She used to be fun."

Simone's mouth puckers into a lemon-twist smile as she moves her woven leather cuff from one wrist to the other. I stop myself from touching the tender patch of bare skin exposed after she's swapped the cuff. "Fun. That's difficult to picture."

I'm gonna say it; the jealousy is real cute on her. But I don't want to perpetrate competition or a girl fight. I'm not one to play games. "I said *used to be*. She's definitely changed, not for the better."

"What happened?"

I examine the end of one of my dreds while I think about it. "Nothing real specific." I rack my brain, because that's a bogus answer. "Well. Maybe not. Okay, so, she was hanging out in my room one night when her family was over for a party—this is a few years ago. We were sophomores?"

"You're asking *me* if you were a sophomore?"

I laugh. "No. We were definitely sophomores. Anyway, she'd never seen *The Breakfast Club*, which, criminal, so we started watching it."

"God, I love that film." Simone grabs her hands and clasps them to her chest, kind of like she's hugging herself.

Her reaction to the mention of John Hughes's work? That's a sign. He used to live up here, too. Never knew him personally, but my folks met him a few times. They say he was everything I'd hoped he would have been. His untimely passing was tragic on so many levels.

I go, "Who doesn't love them some J-Hu? That's what I call him in my head 'cause I feel a kinship. Oh, know what else I love? Opening a movie with a crawl—you know, that text graphic where you read the backstory? Like in *Star Wars IV, A New Hope*, which was the first in the theaters about forty years ago, but obviously not the first part of the story. George Lucas's staying power is amazing when you consider—"

"What about Mallory, now?" she prompts, trying to bring me back to this galaxy and not the one far, far away.

"Oh, yeah, I remember she got pissed off about halfway through and I was all, 'What's up?' She goes, 'This movie is fucking bullshit,' which, shocker. She wasn't usually one to swear. Also, even the most pretentious film critics agree it's his best work. So I'm like, 'Why is it bullshit?' She goes, 'Because it's not accurate. Maybe back in John Hughes's time, everyone was all about being one thing—the brain OR the jock OR the princess—but now? No. No way. *Now*, it's like people expect us to be all of these things at the same time and it's just so fucking hard.'"

Simone's face softens and she stops fiddling with her jewelry. "That's truly depressing."

"Right? Like major insight into her world. Anyway, after that night, we were less tight. She got kinda bitchy with me, cold, ignoring me in the halls and stuff, especially once she started getting serious with Liam, and then our families stopped hanging out. I was like, *whatever*. Haven't really talked since then."

"Not at all?" she asks.

"Nope."

Was she embarrassed for letting her guard down around me? We'd swiped a couple bottles of wine and I always say a drunk man tells no lies. Maybe I accidentally peeked behind the curtain all *Wizard of Oz*–style and that made her mad? Maybe she freaked out that she'd shown me too much of her soul or something, suddenly all naked and exposed like that part of Simone's wrist where I can see the pale blue veins under the surface of her skin. Mallory's not the kind of chick who gets off on allowing you to see her vulnerabilities, or anything less than Stepford-perfection.

Simone watches Mallory blow past us with nary a glance in our direction. "Certainly in her own world right now, isn't she?"

I reply, "Yeah, I've seen her run the stairs a million times—I promise you we're invisible. You know, if I were making a movie about her life, I'd open with a black screen and all you'd hear is her thumping and heavy breathing from running the bleachers. Maybe there'd be a grunt here and there. I'd let it go for a minute or two and people would be like,

'Sex scene!' but, no. I hate when directors start a movie or TV show like that, by the way. Too cliché. I'm all, *stop it with that amateur shit*. Anyway, the big twist would be to see that she's not gettin' down, that there's no pleasure there. Instead, she's torturing herself, and that would show the audience so much about who that character is."

She bites her bottom lip before saying, "You see everything as it would play out on film, don't you? My mum's just like that."

I pull back and look at her sideways. "Whoa, it's *super hot* when you tell me I remind you of your mom."

She gives me a shove and I tickle her in return. She shrieks with laughter and says, "Stop! No! I'll wee myself. Too ticklish! Can't do it! Swear to God, I'll piss all over the place."

I pause. "So what you're telling me is I'm like your mom *and* you're going to pee? Oh, you're pushing *every one* of my erotic buttons. *Dear* Penthouse *Forum, I never thought it would happen to me, but I was hanging out with this girl who—*"

Before I can complete my thought, I spot a guy in a Lou Malnati's shirt at the bottom of the bleachers so I excuse myself and head down to grab our pie. Can't study hungry, right?

I tell Simone, "Hold that thought, *my daughter*, be right back."

I amble down to the field and then give my favorite delivery driver a half-bro hug. Sometimes I feel like I see him more often than my pops. "S'up Rico?"

Rico slaps me on the back. "Owen! Good to see you. Double pineapple, pepperoni, and ricotta? Didn't even have to look at the name on the order to know it was you."

I shrug. "I'm a creature of habit." Sure, there are lots of other tasty combos, but this one is the best. Trust me, I've tried 'em all. We bullshit for another minute or two before I head back up with the pie.

Simone clutches her stomach.

I ask, "You hungry or you guarding the fortress against marauding ticklers?"

"Starved. Absolutely famished. Christ on a bike, that smells amazing."

I reply, "See? Who says I don't know how to show my woman a good time?"

Simone peers up at me from behind her bangs. "I'm your woman, then?"

Emboldened, I say, "You tell me."

She flushes and her hands fly up to her cheeks, which are bright pink. She doesn't actually consent, but I feel like this is a definitive answer. Maybe we'll become a *thing* and we'll inspire a one-name couple moniker, like *Bennifer*. They'd call us *Simowen*, which sounds all badass and exotic, with beaches and tropical birds. It's kinda perfect.

Pizza forgotten, we grin at each other like a couple of morons until Mallory pounces so hard on the riser that the aftershock knocks over my soda. I laugh and right my can, saying, "You're stomping on these stairs like they owe you money, girl."

Mallory practically falls over as she stops in her tracks.

She watches as I take a slug of my soda and a drop spills onto my awesome vintage Quint's Deep Sea Fishing T-shirt, a nod to *Jaws*, one of the greatest movies ever made. The way Spielberg built tension in so many ways, like the underwater camera POVs and John Williams's score? Epic filmmaking. First flick to break the hundred-million mark at the box office.

Mallory narrows her eyes at me. "Is there anywhere else you need to *be*, Owen?"

I look around, from the trees tinged in golden light to the cardboard box full of the best pizza on earth to the fascinating lady at my side. Robert Frost wrote a poem in which he claimed that nothing gold can stay, but I feel like he might be wrong in this instance. I lean closer to Simone and tell Mallory the truth.

"Nope. This is *exactly* where I need to be."

Braden
3:45 PM
u around?

Mallory
running stairs, where r u?
3:45 PM

Braden
3:46 PM
weight room. can u text when ur done?

Mallory
...
3:47 PM

Braden
3:50 PM
never mind, will email u later

12

MALLORY

OH, HONEY, DIDN'T anyone tell you that ironic T-shirts are so last year?

"Cheers, Mallory!" Simone raises her soda in greeting while leaning in to Owen Fucking Foley-Feinstein.

Of course she'd be into him.

Of course she would.

My heart's racing in my chest and rivulets of sweat stream down my back. I hop from one leg to another so that the lactic acid doesn't have a chance to collect in my calves, causing a cramp. Anyone else and this wouldn't be my business, but I feel like I need to interject. I say, "Can I talk to you for a second, Simone?"

She pats the spot next to her. "Have a seat."

I shoot a pointed glance at Owen. "In private."

Shrugging, she replies, "Okay. Shall I come up, or would you prefer to come here? Wait, on second thought, I'll pop around to you. You've done enough up and down. I'm exhausted just sitting here."

Please. Like she knows exhaustion.

Like I didn't witness her sitting there in Constitutional Government class today, all unapologetic, all, "Dreadfully sorry, didn't get to it," when the teacher was collecting our homework. I wanted to scream, "If you have time to sleep, you have time to work!"

You can survive on three hours of rest a night. Ask me how I know.

She stands and brushes the dust off her weird front-snapped pants with the low crotch. They're cut like she's trying to accommodate an adult diaper. Again, she did this to herself voluntarily? I thought Europe was the fashion capital of the world!

She moseys up to me and it's all I can do to not just unleash on her. What is she *thinking*, just wasting the afternoon with that loser? Who does that during her *senior year*? And how is it that she's gotten involved in exactly nothing since she's been here? Mr. Gorton told me this in confidence because he was worried; his concern was that *I'd* somehow fallen down on the job as tour guide explaining expectations and it's reflecting badly on him, me, *and* the school.

"Trust me?" I'd replied to him. "Not *my* doing."

Seriously, though, she's in no extracurricular activities. Zip. Nada. Nothingburger with a side of zilch sauce. She's going to have a big fat goose egg to record on her college applications. I mean, when I do finally lie down at night, I can't sleep because I'm overwhelmed. Every second of my day is booked and I still I feel like I'm not trying hard enough and here's this girl who's got *zero* going on and she's just sitting around, calm as can be, not turning in homework and swilling high fructose corn syrup with assholes like it's her job!

UNFAIR!

"You're sweating a *lot*—do you have a towel?" she asks,

looking at me like I'm a bug on the business end of a microscope.

I swipe at my forehead with the back of my hand and run a fingertip under each eye to catch any stray mascara. "I'm fine."

"We have loads of napkins," she persists.

This is not how this conversation is supposed to go; this is not about me. I need to take control. "I see you're hanging with Owen," I begin. "Are you sure that's the best idea?"

She cocks her head. "Meaning?"

Damn it, is she going to play dumb?

Am I going to have to break this down for her?

Owen is headed exactly nowhere in life. Trust me, I know him. I'm *glad* our parents don't get together anymore. He was the worst influence. He loved to spout drivel like, "Get off the treadmill, Mal. Literally and figuratively." As though *I'm* somehow having a problem? I'm not the person who's all *Welcome to Losertown, Population: You.* He's the one throwing off the stats here, not me. I'm setting the curve, the goddamned standard, while he's part of the 2 percent of NSHS students who likely won't go on to college, despite everyone's best efforts to prepare him for the real world.

If he's lucky?

If he's lucky, he moves to LA after graduation, gets cast on some lame MTV reality show, has an on-camera threesome in a hot tub, and then spends the next ten years tending bar and living on people's couches while he milks his infinitesimal bit of fame until he's eventually sent to rehab and then moves back home to his parents' house.

Then we'll all be embarrassed when we see him at our class reunion when he's, like, "Hey, remember how we used to par-*tay* back in the day?" And we won't because we'll have been too busy becoming neurosurgeons and litigators and tech gurus. Or, investment bankers, like me.

Ugh.

But I don't say any of this.

Instead, I say, "Meaning, are you sure that's a good idea?" I gesture down at him with the tip of my right sneaker before I return to my light jog-in-place.

"Why? Because of the weed?"

Oh, good, so I don't need to explain. "Obviously."

She surprises me by snorting. "Um, Mallory? Snoop Dogg stayed at my house when my mum was photographing him for *Vanity Fair*. Trust me, I'm familiar with controlled substances. I tried an edible brownie once, giggled the whole time and I'm *not* a giggler."

I must be giving her the impression that I'm interested, because she continues.

"My best friend, Cordy, and I inhaled about six bags of crisps apiece and she encouraged me to tell everyone on Instagram that I loved them. Which ended up being massively humiliating, by the way. Mr. Knapton, our math teacher, was so amused when Cordy and I showed up in his Algebra II class that Monday morning. He said he was glad at our enthusiasm about his first attempt at making sourdough bread because no one at his house cared much for the loaf. Too spongy."

So, what are we, girlfriends now?

Except that it kind of feels good to stand here and catch my breath for a second. If her boring story is the price of admission, so be it.

"When I woke up the morning after, I felt like I'd swallowed the whole Dead Sea. Wait, you look confused—the Dead Sea? The water has a mad-high salt content? You almost can't drown in it, no matter how hard you try to go under, because the sodium changes the buoyancy. See, now I need Mr. Knapton here to explain because I'm not saying the math-y-science-y part right. Anyway, drugs aren't of interest. *Not my jam*, as you say. Ergo, I'll be fine around Owen. He can't corrupt me—I'm incorruptible by choice."

Gripping one ankle in a quad stretch and then the other, I tell her, "Great, then I'll cross losing you at Coachella off my list. Can you explain to me then how you have a free afternoon to do nothing?"

"We're not doing nothing, we're getting a bit of sun before tackling this mountain of books," she replies, pointing in the vicinity of her satchel. "We're taking a little break *before* we get to work."

"Why?"

"*Why?* I dunno, specifically. Don't you ever feel like eating your pudding first?"

Pudding? *No.*

I say, "Don't you understand how important it is to appear well-rounded to university admissions officers? Colleges aren't just judging you on your grades—your homework's a part of that, you know—they also want to see your extracurriculars."

And, it can't be said enough, college is the big dance.

College is *everything*, which is why there's so much *pressure* on us about it. Our future is all we think about, our singular obsession. Part of the problem is some parents (particularly the narcissistic, self-involved douchebags, i.e. Liam's dad or my mom) see us as status symbols and as an extension of their "personal brands."

We are the feather in the cap that is their Facebook status update.

They don't understand that *we* are not *them.*

When they look at how hard they've had to work to live in

North Shore, their expectations naturally are so much higher. What that means is that even though Southern Illinois University may have been fine for, say, Liam's father, damn it, *the kid's* going to Princeton. What's so ironic is that Generation X—our parents' generation—is best known for being "slackers." Yet they're the ones who are such taskmasters now.

How is that okay?

With our folks, it's like their self-worth has become inexorably linked to ours. If we aren't out there winning, if we aren't out there overachieving, if we aren't representative of the very highest standards of success, then there's hell to pay. Like *they're* somehow flawed if *we* don't get in early decision at Princeton, if we don't crush our ACTs, if we don't win a state title.

I'm like, *when the fuck did they ever win State?* How come it's incumbent on us?

I always regret it when I ask that question out loud, but it's like I can't help myself.

Simone shrugs. "Meh, don't particularly want to go to college. It's not as big a deal in Europe. Half the kids end up in skilled trades instead, which are viewed with much more respect over there than over here. I plan to design jewelry for a living. Technically, I don't need a degree for that. And, if by some miracle I were to be admitted to university, I'd take a gap year first."

Her attitude is so askew, so cavalier, that I accidentally let out a bark-like noise in protest.

Owen looks up at us, confused. "You guys have a poodle up there?"

Idiot.

I seem to be amusing Simone, like I'm the clown in this situation. (*I'm* the clown? Have you even *looked* at your pants?)

She says, "Would you feel better if I told you I agreed to take photos for the school paper?"

"YES, so much better!"

I practically collapse with relief. I didn't realize I'd been so tensed up. I feel like I can check one tiny box off a to-do list that's presently about eight miles long. As a peer counselor and as the leader of *Novus Orsa*, it's my duty to make sure she's getting the most out of North Shore, as it's given us so much. How is she not wildly appreciative of being here? A North Shore education is like someone handing her a billion-dollar check and instead of falling to her knees in gratitude, she's like, "Can I have this in small bills instead, then? I'd like to buy a Kit-Kat."

I don't relax for long, though.

I say, "You know, the paper's very competitive. Most students have to try out for it. Hmm…wonder if they just wanted you because they're hoping you'll introduce them to your mother? Like maybe she'll offer them internships?"

Can I legitimately check off this box or are the kids on *The Round Table Express* just trying to use Simone for her connections? I'm concerned. Does this count as an accomplished mission? Am I shirking my duties or not?

Now she's confused. Ugh, does she have to telegraph every single one of her emotions across her pasty, freckled face? God help her if she ever plays strip poker. "You're saying you *don't* want me to take pictures for the paper?"

I grip her arm to emphasize the importance of this first step. "No, do it, definitely do it. You need the experience for your apps. You'll need more, though, much more. Let me think on what else might be a good fit for you. I'll hit you up in Government with suggestions." After I let go of Simone,

I squat and cross my right calf over my left thigh to open up my hip flexor.

Owen shouts, "You look like the number four!"

"Do you ever stop moving?" Simone asks.

Why do I have the feeling she's judging me? Is she judging me? IN THOSE PANTS? I'm only trying to help. I reverse positions to stretch the other hip.

"No. Okay, I think we're done."

"Then this was...enlightening?" Simone says. She starts to shuffle back down to her spot on the bleachers, hampered by her horrible sartorial choices.

Oh, she's *definitely* judging me. She's awfully smug for someone who probably can't even get into the University of Iowa. Before she sits, a light breeze musses all the unshaved portions of her hair.

"Wait, one more question. Your bangs—they're blue now."

She grins. "Dip-dyed for school spirit. Go, Knights! See you later, Mallory. Have a nice run."

She sits back next to Owen, who passes her a fresh Coke from a Styrofoam minicooler. Sweet Jesus, a *second* can. I have diabetes just imagining two sodas in one week. I shudder as I contract my hamstrings.

Seriously, though, that was outstanding advice on my part. I feel like I can count our conversation toward my time commitment to volunteer peer counseling for the week, maybe a fifteen-minute increment if I round up like attorneys do. When my father speaks to a client, even if it's for two minutes, he rounds it up to the full fifteen. He says otherwise the accounting on his billable hours would be out of hand. (Yes, he has people who do the bookkeeping, but still.)

Now, let's get back to the stairs. Wasn't I on eight hundred and twelve? I quickly flex each of my calves and stretch out my quads again.

Here were go.

Lots of energy, Mallory, I say to myself. *You just had a rest. You should be raring to go.*

Eight hundred and thirteen. Eight hundred and fourteen. Eight hundred and fifteen.

I ease back into my groove.

It's going to be okay.

See? I already helped Simone. I can totally do difficult things. I'm good enough. I can be in control. I'm *in* control. I'm not *slipping*, regardless of what my mother says. Listen, I *needed* to eat that half tuna sandwich; I blacked out in the shower after practice that day! And I made up for the calories on the elliptical.

I'm *going* to be accepted to Princeton.

They'll take me, they have to. I'm the full package.

Nine hundred and nine, nine hundred and ten.

My calves burn with the sting of victory and I'm breathing hard. Sweat is pouring off me once again. This feels good. This feels right. I am the master of my own universe. This is all about me right now. I'm doing everything I can to ensure my own personal best, even if Liam isn't.

Of course he blew off the stairs again today.

Of course he did.

Thing is? If Liam isn't striving, if Liam decides to sit this one out, that's his problem. I can't have him hold me back. I'm not committed to him. I'm not *married*; I'm seventeen. I have to do what's right for me.

I'm all about Team Mallory.

After all, winners never quit and quitters never pepperoni. Um…

Quitters never pepperoni?

Wait...*what?*

I find myself stopping short again and this time I can't control the momentum of my body pitching forward. I go down hard on my left knee, landing with a thud on the metal riser.

"You okay, Mal?" Owen asks, motioning like he's going to get up. *Pfft*, like I'd take Dr. Feelgood's help.

"I'm fine!" I say, holding up my leg. "See? Not even scraped."

The pain in my left knee radiates all the way up to my hip and down to my foot. I keep my face very still so that I don't wince as I shake the left side harder, trying to increase the blood flow. I bend my knee a few times and it seems to be operating normally.

So I'm golden. I am. As always, I *play through the pain.*

They resume what they're doing, which is eating a freaking deep-dish pizza from Lou Malnati's. I can smell it from here. Look at how those strings of mozzarella are stretching, like, a foot long. Simone takes an enormous bite, just crams it right on in, and a chunk of pineapple falls onto the riser, landing with a moist *splat*. Ugh.

Bringing a *goddamned pizza* to where people are working out?

Who does that?

What is wrong with them?

Why is my mouth suddenly watering?

Which step was I on before I fell?

Nine hundred and...?

The Metra train blows its horn as it chugs down the tracks behind the school and the sound makes me tense. Then again, that sound always makes me tense.

Okay, I need to focus.

I'm off my game today. I'm mad that Liam's MIA again.

115

Where does he even go? Unacceptable. Plus, Braden was acting seriously weird last night, like, lingering outside of my
room when I was trying to finish my work after I'd shut my
bedroom door. I was probably more dismissive with him than
necessary, but I was looking at maybe getting two hours of
sleep and I literally could not handle one more thing. Then
earlier today in the hall outside of my Italian class? He was all,
"Can we please talk?" and I told him I was late for a meeting
with Mr. Gorton and that I'd circle back to him later.

I didn't have a meeting; I was just avoiding the conversation. I mean, what does he even want to talk *about*?

I'm sure I don't want to know.

Or maybe I do.

Shit.

Why is my relationship with Braden so confusing? I consider him my third brother, so why don't I have the same kind
of fraternal vibe toward him like I do with Holden and Theo?
Feeling like this, if he were my actual brother, I would need
all the therapy, you know?

I've been avoiding him ever since our conversation last
week, not because he was wrong, but because I fear he was
right. He'd invited himself into my room that night, sitting
down at the end of my bed, taking off his hoodie and getting all comfy. One of the cats immediately hopped on his
lap and curled up there. This was sort of funny because Liam
is so desperate to win over the cats and they sort of hate him
for making the effort. They think he's a try-hard.

"You're not happy," Braden said.

"If you mean I'm not happy you're bothering me, then
you're right," I replied, but I said it with a smile. I swatted
him with my notebook for emphasis.

He swallowed hard and I noticed his jaw was clenched,

like he was biting down really hard. "No, Mal, I'm serious. Things aren't right with you and Liam. You guys fight every time I see you lately and then Theo tells me you do nothing but complain about him when you're apart. That's not healthy. You're miserable. Be with someone who lifts you up, not brings you down. Don't waste your time on someone who makes you miserable. It's bad for you and it's hard on everyone around you."

"What are you talking about?" I replied. My voice came out at a higher pitch than usual, making me sound screechy. Not cool. I cleared my throat and tried again. "What do you mean? I'm super content. I'm exultant. Jubilant. Blissful. In fact, I'm every SAT word for happy. And I promise you, no one around us is miserable."

Except maybe…the crowd at the lunch table (mostly named Jasper) who wince when I get on Liam about running the stairs, or when he complains that my salad is basically water and human beings need more protein than rabbits do. And then there was the time he didn't defend me when the JasHole's *skank du jour* coughed "Pro-ana" into her napkin. That was shitty.

So maybe I've nagged him a little too much about working on his Common Application and then he tells me to stop being so bitchy and I get super frosty, saying I'm not a bitch and he's all, *I didn't say you were a bitch, I said you were being bitchy*, and the whole thing dissolves into an argument about semantics.

And maybe that's happened more than once.

Or he tells me not to be so curt when randoms try to talk to me and I counter that he could maybe try being less friendly when his fangirls get all handsy whenever they find an excuse to be next to him.

Fine, we might have our moments, but misery-inducing?
No.

Braden gave me this look that made something stir in my
stomach, but I tried to chalk it up to having only ingested two
Vanilla Almond Quest bars all day. (Guess what Liam? Forty-
two grams of protein, which is just shy of the RDA of forty-
six for someone my age/size. Boom. How ya like me now?)

"You trying to convince me or yourself?" Braden said.

Through gritted teeth, I said, "I don't *need* to convince
anyone. If you can't see that we're perfect for each other, then
that's your problem, not mine."

He placed a palm on my knee, which somehow made me
think of the perfection of a pat of golden butter melting into
a warm muffin. Maybe I was hungrier than I'd admit?

He said, "Just because you *look* right for each other doesn't
mean you are. Life's too short to stay with someone for the
sake of appearances. Don't do that. I feel like you'd be better off apart."

I bristled. "And you are inserting yourself into my business *why* exactly?"

"Because this has been on my mind for a while and I
couldn't not say it to you. Honestly, it all goes back to Macey.
I've been thinking about her a lot."

I felt a pang of jealousy, quickly followed by self-loathing.
What kind of person does that?

Braden explained, "She let Weston walk all over her. They
were so unhappy together. She and I went way back. We were
friends ever since our peewee soccer team, but I didn't say
anything to her because Weston's my *boy*. Bro Code. Now I
wish I had. Wish I'd interfered. Wish I'd told her, *you deserve
more*. I'd rather have both of them furious with me, but both
of them *here*, you know? Macey's..."

He stopped and took an uneven breath. He didn't seem like he could say the word *suicide*. "Macey's *passing* hit me pretty hard."

I couldn't look him in the eye, instead fixing my gaze downward to where his giant paw rested on my knee. The weight of his hand on my leg felt like the only thing keeping me tethered to the earth; without it I might just fly off into the stratosphere.

"It hit us all hard," I replied, more to myself than him. Macey was so full of life, so quick to make everyone feel comfortable, so eager to please. We hung out a lot in chorus in junior high. While we didn't have any classes together at NSHS, we remained friendly. She'd crack me up, the way she'd run around in her overall-shorts, paired with her endless supply of ridiculously patterned socks, perpetually showing off her Irish Dance moves.

Despite his size, something about our conversation made Braden seem smaller, almost fragile somehow. "Something about her being with Weston, like, diminished her spark. They weren't better together. They were wrong as a couple. I know now she was struggling with depression and her choices weren't Weston's fault, but still. They were bad together and I didn't intervene. If I'd said or done something, maybe we'd have a different outcome. That's why I'm here, right now, telling you I'm seeing the same kind of thing with you and Liam. You guys need to go your separate ways. Please. I don't know what I'd do if anything happened to you."

For some reason, I couldn't acknowledge any kernel of truth in his observation. I could tell he wanted me to open up, but instead I shut down, retorting with, "You know nothing, Jon Snow." Then I put on my headphones and ignored him until he finally took his hand off my knee and quietly left my room.

I've hated myself for how I handled our conversation, to the point that it's impacting my studies and my state of mind and my workout. That wasn't fair.

Liam and I will be okay.

Mostly.

Eventually.

We can even be perfect if we just work a little harder at it.

I shake my head, pushing away thoughts of Braden, particularly the part where his hand on my knee felt so profoundly right, like a second skin, like coming home.

Head back in the game, Mallory, I say to myself. *Keep moving forward.*

I flex my legs and get ready to run the stairs again.

Wait, what number was I on?

You know what?

Screw it.

I'll just start over.

One. Two. Three.

Mallory 7:45 AM

sorry 4 last night, been thinking abt what u said, u may be right

Liam 7:46 AM

what r u talking abt?

Mallory 7:46 AM

shit-meant 4 braden

Liam 7:47 AM

right, bc why ever bother to apologize to me?

13

KENT

"YOU'RE SHITTING ME."

Stephen stops in the street, too overcome with incredulity to take another step. I'm totally there with him, save for I'm still actually moving.

"I shit you not, Stephen," Simone replies.

I'm clutching my head in disbelief, elbows jutting out on either side, shocked. How can this *be*?

I say, "Simone please, explain a scenario in which that's even a vague possibility."

"You act like we're somehow opposed or trying to avoid it," Simone says. "We're not. Far from it. In fact, living close to Chicago was a huge selling point of the whole book project."

"Boggled." I point to myself. "Do you see this handsome face? This is the face of a man who is boggled."

Sometimes it's easy to forget I'm a man, even though I'm eighteen. Because I look so much younger, I make it a point to remind myself and those around me. I'm old enough to vote, to die in some far-flung war, or to pick up a pack of Camels at the gas station, yet waitresses often still hand me the kiddie menu. I let that one slide, though.

(You heard me, Denny's, *Imma* enjoy your chicken fingers *and* grilled cheeses at the discounted price, TYVM.)

People probably peg me for twelve when they don't know me. Hell, I don't even need to shave yet. (Still do, though, in case it helps.) I claim to be cool that this baby-face gets me cheaper tickets at the movies and keeps my Physics Olympics competitors from realizing I'm a serious contender until it's too late, but that's not entirely true. Guess it's kind of like baggage that I've learned to navigate. No, I don't love looking like a preteen, but I don't let it define me.

My mom says the men in our family are late bloomers. She swears they all fill out by the time college rolls around and that my Uncle Dave grew eleven inches when he was a senior in high school. My Nana Swenson had to buy him new pants every month that year because they kept turning into floods on him. Hope this happens for me. I'm not about going through life in a booster seat, you know?

"So no Field Museum? No Michigan Ave?" Stephen demands.

"We've been down to Devon Avenue, does that count?" Simone asks. "We had to go to Patel Brothers to pick up specific Indian ingredients to make *rava kasari* for Janmashtami."

"Those are what now?" I ask.

"Well, one's a type of pistachio dessert and the other's the holiday that celebrates Krishna, the eighth avatar of Vishnu."

"You guys are Hindu?" I ask.

"Sort of. For mum and me, it's like Hinduism is less about religion and more about cultural traditions. That's why we also decorate a tree and load up on figgy pudding at Christmas."

"Best of all worlds, right?" I say.

Stephen's not even listening to us. He's still too wound up

123

about her visiting downtown proper. "*Pfft*, West Rogers Park is barely within Chicago limits. Doesn't count. What about the Sears Tower? You *have to* have been there by now, right?"

By simple association, Stephen reads younger, too. I'd put him at about fourteen when he's with me…which is pretty much always.

"Is that the Willis Tower?" she queries.

"*Bzzzt*, no," I chime in. "If you're from Chicago, it will *always* be the Sears Tower, forever and ever, amen."

She tells us, "You act like we've avoided downtown. We just haven't gotten there yet. We've lived here a little over a month and we spent the first couple of weeks settling in. Plus, we have Warhol and we couldn't leave him for that long at first. He's only now become crate-trained."

"No Art Institute? No Museum of Contemporary Art? Hasn't your dad had his stuff on display there?"

Stephen is about ten paces behind us, still rooted in the same spot, utterly dismayed that anyone would overlook the gift that is Chicago proper. Truth? I'm pleased to see Stephen appalled right now. Psyched, actually. Glad to see him *feeling* anything. I like witnessing some genuine passion.

Sure beats the dull funk he was mired in last week.

I knew there was something wrong when I said that Tupac's song "Dear Mama" was trite. (I admit it; I was trying to bait him, that's *how we do*.) Instead of firing back with any number of facts, like how *Rolling Stone* placed it at Number 18 on its 50 Greatest Hip-Hop Songs of All Time list, or that it was nominated for a Grammy as a Best Rap Solo Performance, Stephen just offered a pitiful shrug and said, "You're probably right."

God, his sulking can be too much. I swear his moods are like emotional ransom notes sometimes, like Crappy Stephen has abducted Happy Stephen and won't let him free 'til I offer up my pound of flesh.

Gets old.

Gets *real* old.

I'm glad Simone rolls with us now; she's great about helping bring him back up, doesn't look at it as a chore, either. I'm not always as generous with him as I should be, but JFC, I'm dealing with my own shit. *You're not the only one under stress, bro.* I mean, he's never had a basketball player rest an elbow on his head, telling him he'd be a great end table.

Yeah, ha, ha.

Real fucking funny.

Stephen's rallying today because MIT confirmed his alumni interview and he says he finally feels like the end is in sight, like all his efforts will have been worth it. No one could be more ready to move across the country/away from his Tiger Mom. Fact. The downside is, he's been talking about how we should room together out in Boston. This is a *bad* idea. I'm telling you, we're still buds right now precisely because I can go back to my own home at the end of the day when I've reached my limit. Hot and cold running Cho 24/7 is a recipe for disaster. But I don't know how to say no, so for now, I smile and nod whenever he brings up the dorms.

Simone is explaining, "Of course we plan to go downtown and of course we will. But right now my father is still having way too much fun hitting warehouse stores."

"Do you guys not have Costco in England?" I ask.

"Yes, but we didn't have the space to buy in bulk so we never went. He's making up for lost time. We own a lot of paper towels now. A *lot*. My father's made it his personal quest to fill all our empty closets with home supplies bought in family-sized packs. Did you know Windex came in gallon jugs? I didn't."

"Speak of the devil," I say.

We watch as her dad pulls up in an SUV roughly the size of the starship *Enterprise*. Simone says he's a total spendthrift and that some accountant keeps a tight lock on all the family's cash, but her dad slipped the purchase past their guy when he was out of the office for Rosh Hashanah.

"Anyone fancy a lift to school, huh? Bet your mates have never seen a ride like this, eh, Simba?" He twirls the pine tree air freshener hanging from the rearview mirror as he nods with pride.

"No, my mom had the exact same model," I say. "Ours was light gray."

"Mine has one now," Stephen says. "Hers is tan."

"I bought a ladies' car then?" her dad asks, shoulders slumping. Poor guy. He looks so flattened behind the wheel. Even his puffy man-bun is deflated.

"SUVs are pretty much unisex," I quickly offer, as I'm so accustomed to trying to bring people up that it's second nature. "Plus, you can use this one to haul a boat. That's why we bought ours."

"Glad the Jewish holidays are over, lest there be watercraft in my family's future," Simone says. I can't tell if she's joking or not because she's super deadpan. (I think it's the whole semi-British thing.)

Mr. Chastain seems to brighten, though. "Well, all right then. Off to Costco! Lots of bargains to be found! Have a good day of class!"

Her dad's posture vastly improves before he begins to pull away.

Simone tells us, "I'm sure once he loads up his cart with

126

sixteen cases of tuna and a few hundred triple-A batteries, he'll be right as rain again. Hope his fascination with shopping in bulk ends soon—he's yet to tackle a single creative endeavor since we've arrived and my mum's worried."

Mr. Chastain roars off and the SUV bottoms out as he crosses over the train tracks. He's got to drive a few miles west to get to the big box stores. North Shore doesn't allow such retail establishments in this town. They don't permit billboards, either. I've lived here so long that now it's weird when I'm someplace that has them.

"The NRA bumper sticker is a nice touch," I observe.

She explains, "Came with the truck. The dealer offered to remove it, but my dad thought it looked menacing in an appealing way. He's profoundly anti-gun, but apparently pro-gun sticker."

I laugh. "Who isn't?"

Stephen sprints to catch up with us. "So you haven't been to Navy Pier. You haven't seen the Bean."

Simone says, "Stephen, what part of 'we haven't made it downtown yet' are you not understanding? And what is the Bean?"

"It's a giant, reflective silver bean-shaped piece of art in Millennium Park," I say.

"You mean Cloud Gate, the Anish Kapoor piece? My parents know the sculptor. He lives in London," Simone says.

"Except no one in Chicago calls it Cloud Gate," I explain.

"Okay, then. Does the Bean *do* anything?" she asks. "Any functionality?"

Incensed, Stephen stops again and puts his hands on his hips. "Does it *do* anything? Are you seriously asking that? Didn't your dad recently exhibit a stadium full of *garbage*? I saw it on the news, with all the old train cars with computer monitors and calculators and stuff spilling out. Reminded me of the roomful of old shoes we saw at the Holocaust Museum on the DC class trip. Friggin' creepy."

"Hey, chill." I step between the two of them, like a referee at a boxing match. This makes Simone chuckle all over again.

"No worries, Kent, I'm a lover, not a fighter. Stephen's right, that's what Dad was aiming for with the exhibit," she tells us.

"Wait, what are you guys talking about?" I ask.

Simone explains, "The installation—called *SegaGenocide*—was a commentary on the death of old technology and our quick-to-dispose society. Dad filled Wembley Arena with antique boxcars, and each was stuffed to the brim with obsolete machinery. One car contained Betamax machines, another Walkman cassette players, there were brick-sized calculators, Atari games, floppy disks, typewriters, etc. The whole thing stretched from one side of the stadium to the other. If seeing the exhibit, even in a news broadcast, made Stephen uncomfortable, then Dad will be chuffed. He believes art should always be evocative."

I say, "Your dad's a weird guy and I mean that in the best possible sense," but Simone's not paying attention to me. Instead, she's totally focused on Stephen.

See?

Even *she's* getting attuned to monitoring and managing his emotional well-being.

She says, "I'm sorry, Stephen. Please accept my apology for any perceived slight. You clearly have very strong feelings for your Bean and I respect that. I would never question the artist's vision, just wanted to know if there was some feature I wasn't to miss."

Mollified, he says, "The Bean looks like it's made from liquid mercury and you can walk under it. Reflects the whole skyline and it's just badass."

She replies, "Well, I can't wait to see it. I'll make it first on my list."

We stop and check both ways before we walk over the railroad tracks. Simone says she's still getting the hang of which way to look before crossing anything here because they drive on the opposite side in the UK. I tell her there are plenty of lights and a protective barrier that comes down when the commuter rail is about to pass, but that you can't be too careful. She's aware pedestrians have been hit by the train before, but I didn't elaborate that these were deliberate choices. She wasn't here at the beginning of the summer so she wouldn't know the details about Paul or Macey, and I doubt anyone's been anxious to tell her. She probably assumes any casualty's an accident.

If only, right?

"You realize this train right here will take you downtown in thirty minutes. No fuss. No muss. Five bucks. That's the price of a coffee. You can walk to the station from your house," Stephen says. "You don't even need to drive and park. The train'll bring you into Ogilvy station and from there, you can either hoof it or cab it to anywhere downtown. Or, when the weather's nice, you can ride the water taxi to Navy Pier on the same route as the big-buck architectural tours."

"Is Chicago paying you a commission or something?" I ask, giving Stephen a friendly shove.

He shoves me back, harder than I pushed him, and I stumble while balancing myself.

(Mental note: seriously, self, double-down on the pushups.)

Stephen tells us, "I'm just sayin', we barely ever get to go into Chicago, what with everything we have going on, so it would be nice if someone took advantage of it."

"He's obsessed with the city. That's because of one time we were down staying with his older sister, Caitlyn," I explain. "She's doing her med school residency at Northwestern Hospital and she and her fiancé, Greg, live in a high-rise. Greg has a boss telescope, real high line. So it's late and they're already asleep and we decide to use the telescope, but it's too bright and we can't see any constellations. We start looking around instead. We spot this beautiful girl in the building across from us. Seriously, she's a total smokeshow. She's eating a turkey leg in her apartment…and then we notice she's completely naked from the waist down. *Boom*, commando! Just maxin' and relaxin' and chewing on her turkey leg, like it's the most natural thing in the world to do *sans* pants."

"That was the greatest day of my life," Stephen confirms with an enthusiastic nod. Poor Stephen. His mom net-nannies his internet usage so closely that he's the only kid in twenty years to comb the library for old issues of *National Geographic* in order to see a single nip.

"I pinky-swear promise you I will hit the city very soon. Maybe Saturday. No more excuses," she says, while linking one pinky to the other for good measure. "My goal is not to peep at the naked, though."

"Go to the Museum of Science and Industry first," Stephen says.

"Thought I had to see the Bean first."

"Go there second. The Bean won't take that long," he replies.

"Any chance you guys can tag along?"

"*Pfft*, I wish. Can't. We have a tournament this weekend," I say. "Gots to get our physics on, son."

Stephen digs into his backpack and pulls out his iPhone, which is wrapped in a case that makes it look like an old cassette. He's so excited, he's practically dancing around us. "I have a surprise for the team. I made the best, most turnt-up playlist for the bus."

The prospect of the interview has him particularly chipper. Elated, even. I like his energy, but I'm wary. He's super mercurial and his temperament changes on a dime. When we studied bipolar disorder in Behavioral Psych last year, I asked Stephen as gently as I could if any of the symptoms seemed... familiar. I mentioned the time he was up for three straight days working on our robot's reticulating arm, and then how he crashed afterward, thrown into a funk that lasted for weeks. He admitted to having his own concerns and promised to talk to his mom about it. I doubt he did, though, because nothing's changed and the mood swings continue. As vigilant as his mom is, she'd have been on it.

When Stephen's down, he speaks in monotone and won't make eye contact, but today his words are animated and full of life. Is it wrong that I think *this* is the guy who's my best friend, *this* dude is awesome?

He tells us, "The playlist is all dis tracks. We're gonna start off super thug with Eazy-E's 'Real Muthaphukkin G's,' then we're gonna pull it back, just a little, with Dr. Dre featuring Snoop and 'Fuck Wit Dre Day.' Then we have Jay Z, Mobb Deep, we'll go sorta new school with Eminem, then back to old-school with Nas, Makaveli, Boogie Down Productions—"

"You should add Nicki Minaj's 'Roman's Revenge,'" Simone suggests. "Cordy and I are mad for that song. We used to sing it together all the time. Our favorite part was the chorus. Suspect we sounded like two damp cats in a sack, but we still belted it out full tilt."

131

Stephen pulls a face like she's just cut the world's most pungent fart.

Now it's Simone's turn to stop in her tracks. "Whoa, why are you looking at me like that, Cho? This a no-girls-allowed list, then? I mean, Eminem's on the track!"

Stephen smirks. "I'd *like* to keep walking to school with you, so *Imma* pretend I didn't just hear you ask that ratchet question."

She raps a couple of lines from the song. "See? What's not to love?" Stephen responds by crossing his arms and staring off into the distance; she's genuinely flummoxed.

I shake my head. "You bring up Minaj, he's not going to acknowledge you. PS, never rap again—it shames us all."

She holds her hand out like she's holding a shopping bag handle and then says, "Can you hear this, Kent?"

"Hear what?"

"No? Then let me turn it up," she says, rotating her wrist to flip me the bird and she sputters with laughter.

I like this.

I like *us*.

We have kickass friend-chemistry. She balances us out. When we roll, we come across as quirky instead of spazzy and everything's more fun. Now, maybe I'm a total prick for even thinking this, but I wonder if her hooking up with Stephen would wreck our new trio? If a love connection would ruin everything? I want him to be happy, but...*fuck*, I want *me* to be happy, too.

I haven't said anything to Stephen, but I've quietly encouraged the whole Owen thing for the past two weeks. Simone says she's confused about how he feels because he hasn't even kissed her yet, but I suspect he's biding his time, establishing a true friendship first. Like he wants to have a solid foundation built before bringing in romance. Doesn't seem like the worst idea to me. (Of course, I'm no expert.)

I tagged along to his short film screening last night with Simone and her folks. I kind of didn't grasp what the movie was about, but that's not a negative. Simone said it was "brilliant," pointing out what was so artistic about the flowers and the wheels and stuff, and then I got it. After spending time with him, I've gained a whole new appreciation for all things Foley-Feinstein. People underestimate him. I forgot that I used to like him and I underestimated him. There's more to Owen than weird hair and a too-casual relationship with soap.

When Owen invited us to his event, I suggested we not tell Stephen because he'd be at his oboe lesson at that time and that he'd have felt bad about missing out, but that's not entirely accurate.

Truth is I didn't want to watch him agonize over every single word, glance, and touch Simone and Owen exchanged and I definitely wasn't up for the Monday morning quarterbacking he'd insist on while doing the postmortem.

Owen's a good dude and he looks at Simone like she's this rare butterfly, almost too delicate to touch. How can she wonder if he likes her? Pretty sure he worships her already and if he's not been quick to make moves, then it's out of respect. Most of the guys in this school aren't like that. Most are total misogynists. You should hear the way they talk in the locker room after gym class. I mean, *I'm* embarrassed, and I'm a Gold Medallion Member at Porn-o-copia.com so I've seen everything…even if I've yet to experience it.

A while ago, my dad decided we needed a father–son talk about the whole porn thing. He sat me down to caution me about images online. He said that the internet would give me unrealistic expectations of what'll happen when I do get a girlfriend. I replied that I'm a five-foot-four future physicist who can bowl a perfect game; the only unrealistic expectation here is that I'd ever even *see* a live girl naked.

I can't complain about the lecture too much, though. When Mrs. Cho busted Stephen after he downloaded an X-rated video on his new phone, his punishment was to *sit there and watch it with her.*

Something like that will FUCK YOU UP FOR LIFE.

Anyway, after the big, awkward porn lecture, Dad took me for sushi, which my mom hates so we never have as a family. Over volcano maki, I told him I do believe I'll eventually find a girlfriend, but probably not in this zip code. He poured me some green tea and promised that the ladies at MIT would recognize my charms. Assured me that I'll have come into my own by then.

Am living for that day.

'Til then, I have a whole harem in my imagination.

(PS, they all look like Mallory.)

My point is, NSHS is *the worst* for most girls. I wanna shout, *You know how much easier your life would be if you liked the* nice *guys?* but they're too distracted by washboard abs and chiseled jaws and Macklemore hair to listen. What am I supposed to say to them? What are my selling points? *Hey, baby, wanna watch me make a robot walk?* It's almost like they're *trying* to hook up with terrible choices. Christ, every Monday there's half a dozen hot chicks crying off all their mascara in the halls because one of the Jaspers used them and abused them over the weekend. (This place is full of Jaspers/Jasper wanna-bes.)

As for Owen? He strikes me as a gentleman. Like, a funky gentleman who might be better served with actual Right Guard and not rock crystal, but still. Washing off patchouli oil is way easier than learning how to be chivalrous.

Stephen scrolls through his list. "*Anyway*, then we're on to Tim Dog with 'Fuck Compton.' He wasn't a huge player in the whole rap game, but this song put Ice, Dre, Eazy, and, really, all of NWA in the crosshairs, so *Imma* allow it. And because I'm not *sexist*," he throws a sidelong glance at Simone, full of shade, "I'll include MC Lyte's '10% Dis'—she's a *female*, just so you know—then Kool Moe Dee, and the penultimate dis, 'No Vaseline,' by Ice Cube."

"Before I came here, I thought *penultimate* meant 'most ultimate,'" Simone muses. "I've been using that word wrong for quite a long time. Ages. This really is an excellent school."

Stephen plows ahead, not acknowledging her comment because he's too excited about his mix to even consider an awkward stab at flirting. "That leads us to the greatest dis of all time... A drumroll, please."

He pauses, expectantly.

Simone and I just look at each other. "Are we supposed to be doing something?" she asks.

"Why aren't you drumrolling?" Stephen pouts.

"Oh, sorry," I say. Simone makes rolling *rrrrrrrr* sounds with her tongue while I beat an imaginary snare drum.

"And the number one dis song is... 'Hit 'Em Up' by 'Pac!"

I drop my imaginary drumsticks and I can feel my mouth narrowing into a thin, hard line.

This is so typical.

This is the exact bullshit he always pulls.

Suddenly, I don't feel so guilty being Team Owen. "Are you seriously not putting Biggie's "Who Shot Ya" on your playlist? That's just insulting and intentional. And wrong. It's wrong and it's insulting and it's wrong."

"Are you saying you feel this is wrong, Kent?" Simone interjects.

While we've been walking and talking (and arguing), we've arrived on campus.

"Don't know what to tell you two, except that 'Pac rules. Don't believe me? Then let's take a simple random sample of our classmates," Stephen suggests.

I roll my eyes so far back that I can see my frontal lobe.

(Mental note: consider other colleges. Maybe I don't even *want* four more years of this, you know?)

Stephen starts looking around at the kids cruising past us on the quad. Mallory and Liam approach from one of the practice fields. While they seem like they belong in Barbie's Dream House together, they're acting more like something out of *Fight Club*. Those two are perpetually bickering. We'll have to work on her attitude when we're married.

(I'm open to going to counseling, though.)

Mallory takes some big strides away from him, as though she's trying to ditch him.

That's right, girl. Walk this way. Come to your new *daddy.*

"Hey, um, you! Mallory! Liam! Real quick—who was better? Tupac or Biggie?" Stephen calls after them.

Mallory curls her lip and replies, "Ohmigod, you're such tools. You need to get a life."

Stephen retorts, "Yeah? You need to get a sandwich."

Liam frowns at Mallory and says, "Take it easy, Mal." He turns to me and Stephen and says, "I'm sorry, guys. She's not really a morning person."

I reply, "Hey, Liam. 'Sup?" I'm extra nice because he would kick my tiny ass from one side of campus to the other if he knew how heavily his girlfriend factored into my active fantasy life. "It's okay. I'm not even worried about her. Would you say that's a vote for Biggie, then?"

Mallory huffs audibly and says, "I can't *even*," before dashing off and Liam hustles to catch up with her. His movement is quick but stiff, like there's some pain associated with having to run.

The next four students vote "Um, who?" and one says "They're Drake's parents," before a music teacher walks past us in the same tweed and leather patched blazer he wears every day, toting a briefcase and a battered old plaid thermos.

"Mr. Conroy, Mr. Conroy! Settle an argument—who was better? Biggie or Tupac?" I ask.

Mr. Conroy removes his bifocals and rubs the bridge of his beaked nose. He has two cottony puffs of comma-shaped hair clinging tenuously to either side of his head. "Hmm… that is a puzzler, indeed it is. I would have to say…my goodness. Such a question and I've not even had my first cup of Earl Grey. If I had to choose, I would opt for…Mr. Shakur."

Stephen begins to bounce on his heels as Mr. Conroy speaks.

Mr. Conroy says, "Admittedly, Mr. Wallace had the better flow, particularly when you break down his rhyming sequence vis a vis his sense of humor. Pairing *birfdays* and *worst days* and *thirs-tay?* Cheeky. He let you in on the joke, that was his power. That was his appeal. With Mr. Shakur, there was something more lyrical, more complex. Heartfelt. Poetic. I feel as though Biggie showed us his personality, he invited us to the party. However, Tupac touched us with his soul and that is the telling difference. Tupac is my decision. Yes. Westside, if you will."

Stephen proves to be a poor winner. He struts around the quad, high-fiving random freshmen, hooting and "throwing up the 'dub," which is a W-shaped gang sign made by splaying the palm and crossing the middle and ring fingers. We learned the gesture together from watching Ice Cube and Da

Lench Mob on old episodes of *Yo, MTV Raps* on YouTube, but *one of us* has enough sense not to do in public.

I mean, dude…*no.*

He carries on for three solid minutes before he returns, beaming, his brow damp with perspiration, to where Simone and I are standing. His grin has taken over his entire face and I can't even see the whites of his eyes. I'm torn between being embarrassed for him and wanting to punch him in his smug face.

The celebration is cut short when we hear the quick bleat of the Metra train's horn, followed by increasingly plaintive pulls, and then the squeal of air brakes applied too late, the sound of metal on metal as the train grinds uselessly against the rails for purchase.

No.

Not again.

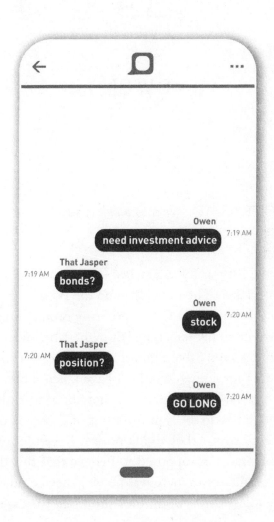

14

——

OWEN

THE NOTE READ, *We're so proud of you!*

Proud of me.

Riiiiiiight.

I took the fifty that was attached to the note and stuffed the bill in my pocket. Then I wadded up the Post-It and tossed it in the recycle bin. If my folks were truly proud of me, they'd have shown up to my screening last night. Mine were the only parents who weren't there out of all the student filmmakers. Why didn't they come? Wouldn't have taken more than half an hour of their day. I taped the flier about it to the fridge weeks ago. They grab skim milk out of there for their coffees every morning; they didn't notice? I even set reminders in their phones. I'm supposed to believe that this thing just snuck up on them and there was no way they could rearrange their schedules? Last month, they promised they were going to be there and then…

Two empty reserved seats, right up front.

I mean, *Simone's* parents were there. *They* showed up. They were all enthusiastic, too, gave me a standing O when it was over, shouting *"Bravo, bravo!"* I'm nobody to them, just some random who's crushing on their daughter.

My parents tell me they're working so hard for *me*. How can that be true when they miss everything that's important in my life? They say one thing, but their actions deliver an entirely different message. They never made an appearance at my lacrosse games, either. Wonder if I'd still be playing if they ever actually came and cheered me on?

So I pulled the money out of my pocket and I examined the bill, front and back. Ulysses S. Grant was sitting there with this look on his face like he'd just been goosed. Was this cash supposed to make me feel better?

It didn't.

But I knew what would. Like Bob Marley says, "Herb is the healing of a nation." In this case, I'm a nation of one.

Jasper Gates meets me under the railroad trestle. His parents are legit billionaires so he's the least likely weed dealer you'll ever meet. 'Course, his forest green corduroys with the white embroidered pheasants are kind of pimp, so I guess that counts. Wait, pimps are for hookers, not drugs.

Whatever.

I asked him once why he dealt—he's not exactly hurting for spending money. He replied that being an entrepreneur runs in the family, which seems as good an explanation as any. I heard his parents spend all their time on philanthropic causes around the globe now, which is badass. But I wonder if Jasper would be dealing at all if they were home more.

The railroad trestle's not far from the school, so it's our usual meeting point. "What's shakin', Kosher Bacon?" Jasper asks as he strides confidently down the embankment. I grudgingly admire his balance. How's he's not slipping all over the place with the dew-damp grass under his slick-bottomed loaf-

141

ers? Guess that's just Jasper for you, everything under control always, not a hair out of place, all gelled back like Gordon Gekko's character in *Wall Street*. There's a whole pack of guys named Jasper at our school, but he's *the* Jasper, the one all the other Jaspers aspire to be, kind of like Heather Chandler in the movie *Heathers*. "Thought you were going soft on me. Where you been, man? You haven't texted in a while."

I haven't bought in weeks. Hasn't been on my mind. "High on life, bro," I reply. "New girlfriend."

He slaps me on the back with one hand and simultaneously takes the fiddy and shoves the Ziploc in my hoodie pocket with the other. "Ass trumps my product? You old dog." Then he punches me in the shoulder, way harder than necessary.

"Whoa," I say, bristling as I rub the point of impact. Not sure if I'm saltier about the assault on my bod or on Simone's character. I haven't laid a hand on her yet because I'm waiting for the right moment.

I say, "She's a really nice girl, it's not like that."

He takes a step back from me, transaction complete. Smirking, he replies, "Figures you can't close the deal. Flaccid-Foley-Feinstein, you're a triple threat."

Sorta of hate Jasper sometimes.

Sucks that he's a necessary evil, so I have to be cool. I take out the baggie and pack my pipe and then I grab my lighter. I offer the full bowl to him first. "You in?" I ask.

He refuses. "I don't get high on my own supply."

"Please, Biggie Smalls, you get high on your own supply all the time," I reply. We used to play lacrosse together and trust me, Jasper was Captain Pre-Game.

He shrugs. "Then I guess I'm a hypocrite. Taking off. See you later, Folsturbater." He sprints back up the embankment, so sure of himself that he travels up the practically vertical face with his paws in his pockets. He won't need his hands free to catch himself if he falls because the Jasper Gateses of this world never fall. This kid lives such a charmed life. He's, like, the luckiest dude in North Shore.

When he's out of sight, I light my pipe, careful to not ignite all the contents at once. Trick is to leave some green. You blaze up the whole thing and that's a one-way ticket to a scorched esophagus and a coughing fit. Rookie mistake. I place my finger over the carb (air intake hole) and inhale, long and steady.

I hold the smoke in my lungs for a solid ten count, and then I blow out a slow stream. A feeling of peace and tranquility washes over me and the universe turns Technicolor, like when Dorothy finally lands in Oz.

The birds' songs are suddenly almost too sweet to bear and the woods around me smell of damp earth, teeming with life. The scene is so moving that I have to swallow down the lump in my throat.

How could anyone be unhappy on a day like this? How could *I* be unhappy? The air tastes like baked apples and the forest looks like someone dumped out a bowl of Froot Loops, with equal parts of green, red, orange, and yellow leaves.

Another hit and I'm cool with my parents again. They do their best. They're trying, right? *A* for effort, if not execution. My mom did come in late last night and kiss me on the cheek when she thought I was asleep. I liked that. And my pops said something about this being the year we finally make it to the Sundance Film Festival. Maybe that'll happen, maybe it won't, but I'm stoked he offered. I'm going to hug him when he gets home tonight. He's a righteous dude.

I am filled with love.

I love my family.

I love being outside.

I love the combination of pineapple and tomato sauce and ricotta and ham. Sounds sick and wrong and definitely not kashrut, but it's *everything*.

I love dogs. We should get a dog because I would really, *really* love him. Like a pug or a Pekinese or a pit bull. Something with a *P*, for sure.

I love Robert DeNiro in *Godfather II*.

I repack the bowl and take another hit.

I love this time of year and I can't wait to show Simone boss old horror movies like *The Omen* and *The Exorcist*. I love that they might scare her and she'll have to climb into my lap.

I could love Simone.

Obviously not yet because I'm building a friendship first. Haven't laid a finger on her. But I could see it happening at some point in the not-too-distant future, though. Maybe Wednesday?

No.

Today.

I'm *absolutely* gonna kiss her when I see her. Screw my whole waiting-for-the-perfect-cinematographic-moment plan. I'm done waiting. Don't care. It's time. At this point, she might not even realize I like her that way, so I plan to show her. *Girl, you are exiting the friend zone in three…two…one…*

I take a fourth hit. This is way more than I usually smoke, but I'm celebrating. All my thoughts turn to Simone. She's been awesome these past few weeks, like interesting and deep and we don't talk about nonsense like clothing or video games. We connect.

Last night Simone's folks took her, Kent, and me out for frozen yogurt after my movie and we spent a ton of time debating about renewable energy sources. Windmills for the win!

Forgot how much I liked Kent. We had some good times at astronomy camp together before seventh grade. A bunch of us from Cherokee Elementary ended up there together. Kent and I were bunk-mates, which was nice. He'd been there the summer before, so he knew everyone. He was supposed to room with Stephen Cho, but Cho's grandfather had gotten sick and he couldn't come.

Kent and I would sit there in the darkened planetarium, clicking our laser pointers, pretending we were shooting Imperial Star Destroyers, his Luke to my Han. Then we came home and Stephen was his shadow. Don't know why, but I just didn't dig Stephen's energy. Too negative or too hyper or too *something*. Always made me feel off-kilter. Ever since then I've lumped Kent and Stephen together. Didn't occur to me that I could hang with one without the other.

Anyway, we got into this epic discussion last night about whether free will is a thing and Kent started throwing out stuff about quantum mechanics and how Heisenberg's Uncertainty Principle proves its existence and I went home with my mind utterly blown. (Kinda wish I'd gone to physics camp now.) So, while I thought the evening was going to be a bad scene after Mom and Dad were no-shows, it ended up pretty good.

Especially the being around Simone part.

Simone knows I smoke sometimes and she's fine with that. She did say she's not interested in joining me because she just can't eat that much sodium. Didn't know what that meant, but I nodded like I did.

Wait…

Is she really fine?

Or is the sodium thing a red herring?

Is that why we haven't moved out of the friend zone?

145

What if her being okay with my smoking is just one of those things you say in the beginning of a relationship, because it's not a deal-breaker, but it's not something you condone? Kind of, *no, it's fine if you leave your empty Starbucks cups in my car,* when you actually mean, *I don't mind having to pick up after you all the time, you goddamned littering litterbug, as you currently possess just enough redeeming qualities that this isn't the hill I want to die on.* Like that.

Does weed make her mad?

Would she be pissed to know what I'm doing right now?

I feel like she might be mad.

Shit.

She's gonna be mad.

She's gonna be real mad and she's gonna dump me before we ever even achieve *Simowen* status.

Can't have that. Don't want that.

I should...quit. I should quit right now. Cold turkey. Detonate the whole habit like the Death Star. I look down at my baggie and it's still full of bud. That's got to go. I take a sharp rock and use it to dig a hole. Once it's deep enough to conceal what's left, I dump it onto the ground and then use my foot to cover it back up with dirt.

Okay, that's better.

Wait, what if it grows?

No, hold up, I'm not Jack and this ain't no beanstalk. Hell, I'd have planted my weed a long time ago if I thought I could cultivate it myself and not do business with Jasper.

What about the pipe, though? What if she gets cold today and asks for my hoodie? I wanna be a gentleman, right? I'd need to cover her shoulders like they do in all those late '80s rom-coms. Giving her my jacket seems like a real Tom Hanks gesture. No one doesn't love Tom Hanks. But what if

146

she reaches in my pocket and feels my pipe? That's not cool. Tom Hanks would never pull a move like that. Need to get rid of it, destroy the evidence.

I take the pipe and throw it into the small stream that runs under the trestle. The current begins to slowly carry it away.

Shit, should I have wiped off my fingerprints? What if someone finds it? Will I go to jail? She won't like me then! I scramble after the pipe and fish it out of the water. I wipe down the whole thing with the corner of my hoodie. I hold it with the tail of my T-shirt as I rub so I don't cover it with new DNA.

Better. Much better. *Mucho mejor.*

I feel like I'm standing outside of myself right now observing the whole scene. As I wind up and pitch, I'm in super slow-mo, like I'm suspended in a vat of molasses or something. My senses are on point, hyper-exaggerated. I can hear the pipe going *whoosh-whoosh-whoosh-whoosh* as it cuts through the air for an endless stretch of time until it finally lands with a juicy splash about three hours later.

Coffee.

I need coffee. I've gotta get it together. I slap myself in the face a couple of times and then I'm mad at myself for hurting me.

Definitely coffee.

New plan. I'll climb this hill and then I'm going to hit the coffee cart for a quad espresso. Then I'm going to drink it real fast, find Simone, and close this deal. Ink that contract, baby.

I start up the embankment but I keep sliding down. When did my feet become skis? This is so trippy. I try again, but this time I bend over and clutch the grass as I make my way up. Grip. Grip the grass. Griiiip. Grrrrriiiipppp. *Grip* sounds like a made-up word. Grrrriiiiippp the grrraaaaasss. Look.

I'm doing it. I'm doing it! I release the grass to give myself a round of applause and when I do, I slide back down.

No applause, O-town. Just grip. Grrrriiippppp.

You know what's hilarious?

Gggggrrrriiiiiip.

I'm halfway up the embankment when I see another dude I know. Wait, he was at camp with us! He wasn't in our same school then, but he is now.

"Greetings, fellow stargazer!" I say, with a lift of my chin. "Can't wave, need to grip."

He doesn't respond.

That's weird. Why didn't he say hey? I'm a friendly guy. He's a friendly guy. Two of us, two friendly guys. Why aren't we being two friendly guys together?

Wait, wasn't he all about the astronomy puns back then? Yeah, he was. I remember he almost wet his pants when I told him my fish in orbit/trouter space joke. He loved puns, fucking *loved* them.

I go, "Hey, how's Uranus?"

I crack myself up, but my words don't even register with him. What's *up* with that? Wait, maybe I'm talking in a whisper and I only sound like I'm yelling in my head? I'll try again.

"What's up, bro?"

Was that shout-y? Felt shout-y. But he says nada. Is he mad at me? Is *everyone* mad at me? Why would he be mad at me? I didn't do anything... Did I? We don't have a beef. We never had beef. But what if we do? What if I wronged him somehow and now he hates me? I feel awful. Am I out there spreading terrible karma, unbeknownst to me?

When did I start using the word *unbeknownst*?

The ground begins to tremble under my grip as I scramble

upward. Oh, *no wonder* he can't hear me. Train's a-comin'. I say, "You can't hear me because of the train!"

I feel better knowing that my old pal is not my enemy. Least that's something, right?

Something.

Something feels off here. What's wrong with this picture? There's something off kilter and I'm not seeing it. Like in the *Highlights* magazines I'd look at as a kid at the dentist office, when one cartoon bear would have an emblem on his fez and the other wouldn't. Like that. Like something isn't right. Like something is off.

I peer up at him. Nah, he looks normal. His usual, maybe a little more tired. Mostly same as always. But something is pulling on the sleeve of my consciousness, though. Something saying *no*. No. NO. What is it?

Can't think, train's too loud.

Train's too loud.

Too loud.

Train.

Oh. Train.

Train.

"Dude," I shout. "Get off the tracks. TRAIN."

0 likes

MalloryGood 11m
where is everyone? ANSWER ME
GODDAMN IT
View all 5 comments

AveryDayAllDay jesus, mal, what NOW?
saw u 2 seconds ago.
SupaFlySpencer im all good
MidfieldNoell noe here, chillin like a villain
EliseALot heard it 2 am sick already
NShoreKnightTheo out of shower after
practice—what up?

15

MALLORY

NO.

The second I hear the desperate pull of the train's whistle, I know.

I know.

I know with every fiber of my being.

How? *How is this happening again?*

The campus is motionless, no one's moving. We're like the world's largest mannequin challenge. No one's talking, not a single word. We're just…frozen.

Bracing ourselves.

The only person who appears normal right now, who doesn't look like she's been punched directly in the gut, who doesn't seem like the whole goddamned world is crashing down around her, is Simone. She's standing there with her two lame friends, smiley and effervescent. Her whole demeanor says, *Now then, what's all this?*

I'm so jealous of her obliviousness, of not knowing what comes next.

I want to be her right now.

I want to be the girl who hasn't yet learned North Shore's dirty little secret. Her ignorance is bliss. Maybe that's because there's a fact that I omitted when conducting her campus tour, an oversight that is in no way, shape, or form small.

North Shore has one of the highest teen suicide rates in the country. Because sometimes being the best comes at a price.

I must be in shock right now because I can't feel anything. I can't run, I can't walk, I can't take a single step. Instead, I'm thinking in facts and figures. Data points are easier to manage than feelings.

I'm rationalizing that suicide is not uncommon in moneyed communities where academic success is valued over almost anything else. Take Palo Alto, a San Francisco suburb like North Shore, where six kids committed suicide between 2009 and 2011. Four more died by their own hands in 2015. In Fairfax County, Virginia, four teenage boys killed themselves in a one-month period of 2014, with fifteen other teens ending their lives in the three years previous. I'm staggered by the numbers. But I'm numb to them, too.

Even though it's an epidemic.

I'm rationalizing that somehow being a part of a problem larger than just this community makes it less terrible. Less tragic. At least that's what I tell myself.

I'm rationalizing that in towns like mine around the country, multiple times a year, kids will acquiesce to that desperate voice inside themselves, the one that tells them they're broken, that they can't be fixed. That their lives are a burning building and they're trapped on the fortieth floor, where it's easier to jump than it is to be taken by the fire. They'll give in to the temporary urge for a permanent solution, the urge to make it stop, for it all to be over.

I'm rational because I'm afraid of what will happen if I'm allowed to be irrational.

This is not okay.

THIS IS NOT OKAY.

If I could *make it stop*, I would.

I watch Simone's innocence slip away as she's briefed on what that sound means, on what just happened. Her broad grin collapses in on itself, replaced with a horrified rictus. Without glancing back at her friends, she takes off across the quad, her book bag banging against her side as she plows through all the static bodies still frozen on the paths.

Welcome to North Shore, Simone; now you're truly one of us.

"Please step inside the building, Signorina Goodman. *Andiamo*," says Ms. DeMamp, my Italian Lit teacher. Her words are sharp, urgent. Her eyes are like two black dots in the middle of a sheet-white face, stark relief to her flashy embroidered peasant blouse.

I start to say "The bell hasn't—" but she's not hearing it. She hustles me through the doorway and shoos me down the hallway. We students need to be herded like cattle into our respective classrooms by clearer heads. And in some cases, the teachers require herding, too.

As I sit down at my desk, I want to turn to my classmates, demanding they tell me *why*.

Yet I already know *why*, at least some version.

The *why* is because whatever problems these kids have are compounded by not getting enough As in their honors classes so they can't become neurosurgeons or litigators or tech gurus or investment bankers and make enough money to buy big houses with rolling lawns and send their kids to whatever schools starts the cycle all over again.

I guess now the question is *who*.

153

We're all suddenly the residents of Panem, waiting to see which tribute is broadcasted.

I move like a zombie through my morning classes, through hushed hallways.

No one knows what happened yet, but the rumors are flying. The true answer is imminent, even though we don't want it. The teachers are the ones tasked with breaking the news. They have a form they're supposed to read; they simply fill in the blank with the deceased's name.

How messed up is that?

This happens so often the school *has printed a form.*

Each of our teachers is given the slip of paper with the name to insert and they all tell us concurrently.

So we wait.

I should be experiencing a mounting sense of dread, a panic that causes me to sweat through my shirt, a fear so thick and bitter and heavy in my chest that I can't pull air into my lungs.

But I can't feel anything.

To feel would be to acknowledge.

I can't acknowledge. I won't acknowledge. Not now. Not yet. Not until.

Right before lunch, we're told that Counselor Gorton is about to make a school-wide announcement this time, rather than our individual teachers.

I steel myself.

The loudspeaker snaps and hums as it comes to life. *"North Shore students and faculty, I…"* Mr. Gorton's voice breaks as he finds the words. *"I have extremely sad news about your classmate who perished this morning. The extremely sad news is…"*

He exhales so loudly that the speaker in the classroom crackles with feedback. I wince. He clears his throat and begins again.

"Crisis stations will be located throughout the school this afternoon to provide grief counseling for those who wish to talk with one of our therapists. Information about the funeral will be provided when it is available, and students may attend with written permission from a parent or guardian."

We all look at each other in confusion. Did he not tell us who? Did he miss that key piece of information? Who? Who was it? We're like a pack of owls in here, all *who? Who? WHO?*

Who the fuck is he talking about?

We hear some shuffling in the background and then the sound of a hand covering the microphone. There's more muffled mumbling and then Vice Principal Torres takes the mic. *"North Shore students and faculty, the extremely sad news is that Braden DeRocher has died. We want to…"*

Nothing he says after that registers.

I am a vacuum. A void. A black hole.

I glance at my phone.

11:34 a.m. That's when time stops.

Collective gasps resonate throughout the whole school, sounding like someone suddenly sucked out all of the air. When the dismissal bell rings at 11:35, girls cluster together in the halls, taking turns sobbing on friends' shoulders and consoling each other.

Meanwhile, I don't shed a tear.

I'm too numb, too empty, too pissed off at the freshmen who are keening like fishwives—a lot of these girls never even *met* him. I know this because he's not just my brother's best friend, he's mine, too. So why are these randoms *weeping*? What do *they* have to feel bad about?

They've never kicked Braden out of their rooms when he lingered in their doorways, looking like he might have something to say.

(Not because they didn't want to hear it, but because they were busy studying for a test they had to ace or else.)

They've never watched his smile fade when they told him to grow up already.

(Not because he'd done anything wrong, but because they were hangry from too much exercise and too little food.)

They've never asked him if he even *had* his own house to go home to.

(Not because they resented having him there, but because they were having their own meltdown and had hoped for some privacy.)

If anyone cries, it should be me. Braden is my surrogate brother who annoys the crap out of me, but whom I secretly adore. But now I won't ever have the chance to make sure he understands both parts of the equation.

Goddamn it.

The boys in school react to the news with stoicism. They're more stiff upper lip, more ashen-faced, save for Theo. He punches a locker so hard that he breaks his hand. Shatters a bunch of bones. The school nurse has me drive him to the ER. Theo will be benched with the injury for the rest of the season.

Our mother has the nerve to be mad at him. Not Theo. I mean she's mad at *Braden* for ruining Theo's season.

I can't.

I can't.

I can't.

NSHS brings in therapists because the whole school is gutted, students and staff alike. How could anyone in Braden's orbit not be?

What's so fucked-up is that this is not our first rodeo, this is not our first time around. We recognize these grief counselors when they appear in their nondescript cardigans, with their salt-and-pepper hair, toting boxes of Kleenex. We've even learned their names because we see them so often.

Mrs. Callahan.

Mr. Regillio.

Ms. Verde.

This visit is going to go down like every other time, where they'll be here for a couple of days, seeking out kids who are actively mourning in the halls. They'll hug us and implore us to feel our feelings. They'll promise us it will get better. They'll tell us to take all the time in the world we need to feel right again.

Except the promise that we can take all the time we need is a tremendous lie, because they're here for two days and then the school expects us to move on because midterms are coming up and the deadlines for early admission applications loom, so, really, we need to pull it together and that's not going to happen if everyone's standing around, feeling their feelings.

Then those grief counselors in their nondescript cardigans with their salt-and-pepper hair pack their Kleenex back into their hybrid vehicles and drive off into the sunset, like nothing ever even happened.

Until next time.

How can they be sent away when we're clearly not done with them?

I try to find out as much as I can from the counselors, but they're so busy when they're here. How can anyone expect three people to process two thousand students' worth of grief in a couple of days?

In the interim, I do what I can in peer counseling, which is never enough. I mean, the whole certification takes twenty hours, and the suicide segment was less than an hour. We're taught to refer those with suicidal ideations, but we're on our own when it comes to helping others deal with the aftermath.

I guess North Shore believes we shouldn't grieve for long, that we're better than that. I mean, do we not breed excellence here?

Maybe I drink too much of the Kool-Aid, because each time, I try to go along with the program. To shut down my emotions, which would consume me if I let them. Maybe the easiest thing is to just trust in our excellence or some bullshit like that. Yet if I do this now, that would mean Braden fell short of excellence, and I don't believe that.

Can't believe that.

If history is an indication, in two days from now, the memorials erected to Braden will have been removed. The counselors will be gone. All the flowers and candles, all the notes and pictures and footballs will have vanished. The administration will have been careful to make sure Braden doesn't look like a martyr.

(Isn't he, though?)

NSHS will be vehement about us remembering that even though Braden's life is over, ours aren't. And again, they'll remind us that college application time is right around the corner.

Like they do.

Like they always fucking do.

The driven part of me will agree that I need to keep pressing forward because Princeton awaits. Braden used to tease me all the time, saying that I wasn't destined to be a Tiger, because I'm much more of a cougar. (Liam's three months my junior.) Then I'll think about everything I have coming up and the cynical part of me wonders *why even bother*?

Right now, I wonder how I'm going to muster the energy for any of what's to come.

This time is different.

This time is so much closer to home.

The two days have passed, and everything I predicted has happened. The counselors are gone. The flowers have been incinerated. The school is trying to maintain a façade of normalcy. But I can't seem to snap back this time, to rally, to forget.

I feel…hollow.

Like an empty husk, the contents long since rotted away, the outside a vacant shell, a brilliant façade.

If losing Braden hasn't been bad enough, the press coverage is making all of this a million times harder. The reporting seems fair enough, but it's the reactions to the stories that are devastating. It's like, "Hey, how 'bout we take one of the worst things that ever happened to you and put it on the national news and let all kinds of viewers offer up their unfiltered opinions on shit they don't understand?"

People who aren't from North Shore are being super harsh on social media, not at all sympathetic. Our teachers implore us to never read the comments, but I can't help myself. I always hope that others have the answer, that they'll make me understand why it happened, that the life he lived then lost was not in vain.

They never do, though.

These strangers, this faceless mob, they're passing judgments based on B-roll of the makeshift memorials in front of Braden's huge, gated house, with its rolling green lawn and driveway full of imported cars. They see pictures of this handsome kid on exotic vacations, like skiing in Gstaad in his silly cat hat, or standing on the beach in Bora Bora, six pack abs on full display, and all they can say is *hashtag* firstworldproblems.

These haters make everything worse for those of us who cared about Braden.

Who loved him.

But never told him.

I feel like I've been cauterized, like my ability to experience emotions has been burned closed. In a bout of self-protection, an attempt to keep myself from falling apart entirely, I've sealed off that which allows me to feel, to staunch the metaphorical bleeding, to protect what's left.

I can't make sense of this.

I have to know *why*.

I have to figure out exactly *why*.

If I can determine this, if I can get to the bottom of *why*, maybe I can pass along the word. I can stop this from happening again and Braden's name will be the last entry on a long, tragic list. So now is the time to be rational. To be diligent. I fight every instinct that's telling me to lie facedown on my bed and sob for the next week.

Month.

Year.

I rally against all the impulses that make me want to pick up his favorite hoodie, which he left in my room the last night we talked, and cling to it like a child with her security blanket.

How can he be gone when his stupid sweatshirt is still in my bedroom?

I need to piece together whatever clues Braden's left, for my brother and for me. Theo is falling apart, so I need to be strong for both of us. I need to be academic about my approach. Systematic.

From a logical standpoint, everyone who knew Braden liked Braden. *Everyone.* There was no bullying, no exclusion, no intentional isolation, none of that stuff you read about in the warning pamphlets that the grief counselors strew around campus like so much confetti in the days that always follow. Braden wasn't like Rudolph in the Christmas songs, you know? He wasn't just invited to join in all the reindeer games; he was the chief instigator. He started the campus-wide snowball fight last winter that got so huge, the North Shore PD had to break it up…but not before they tossed a few as well.

He came up with the junior class prank, too, convincing us to steal every fork in the cafeteria before school let out for summer and leave them at a designated drop point. He had them welded into one giant fork, which he deposited in the middle of the quad on the last day of class, along with a sign that read GET THE FORK OUT, SENIORS. No one knew he was the mastermind until it was over, because he communicated with the student body with anonymous Insta-Chats using codename *Monsieur Fourchette*. He didn't even tell Theo or me.

I guess he kept more hidden than we realized.

Braden is—no, goddamn it, I must stop that—*was* the nicest guy. Goofy. He loved to make us laugh, except he never said "love," he'd only say "heart," as in, "I totally heart the new Chainsmokers' song." He'd go out of his way to make us wince with his terrible puns. And he wasn't afraid to be the butt of the joke. He used to wear a knit cap with a cat's face embroidered on the front, complete with ears that stuck off the top and a tail hanging down the back. People couldn't help but smile when they saw this huge linebacker cruising around the halls in a little girl's Hello Kitty hat.

161

His hoodie catches my eye and I pick it up for the first time since…

Since *then*.

As I do, a pink cat hat, complete with tail, falls onto the floor.

My heart starts pounding so hard that it feels like it's trying to escape from my throat, and my knees go weak. I have to clamp my hands in my armpits to keep myself from picking up the hat and inhaling his essence—clean cotton and ocean breeze and wintergreen Tic Tac.

I practically run to the other side of the room, as though his Hello Kitty hat is a horcrux, full of dark magic, a cursed object. But, logically, what kind of spell could a bit of yarn cast?

The worst has already happened.

I curl up on the padded window bench, pressing myself against the cold glass, as far from Braden's hat as I can get. I decide to double down on my efforts to understand why this happened. That's the only way through.

I need to be smart. I need to muster all my resources.

Braden was smart. Mostly honors classes, with a couple of APs as well. And a talented athlete, so gifted, so nimble for his size. The Knights have been crushing it this season, thanks to him. He's had scouts sniffing around since ninth grade, so he absolutely could have played in college and maybe even beyond. He had so many options.

Was he hit too much, too hard on the field? Had he suffered a head injury? That doesn't make sense; he was far more likely to be the one knocking down opponents.

This doesn't add up. This dog won't hunt.

In my mind, in anyone's mind, really, Braden was not motivated to kill himself, even though Theo says no one really knows what's happening inside someone's mind.

Were there clues? Did we miss them?

Was there a reason Braden was always at our house instead of his own? I'd just assumed he'd had more fun with us than without. The few times we hung out at his place, his parents seemed cool and laid-back, more like pals than parents. He never complained about them; he rarely even mentioned them.

Theo and I have talked about his home life again and again for the past few days and we're coming up with nothing, no triggers there. Is it possible he was mad at his parents? But how? They were barely ever around. In fact, Theo and I once joked about being jealous that his folks weren't overly invested in his success.

Braden laughed right along with us.

He laughed all the time.

But what if all that good humor was the brave face he put on while something unspeakable raged inside him? The bitch of it is, I'll never get to ask him now.

I should have and I didn't and I can't forgive myself for that.

Theo's been suggesting his death was a freak accident. When I first heard the desperate pull of the train's horn that morning, that insistent shriek that sent shivers down my spine, the worst sound in the world, I'd hoped it was an accident.

But part of me already knew.

History always repeats itself.

Still, the idea of an accident has been easier to swallow. An ill-timed crossing, a devastating mistake, a mathematical miscalculation spurred on by the arrogance of youthful invincibility. There's a certain solace in that which is unintended, involuntary, a cruel sleight-of-hand.

Deep down, do I buy that we lost Braden to a terrible twist of fate?

No.

Yet the theory gives Theo a modicum of comfort, so I encourage him. And I try to make myself believe this fiction until it finally feels like fact.

We've just learned there was a witness who saw everything.
Owen Fucking Foley-Feinstein.
Braden's death was not an accident.
I just...can't.

16

OWEN

I CAN'T.
I can't.
I can't.
I can't.
I can't.
I can't.
I can't.
I can't.
I can't.
I can't.
I can't.
I can't.
I can't.
I can't.
I can't.
I can't.

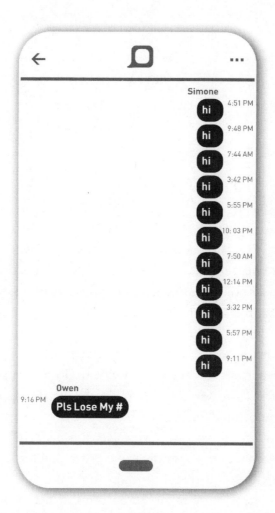

17

—

SIMONE

"WHAT ARE YOU in for?"

"Pardon?" I glance up from my Financial Management textbook. I've thrown myself into my studies for lack of knowing what else to do. Sometimes the easiest thing is to get lost in a book, regardless of the subject matter. Words are always a source of comfort, a true north.

Currently, I'm discovering the nuances of investment strategies, which is both fascinating and terrifying. Thus far, I've learned what not to do and why not to do it. I'm suddenly very grateful for Mr. Hochberg's firm hand. Suspect he's wholly responsible for the fact that we're not homeless.

But I'm not the only one who's circumspect right now. In fact, the whole campus is mired in a proverbial fog. Everyone here is so sad, so quiet.

But no one is more of all these things than Owen.

Owen witnessed what happened to Braden. He *saw* it. Was standing right there. I can't even imagine what he's going through…largely because he won't talk to me. He has utterly and completely withdrawn from everyone, particularly me. He ignores my texts and calls and emails, refuses to come to the door when I knock. He's barely attending school and when he's here, he just looks past everyone, even his closest friends, like we're invisible.

"Mum, what can I do for him?" I asked last week after my millionth ignored text. "I want to reach him, I want to see if he's okay. I want him to know I'm here. Do I just camp out in front of his place? Do I bring a pizza? Do I make him talk to me?"

"Grief is a tricky creature, Sims."

"I'm desperate to help! He doesn't have to be my boyfriend, I would never put that kind of pressure on him right now, but I'd at least like to be his friend. What else can I do?"

"Simba, you've been very clear about extending your hand. Understand Owen's not obligated to take it, regardless of your fine intentions. It's possible he's one of those who heals more quickly on his own. Some people rush to others for solace—people like you," she said with a small, sad smile as she brushed my hair out of my eyes. "For others, they need time and privacy. Space. They need to process inside their own heads, without any external input. Your efforts might be driving him farther away. At this point, you have to respect the boundaries he's erected."

"I just feel so useless, so rejected."

Mum took a deep breath. "Sim, precious girl, *this is not about you*, even if you feel like it is. Let him go for now. Give Owen a month or two, he may find his way back to you."

"What if he doesn't?" I asked, my lip quivering.

"Then he doesn't," she said, but not harshly. Then she hugged me to her and I started to cry.

I *hate* losses. I can't stand to give up. But from what Mum said, it sounds like my being stubborn isn't helping anything.

So that's it with Owen, even though the idea of leaving him alone makes my heart twist up like an origami swan.

Still, I'll respect his wishes. I won't be one more complication in his life, but I will be here if he changes his mind. I hope desperately that he does.

The boy next to me, Liam, I believe, repeats his question.

"I said, what are you in for?" He shifts in his seat, attempting to get comfortable in one of the rigid wooden chairs outside the guidance offices, but they're designed in such a way that this is impossible. Not by coincidence, I'd imagine. He keeps stretching and repositioning his long legs, but can't seem to find a situation that's suitable.

I reply, "I'm *so* sorry, I don't understand the question."

Liam grins at me. I notice that one of his incisors is a teeny bit more prominent than the other, and he suddenly reminds me of my first crush. At the time, Cordy was mad for the boys in One Direction—she wasn't picky, didn't have a fave—but not me. I was all about David Bowie. My parents found that hilarious, because he was *Mum's* first crush, too.

I'm glad to see a person here with a genuine smile. To be honest, this may be the first one I've seen from the student body since Braden died. Kent says that life gets back to normal within a week or two, or at least that's what's happened every other time.

How incredibly sad is it that "every other time" is a *thing*.

Liam says, "You clearly do not watch enough shows about the American penal system. That's what you're supposed to say to a fellow inmate to find out what crime they've committed."

"Huh. I did not know that. Not sure I've heard anyone ask that on *Orange Is the New Black*," I reply. "But then I've only seen one season. Question—am I supposed to *like* Piper? Because she whines quite a bit and it's off-putting. I'm rooting

170

for her to be shanked in the shower. Is that awful? I prefer everyone else, particularly Taystee."

"Ah, so you're avoiding the question. You must have done something serious." He cocks an eyebrow as he leans in and I notice that he smells clean and fresh, like lemon soap and pine trees. I'm grateful that waves of Axe Body Spray don't waft off him like so many of the boys in the halls. Whoever invented that stuff should be imprisoned with Piper.

When Liam speaks again, he's assumed a (terrible) German accent. "Ve haf vays of making you talk."

My bottom's gone numb in this punishing chair. I've been here only a few minutes, yet this furniture is crippling. I tell him, "Five more seconds in this cruel seat and I'll sing like a canary."

"Funf, vier, drei, zwei, eins..." he counts.

Liam is a friendly sort, isn't he? I've heard that about him. People keep saying he's a shoo-in for Homecoming King, which is essentially a popularity contest. Well, if the most popular person is someone who's very nice and a bit cute with his small dimple, then he has my vote.

I divert my attention back to my book. I'm washed in a wave of self-loathing about noticing if Liam might be cute.

What is wrong with me?

I feel as though I should be in mourning for what might have been with Owen. Yet I know Owen's devastated. How could he not be? I so want to support him so he can be *less* devastated, but that's the wrong call, says Mum. Still, how can he not want caring people around him? He told me his parents are never there, so I just imagine him rattling around that big house, all by himself, and it makes me want to sob. I would be so devastated to deal with something like this on my own.

Wait, that's not fair. I've never experienced anything even a fraction as tragic as what he witnessed, so I can't say how I'd feel, can't promise I wouldn't close up, circle the emotional wagons. Perhaps I'd shut down, too. Perhaps he's not allowing anyone in because it's all too raw.

The message I tried to offer again and again to no avail was I'm his friend and I want to be there for him, but he has to *let* me.

In so doing, I suspect I've made it all worse.

Am I doing it *all* wrong here, I wonder? Should I be more guarded around people? Do I give off the wrong idea? Do I perpetrate the fiction that I'm interested in more than I intend? Cordy says I'm a terrible flirt, but I don't see it, especially as that's rarely my intention. Plus, I don't have the confidence to consciously flirt. Rather, I'm genuinely interested in people and maybe that comes across as something else, something I don't mean. I'm a tactile person, always touching—do I invade other people's personal space too much?

Perhaps I misjudged Owen's signals. Perhaps everything was one-sided and I misinterpreted the situation. Would not be the first time. Last night on Skype, Cordy reminded me of the Alastair business a few years back. I thought he and I had been Facebook Official for weeks, always running about together...until he introduced me to his boyfriend, James. I truly thought Cody would hemorrhage from laughing so hard back then. She says I'm too naïve for my own good.

I think the problem *is* me. I sigh with frustration.

"See?" Liam says, responding to my exhale. He's still working the German accent. Christ, I'd forgotten he was next to me. "Knew you vere in for somethink bad. You vill speak or not?"

I explain, "I've a committed a number of crimes, apparently. First, I haven't taken my ACTs—"

"Whoa, you haven't taken your ACTs?" he exclaims, accent abandoned, eyes flying wide open. Brown. Huh. Funny, I'd have pegged him for having something in the blue or green category with all the golden hair and tawny skin. He seems the sporty type. He strikes me as very California, if that's an apt way to describe someone who lives in the center of the country.

Who does he remind me of? Someone…familiar. Ah, *of course*. I snort inadvertently.

"You *must* date Mallory because you sound exactly like her."

His lips flatten into a thin line before he rearranges them into another smile. "Sorry. Natural reaction. I'm just surprised is all. We started doing practice ACTs in eighth grade, and the real thing in ninth, so meeting someone who hasn't taken one? That's like running across a unicorn or someone who doesn't have a driver's license."

I shrug. "Afraid I don't have one of those, either."

At home, I mostly take the Tube when I need to get somewhere, or I ride my bike. I rarely drive my parents' car because traffic in London is ridic. Granted, there's loads of free parking in North Shore and the traffic in town is kind of nonexistent, but I can walk anywhere I need and the whole wrong side of the road business makes me nervous. I need a few driving-here lessons to be comfortable. Owen was going to help me.

Sigh.

Still, getting a license *is* on my list. In fact, I've started a list of all the American Must Do things. There's already so much on the page that it's daunting.

Liam looks me up and down, incredulous. "What? No license? Are you from the moon or something?"

I close my book and slip it back into my satchel. "Yes. Exactly there. You've nailed it. Did my accent give me away? So hard to shake that Lunar Lisp."

"What's your name, Moon Girl?"

Pity that this one has a girlfriend as blond and lovely and focused as Mallory, because he's a delight. While he's not flirting with me, he *is* talking to me like I'm the only person in the world. He's not glancing at his phone or looking around to see who might walk in next. He's all honed in on what I'm about to say and that's a lovely trait, extraordinarily polite, deeply mindful, which I appreciate.

"I'm Simone Chastain. Pleased to meet you."

"Liam Avery." He seems amused when I extend my hand, but he gives it a solid shake, lingering for just a second before letting it go. His palms are neither too sweaty nor too limp. While a bit rough and calloused, they're also firm and warm, exactly the kind you'd want to hold while, say, watching a scary film or killing time wandering around a park on a chilly day. He maintains eye contact the whole time, too, which feels oddly intimate. For a second, I feel more like we're navigating a first date and less like we're queued up to chat with our guidance counselors.

And that is *very* wrong.

I quickly pull my hand away.

"Yes, Liam Avery, I've seen your posters," I say. "I particularly like Liam Avery: The Man Your Man Could Smell Like, especially with that picture of you on the boat and the caption 'I'm on a boat!' A dated reference, but not irrelevant. Or the one where you're on the soccer field, superimposed over the Apple logo with Beauty Outside, Beast Inside?"

Shit, is *this* the accidental flirting Cordy says I do? Not my intention, particularly not now.

The tips of his ears turn red. "My mom used to run an ad agency and lives for this kind of stuff. She and Mallory came up with the posters. I was their unwilling accomplice."

"Personally, I pity the competition. Who's going to vote Weston 4 King or Josh [who] Is 'N It 2 Win It when they can Keep Calm and Liam On? No contest."

A guidance secretary enters the waiting area. "Miss Chastain? Mr. Gorton is ready for you."

"That's me." I rise and grab my heavy bag, hooking it over my shoulder with a small *oof*. Liam gets up, too, even though he's not yet been called. Bonus points for being polite.

"Good luck in there, Moon Girl. Hope you're granted time off for good behavior." He shoots me with pretend finger guns before he sits down again.

I find myself smiling when I enter Mr. Gorton's office.

"Good day, Miss Chastain. Please be seated."

I note that the chairs in here are decidedly more comfortable than the ones in the waiting area. I guess they couldn't be worse.

"Howdy, partner." I doff my imaginary ten-gallon hat at him, inspired by Liam's Wild West gesture.

Mr. Gorton seems nonplussed, but doesn't question my suddenly speaking like a cowboy. Where *did* that come from? Perhaps Liam made me a tiny bit bubbly inside, which doesn't feel like my MO. Then again, I don't have an MO.

Of course, Cordy tells me I'd be more attractive to boys if I could develop some Daddy issues.

(She truly is a font of terrible advice, but I love her dearly.)

Mr. Gorton strikes me as one of the lesser characters on *Mad Men*, perhaps a Ken Cosgrove–type, all tidy and buttoned-down and spit-shined, with neatly parted hair and very starchy shirts. I feel as though the clocks are precise to the second in his world.

He opens a manila folder, placing it on a desk that looks to be neat as a pin. In fact, I'm impressed by how squared away his whole office is, not a pencil out of place. I bet he's never had to drink milk out of an old spaghetti sauce jar at his new house because no one's unpacked proper glassware yet. Of course, right after the whole Ragu incident, Dad went out and bought a gross of new tumblers. A gross! We had no drinking apparatus and now we have every glass in the universe.

Mr. Gorton clears his throat. "Yes, well, much to discuss. Let's begin with the most pressing part, shall we? ACTs. I can't stress enough how important these are. Colleges won't even consider your application without SAT or ACT scores. We've registered you for the test—and paid the fee for the late registration, your parents will need to send a check, make it payable to the school—and you'll sit for the ACTs on October 24th."

I protest, "Begging your pardon but you didn't even clear this with me! What if I have plans that day?" I don't, but what if I did? Very presumptuous on his part.

His wire and tortoise shell glasses make him seem far older than he probably is. I'd guess he was fifty based on his demeanor, but he's probably barely thirty. Suspect this is intentional, to seem like more of an authority to the students. Muss his hair, skip the shave for a few days, and give him cool shirt and a pair of Chucks, he might even pass for our age.

He tells me, "After you take the test, there's a three- to eight-week lag period for the results to be released. Let me be clear here. This is the *first semester* of your *senior year*—eight weeks is practically a lifetime. You cannot afford to wait any longer, it's imperative you take the ACTs now. You're already desperately behind the curve."

Mr. Gorton's cheeks begin to flush and little balls of spittle form in the corners of his mouth. I don't want to stare, but I'm drawn to those tiny spheres of foam wedging their ways into the ends of his lips. They're so incongruous with the rest of his buttoned-down visage. Would it be rude to hand him a Kleenex?

"Behind the curve for what, exactly?"

"For admission! For starting in the fall."

I shrug. "If I go to university at all, I'm taking a gap year."

Mr. Gorton deflates like one of those blow-up Santa yard ornaments on Boxing Day. "We don't advocate gap years here."

"Why not? Loads of my friends have taken them. They're marvelous, great fun. People at home do them all the time."

Every friend that's taken a gap year has loved it. In my head, it makes sense to take time to be a kid before vaulting forever into the world of grown-ups. I don't understand the rush here to have the future all mapped out before you're even legally allowed to vote or drink or smoke.

Mr. Gorton says, "Gap years slow students' trajectories—they throw them off course."

"What if you've no clue as to what course you should be *on*? Wouldn't a gap year be incredibly useful in that respect? Sometimes people aren't fully baked—they need a bit more time in the oven, you know?"

I thought I'd be immune to the pressure here, but it's starting to impact me, put me on edge, particularly now that I don't have Owen's calming influence. The pervasive anxiety in the atmosphere is making me more quick to escalate, prone to argue.

I don't like it; definitely not mindful.

"Here's what we suggest—take your ACTs, apply to college, and if you insist on a gap year, defer your acceptance."

What?

"How is this a good idea?" And how could I select a college when I'm not even ready to pick a continent?

"Beg your pardon?" He rests his elbows on the desk, steepling his fingers.

"How does your strategy benefit anyone other than NSHS? Let's say my applying would help maintain the college acceptance statistics, but how would that benefit *me*? If I'm uncertain about university, why in the bloody hell—sorry, heavens—would I make a commitment? That's nonsensical. While I don't want to be a pain, I have to ask—is this not ludicrous?"

"You're not understanding the bigger picture."

"Then please paint it for me," I request. "I'm not trying to be difficult, I genuinely want to understand your point of view."

His foot taps out a frustrated beat beneath his desk. Suspect this conversation is not going well for either of us.

"My point of view, Miss Chastain, is that 98 percent of our students go on to college right after high school. Our goal is 100 percent. If this were a bad idea, we wouldn't be pushing it."

"Right, but what does it look like a year after this most excellent, well-bred 98 percent graduates? How do they progress in college? Is it smooth sailing? Do your alumni continue the patterns of success set up here or do they arrive at uni and just lose their minds after four years of such discipline? And doesn't anyone want to be, say, an electrician or plumber instead? If that's more their aptitude? Those are excellent jobs in Europe, highly respected. We'll always have lightbulbs and toilets. Why is everyone so hell-bent on college here? Without, say, welders or masons, university buildings wouldn't even exist."

Mr. Gorton is visibly uncomfortable. "Because of our rigorous standards, students establish the groundwork for success here. That's our job and we do it well. How students use these tools after graduation is their responsibility."

So some *do* flame out from burning too hot in high school. Interesting.

Kent believes a lot of the NSHS suicides are the result of students having too much academic pressure, and that makes me want to weep. There's something profoundly wrong when kids feel like they have no other alternative when they don't reach their goals.

That is not okay.

THAT IS NOT OKAY.

I am on fire right now. "Mr. Gorton, I wholly disagree. The solution this school proposes is to work *harder*? Be *more* goal oriented? Have a keener focus? Aren't we all still reeling from a terrible tragedy here? Wouldn't everyone benefit from dialing down the heat a degree or two? Why is this school so intent on pushing people forward when a tiny break, a small reprieve, could be the one thing that makes a difference between life and death? I think that—"

Before I can complete my thought, he starts talking, saying, "The other reason I wanted to speak with you is about your extracurricular activities. You're dropping out of the newspaper? Terrible idea, you need this activity for your applications, it's a must-have. Good colleges only admit students who are engaged, who demonstrate leadership positions. So why are you considering this impulsive and detrimental move?"

I nod. "Artistic differences."

"Damn it, Miss Chastain, you're seventeen years old, you have no right to claim artistic differences!" He bangs a fist on his desk, which takes us both by surprise. Cold coffee sloshes out of his cup and splashes onto the manila folder containing my information. He quickly extracts some Starbucks napkins from his drawer and sops up the spilled brew.

Oh, no. I really have gotten under his skin. Before I can make it right, he beats me to an apology. "I'm so sorry, that was inappropriate. Please forgive me, we've all been on edge since what happened with Mr. DeRocher."

When Braden DeRocher stepped in front of the train that awful morning a few weeks ago, most people froze. Not me. I went dashing to the newspaper office to grab a proper camera. I ditched most of my morning classes to document what was happening. Nothing gristly, but I felt that this was a pivotal moment and it was my duty as a newspaper staffer to record everything.

Choking back tears, I snapped shots of the rescue personnel and the emergency vehicles, of the forlorn sneaker by the side of the tracks, still white from being earmarked for back to school. I focused on the crowd of commuters, each one wearing a different expression, most of them in various stages of shock and disbelief, but a few who seemed almost relieved at the news that it wasn't their kid. That their ticket wasn't the one pulled.

Over the next few days, I took shots of the grief counselors in their nubby jumpers, of the chalk drawings scrawled all over the school's sidewalks, declaring the students' love for 'The Roach'—I guess that was his nickname. I captured images of the custodial staff going along after the students and collecting all the mementos they left at the ersatz memorials around his now-dented locker. I snapped THE ROACH spelled out with Solo cups inserted in the chain link fence around the back of the practice field and of the poster boards with their declarations of "hearting" him stuffed in the bins.

Every single picture broke my heart but also told a story, one the school newspaper refused to report. My shots were summarily rejected so I tendered my resignation.

In my opinion, we can't go on pretending this didn't happen; it's unhealthy. I had no clue these tragedies occurred with such frequency here and I wanted to do something—anything—to make it stop. I felt that pushing reality under the rug was the wrong call.

Mr. Gorton uses one of the napkins to blot at either side of his mouth and he suddenly seems tired and beaten, far closer to fifty than thirty. "Let me explain something to you about the Werther Effect. Are you familiar?"

I shake my head no.

He sighs before he speaks, like he's steeling himself for the explanation. "The Werther Effect is where others are inspired to imitate suicidal behavior after seeing it reported in the media." He reaches into his desk and retrieves a pamphlet, then hands it to me.

He says, "There's such a prevailing belief that suicide is 'contagious' that the World Health Organization has set up specific guidelines for reporting on these stories. The overarching message is that of *restraint*. No sensationalism about the suicide. No prominent placement or explicit description. No particulars of the site where it happened. Actually, no use of the word *suicide* in the headline should be permitted. *Definitely no footage of the scene*, Miss Chastain. So, your pictures, regardless of the quality, of the 'artistic intent,' are inappropriate for so many reasons."

181

I begin to shrink in my chair, clutching the pamphlet, as he continues.

"The media, *including the school newspaper,* has to do everything it can to avoid glorifying or romanticizing the notion of suicide *to keep it from spreading.*"

I feel two inches tall. Why, why, WHY is my first impulse always the wrong one?

"Did you notice how the memorials were removed after two days? There's a solid rationale behind that—many of the students didn't know Mr. DeRocher and seeing evidence of his suicide every day is jarring. Disconcerting. For those in mourning, encountering something about the deceased reopens that wound. We're not trying to 'cover up' Mr. DeRocher's death, nor is our intention to 'censor' you. I believe those were the words you used with your journalism advisor?"

I sink lower into my seat. I want to spread open the pamphlet and cower behind it. If crawling under the chair were a possibility right now, I'd do it.

He says, "We're attempting to keep the emphasis off the story, because the more we focus on someone else's suicide, the more it puts the option on the table for another student. Does this make sense to you, Miss Chastain?"

Christ on a bike. I'm an arsehole. I came in here all self-righteous, spurred on by my nice chat with Liam, embracing my inner cowgirl, ready to take on the world. I was so convinced of being right, of needing to express myself as an *artist,* that it never occurred to me that my own actions could be detrimental.

I say, "I... I sort of want to die now."

Mr. Gorton blanches.

I quickly amend my statement. "I keep stepping in it, don't I? Again and again."

He gives me a weary smile. "Happens to the best of us."

I clap my hands together. "Right, new plan. I'm going to find some ACT prep work and spend the next few weeks getting ready for this test. But first I'll swing by the journalism room and apologize to Mr. Tompkins. I'm sorry, I'm so very sorry—I didn't know. Does that cover everything in your file?"

He glances down at his note. "It's a start."

I can tell we're not done talking, although we're through with this particular conversation. This doesn't mean I can't take my gap year or that I have any clue as to what I'm meant to do as an adult. Nor does it mean he won't try to convince me about how important college is. But for the moment, I want to meet him in the middle. I want him to have a win. How hard have the past few weeks been on him? Poor man. So if Mr. Gorton feels I should have the test in the bag in order to keep my options open, then I will.

I mean, I was wrong—so unimaginably wrong—about the photos, so it's possible that I don't have every last bit figured out just yet.

18

===

MALLORY

WELL, THAT'S IRONIC, I think. *My friends are all wasted, too. And I also hate this* ~~club~~ *party.*

Snakehips is blasting from the JasHole's elaborate sound system. The components look like something out of NASA and the subwoofer's the size of a coffee table. The heavy bass radiates up every vertebra in my spine. Anyone else would just play music on their phone with a couple of portable Bluetooth speakers, but not Jasper.

Of course not Jasper.

The crowd raises their glasses and sings along. Everyone, that is, except me. Not feeling it.

You'd think that no one on a team would drink, given the consequences of being caught. NSHS has a zero-tolerance policy and if you're found at a party where there's liquor, boom, that's it, your athletic career is over, no questions asked, do not pass go/do not collect two hundred dollars, even if you're not imbibing yourself. Were this party to get busted, our entire men's soccer, water polo, and lacrosse teams would be decimated, as would most of the women's field hockey and cross-country teams. PS, shake a pom-pom goodbye at the entire spring sports cheerleading squad, save for Brooke, who's only home because she had her wisdom teeth removed today.

You'd imagine no one would take the risk, yet here we are.

Really, though, it's not like the cops would show up. Jasper's house has a solid half mile of winding, brick-lined driveway from the ten-foot-tall iron gates out front and he's stationed two freshmen from the soccer team to stand guard. Plus, this place sits on about six acres, set high on a cliff over the lake. His parents are out of the country and there are so many trees on either side of his property that you can't even *see* the neighbors, let alone hear them.

Although everyone in North Shore does well, Jasper's folks are extra rich. Super rich. Fuck-you-rich. Lucky-sperm-club rich. If anything were to happen, his dad would be on the horn with his BFF (the governor, natch) and that would be it. Non-issue. Membership has its privileges. Plus, his family's, like, beloved. They spend all their time flying around the globe, doing stuff like building wells for developing countries. But I wonder if Jasper would be less of a JasHole if they ever spent time any time here?

I've been nursing the same vodka and diet cran since I got here. I've had, what, two sips? Mostly I'm just holding the glass so the JasHole's not all, *Mallory, why aren't you partying*?

I'm so not into this.

Noell, a midfielder on my team, comes up to me, throwing an arm around my neck. She's so enthusiastic that she practically puts me in a chokehold. Her auburn hair is parted down the middle and coiled into two matching buns on top of her head. She smells like artificial peaches. I can't tell if that's from her body lotion or her gum. She starts singing right in my face and I can practically see down her throat. I wonder why her parents didn't spring for the white porcelain fillings instead of the metal ones? Why buy your kid new boobs and then cheap out on her smile?

Noell finishes her drink and tosses the empty cup over her shoulder. I'd be all, *Were you raised in a barn?* except that's what everyone else is doing, too. Jasper's house is trashed and I mean that literally. Bottles and cans litter the floors and there are random pizza boxes and McDonald's bags everywhere. All this garbage can't just be from tonight. How long have his parents been away?

A framed, signed Stan Mikita hockey jersey hangs crooked on the wall and there's stuffing coming out of one of the leather club chairs. The cabinet doors on the built-ins hang open, one of them off its hinges, with hundreds of DVDs and Xbox games spilling out across the floor. Looks like a Best Buy after a Black Friday riot.

Unprotected discs are all over the place—on the carpet, stuck in the drywall, peeking out from beneath the pool table—although the bulk of them seem to have landed in the plastic basket that's half-full of dirty(?) clothes, like a game of indoor ultimate Frisbee broke out at some point.

For a moment, I wonder who's going to put this place back together before his parents return from Prague. Then I remember the Jaspers of this world always have someone around to clean up their messes for them.

Noell howls along to the song. Yeah, girl, you *do* drink too much and you *are* wasting your Friday night.

I raise my Solo cup and pretend to take a sip before extricating myself from Noell's monkey-grip. Satisfied with our interaction, she *grand-jetés* over to Spencer, the team goalie. Those two hop up onto a coffee table, where someone hands Noell a fresh glass of something orange. They begin waving their cups around as they dance and shout. Despite the freezing temps, they're both in tiny tanks and miniskirts, their feet bare. I'm wearing leggings and a turtleneck and a sweater and Uggs and I'm still frigid. They begin to grind on each other, less because they're bi, and more because they're thirsty for attention.

I can't help but roll my eyes.

A couple of water polo guys notice—both named Jasper—and start pitching cups at them. Spencer handily deflects each one without spilling a drop of her beer. Her quick reflexes are why we're going to crush Naperville North next Wednesday.

So there's that.

How can everyone cut loose right now? How are they ready to resume their normal lives? How are they not awake all night, every night, trying to figure out why Braden might have done it? He was friends with everyone here. How are they happy? How is that possible? He's *gone*. And it's only been a few weeks. They're just doing keg-stands and pounding shots and dancing on tables, like nothing happened.

How are they not consumed with regret?

Regret for not having seen the signs.

Regret for not being a better listener.

Regret for being too much of a chicken-shit, for getting so wrapped up in appearances, for wanting to make hashtag *BarbieandKen* happen so badly that I never indicated that his crush was reciprocal.

Goddamn it.

Maybe vodka is the answer.

I take another drink but can't even enjoy it because I didn't budget for the calories and I'm too tired to do extra crunches when I get home.

As if trying to deal with losing Braden weren't enough, our

applications for early decision are due in a couple of weeks. Why is everyone screwing around in Jasper's game room when we should be working on our essay questions? Who fucking cares if his dad owns an arcade's worth of vintage Ms. Pac-Man machines? Liam was so psyched to play them, but I was like, "Uh-huh. Be sure to mention all the bananas your avatar ate on your Common Application, 'cause that's impressive."

He didn't even reply; he just walked away. He keeps pretending to hobble around me, too, like he's in oh-so-much pain. He's only doing that to get out of stuff that's hard or boring. Or maybe he's been trying to get my attention because I've been so focused on unraveling Braden's reasons.

Whatever.

I'll be submitting my app as soon as I write my personal essay for Princeton. I already completed my whole Common Application and took my ACTs and the two SAT subject tests. I hit the top ninety-sixth percentile in each, yet my mother wanted to know why they weren't higher. I told her I could show her the math behind the percentiles, but someone who went to *Arizona State* might not understand.

(She was furious, but at least I made Theo laugh.)

I have glowing personal recommendations from four of my teachers for my app as well. I only needed two, but I always cover my bases. Glad I did—I sort of feel like Ms. DeMamp was being backhanded, "complimenting" my intensity and drive.

I worked with an admissions coach to answer the fill-in-the-blank portions of Princeton's form. The coach explained that although Princeton wants me to be authentic, there's honest and then there's *honest*. Each answer paints a specific picture and it was his job to ensure my responses were in line with best presenting myself. For example, with Favorite

Book, I couldn't write, *Who has time to read for fun?* (or *Pretty Little Liars*) so instead he had me talk about Aldous Huxley's *Brave New World*. I went all counterpoint, elaborating on the benefits of being an Alpha. I'm sure most people claim to side with the Savage because of his humanity, but given the choice, wouldn't we prefer to be born superior?

My coach vetoed my original Favorite Line from a Book or a Movie. He said it's cliché to pick Fitzgerald's quote from *The Great Gatsby* about beating on, boats against the current, so I went with "'Dear God,' she prayed, 'let me be something every minute of every hour of my life'" from *A Tree Grows in Brooklyn* because it's apt and it is how I feel—really, it's how I live.

I tied the quote in with an early memory of my mother reading this novel to me and how *A Tree Grows in Brooklyn* inspired a lifetime love of the written word.

Except that's total BS.

The only thing my mother ever read to me was the label on a package of Chips Ahoy when she thought I was looking thick in seventh grade. "Sugar?" she'd shrieked. "High fructose corn syrup? Partially hydrogenated cottonseed oil? This is why you're fat, Calorie Mallory."

Is it any wonder I dieted myself out of that moniker right quick?

Speaking of, Jasper refuses to call any of his friends by their real names. Everyone he likes gets a nickname. A Jasper nickname is a badge of honor.

Try to guess what he calls me.

"Yo, Mallory!" he hollers. His cheeks are flushed red and his normally slicked-back brown curls are all over the place. He's basically a big, drunken Labradoodle. Today his pants are embroidered with little pumpkins, presumably in honor of it being fall. His oxford shirt hangs open and he has a striped rep tie wrapped around his head like a sweatband, as though he's a competing in the Preppy Hunger Games. "We're doing body shots and we need a body—c'mere."

"I'm good where I am," I reply with a tight smile. I plant myself on the couch.

"Don't be lame, the Knights need you! Your stomach is like, convex, and you'll hold the most tequila."

"Concave," I correct.

He shrugs. "Same diff."

"Nope, not even a little bit."

"Mallory, you're being a major buzzkill," he says. "Didn't you used to be fun?"

"Jas, I'm, like, the most clothed person here," I argue, pointing to all my layers. "Go find someone less dressed. So, basically anyone else."

"*Pfft*, be like that then," Jasper replies. "Yo, Noell, My Belle! Body shots!"

Noell hops down from the coffee table and yanks off her tank, flaunting her new assets, housed in a Victoria's Secret push-up bra. This evokes a spontaneous round of applause from the water polo Jaspers.

"What?" she says innocently, wrapping her shirt around her neck like a towel post-workout. "I don't want it to get wet."

Flo Rida's "Wobble" comes on and Jasmine from the JV cheer team squeals. Her name is actually Margo, but she resembles the Disney princess so closely that it was inevitable that Jasper gave her this nickname. She hurls her arms up and out with the high-V of victory in someone *finally* playing her jam. (Which isn't hard. Nine out of ten songs are her jam.) Her gesture knocks Dane's beer out of his hands and I end up covered in foam and Natty Light dregs.

"Ohmigod, I'm like *so* sorry!" Jasmine says.

"No prob," I reply, and it truly isn't.

Because now I have the perfect excuse to leave.

I don't bother looking for Liam to say goodbye. I'm sure he's too wasted to drive me home at this point and I'm not into spending time with him anyway. I thought he'd be my rock over the last few weeks, but that hasn't happened. Lately he's been avoiding me, saying I have to let go, that I can't keep going over the circumstances around Braden's death, dissecting every piece of information in the hopes of finding some kind of clue.

Sometimes I wonder if he even knows me at all.

I order an Uber, which should be here by the time I make it to the end of Jasper's driveway. Uber has been my mother's most favorite invention ever. Before I had the LR4, setting me up with an account allowed her to not have to even pretend to be invested in my comings and goings.

I exit through the double front doors and head over to the giant three-tiered fountain Jasper's folks imported from Milan. When we would come here for birthday parties as little kids, all of us would ask our parents for coins and we'd toss them into the water while making our wishes. Years later, Jasper admitted he'd fish out all the money and spend it on candy. That still makes me mad—it's like he was stealing our hopes and dreams.

The fountain is illuminated by underwater spotlights, located in a circle of grass in the middle of Jasper's driveway. I dip my hands in the freezing cold water and press them to my face, wiping away stray bits of froth from the beer. The water smells vaguely of algae. I'm tempted to toss in a coin but don't because Jasper would probably swipe it anyway.

And wishes can't bring back Braden.

I sprint down the drive and away from the house before someone can stop me from leaving the party. No one follows me. I'm not sure if I'm relieved or disappointed.

At the bottom of the hill leading up to the house, the freshmen assigned to gate duty are huddled together with a fifth of peppermint schnapps. They're watching YouTube videos on their phones—looks to be shouting goats.

"You outta here, Mallory?" one of them asks, putting his video on mute. I don't know his name, but he knows mine. Whether that's because of my own merits or due to dating the team's star is undetermined.

"Someone spilled a beer on me. I smell like the Anheuser-Busch factory, so I'm leaving," I reply.

"That sucks, man!" says the other freshman. He holds up the bottle of schnapps. "Hey, you didn't happen to bring one of those beers with you, by any chance? This is like drinking mouthwash."

"Unless you want to wring out my sweater, then no."

I exit the pedestrian gate just as my Uber arrives. I open the door to the Audi and slide in back, and am immediately surrounded by the scent of new leather and luxury. "Hi, I'm the one who called. I'm going to 221 Morningstar, please."

The driver looks at me in the rearview mirror. "That you, Mallory?"

"Um, yes?" Kind of a random question. I mean, didn't he receive all my details when I placed the order?

"No way! It's me, Mal, Jeremy Jones!"

"Wait, Jeremy? *Rugby* Jeremy? From NSHS?" Jeremy was a senior when I was a freshman. He was tremendously popular back then, and another one of the all-arounders, meaning he excelled at everything—sports, academics, extracurriculars, music, in specific—and had an unparalleled social standing.

Pretty sure he was Prom King that year, too. "Hey, don't you go to school back East? Is it...Cornell?"

"Close. Dartmouth."

I'm confused. "But you're here. Did you graduate early?"

"Nah, I'm taking some time off. The whole thing was..." He exhales loudly. "Was like, *a lot*, you know? I wasn't used to all the freedom. They sort of expect you to be self-disciplined. I got there and I kind of, I don't know, imploded on myself like a dying star."

"I'm really sorry," I say.

He shrugs. "Don't be. S'okay. More than okay. I'm taking a TV-time-out right now and it's sorta awesome. I feel like this is the first break I've had in a very long time. I'm living at home to save up some scrilla and then I'm moving to New York with some bros. We're gonna start a ska band."

I'm not sure how to reply, but it doesn't matter because he keeps talking.

"I'll bartend until I either figure out what's next or blow up, like, worldwide. Ska's gonna make a comeback, bank on that. If music doesn't work out, I have some buddies who work on an organic farm in Vermont. Either way, the future's gonna be great."

Um...bartending or farming? Neither option sounds promising to me. However, a degree from Dartmouth? *That* smacks of possibilities. It's my second choice if I don't get into Princeton early decision.

Jeremy swerves to not plow into someone who's just emerged from the shadows directly into our path, almost like he was trying to get hit.

"Asshole!" Jeremy yells, less out of anger than fear.

The guy doesn't even look up, like Jeremy shouting at him doesn't even register. Oh, wait. I *know* him. He's in my class.

193

That's...um...what's his name. Simone's buddy. Spiky hair. Too much gel. His mom does Pilates and yoga with mine and somehow they manage to make it into a competition. Somebody Something Chang? My mom says the kid's supposed to be a genius, but how smart can he be, wearing all black and walking in the street in the dark?

"Not cool, dude!" Jeremy calls as we drive away. He messes with the radio until he finds an oldies station. They're playing "How You Remind Me," which prompts a running commentary on how Nickelback never got their proper due. Once after I'd fought with my mom, Braden sent me a shot of her with a Nickelback tattoo photoshopped across her cleavage. I literally wet my pants from laughing so hard. For weeks, every time she'd get on me, I'd picture her ink and then I'd feel better.

I miss him so much.

"This you?"

Jeremy pulls up to my place, a pitch-black French country-style home on a cul-de-sac with a whole bunch of other French country-style homes. My development is newer, but the builders tried to infuse the neighborhood with Euro charm, so our streetlights are gas lamps and every house has a steeply pitched roof with lots of gables. The neighborhood's supposed to look historic, but with so few mature trees out front, it seems vaguely off-kilter. Every enormous home is so perfectly appointed, so neat and symmetrical, with roses trimmed just so and ivy framing every window, it's like someone enlarged a bunch of dollhouses and made them life-size. A few years ago, one of my neighbors erected a cheap fence and the neighborhood has yet to stop complaining about it. The Leonards are afraid to show their penny-pinching faces at our block parties now.

"Yeah, thanks."

"It's pretty dark," he says. "Need me to wait until you get inside and turn on some lights?"

"I'll be fine."

"Cool. Okay, catch you on the flip side, Mal."

I exit the car and start walking down the darkened bluestone path to my front door. *That was odd*, I think. If I recall correctly, Jeremy was mover, a shaker, a big man on campus. I could see him leaving college early to go all Zuckerberg, and not to drive an Uber, even if the car in question's a shiny new Audi sedan.

How did he get there? Why couldn't he translate the discipline he learned at NSHS to college? Did he peak in high school? Where did he go wrong and how might I avoid a similar fate? I feel like there's a lot more I should have asked him. Like this was a missed opportunity, a Ghost of Christmas Future.

He must be reading my mind, because he rolls down the window and calls after me. "Hey, Mallory?"

I turn back to him. "Yeah, Jeremy?"

What kind of wisdom do you have for me? What caveat? What piece of information can you share that will inoculate me from suffering your same destiny?

How can I save me from myself?

Jeremy breaks out that crazy-big Zac Effron smile that used to make all the freshmen girls swoon, including me. "Make sure you rate me five stars on Uber!"

He peels away as I open the front door. "I'm home," I call, but my voice echoes through the empty house. I figured Theo wouldn't be here, as he's at an away football game and won't be back until late. Even though he's benched with an injury, he insists on suiting up and being there. My dad's out of town on business—again—and my mother? I could check her Instagram feed to see what she might be up to, except I don't care. Not into witnessing her waving around glasses of wine with her girlfriends, displaying too much skin, flirting with businessmen who may or may not be married, all while squeezed into *my* J Brand jeans.

Plus, I'm mortified every time I see her posts. *No, Mom, you're not too old to go braless* at all.

I should just appreciate the quiet.

I strip down to my underwear in the laundry room and toss everything into the washer. I put in the detergent and extra fabric softener, then set the temperature to hot. I assume that will wash away all the beer-whiff. I pull on a pair of pajamas from the basket of clean clothes our housekeeper, Marta, folded (and left) on top of the dryer.

I go to the double-door fridge and peer inside to find a wrapped plate with a Post-It reading *Theo* on top. My mother left him a hefty rib eye steak, richly marbled with fat and branded with grill marks, served with a heaping side of au gratin potatoes, oozing with cream and topped with crisped, brown, buttery breadcrumbs. Maple-bourbon glazed carrots and jalapeño cornbread complete the entrée, and there's a large ramekin full of crème brûlée dotted with fresh raspberries next to it. Obviously she didn't cook this, as the bag from the delivery service sits empty on the kitchen island. I look deeper into the fridge to see if she ordered anything for me, even though I know the answer long before concluding the search.

For a moment, I consider scarfing down Theo's entire meal, but then I'd hate myself more than I already do. I settle for a bottle of water, a handful of baby carrots, and one thirty-five-calorie wedge of Laughing Cow Creamy Light Swiss.

Once upstairs, I recline on my comforter, which is snowy white with silver piping, and I shove a couple of pillows behind my back. My black cat Dora hops up next to me and curls against my leg. Yes, Dora as in *the Explorer.* (Don't laugh, I was eight when I named her.) Don't know where our other cat, Boots, is. He and Dora were littermates and they have hated each other their entire lives. In retrospect, we should have named him Swiper.

I flip open my Mac Book Pro to view my incomplete Princeton essay.

Or, that's what I mean to do.

Instead, I find myself on what's become my default—staring at Braden's Instagram feed. I've spent the last few weeks enlarging each shot to see if there's anything, anything at all I missed. In last year's shot at Homecoming, I notice his smile doesn't completely reach his eyes. Was this a warning sign? Should I have known?

After I've inspected another twenty or thirty pictures, I pull up the log-in screen for his email. I type in BradentheRoach@northshorehs.edu and then pause over the password box.

I know that breaking into his email is a gross invasion of privacy and I'm disgusted with myself, yet I'm compelled anyway.

I'm compelled to know *why.* I mean, what if he drafted a suicide note and forgot to press Send? Or, what if he read something that sent him over the edge?

Then I remember something—in his final text, he said he'd email me. I never got that email.

I *have* to see what's in his email account.

I've already tried a bunch of possibilities, like his birthdate, his first dog's name, his football position, but none of them have worked. The NSHS email server tells me I have one more incorrect log-in before the account is locked without additional verification, so I can't keep guessing. The next password I input must be right or that's it.

I feel a trickle of sweat roll down my back, weird because I'm not hot. Yet my pajamas are clinging to my clammy skin and I'm on the edge of hyperventilating.

I'm at a loss so I click shut the window.

No answers today.

I gather my hair into a damp ponytail and I tab back to my Princeton essay. I've already filled out the particulars on which of my extracurricular activities was important and meaningful and why (peer counseling—because I love it and it's the only thing I do that actually matters), and the section on how I spent my last two summer vacays. (Spoiler alert— the activities were enriching.)

My plan was to answer the second of five choices of essay questions, which is based on a quote from Omar Wasow's speech at the 2014 Martin Luther King Jr. Day celebration on campus. My coach says bemoaning white privilege is a homerun swing to admissions directors, especially coming from *this* zip code, so that was the tack I intended to take. Yet in reading this question again, I can't remember any of my talking points. And somehow it feels wrong to use my privilege as a tool, you know? I've already benefitted from it more than enough.

My eyes are drawn to the first question—*Tell us about a person who has influenced you in a significant way.*

That's the question I should answer. I glance at the notes from my admissions coach. He said I should write about someone who moves me, who inspires me, who makes me feel like I could be a different person, a better person. He suggested I use Hillary Clinton and he helped me come up with a bunch of supporting arguments.

But hers is not the name that's on my mind.

Hers is not the name on my lips when I wake from a turbulent dream.

The mention of her name neither causes my pulse to race nor sits like a stone in the bottom of my stomach.

I pull at my pajama top. The fabric feels humid and oppressive, despite how cold my room is.

What if I were to answer with what's in my heart? What if I were to answer honestly? Not *honest* honest, with a wink and a nod, but just regular old honest.

Focused on Braden, I take a deep breath, positioning my shaking fingers over the keyboard.

I begin to type.

Sometimes the pressure to be perfect causes us to crack in the most devastating of ways.

19

KENT

"YEAH, I DON'T feel good about it."

"Come on Stephen, we never do anything like this. We'll have fun," I say in my most persuasive, authoritative voice.

No dice.

As we walk east toward the biggest homes on the lake, he stops under a streetlight and crosses his arms over his chest. Oh, good. He's going into statue-mode again, that's *just* what we need.

Simone says, "Check out how the light reflecting on Stephen's hair gives him a halo! You're downright cherubic-looking, that is, if angels wore Death Row Records T-shirts."

She fails to convince him to budge and I quietly cluck my tongue. Aw, Simone. Sweet, naïve Simone. Stephen's bought himself a one-way ticket to Funk Town and it'll take more than a throwaway compliment to pull him out of it.

Simone then pokes Stephen and he goes rigid, which I'm sure is the exact opposite reaction she hoped to inspire. We need him to *move* not to *freeze*. When her fingers grazed his arm, he became a turtle retreating into his shell. She's still way too new at handling Stephen to know that being all touchy-feely-jokey is the wrong move.

She persists. "What's the matter? The boy in my study hall said it would be fun when he invited me. You allergic to fun? Do we need to find a fun EpiPen to inject you, just in case small traces of fun spill over and contact your skin?"

Stephen lets out a ragged breath. "Yeah, but you're *dope*, Simone, you have a tattoo and everything."

He begins walking again, ever so slowly, literally dragging his feet as we head to the party. Technically, while this is considered movement, he's still impeding our progress. At his .0001 MPH speed, we won't even arrive at Jasper's before the town's curfew.

Stephen shuffles and argues, "The cool kids and athletes don't want us at their party. We don't matter to them. We don't exist. If we died tomorrow, they wouldn't even care."

"Stephen, what an awful thing to say, especially in light of everything! Of course you matter. Of course you exist. Everyone cares," Simone argues. "We care so much."

Stephen's super sad-trombone right now, but I wonder if he doesn't have a point about not being wanted there?

"Wait, how *do* you actually know anyone will be happy to see us there?" I ask. Do I need convincing we'll be welcome, too?

She replies, all matter of fact, "Because Jasper invited us."

"Um, *no*," Stephen says, "he invited *you*, sis. I feel like his crowd is going to thrash the two of us just for showing up."

"Every shitty '80s movie can't be wrong," I add. "The nerds always get their asses handed to them when they breach a popular-kid party." I find myself mentally pumping the brakes, too. Maybe going to a party *is* a bad idea.

Wait, hold up, I say to myself.

No.

I refuse to be dragged into Mr. Cho's Deep Dark Hole of Dire Doom again. I feel like attending this event may be my line in the sand. Do I want to keep hanging on the side of the beach where it's calm and safe and nothing bad ever happens, but nothing interesting does, either?

Or am I willing to take a risk and see what's on the other side of the line?

Maybe I'll get my ass handed to me, but what if I don't? What if the reward's worth the risk? What if there's an awesome, I don't know, *clambake* or something on the other side of the sand? Ooh, or Mallory in a bikini? And what if the popular people *like me* once they get to know me? We were all friends as kids. Maybe we could hang out again. I let Stephen talk me out of doing stuff so often that our default mode is to turn and run. We reject everyone long before they can reject us.

So, what if we *don't* run tonight?

Stephen has worked himself into a full-on lather. "You think those films were based on nothing? They were written as some dork's revenge for having *this very thing* happen to them in high school. Seriously, name me any big writer/director right now and I will show you a guy who stayed home on the weekends to watch *Star Trek* reruns as a kid. I will show you a nerd. Thesis statement, Wes Anderson, J.J. Abrams, Quentin Tarantino. *Quentin?* His name is *Quentin.* He got his ass kicked on the reg in high school, I guaran-goddamn-tee it."

With far more patience than I can muster, Simone says, "Jasper said, 'Hey, come to my house on Friday. Bring your friends.' At no point did he mention or imply he planned to kick anything but *back.* Didn't specify who to bring and he always sees me with you guys before study hall. Do the math. I can't imagine you two showing up is going to be a shock."

"This is ridic. Stephen, you're being a huge wuss, bigger than usual," I say with a fair amount of venom in my voice. The gloves are off now. I don't care if his *widdle feelers* are hurt. This is some bullshit right here. I'm very tired of him dictating our everything.

"Sorry. I'll try not to be so *ridiculous*." His words come out full of peevishness and completely lacking in remorse. If I didn't know better, I'd guess he's *enjoying* screwing up our night. Negative attention's still attention.

I pull out the big guns—quoting Yoda. "You'll *try* not to be? 'Do or do not, there is no try.'" I tug Stephen along by his sleeve to speed him up, but he's suddenly immobile again.

"You know what? No. I'm not going," he says. He turns around and heads back in the direction of our houses.

"Are you fuckin' kidding me, man?" I exclaim. This is exasperating. "Why are you freaking out like this?"

"Because *fuck you*, that's why!" He takes off in a run.

Simone looks to me for guidance. "Do...do we go after him?"

Line? Meet sand.

"You know what? *No*. If he wants to be a drama queen, let him. I can't even deal with his moods right now. His flouncing is so past the expiration date. You hear about the hissy fit he threw at the last meet? He was so hysterical that his behavior almost made the judges forfeit our win. Luckily our coach talked them out of it. We *cannot* encourage this kind of behavior. He's got to learn to control himself or he's going to have no friends left."

We watch Stephen retreat, the thwack of his sneakers sounding hollow on the asphalt. "Is that the best idea, though?"

Simone asks. "I feel like he's going through something but between trying to get Owen to speak to me and my ACT test prep, I haven't been around much."

I start walking in the direction of the party. "Like any of that is your fault? No. Nuh-uh. This is not on you. And this is not on me, either. For the first time in my life, I'm not gonna kowtow to him. I'm not gonna let him make all the rules. He wants to storm off and sit home alone on a Friday night, *let him*." To emphasize my point, I slip into my rapper persona, DJ Wonderbread. "*Imma* meet me some girls. *Imma* mack on drunken cheerleaders. *Imma* find some ladies to be part of my Tunaverse."

Now it's Simone's turn to stop. "Your *what?*"

I drop the persona.

Yeah. I should probably confine DJ Wonderbread to my bedroom.

"Did I catch that right?" she says. "Your *Tunaverse?*"

"My Tunaverse—it's kind of a line from a Run-D.M.C. song? They refer to their groupies as the Tunaverse in 'Down With The King.'"

Simone gives me a sidelong glance. "Huh. Never considered you a misogynist, Kent."

"I'm not, I swear! Honestly, on the whole rap-sexism spectrum, Run, Darryl, and Jam Master Jay trended fairly female-friendly. They were never all, 'bitches and hos.' Mostly, I think they were looking for a word to rhyme with 'universe.' Sure, there were better choices, like *curse* or *asperse* or *adverse* or *reimburse* but maybe they were in a hurry to finish the song? Studio time is expensive. That's why Rick Ross could rhyme *Atlantic* with *Atlantic* in 'Hustlin'. So if you look at it in that context, *Tunaverse* makes sense."

Wait, they are saying Tunaverse, right? Not tune of verse?

Because I'm really going to feel dumb if I've been singing the lyric wrong all this time.

No, it's gotta be Tunaverse. I'm sure of it.

Simone purses her lips and starts to speak a couple of times before actual words come out. Putting her palm on my forearm, she asks, "Kent, let me figure out a nice way to say this—you reckon maybe referring to women as your 'Tunaverse' is why you don't have a girlfriend?"

I nod decisively. "Distinct possibility."

"Cool. If you're comfortable with that, then."

We cross Whitefish Bay Road and head down Eastminster, where the houses are spaced football fields apart, with lawns large enough to host a polo match. The silence out here is profound, but not oppressive, and the only sound is that of our breath and footsteps.

Although the moon's not yet risen, we can still see clearly because the stars are lighting up the sky like a handful of diamonds spilled across a swath of indigo blue velvet. Gazing up, I seek out the Pleiades, also known as the Seven Sisters, which is my favorite fall constellation because it's so luminous. The ancient Greeks used to know it was time to sail again when they'd see this star cluster appear. Only the six brightest stars are visible with the unaided eye, but the myth is that virgins can see seven.

Braden used to joke at astronomy camp that he and I could see all seven. Remembering this feels bittersweet.

"So...back to Stephen," Simone prompts. "What's that all about?"

I explain, "You've already figured out that he's high-strung. This time of year is especially bad because he totally freaks around midterms. Like if there were a giant Easy button on the wall? He'd hurl himself against it to make everything better. Plus there's the whole factor of his mom. Mrs. Cho is kinda relentless. You know; you've witnessed her in action."

She laughs. "Um, yes. Believe me, we'll *never* place our fallen leaves in plastic bags instead of paper again. I mean, we are sort of idiots when it comes to neighborhood stuff, so I understand why she's been merciless with us. But why's she like that with poor Stephen?"

"Eh, maybe she feels like she's gotta be extra-hard on him because his dad is always away on consulting engagements?"

"I guess. Still, your dad travels all the time and your mum is equally bossy, no offense—"

"None taken."

"And I don't see you regularly freaking out," she finishes.

I shrug. "True dat. I'm better at managing her expectations. Like tonight? I told her I was going to a party and she insisted I wear a tennis sweater. *A tennis sweater.* I'm sorry, is it suddenly 1984? Is Jake Ryan gonna be there? But I didn't argue, I said, 'Great call,' and just pulled it on. Then I borrowed this NWA T-shirt from Stephen when I got to his house. She was satisfied, I didn't have to spend the effort arguing, and now I'm not showing up at a party dressed like a villain in a John Hughes movie. Problem solved." I point to the hateful garment currently tied around my waist.

(Mental note: put sweater back on before going home.)

"Why can't Stephen try that?"

"Because he doesn't want to. What he wants is to change the way things are instead of accepting reality and finding a way to navigate around it. With someone as strong-willed as Mrs. Cho, that's never gonna work. You can't charge at her head-on. It's like bullfighting. You can't be all, 'Come at me, bro' because the bull's got more brute force. Gotta dance with your red cape, gotta finesse the bull. Outsmart him. Distract him. What our boy doesn't realize is he's just like his mom, just as stubborn, equally unrelenting, unwilling to compromise. He wants to go *mano a mano* with the bull and the bull's always gonna win because its strength is so disparate."

"Does he listen to you when you tell him this?"

"No, never has. He insists on running into brick walls and then gets mad every time he discovers that the wall's so damn hard and solid. He'd rather bemoan how unfair it is that the wall exists, than dig under or climb over. As his friend, it's frustrating to stand there and say 'Dude, there's a door in the middle of the wall—just go through that instead,' and he won't because he's too wrapped up in being angry the wall was ever built."

"Poor Stephen, that sounds exhausting."

"Uh-huh. That's why he's always stressed. This year's worse than usual with our MIT early action apps hanging over our heads. He has his paperwork completed, but he's all panic at the disco about the face-to-face with an alumnus interview next week. He was so psyched when they scheduled the interview but now that it's coming up, it's become too real. He's worried he'll crash and burn in front of someone. He says he presents better on paper."

"Then how do we convince him that it's okay to use the door?"

"You tell me. I've been struggling with that question ever since we met at Montessori when we were three."

"You know what would help him *so much* right now?" she asks.

"What's that?"

"A BEER. I understand that America's a lot more stringent about youth and liquor, but if anyone needed an alcoholic beverage... I mean, *damn*."

"I feel ya."

We walk in silence for a couple of minutes.

"Hey, Simone?"

"Uh-huh?"

I can't look her in the eye as I pose my question. "They're not going to kick my geek ass like in a shitty '80s movie, right?"

"I've got your back," she promises, giving me a quick shoulder hug, and I believe her.

Yes, I made the right call, Stephen be damned. I can't figure it all out for him; he's gotta want to do it for himself. And this party is going to be great. Way better than playing World of Warcraft, anyway. Maybe this night won't change my life, but I feel it's a big step in that direction.

She adds, "As long as you stop saying Tunaverse."

20

STEPHEN

THEY'D BE SORRY.

If that car had hit me, Kent and Simone would have been so sorry.

Or would they?

Would they even care?

Real friends don't make you do the kind of thing that's destined to fail, that scares you to death. Real friends don't *abandon* you. Real friends are there for you. Real friends aren't all *later, dude* when you're clearly in distress. Real friends chase after you. Real friends ask what's wrong and listen as you explain and then try to make you feel better.

Tonight was a test and Kent and Simone failed. Big time. They made it clear they only want me around if I'm being "cool," if I'm low-maintenance, laughing and joking and, like, riffing on Biggie. But I can't be up all the time. It's hard for me to be "on" sometimes. Or, a lot of times.

I should have known Kent would be a traitor. That's his nature. Look at how he went to astronomy camp without me TWICE. The first time, my mom decided I was too young for sleepaway camp and the second time, I had to bail because my grandfather was sick. What bullshit. That camp was *my* idea—he wanted to go to computer camp! Then I barely heard from him either summer, and whenever I did, his emails were nothing but *Braden and I this, Owen and I that, Braden said, "I enjoy constellations, I mean it, I am being Sirius."*

Freaking lame.

So I worked on my own awesome pun that second summer. When he came back I told him, "I bought Stephen Hawking's new book on antigravity and I just can't put it down." He looked at me and shrugged and said he hadn't seen it; he was too busy to read at camp. He didn't get the joke. I'm surprised he even deigned to hang out with me after his perfect BFF summers with Owen and Braden were over.

What's so ironic is that for the past few weeks, Kent's been super distressed about Braden, agonizing if there was something he could have done.

Riiiight.

Braden got sucked into the cool crowd the minute he started playing football in junior high and that was it for our crew. He and Kent hadn't even hung out in years. So for Kent to think there was something he could have done? Like somehow the outcome would have been different if Kent had, I don't know, followed him on Snapchat? I'm sure Braden would have been, "That Kent sure is a lifesaver."

Don't get me wrong, I feel terrible about Braden. What a fucking waste of talent and opportunity and, just, everything. My point is that Kent overestimates the impact he might have had.

Meanwhile, I'm right here, heartsick due to Simone's rejection and out of my head about midterms, sweating bullets over my interview. But does he have a minute to spare for me? Does he have a supportive word for me? Is he even patient with me anymore?

211

No. Hell, no.

You know what? I'm blocking both their numbers right now. That way when I don't hear from them I won't be disappointed. That's it. That's my line in the sand.

I pull out my iPhone and make the changes.

Bye, Felicia.

There. Done. That's better.

So why don't I feel better?

You know what the bitch of it all is? The bitch of it is that if Braden was beloved before, now he's practically canonized. He's more popular in death than he even was in life. Girls are going around with the #31 from his football jersey drawn on their hands in ballpoint. All the guys on the team slapped roach stickers on their helmets. A huge group of kids did a flash mob in his honor at the pep rally today. Saint Braden's gone but in no way forgotten. People are talking about him like he's the second coming of Paul Walker and Jesus H. Christ combined.

And now I'm the lowest person on the face of the earth because I envy a dead guy.

How pathetic am I?

No wonder my friends don't want to be around me.

I wouldn't want to be around me.

So…that's why when I heard the car coming up behind me, I didn't rush to get out of the way. I could have easily moved onto the sidewalk, but I didn't because for a split second, I thought, *Why not? Why fucking not?*

Suddenly, I understood what Paulie and Macey must have been feeling in their last moments. Like, they just didn't want everything to be so hard anymore.

Wouldn't *that* be the most fitting end to this night—a *real* car wreck to go with the proverbial car wreck that is my life.

21

OWEN

I DON'T KNOW how to live with myself.

I should have been faster.

I should have tried harder.

I can't sleep. I can't eat. Can't talk to my friends.

I can't look at texts, or answer calls; everyone asking me if I'm okay, like I'm the victim, like this somehow happened to me.

Am I okay? No, I am *not* okay.

I am not okay.

I was on the cusp of everything and now I have nothing. Because I deserve nothing.

I should have been the hero but I was too weak.

Too slow.

Too worthless.

Too high.

I don't deserve to keep living my life like nothing happened. I don't deserve normal. I don't deserve a future. I don't deserve to wake up to music. I don't deserve the right to pick up my camera, to play my guitar.

I don't deserve to be happy.

I don't deserve anything.
I failed.
I failed Braden. I failed myself.
I can't.
Something has to change. I can't go on like this.
I can't.
I can't.
I'm all alone and I can't.
I can't.

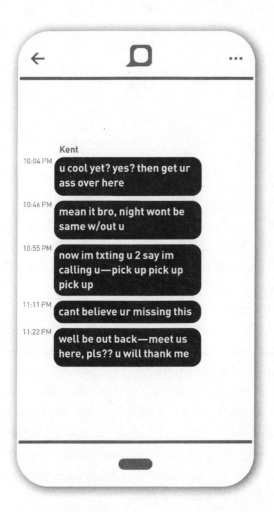

22

SIMONE

"MOON GIRL!"

"Liam!" I squeal. In fact, I squeal so loudly that I practically slide off the back of the couch on which I've been perched, watching a bunch of Jaspers play ultimate Frisbee with a *Die Hard* boxed set.

I add, "Yippie-ki-yay, motherfucker!"

Look at me, squealing and quoting Bruce Willis movies and speaking in exclamation points! I suspect I'm buzzed. Not my fault, really. The beer here's so cold, so refreshing, not like those thick, tepid, metallic glasses of bread they serve at pubs at home. Whatever's in my plastic cup is chilly and light and doesn't make me feel like I've just swallowed fifteen slices of pumpernickel. That'd make anyone giddy, I recon.

"Never seen you at one of Jasper's bashes before."

"Never been invited before," I reply.

"His house parties are the best."

"Wait, are you saying this is Jasper's *actual* home? He lives *here*? He didn't rent out the Playboy mansion?" I glance around the sprawling room, shocked that it could be part of someone's residence. I simply assumed we were someplace fancy that wouldn't return Jasper's security deposit.

"Nope, this is his place. He mostly has it to himself, though. His folks spend a shit-ton of time traveling."

"That sounds so lonely," I say. I can't imagine being on my own that often. I'd desperately miss my family, but people up here seem used to it. I don't know how it doesn't bother Kent and Stephen that their dads are gone every week from Monday morning to Thursday night.

There's not a second that goes by where I don't need both my parents. I require my mum for a million different reasons every day. And I can't imagine not endlessly talking with my dad. I believe we're so close because we've always lived in such small spaces; we can't help but be enmeshed in each other's business. Even now in our big house (well, not big compared to this palace/chateau/castle here) we tend to cluster up, never leaving one another by ourselves for long. "That must be terribly sad for him."

Liam thrusts his chin in Jasper's direction, where he's busy being dry-humped by two girls in tiny skirts, dancing on either side of him. "He looks pretty broken-up."

I laugh. "Fair enough. Tell me, are we celebrating anything specific tonight? What made him throw this to-do?"

Liam gives me a sly grin that just reveals that bold incisor. "Other than 'because he can'? He's letting everyone blow off some steam before midterms. Also, Thursday's our last game before regionals, so this week's going to be intense."

He takes a seat on the back of the couch next to me and sort of leans in so his shoulder is touching mine. I'm not sure how to interpret his body language. This feels like flirting, but he has a girlfriend, so I'm obviously wrong.

217

"Shall I wish you luck, or is that a bad omen? Do I say something like 'break a leg' instead?"

"How about you come to the game and cheer us on?"

An invitation to watch him play? That also seems a tiny bit flirty, but again, is probably just my buzz. "Not sure that I can. You see, *someone* gave me loads of grief about not having taken my ACTs, so now I'm tied up with test prep. Couldn't fit being a cheerleader into my cram-packed schedule of trying to choose the *best* answer."

The whole family has gotten into the act of readying me for the ACTs. After dinner, we sit at the table with Mum's laptop and Dad and I compete against each other for the correct answer.

Let me just say this—it's a blessing my father's already found his professional calling, even if he's not worked much lately. Dad argues every answer he biffs, too, so we're not plowing through the prep as quickly as we should. But he's having a fine time and I feel like I'm learning when I hear his rationale, so I see no reason to stop.

Of course, when he does manage to get an answer right? He showboats like an NFL quarterback scoring the winning Super Bowl touchdown. (Yes, Dad's rediscovered American football—LOVES IT. Calls it "the *real* football," having completely abandoned his longtime obsession with footy and Liverpool FC.) Even Warhol gets into the act during our quizzes, barking and tearing around the table.

Liam nudges me with his shoulder. "If you change your mind, let me know."

I take a sip of my beer so he doesn't see me blush. Stupid half-English skin, broadcasting my every emotion. I ask him, "Will you miss it? Soccer? When the season's over, will you still play for fun?"

He darkens. "This year? Nothing about soccer is fun."

"Why's that?"

"The team's largely seniors, so it's doubly important that we win because for most of us, that's it. Not many are playing in college, by choice. We want to go out on top. Like, I don't even know what would happen if we don't bring home the W."

"Bring home the W?"

"The win," he says. "Like on the flags for the Cubs' wins."

Something clicks inside my brain. "Ohhh, *the W* stands for *the win*; that explains *a lot*. So much, in fact," I say.

"What do you mean?" he asks.

"Promise me you won't laugh?" I ask.

He shakes his head. "I promise you I *will* laugh, but tell me anyway."

I explain, "Well, ever since we got here, we've spotted all the W flags hanging from people's flagpoles and letter-boxes."

"Mailboxes?" he says, trying to suppress a snicker.

I glower at him, but I'm not seriously mad. "See? You're already laughing at me."

"Uh-huh, just as I told you I would."

"Anyway, we didn't understand why everyone was hanging their flags. We were all, like, 'Is this a new form of protest?'"

Liam cocks his head and peers directly into my eyes. There I go again, feeling squishy inside. "I don't follow."

I explain, "We thought they were hoisting the W in praise of former President George W. Bush."

His entire body convulses as he holds in his laughter, trying to maintain a straight face. "You thought Cubs Win flags were a form of social activism?"

"That's about the size of it, yes." When I face-palm in utter mortification, my hair gets all tangled.

The sides of his lips are curling up, but he manages to not emit a single guffaw. He tucks a stray lock behind my left ear, telling me, "You are too cute for your own good."

!

!!

!!!

I mentally begin to take notes, as I want to remember every word for when I Skype with Cordy. I need her to tell me if he's flirting. At this point, I'm pretty sure *I* am, though. The drinks have made me forget my troubles and now I feel all fluttery inside, like I'm filled to the brim with fizzy water... or Natural Light. Same difference.

He holds up my wrist, which is encircled by loops and loops of beads. "I like this. You didn't get the memo about the Return to Tiffany bracelet? Every girlfriend demands one on her birthday. Pretty sure it's in the manual."

"Afraid not." I can practically feel an electric charge passing from his skin to mine. "This is a Tibetan prayer bracelet."

"That mean something special?"

"To practicing Buddhists, yes. The bracelets are used to keep track of prayers. See, there are 108 beads, which is how many times they chant their mantras. They move their fingers along the beads so they can concentrate on what they're saying and feeling, rather than being distracted by remembering what number prayer they're on. I made this one with seeds from a Bodhi tree. You feel how the texture is all nubby?"

Liam rubs the beads and I try not to squirm under his touch. *Be cool*, I tell myself. *Act like you've been here before.*

I continue in a rush, "I bought them on the street in Marrakesh for a song. You don't have to use Bodhi seeds though— you can grab any stone or seed. But I like Bodhi seeds because this tree is sacred in India, so it's extraspecial to me. Story is that Buddha was sitting under one when he became spiritually enlightened."

He looks at me like I've just spilled the most delicious secret. "That's so badass. Wait, hold up—you *made* this?" he asks, turning my hand this way and that.

"Yep. Here, check this out—the last bead, the anchor?" I point to a smooth piece of jade I've strung on the end, with loose strands forming a tassel on the bottom. "This is a guru bead. This one isn't counted. It's the end marker. Buddhists skip over it and begin their prayers anew."

"Where have you been?" he asks.

I shrug. "Everywhere. Name a continent and we've set foot on it, save for Antarctica. We do have plans eventually, though, as we'd very much like to hang with the penguins."

"That's not what I meant." He's still hanging on to my hand as he rubs a thumb over my knuckles.

"Then what did you mean?" I ask. My stomach flops again he gazes directly into my eyes. Hold on, is he going to lean in to kiss me? Is that possible? I think *yes*. I can feel his breath brush my lips as he exhales.

Before he makes contact and before I can reciprocate (suspect I would reciprocate him rotten, FYI) he catches himself, perhaps remembering that he has a girlfriend who is, sadly, not me. He jumps to his feet and says, "You're empty. Lemme get you a refill."

He returns with one glass of beer.

"Nothing for you?" I ask.

"No, I'm being careful. I'm taking meds for my jacked up ACL. In a perfect world, I'd rest it, but with the upcoming games, that's not an option. Advil wasn't cutting it, so I'm on something stronger. Drinking with pills is a little too Amy Winehouse, you know?" He takes a prescription bottle out of his pocket and taps out several thick, white oblong tablets. He pops them into his mouth and crunches down.

I shudder. "Oy! Doesn't that taste like poison?"

He nods. "Works faster if you chew. And yes, tastes like ass, so I will borrow a sip." He takes my beer and rinses his mouth, but swallows everything instead of spitting. "The doctor is *in*."

Kent comes dashing up to us, carrying what looks like a crystal vase full of beer. "They were out of cups," he explains.

For someone who's never consumed alcohol before, he's taken quite a shine to it. He was shy at first, all tensed up, but once he realized no one was going to thrash him like an '80s movie, he came to life. He was surprised that people knew him and I was like, "Didn't you grow up with all these folks? Like they were going to forget?"

Don't know why Kent never goes to parties—he turned into a complete social butterfly once he had a few drinks. Sometimes confidence comes in liquid form. I've been watching him whip and nae nae all night—the kid's got moves!

He falls down on the couch next to me and I'm impressed at how he's able to keep his beer from sloshing all over the place.

"No shit, Simone, this is the greatest night of my life. That hot girl Noell? She saw Stephen's shirt and was all over me— said she just watched *Straight Outta Compton* and it made her cry when Eazy-E died. She said seeing me in this shirt was like, fate."

"Fate *how*? Does she want to rap professionally?" I ask.

"Who cares, *she stuck her tongue in my ear*! I don't know what that means, but I liked it. *A lot.* How's our boy missing this? I've been texting him all night. Now I gotta thank him for the loan! This shirt changed my life. Also beer. But mostly this shirt. Where is Stevie-boy? He's ignoring me. Let's send him a Snap and convince him to get over here."

I ask, "Liam, you want in on this? Your presence might be helpful, if you don't mind."

"Which Stephen?" he asks. "Stephen the hockey player or Stephen the genius?"

I reply, "Genius."

"He keeps ruining the curve in our Quantum Mechanics class."

"Typical," Kent says, but with obvious pride in his friend. "Let's go for it."

The three of us huddle together while Kent pulls up Snapchat, his arm extended far enough for all of us to be seen in the shot. "Yo, Stevie C, DJ Wonderbread in the hizzy!"

"DJ *Wonderbread*?" Liam asks out of the side of his mouth.

"Shh, we're rolling," I whisper back.

"Get your flat ass over here, bro! We are *throwing down*! We're drinking out of home décor!" He holds up his vase, now spilling half of the contents onto his lucky shirt. He doesn't seem to notice. "You gotta come! You gotta!"

The hot girl, ostensibly Noell, photobombs our Snap by lifting her shirt and flashing Stephen her paean to plastic surgery.

"Woo! This is an epic night, see you soon! DJ Wonderbread out!"

With that, he stuffs his phone in his pocket while Noell climbs onto him piggyback-style. "Can you carry me upstairs like this?" she asks, breathing heavily into his ear.

I've never seen Kent hoist anything heavier than a textbook, but I have a feeling he's going to soldier through. They run off.

Liam suggests we get some air. I don't know if this is code for something else, but I'm game to find out.

Wait, am I interpreting *this* wrong, too? I so misread Owen's signs. Argh. He's still icing me out, so I'm listening to Mum and giving him a wide berth. Kent made the point that you can do only so much for people who steadfastly refuse your help. At some point, you let go for your own sanity. So I guess I'm free and clear to join him outside.

Liam leads me through a maze of perfectly appointed rooms until we reach the kitchen. He takes a fancy blue bottle of sparkling water from the fridge and we head out to the patio, where we grab a couple of padded metal lawn chairs overlooking the pool.

The music from the party seems to have followed us. I look around for the source of the sound and discover that the large, decorative rocks out here are actually speakers. So posh! The Weeknd's "Can't Feel My Face" plays as we settle in.

...be beautiful...

The water in the pool must be heated, because great swaths of steam are wafting from it. The mist envelops the whole patio in a dreamy haze. In the distance, I can almost make out the lake at the bottom of the bluff. I bet if we walked closer to the edge, we could hear the water lapping against the shoreline. Who knew a lake could have waves? The air has a nip to it, so we each wrap up in the plush green-and-white-striped towels that are stacked in a ginormous terry-cloth pyramid inside the pool's cabana.

"So..." Liam begins. "What's next?" His speech is slowing and his eyes are becoming a bit glassy. Whatever he's taken must be strong. Hope it's helping what ails him.

"What's next tonight? What's next tomorrow? What's next for the rest of my life?" I ask. I stick my feet under the towel because my toes are ten little ice cubes. "Please be more specific here. For example, tonight, I'm going to go home, eat all the hummus in the fridge—doesn't that sound amazing? I'm famished! Then, off to bed in footed pajamas with my dog. Tomorrow I'm prepping more for the ACTs and I also need to order a birthday present."

Stephen's turning eighteen in a couple of weeks. I've already made him a tooled leather necklace with a Tuareg amulet on the end, which tribe fathers used to give to their sons for protection. The amulets were meant to guide these young men in times of confusion. Could there be a more apt description of senior year? I'm also buying him a version of the black Compton hat that Eazy-E made famous. Only, instead of *Compton*, I'll ask the designer to spell out *North Shore* in Gothic calligraphy. I figure his mum couldn't possibly protest that and I'm sure he'll love it.

I conclude, "For the rest of my life? Don't know. That's wide open. We'll see where the road takes me."

"What's that like?" he asks. He sounds wistful.

…can't feel…

"What'd you mean, then?" I reply. I sound far more English when I'm drinking.

He scrubs at his eyes with the heels of his hands. "To not have every second of your life mapped out for you. I've been on the same course since I was ten. *Ten.* Like with the soccer? Soccer wasn't even my favorite sport, I wanted to swim. But I wasn't fast enough."

"For what?" I ask. "For sharks? You look to be in one piece."

He offers me a wry smile. "Fast enough for my dad. Fast enough to be the star of the swim team, I guess. Everyone said, 'Oh, Liam's so great at soccer, *that's* his sport.' Didn't have a choice. I was forced into it. Around here, you're put into a

225

track when you're too young to know enough to say, 'Nope, not into that.' Then you're, like, swept up, moved along. You can't go against the tide of what someone else decides should be your life. 'Play soccer, Liam.' 'Class President would look great on your transcript, Liam.' 'Make sure they elect you Homecoming King, Liam.' So now I'm here and I'm doing everything everyone expects of me. Like it or not, I'm the one the team is counting on to bring us the W. Which stands for *win*."

"Which stands for *win*," I repeat, because I'm not sure what else to say.

…with you…

"Then next year, I'm probably off to Princeton."

"Amazing," I reply. I know the Ivy League is the holy grail for the Knights.

"Not amazing. New Jersey is *cold*. Real fucking cold. Cold as Illinois. I want to go to college somewhere warm. Studying outside in January? Getting a tan? That appeals. University of Arizona, UCLA, Gainesville, someplace like that. But I don't have a choice. At what point do *I* get to be in charge? When can I call the shots? When am I allowed to finally steer this ship?" More to himself than to me, he adds, "They act like I'm going to lose control and crash into the rocks. So what if I did? What then?"

Before I can answer, the door from the kitchen bangs open and something pasty-white whizzes past us. We hear a Tarzan-type yell, followed by a huge splash. A brief-clad Kent has launched himself off the diving board into the pool, with a half-dressed Noell on his heels. She shouts, "Tunaverse!" before she hits the water. Another girl runs up behind them and hops in, too.

Liam looks at them and then looks at me. "Fuck it. I can't control the future but I can still swim if I want." He rises from his chair, a bit unsteadily, and pulls off his T-shirt and hoodie in one fluid motion before dropping his pants.

Blimey.

He has those cut oblique muscles on either side of his stomach, a la David Beckham. I love those. A lot. My hand takes on a mind of its own, reaching in the direction of his abs. Before I can connect, he begins to sprint away. Pity.

Over his shoulder, he calls, "Last one in's a rotten egg."

What else can I do?

I strip down to my camisole and knickers and I'm in the pool, too.

The whole party moves outdoors and everyone starts jumping into the warm water, some of them fully clothed, and some of them completely bare-assed. (Maybe that's just Jasper?) We chicken fight and relay race. We play round after round of Marco Polo before we collectively decide we're freezing and head inside.

Liam and I never finish our conversation, but maybe splashing is more therapeutic than talking. His medicine knocks him out fast once we're back inside and when Kent and I leave, he's snoring on the couch in the living room. He looks to be at peace.

We practically jog home because we're both in damp underwear and chilled to the bone. Kent is suddenly grateful to his loathsome tennis sweater. We live close, so we don't have much time to download, save for him repeating over and over that this was the greatest night of his life.

Only after I'm snuggled under my duvet with a bully puppy do I realize Stephen never showed.

What was he was doing instead?

23

MALLORY

"CAN'T YOU AT least pretend to be happy?"

I say this through gritted teeth. For everyone watching me in the stands, I'm beaming, radiating joy, but that's just on the surface. Inside, I'm a mess.

In a fit of serious passy-assy, last year's queen jammed the bobby pins directly into my skull as she was adjusting my crown. (Like it's *my* fault Kaya gained the Freshman Fifteen at Oberlin?) Instead of responding, I just smiled and waved, like I was a good little Miss America contestant or something.

No one ever considers how the pageant winner holds it together when all of the also-rans smear her face with their lipstick in the final thirty seconds of the telecast. She's forced to stand there with her bouquet, trying not to cry off her fake lashes, feigning delight when the runners-up give her the kind of intentionally violent congratulatory kisses that wreck her 'do and dislodge her tiara.

In this scenario, the losing contestants return to their At-lantic City hotel rooms and order, like, fifteen pizzas, while the winner's obligated to spend the next year under the constant public scrutiny to not gain an ounce, lest she wind up on the cover of *People* for porking out.

Some prize.

Liam replies through his own clenched teeth. "Why does it matter if I look happy? Wasn't this all about you anyway?"

I blow a kiss to the crowd. Under my breath, I reply, "These pictures will be in the *Round Table*, in the yearbook, probably in the *Herald* and on *North Shore Daily*. Please pretend you're grateful."

And most definitely pinned and featured prominently on my mother's Facebook timeline, with the caption *"She gets it from me, of course!"* Maybe she'll even snap a selfie later wearing my crown.

By "maybe," I mean "absolutely."

Liam finally plasters on a fake grin. When I glance up at him, I notice his eyes are bloodshot. "Better?" he asks.

Flashes go off all around us. For a minute, I feel like we're on the step-and-repeat at some glamorous Hollywood event, instead of standing on the fifty-yard line during halftime at Homecoming.

"Yes. Was that really so difficult?"

He gives an almost imperceptible shake of his head. "You have no idea."

Why are we talking to each other like this? Why is this suddenly *hard*?

Being with Liam was never supposed to be challenging. Liam is meant to be my respite, my safe space. In theory, anyway. Really, we've been together more out of habit than anything else for the past few months. Something between us changed over the summer.

I wonder if we're not getting along because, in some small

way, I used him to bring me here, to this moment, to stand on this dais in this crown?

If that's factual, then I don't feel good about the win for so many reasons.

Truth?

I *needed* to ride Liam's coattails. I couldn't be elected Homecoming Queen on my own; I'd only win if I were part of a package deal, like with Junior Prom. Even my mom knows that. (In fact, she likes to tell me so. Often.) I mean, Liam is a demigod here. Mr. All-Around. Class President, star of the soccer team, and within three tenths of a point of making valedictorian. (Why did he opt for Honors Humanities and not AP? WHY? The weight in those grades would have made all the difference. I asked him, "Did you *want* to hand off the graduation speech to Sri Kapur?")

Or maybe I just felt like I needed some of his light reflecting back on me.

Liam's the one who's the full package, not me. I'm a pale substitute, an also-ran. Everyone loves him, from the underprivileged kids he coaches during the off-season to the hairnetted lunchroom ladies. The old gal with the unfortunate birthmark saves the biggest slice of pizza for him every week! He even says hi to freshmen in the hallways, not because he has to, but because he wants to. He learns people's names *on purpose*. He exudes goodness.

Everything I've sacrificed, everything I've worked for has led up to this moment and he and I are finally here, experiencing our (literal) crowning achievement. Instead of feeling amazing, like I finally reached that mountaintop, like everything will be easier from here on out, my sole emotion is rage.

I want to punch Liam right in his Prince Charming square jaw.

I want to knock his canted incisor back into place with my clenched fist.

Did he think I wouldn't hear about how *thirsty* he was for Simone Chastain after I left Jasper's? Trust me, I heard. He didn't cross the line with her, but still. Everyone was stoked to fill me in on exactly how cozy they looked. At least I didn't see all the hashtag *troubleinparadise* Instagrams until after I submitted my essay that night. That's something, I guess.

What makes me feel like the worst person in the world is that I don't care that much about losing Liam.

Not anymore.

I'm more concerned about losing face—I feel like that's all I have left.

This is a legit crisis. I wonder, could I fend off the pending catastrophe that is our inevitable breakup? What if I went all Olivia Pope? You know, Team Proactive instead of Team Reactive? Got ahead of the story? What if *I* dumped Liam and not vice-versa? Would it be weird next year at Princeton to not have him as my boyfriend? I'd be on my own, but maybe that's not a bad thing.

The applause has died down and we hold hands out of habit as Principal Gottfried escorts us off the field. As we walk past, people yell stuff like, "We love you, Liam!" and "Way to go, buddy!" and "All hail King Liam!"

No one calls my name.

With a few final waves to the crowd, the principal peels away from us to make more announcements before the second half begins. Then we're out of the spotlight and under the bleachers, alone in the hallway by the team's locker room.

If I'm going to be the one to end this, I should probably do it soon.

Question, though—if I'm ready to lose him like a bad habit, why do I feel like all the wind's been knocked out of me?

Am I being impulsive? Am I overreacting out of jealousy? Am I playing it off like I don't care to self-protect? Am I pissed because no one ever comments how cozy he and I are together anymore? Am I just a thousand percent more scattered now because of Braden?

If I'm being honest?

Yes, yes, yes, yes, and yes.

Of course, I could try to make us work again. We were perfect together once. We were hashtag *BarbieandKen*. Liam made me laugh and I gave him focus. We balanced each other. I helped him reach his true potential and I feel like he made me more approachable. He could talk to me about how his dad was so hard on him and I understood because of my mom. He'd come over so stressed-out, and after an epic hang, he'd be relaxed again, more like himself, and I'd feel better, too.

What if I'm looking at this wrong? Liam was my first love. Liam was my *first*. He says I was his, too, but let's be realistic. I mean, (a) girls have been up in his grill since sixth grade, and (b) soccer camp was co-ed. Was he *really* a monk up there in the north woods of Wisconsin all those summers with athletic girls in tiny shorts and sweaty tank tops? In retrospect, doubtful. Also, he has too many *moves* for me to be his first-round draft choice. He's all-pro, none of this amateur business. Like…the internet can only teach you so much. He's had hands-on training.

Maybe I should just say that I'm sorry for how weird it's been. How weird I've been. Recommit to us. This fall has been hard, so damn hard, and no one is himself or herself right now.

Instead of falling apart, we should come together. Be there for each other. Make *MaLiam* Great Again.

Like old times.

Before I can say anything, Liam pulls a prescription bottle out of his sport coat's pocket and shoves a couple of tablets in his mouth.

"Wait, are you sick?"

Would a better girlfriend even have to ask? Wouldn't she know?

I've never seen him take anything stronger than a gummy vite, yet here he is, swallowing pills dry, like he's a junkie on *The Wire* or something. Seriously, I didn't even realize someone could take meds without liquid; I thought that was just a television device when the director doesn't want to break the flow of the scene by forcing the character to locate a water fountain. This is brand-new and seriously concerning.

A while back, Theo mentioned some teammates were self-medicating with opioids because they thought being immune to pain made them play harder. This shocked me but I'm not sure why. Everyone up here has a script for something. The few of us who aren't diagnosed ADHD have been known to borrow an Adderall or two during midterms; it's what you do to get through. But messing with opioids? That's kind of hardcore.

"Where do they even get them?" I asked.

"Are you kidding?" Theo replied. "Way easier to steal pills than alcohol. Everybody's parents have Oxy or Vicodin sitting around in their bathroom. They lock the liquor cabinet, but the medicine cabinet? That's wiiiiide open. Check out Mom and Dad's bathroom if you don't believe me."

I peeked and he was right—there was a shelf full of stuff

left over from when Mom had her tummy tuck...her cheek implants...her lipo. (I could go on, but you get the picture.)

Theo explained, "What's scary is they start looking for the same high elsewhere when they can't get more opioids. If they can't score more from home, they go to Jasper. If he's not holding, they head a few miles up the road for heroin, which is basically the same thing, but not controlled by the FDA. You know you can get it in pill form now?"

"*What?*" Again, shocker.

"Yeah, it's true. North Shore kids won't go near a needle because it's low-class, but they will swallow, smoke, or snort shit all day long."

I made Theo promise me he wouldn't take anything. Then, for everyone's protection, I told Dad I'd heard all about the opioid/opiate connection in an Organic Chemistry lecture. I suggested he lock our meds in the safe. I mean, I trust Theo, but his friends don't always make wise decisions.

Obviously.

I can feel a lump forming in my throat.

Oh, please tell me Liam isn't doing this now. Please tell me I haven't been so self-involved that I missed the signs.

Damn it, I have, haven't I?

When did he originally hurt his ACL? Right before school started? We'd already begun to grow apart, but then he started skipping stair sessions with me and the rift between us deepened. The timeline of us falling apart makes so much sense now. How could I have been so stupid?

What do I now? I can't just abandon him; I owe him more than that. I care deeply for Liam and I don't want him headed down the wrong path. He has far too much to lose. Maybe my job as his girlfriend is to be there for him, to talk him through the rough spots. Am I his antidrug?

My mind keeps flashing back to Braden, agonizing over the times he may have been reaching out and I wasn't cognizant enough to extend the hand he needed.

I don't want to fail again. I have to try harder.

Wait, no, *do or do not, there is no try.*

I've been digging into my research lately, trying to figure out if Braden displayed any warning signs that Theo or I should have spotted. As I replay every conversation, each interaction, I can't put my finger on anything specific.

I always thought Braden was an open book, so open and free with how he felt.

But the reality is, he must have been a master at keeping his deepest feelings inside. He didn't talk about being sad or depressed. He never said anything about sensing he was a burden or that he didn't have any reasons to live. He didn't isolate himself or give away his prized possessions.

Unless…he left me his hat on purpose.

Of course, now I know a lot more about risk factors. I see how detrimental it was for him to experience Paul's and Macey's passing in such rapid succession. Their deaths put him at risk. And his death puts us all at risk.

I wasn't proactive enough with Braden and that's a lesson I'll never forget. I *won't* fail again. I *will* be better at looking out for Liam.

In my never-ending quest for answers, I ran across this song about a guy who prevented a bunch of people from killing themselves. The song called him the gatekeeper. But I couldn't listen to it more than once—made me feel guilty, like I'd fallen down on the job.

From this second forward, I'll be Liam's shepherd, his sentry, his gatekeeper. He deserves that.

So, in the gentlest manner possible, I place a palm on the

pocket where Liam's stashed the pills. "We should talk about these."

Apparently all he wanted was for me to be invested, because he immediately softens. He shuts his eyes and hangs his head, which makes his crown slide forward. I right it for him. His demeanor is that of a child trying—and failing—to pass as a full-blown adult.

He says, "I've probably been taking more than I should. I'm starting to depend on them and I'm kind of scared."

"Would you feel better if you told me about everything? No judgment, pinky swear."

He nods slowly, but doesn't say anything. He's wearing his shame like a cloak, can't even meet my eye.

"Can you stop taking them if you want to?" I ask as kindly as I can. Now is not the time for him to feel like I'm lecturing him.

His response is another sad shake of the head. He says, "I'm not sure," and then puts his hands on my waist. He pulls me to him, so I hug him back. He rests his forehead on my shoulder. This is better. We always fit together so well.

"Okay, we can fix this," I say, my voice full of a confidence I don't feel. Yet I will fake it until I make it, for his sake. "We *will* fix this."

Because I refuse to lose anyone else.

Wait a minute…was *Braden* taking opioids? A chill runs down my spine. Is that what happened? That certainly would have been a risk factor. Was he making runs up the road for illegal purposes? Was he addicted? Are pills like Liam's the reason that he killed himself?

I have to know.

"Liam, do you…" His eyes are welling with tears. He's never broken down like this, not even after the time his dad threw him into the garage wall for missing soccer practice when he'd stopped to change an old lady's flat tire. "Do you have any idea if Braden was taking the same thing?"

If he was, then I need to act fast. Clearly the pills messed Braden up and I can't let that happen to Liam. He's too good, too pure, too important to let slip through the cracks. Not just for me, but for everyone.

Braden's death rocked North Shore; Liam's would destroy it.

Liam's whole body goes rigid in my arms before he takes a big step away from me. He switches from broken to vitriolic in a heartbeat. "I should have known Braden would be your priority. Jesus Christ, he's not even with us anymore and yet I'm still playing second string. Spoiler alert, I'm never going to be him, Mallory. I can't compete with him and what's more, I don't want to."

"Liam, no, I'm so sorry. It's only because we're talking about it, I was trying to assess—"

"Enough," he snaps.

"Liam, please, let me help you." I reach for him and he bats away my hands.

"Get off my jock, Mallory."

"You don't understand, I was just asking—"

He doesn't allow me to complete my thought. He is livid, angrier than I've ever seen, and he's practically spitting as he lights into me. "Enough, okay? *Enough.* I've had enough of your *'just asking.'* Christ, Mal, you're worse than my father. You're relentless. 'How's your application coming? When are you going to run stairs? What's your plan for tackling the research paper? Why aren't you in AP Humanities? How are you going to deliver the win at State?' I'm under enough pressure every single fucking day without *my girlfriend* adding to it, especially one who's obsessed with a dead guy. Guess

237

what, Mallory. I'm *here*. He's not. But seems like you made your choice anyway."

Suddenly I'm shaky and I want to vomit, and not just because I've consumed nothing but celery and rye crackers this whole week. My stomach is swimming in acid and my esophagus burns. He's right, isn't he? What is that expression we talked about in English class? Hell is the truth discovered too late?

"Liam, this isn't you," I plead.

"I can't, Mallory. I can't even deal. With any of this." He whips off his crown and throws it against the cinderblock wall outside the men's locker room. Because it's plastic, it just bounces, although a few of the fake gemstones come loose and scatter. "Our 'relationship' is completely fucked up—I keep doing the same thing with you and expecting different results. Well, the train is pulling into the station and I'm getting off. We're done."

"Liam, don't be like this."

"Later, *Queen* Mallory."

With that, he stalks out of the hallway and, ostensibly, my life.

I have no clue how to handle this, how to process, how to break down what just occurred. I'm honestly not sure if I'm more upset that we're over or that he's right about Braden, but that doesn't matter now.

I don't know what Liam's taking or how long he's been taking it, but I think he's in trouble. Yet I can't just go to his parents and level accusations, not without all the facts at my disposal. Anyone else's parents, yes, I totally could/should/ would, but his father isn't a rational person. His dad hasn't raised his hand to him in a year or so, but these are extraordinary circumstances. If his dad kicked the crap out of him for being a Good Samaritan, I can't even imagine what might happen if Liam were actually screwing up. That would be such a shitstorm, particularly if he hasn't done anything wrong.

I can't do that to Liam.

Because I'm at a loss, I proceed the only way I know. I keep up appearances. I straighten my crown and adjust my dress before marching up to my spot in the stands. As I head towards my friends, I act like everything is as perfect as it looks.

Like I always do.

As I navigate to my seat, people offer congrats on my win.

I smile and I nod and pose for pictures, radiant in my victory, flashing that winner's smile. I come across so damn happy.

But I wonder how much happier I'd be if I could just go home and order fifteen pizzas.

24

OWEN

"BUDDY? YOU IN THERE?"

My dad turns on the light and enters my room when I don't answer his knock. He's still dressed for work, wearing what he calls "venture capital casual." His navy chinos have a razor-sharp crease down the front, his checkered plaid shirt's custom-made by an English tailor, and his sweater vest is vicuna, which comes from some kind of llama in Peru and costs 'bout as much as a trip down there.

He and I have the same untamed curls—we look a lot alike, actually—but he keeps his hair clipped real close to control it. For the amount of effort I've put into grooming lately, I'd have dreds now whether or not I wanted them.

"Why are you in the dark, pal?" my father asks. He never comes in here, so this is kinda odd. He sort of has to wade through all the debris on my floor before he reaches me. He sits on the end of my bed, real formal-like, probably to keep his pants nice.

"I fell asleep," I say, but that's a lie.

Truth is, after the sun went down, I just didn't have the

energy to switch on a light. I thought it was around dinner-time but it must be late if he's finally home.

Did I somehow drift off?

I don't sleep now. Can't. The insomnia's almost crippling. Plus, every time I shut my eyes, I have visions of a speeding commuter train. I see an empty shoe by the side of the tracks. And on those rare occasions that sleep comes, my dreams are violent and terrifying. In them, I'm either trapped or climbing a hill that grows taller with every step I take. I don't ever reach the summit, yet I can't stop my ascent, either. It's torture. In sleep, I'm Sisyphus, perpetually trying—and failing—to shove that boulder.

Every day I look like I've been punched because the circles under my eyes are black. Now they match how I feel. At least people are leaving me alone finally. Suspect my hygiene makes it easier for everyone to avoid me. Wasn't intentional, but seems to be working so I'm rolling with it.

At first, everyone at school was all, "We want to be there for you."

Why?

I'm still here.

We shoulda been there for Braden.

Simone was relentless for the first couple of weeks, couldn't understand why I didn't want to talk, why I wouldn't let her in. It's not that I don't want to be around her; it's that I don't *deserve* to be around her.

I don't deserve to have something nice going on in my life. I don't deserve affection. I don't deserve love. So I had to be so shitty with her that she'd finally stop trying to come around. It's gonna be a long time before I can even think about girls again.

I've given up everything that I like, everything that brings

241

me joy. I don't listen to music. Haven't touched my camera, my guitar, my computer, etc. in weeks. Mostly I just hang out on the bleachers when I'm not in class. It's cold now, so I sit out there and shiver. I want my physical discomfort to match my spiritual distress.

I shouldn't be allowed to be a happy camper. I figure I was under the tracks for a reason that morning. Fate placed me there. There's a French proverb that says, *"You often meet your fate on the road you take to avoid it."* I had one job, which was to save Braden, and I failed.

Big league failed.

I'm always going on about saving the whole world, but I couldn't even save one guy.

"You hungry?" my dad asks.

I can't remember the last time I ate. Haven't been hungry. I must be losing weight because my pants are all too big. They sort of hang at my hips now and my face looks gaunt. Haunted.

"Nah," I reply. "I'm fine."

"You sure?" he asks, inching nearer. "You don't look fine. You're giving off a Christian Bale in *The Mechanic* vibe. Remember when he dropped something like sixty pounds for the role?"

I don't say anything.

He puts his hand on my shoulder. "That's not a criticism. Your mother and I are worried, O. You're really going through something. Feels like you're shutting us out. Well, guess what, kiddo? Shutting us out? No longer an option."

I'm still quiet.

My dad shifts even closer to me and is now sitting in a way that's absolutely messing up his pristine pants. He doesn't seem to notice. "We haven't been around enough, buddy, and I'm sorry. You're just such a self-sufficient kid, so cheerful, that we figured you were fine with our schedules, that you were always okay. But you're not okay and it's on us. We owe you an apology."

I can't find any words.

He continues, "In our heads we always thought, 'If we work hard enough to give him everything, he'll be happy. He'll be successful, he'll find his way.' But your mom and I have had our priorities wrong. We see that now and we're going to fix it. Starting next week, family therapy. All of us, no excuses. We're going to get through this together. As a team. Team Foley-Feinstein, which is a terrible team name, yet here we are."

I nod, but I don't add anything...because I can't speak— the lump in my throat won't let me.

He says, "You assume that we adults have it all figured out, right? Wanna know a secret? We don't. We're under the same kinds of stress as you in this community. We feel it, too, the pressure to achieve the most, to have the biggest house, to rack up the most accolades. It's like, the one with the most toys wins. That nonsense doesn't end in high school."

My dad might finally get it.

"It should, though, so Mom and I have made a conscious decision to stop the insanity. Like it or not, pal, we're going to be around from now on. We're going to be more of a family, with weekends and conversations and trips we actually take, as opposed to just book. And if we slip up? Then you call us on it. How does that sound?"

I swallow, hard, finally replying, *"The Machinist."*

"What's that, bud?"

"The Machinist is the movie you mean. *The Mechanic* is a Jason Statham flick about an elite assassin."

"Huh," he says, running a hand across his chin. "I don't think I've actually seen either of them. Tell you what, I'm free this weekend. Why don't we watch them both together?"

"I'd really like that."

He tells me, "You know, Eckhart Tolle says we should realize deeply that the present is all we ever have. I say we start being present together, kiddo, starting now. Sound good?"

I nod. "That would be...badass." My dad hugs me real tight, and I don't fight him, I just lean on in. When we separate, I say, "Sorry if I reek."

His nose twitches. "Oh, is that you? I sort of assumed the smell is whatever your mother's cooking right now."

Wait, she's home, too? I'm getting the sense that they truly mean what my dad's saying and that kinda feels like a miracle.

Maybe things *will* change.

Maybe we've hit the peak of the hill and it will get easier to roll my boulder from here.

"Mom's *cooking*?" I ask, incredulous. "Does she even know how?"

He laughs. "From the smell, I'm guessing *no*."

I inhale and my nostrils suddenly fill with the smell of burning, with hints of fish and feet. "What's she making?"

"Gluten-free pasta and meatless quinoa meatballs."

I take a beat.

"I thought you were hinting that I need to *gain* weight."

He nods as he rises. "I do. That's why I ordered your favorite from Malnati's, just in case. Also, someone named Rico says hi. So we'll be eating something in the next half hour, but I'm not sure what. You ready to come down?"

"I...think I'm gonna hit the shower first. Feelin' kinda gnarly."

"Don't let me stop you."

"It's time?" I ask, afraid to verify exactly how gamy I am.

He's smiling as he replies, "Oh, yeah, buddy. It's time." He watches me from the doorway as I gather up some clean clothes Mom must have snuck in here. "Listen, I don't expect everything to be different overnight, Owen. Please don't think your mom and I expect you to be magically better right away. You've been suffering for a while and it'll take some time to get back to normal, or, to figure out what our new normal is. Just know that you're our priority. We're committed. Whatever you need. We love you, pal."

I am not out of the woods, not by a long shot. But this is my first step in that forest. Like Desmond Tutu said, *"Hope is being able to see that there is light despite the darkness."*

"Love you, too, Pops." I hold up my fist in solidarity. "Team Foley-Feinberg."

"Team Foley-Feinberg," he repeats.

Suddenly, my mom's voice comes across the in-house intercom system. "Hey, guys…do we own a fire extinguisher?"

25

SIMONE

"BRILLIANT, WARHOL, RIGHT nice job, mate!"

Earlier, I had to close my bedroom door after the hundredth positive affirmation. While I'm thrilled that Warhol's taken to his dog training, the noise is interfering with my ACT prep. The test's in the morning and this is my last chance to cram.

I feel ready. I hope I am, anyway. At the start of the school year, I didn't care about university, but I must have *become* concerned through osmosis. Application fever has hit NSHS hard; it's impossible not to be swept up in the frenzy.

I even begged off the Homecoming festivities tonight. Kent told me I didn't have to miss it. He said I need to master time management during the test. That didn't require staying home from social events so much as it just required a watch. Still, I'd hate to be sorry I didn't give up one night if it makes a difference. I can't pinpoint *why* I'm bothered it might make a difference, yet here we are.

As for Stephen, well…he hasn't said anything to me. He has his MIT interview soon and Kent and I both fear it will go badly. He won't talk to us about it, or allow us to help, and that does not portend good news. (Ten points for my use of *portend*. I feel like my prep has been efficacious.) (Ha! Ten more points for *efficacious*.) What I'm saying is that Stephen's been more taciturn than usual. (*Taciturn!* I'm going to slay this test. Wait, is there even a vocab section? Or is that just the SATs? Shit.)

Anyway, I suspect Stephen is jealous of Kent for hooking up with the field hockey girl. Kent tells me he and Stephen have always been matched in every respect, from overbearing mums to performance on Common Core Learning Standards to "Call of Duty: Black Ops" scores, so Noell has tipped the scales, even though she started ignoring Kent the minute she sobered up. Kent insists that's a bell you can't un-ring, so he's still gloating about having become a man.

What does *become a man* mean exactly? Don't know. I've not asked for details, even though he's dying to tell me.

"Well done, Warhol!"

I can hear their muffled voices downstairs, despite a closed door. It's a bit shocking that my parents are involved with anything as mainstream or pedestrian as dog obedience, but I'm glad. When we found out that bringing Warhol back to England would be near impossible—importing pit bulls is banned—my folks sought out a loophole. Now they're training him to be an emotional support dog. They've already bought him a snappy service vest and Warhol loves it almost as much as he loves wearing his sweater. I believe parading around in his support uniform makes him feel important and hard, like one of those tough German Shepherds you see patrolling the airport. (Wearing the sweater just makes him feel smart and fashionable.)

The trainer's been buzzing the doorbell for the past fifteen minutes to get Warhol used to sudden noises. More unfortunate, my father realized he's able to change the sound the doorbell makes so I've been subjected to the opening bars of "America the Beautiful" over and over. I find myself humming about purple mountain majesties while I'm trying to study and that needs to stop right quick.

The bell rings again.

"Oh, beautiful for spacious skies..."

Enough fruited plains already!

A moment later, Dad shouts, "Simba! C'mon down, love!"

"I'm *busy*. Listen, I'm glad Warhol sits when someone comes to the door, but I truly don't need to see him do it *again*."

"Well, he's terribly clever so you should. That's not it, though. You have a visitor."

Who would be here? Stephen's MIA and, besides, Mrs. Cho would never let him out after 9:00 p.m. the night before a meet. Kent was headed to the game and then the dance, in the hopes that Noell might get drunk and give him the time of day again. Owen's been clear about his feelings, so...that's it, the entirety of my inner circle. I have friends in my classes and on the newspaper, but we're not tight enough for a late visit, especially unannounced.

Must be Kent. Suspect I'll be hearing every dirty detail of his newfound manhood soon, whether or not I want to. Might as well be done now.

I tighten my robe and head down the stairs. Didn't bother to dress after my bath or mess around with makeup, so I'm bare-faced with a towel still wrapped around my hair. Kent will have a tremendous laugh, seeing me like this.

Except it's not Kent standing in my entry hall; it's *Liam*.

!

!!

!!!

249

I spot him before he sees me and I fly back up the stairs before I'm noticed. "I'm just out of the bath!" I holler. "Down in two shakes!"

I quickly ponder the contents of my closet. What outfit makes me look the most nonchalant? The most insouciant? (No time to congratulate myself on my outstanding word usage, though.)

I settle on an old pair of Levis with holes worn in the knees and a faded black skull-embossed Misfits T-shirt from my dad's punk rock days. Mum's always after me to toss the natty old thing, but it's so beautifully and genuinely tattered that I can't bear to part with it.

I twist my hair into a messy topknot and brush on some gloss, pencil in my eyebrows, and finish off with a bit of mascara. (I resemble a mole without certain cosmetics.) I slip on my shoes and spray myself with a quick spritz of perfume.

I glance in the mirror—not bad for five minutes.

I head down the stairs again, pretending I don't know who's here. "Kent, I thought you were going to the—oh. *Liam.* Hey."

He hits me with the kind of slow, lazy, Bowie-esque grin that lights up the whole front hallway. The sheer wattage of his presence makes me feel melty inside, like a bar of chocolate left on the dashboard.

My parents are hovering around beside Liam, like…well, like parents.

"Hey, Moon Girl."

My mum cocks an eyebrow in my direction. She's not succumbed to any of those horrible chemicals many women of a certain age shoot into their foreheads, so she's still able to make expressions. Cordy's mum has a whole chemistry lab injected into her face. You have to listen to the tone of her voice to figure out if she's cross or happy or sad; it's too weird.

"Mum, Dad, um, Warhol—this is my friend Liam."

Dad offers a curt nod. "We met."

Huh. My folks are normally more gracious. They're incredibly chatty! I came home last week to them entertaining both the UPS and FedEx men at the kitchen counter. Such is their cheer and effusive nature, they brought détente to the hyper-competitive overnight shipping industry.

"Hope you don't mind me dropping by. Ran into Kent at the game and he gave me your address. Wanted to wish you luck for tomorrow."

"Ah," I say, because any other words escape me. I'm afraid if I open my mouth to say too much, the butterflies in my gut will flutter out and then that would be terribly awkward.

"Don't you need to hit the sack soon. Simba?" my dad asks. His voice has an edge and he makes no motions to indicate he'll afford us any privacy. Mum stands next to him, arms crossed, lips downturned, appearing equally stern.

Um, did I stumble into a bizarre alternative universe here? Did I fall asleep and wake up in *The Twilight Zone*? Who are these *strangers*? I can't believe Liam hasn't had a cup of tea thrust at him at a minimum. My God, Dad sent both the delivery men away with a couple of his original watercolors! (Ooh, Mr. Hochberg had a right fit over that.)

Mum can't be thrown by the fact that there's a boy calling for me. I mean, she put me on birth control when I confessed my crush on David Bowie. I was all, "Wouldn't that be terribly illegal?"

"Doesn't matter," she'd said. Claimed she wanted me to be safe and ready for my "sexual awakening." I replied that, again, didn't need to be on the pill, but wouldn't mind an iTunes gift cert if she was looking to throw around a bit of cash. So why are they both being so inhospitable right now?

I'm not even sure they aren't some ill-programmed clones swapped out for the real thing.

Wait, are they *scowling*? I swear they're scowling. S*omething* is amiss here. I've never had a set bedtime or a curfew or any of the parental rules and conventions that drove all my friends so mad. Cordy would always cry, "My mum's so strict!" and I'd listen and sympathize, but truly could not empathize. In fact, I couldn't even imagine.

But, now? Now I have an inkling.

I feel the need to move the party away from these two. "Liam and I are going to go chat in the TV room, unless you have an objection?" I say. I can't decipher the look that passes between them.

"Fifteen minutes max, Sim," my mum says, tapping the face of her watch. "You have an early morning and a big day." Such is their consternation that Warhol, who's taken a shine to Liam, doesn't even frolic.

While I'd like to get to the root of their reactions, I'm far more interested in discovering why Luscious Liam is here.

"We'll have a word and be up in two shakes," I say as I lead him to our finished basement. We lived here three days before any of us realized that this part of the house was more than just a grotty old cellar that housed the mechanicals. There's a whole bar setup and a posh extra kitchen, as well as a state-of-the-art screening room with built-in movie theater seats and a popcorn machine. Dad couldn't stop exclaiming when we discovered this portion, crowing about how he has dreams where he discovers new rooms and never knew it could be a reality.

"Nice place," Liam remarks.

"Thanks," I reply, even though what I want to say is WHY

ON EARTH ARE YOU HERE AND DO YOU FANCY ME BECAUSE I LIKE YOU SOOOOOOO MUCH.

I manage to hold myself together, though, as I ease onto the couch.

"You want some popped corn?" I ask, gesturing toward the machine. "I can make it just like the theater does."

"I'm good," he says. He settles in the seat next to me. I tuck my legs under myself and angle so that we're facing each other. My bare knees show through my jeans. Did I shave them? Please tell me I remembered to shave them. Stubble will not do. "I wanted to talk to you, Moon Girl."

"Uh-huh, of course." I try to sound cool, but I'm so nervous right now that I can't catch a full breath. I suck in little gulps of air here and there. Is it possible to drown on dry land? I pray I don't find out.

"I broke up with Mallory."

"I'm sorry," I reply automatically, even though I'm actually thinking YES, YES, YES, PRAISES TO YOU, CHRIST *AND* YOUR BIKE!

I find myself suddenly designing the kind of commitment ring that Brazilian men give their intended before proposing marriage. I picture braided platinum, with an inset moonstone.

Stop that, self, you're being too ridiculous. Also, we're not in Brazil. And we're still minors.

"Don't be, it was a long time coming. We just weren't right together anymore. Everything had become so complicated and heavy and just…wrong. The minute I ended it, I felt euphoric, like I was free. That's when I realized the only thing I wanted was to see you. Being with you is easy."

"I'm terribly easy," I agree. Then I snort and clamp a hand over my face. "That's not what I meant."

He grins and my innards arrange themselves into a Gor-

253

dian knot. "What I'm trying to say is that I want to be around you. I feel like I can be me, no expectations, no demands. I can't..." He searches for the words.

"Feel your face? Particularly when you're with me?" I say, paraphrasing what I already consider *our* song.

He smiles, activating his dimple. (Would it be bad manners to place my tongue in that divot?)

He says, "I've been gravitating toward you and now I don't need to fight those feelings."

I nod. Saying nothing is probably the better strategy. I'm having to remind myself to breathe. This is so surreal, having a boy I fantasize about just materialize at my house to confess his hidden feelings about me. Maybe my dad dreams about undiscovered rooms, but this is how *my* dreams unfurl.

Wait, did I pass out while reviewing my prep work? Is this all a product of my imagination, brought on by too much maths? Am I actually face-first on an open Kaplan book right now, a slight trickle of drool leaking onto the pages?

Liam reaches over and threads his fingers through the back of my hair. Oh, that's nice. My topknot comes undone, but I don't mind. He says, "All I could think of doing was this." With that, he pulls me close to him. Our foreheads are pressed together. The heat generated from where skin touches skin gives me goose bumps. He gazes deep into my eyes for what feels like a lifetime before he begins to kiss me.

!

!!

!!!

His kiss is like none I've experienced, hard, but a good hard, and not like all those other times where I worried about the guy's braces catching the side of my mouth, or if he could smell the curry I ate at lunch, or if I was even doing it right.

Liam's kiss has rendered me weightless, transporting me to another dimension in time and space. I feel like I'm swimming underwater, arching and flexing in an endless, warm emerald pool. My limbs are liquid and free, like I've become one with the sea. I've lost all sense of equilibrium. I'm flying and floating, careening at a hundred miles an hour yet concurrently standing still.

Or maybe that's just the oxygen deprivation, because at some point, my lungs forgot to function.

I pull away first and try not to gasp for air, a goldfish leapt from its bowl.

Liam's hand remains firmly on my neck, keeping my face tucked up close to his. He cups my cheek in his palm. We're taking quick, shallow breaths in unison, our hearts beating with the same tempo. I feel his pulse racing alongside mine. I want to crawl inside this moment and live here for all eternity.

"That?" he says with a smile that slowly plays across his lips. "Was *everything*."

His skin is flushed; I'm sure mine is, too. My lips tingle—I can still feel where he pressed against them. I'm gripping the lapels of his sport jacket, yet I don't remember reaching for him. My body instinctively wants to pull him closer as it's all I can do not to climb onto him.

I suddenly understand why Kent wants to dish details now.

Liam buries his head against my neck and begins to kiss me again and I'm almost overwhelmed as my pleasure morphs into desire. The notion of "going too far" wasn't ever an issue with the boys I snogged…that is, until now.

Oh, I could make very bad decisions with this one.

I grab a handful of his hair and pull him closer. He pulls me right back.

I didn't realize that toe-curling was an actual thing, yet here we are. The ends of my feet are clenched into little bunches inside my shoes. I'm desperately tempted to kick them off, followed by everything else I'm wearing.

"You smell incredible."

As I'm still *me*, I'm obligated to deflect and break our trance. Cordy's right about my lack of game. I explain, "I'm wearing CB I Hate Perfume. Christopher, the guy who created it, is a family friend. He used to drive a cab and he hated how people reeked of the cheap stuff. He despised being accosted by all the commercial fragrances. Long story short, his bad experiences inspired him to whip up really unique scents."

Christopher should attempt to bottle the pheromones whizzing back and forth between the two of us. He'd make bank. As Liam gazes at me, I notice that his irises are different shades of amber and caramel and hazelnut, like a terribly sumptuous bar of Swiss chocolate. I used to think brown was boring, but suddenly it's my favorite.

Again, because I'm destined to ruin every romantic moment, I continue my CB infomercial. "I'm wearing Just Breathe, which was a limited edition. What you're smelling is a mix of bamboo and, um, green tea and—"

Liam saves me from myself by kissing me again. I'm swept away. His kiss is as sure and steady as the return of the tide and just as powerful. When his tongue touches my bottom lip, I respond in kind and we find ourselves woven together like a Brazilian commitment ring. Everything about his mouth on mine is right and formidable and all-encompassing, like I was put on this earth to live out this moment. I'm drawn out of my seat and onto his lap and he holds me harder, closer, as I grip his waist with my legs, his hands traveling from my hair down the length of my body, finding purchase on the bare stretch of my lower back where my shirt has ridden up.

I never want him to stop.

Still, my nature, my singular compulsion, is to wreck this moment. "And sandalwood and forest and a little bit of incense," I finish once we've pulled apart.

What is *wrong* with me?

How is it that I've taken the most romantic/erotic moment of my life and turned it into a *Sephora* advert? Cordy's going to love hearing about this. Yet I can't shut my fool mouth.

"When Christopher asked me my favorite scent, I told him I wanted to recreate what I smelled when strolling the souk in Marrakesh, so this is what he picked."

HOLY CRAP, SELF, STUFF A SOCK IN IT.

Instead of commenting on what a silly little fool I am or, perhaps, coming to his senses, Liam sweeps my bangs out of my eyes and tangles his hand in my hair again.

"Can I see you tomorrow night?" he asks, tracing his finger down my jawline.

Wait, he wasn't thrown by my rattling off details like I was some sort of *Marie Claire* listicle come to life? My self-sabotage didn't mar the moment? Is it possible that he cares for me not *despite* my own nature, but *because* of it?

I take my first proper inhale in about ten minutes and reply once the oxygen returns to my brain. "Yes."

"All right then, off you go!" my dad bellows down the stairs. "Chop, chop, Simba!" He sounds like he means it, too.

"That's my cue," Liam says. But before he gets up, he runs a thumb over my tender lower lip while his eyes search my face. Ripples of pleasure cascade down to my curled toes. "To be continued."

And what do I say in response? Which words do I pull out of my now-expansive lexicon to express exactly how on-board I am with his newly confessed sentiments?

"Okeydokey, artichoke-y."

NO GAME. NONE.

Cordy will die, and legitimately so.

After I see him to the door, I'm giddy as I step into the kitchen to chat with my parents. (The trainer must have left while we were downstairs snogging. Again, WE WERE DOWNSTAIRS SNOGGING!)

I want to recruit my folks into helping me send out a Twitter status, addressed to all of North America, exclaiming LIAM KISSED ME AND I KISSED HIM BACK. They're going to be so glad for me! I can't wait to tell Mum everything! Liam is LOADS more appropriate than David Bowie.

I try to slap the grin from my face; I am wholly unsuccessful.

"So," I begin. "What'd you think?"

"Simba...your friend is on drugs," Mum says.

This is not what I expected to hear. I lose the smile right quick.

"Beg your pardon?" I ask.

"That boy, your *friend,* is high," Dad adds. He's all white-lipped and rigid as he says this.

"What?" I fume. "Have you lost your collective minds? Liam's an elite athlete—the last thing he would do would be to ingest an illegal substance. He's not *high.* He had a sports injury and he's taking medicine, like Tylenol or something. That's it. You're both being incredibly irrational."

"Simmy, no," Mum says gently. "That's not what Tylenol looks like."

Dad is a lot harsher. "He's jammed out of his head, Sim. That boy was *off to see the wizard.* He was *not of this world.* He was *flying.* You have to trust me, been there, done that, sculpted the goddamned fetus out of it."

I know exactly what the problem is here; the problem is not me.

The problem is that since we've been in America, my dad has lost his spark. He's not created a damn thing and that always puts him in a right foul mood. Last week, I thought he was finally inspired when I saw these huge lists written out on the wall of his workshop.

Turns out, he was simply trying to organize his fantasy football picks.

Mum's concerned, too. He's not himself when he's not enmeshed in a project; it's like his creativity is replaced with anger. The last time he was blocked like this, he went to war with the greengrocer on Drury Lane, saying Mr. Saccomandi was passing off factory-farmed leeks and beetroot as organic produce. Was quite a whole to-do there for a while, until he finally took that trip to Peru and came home inspired.

Mum and Dad eye each other before Mum starts to speak. "Simmy, sweetie, your Dad and I… Well, we're older and wiser than you. We've been around the block. You have to trust us when we say that Liam was not right-minded. His pupils were little pinpoints and he was all ruddy and breathing hard—*none* of that is normal. *All* are signs of drug use. Bad ones, not just a blunt at a party."

I want to stomp my feet or throw a knickknack or something, which is not at all like me. I can't even recall the last time I wasn't on the same page as my parents; maybe that's why I feel like overreacting. I'm boggled by the very unfairness of their accusations. No one should be projecting his or her own shortcomings onto this perfectly lovely boy.

I calm myself and try to express my feelings. "I disagree. Those are completely *normal* reactions for someone who's coming over to tell a girl that he likes her. Can't you trust my judgment?"

"We trust *you*," Dad says. "Always have. We don't trust

him. Who comes to a girl's house when caned? My God, the lack of proper judgment is astounding."

"Are you serious?" The urge to stomp is back. "He's not *on* anything! And, hypothetically, what if he did experiment with something, just the once? You're such hypocrites! Or did you forget traveling to Peru for the sole purpose of taking ayahuasca just last year?"

I'm referring to the hallucinogenic plant that's cooked down into a tea and administered by a shaman. Chugging the elixir is supposed to give users insights regarding their earthly purpose and users have told stories of visiting different spiritual realms. Mum said it mostly made her throw up in a bucket and appreciate first world bathrooms, but Dad said this was what inspired him to create *SegaGenocide*.

Thank God it did. The veg weren't nearly as fresh at regular supermarkets.

"That's a single instance," I add. "I know all about your lives back before I was born. People have written *books* about your crowd! I mean, if you Google 'cocaine' and '1990s,' your picture appears first, Dad! You both used to chill with Keith Richards! Honestly, how I wasn't born with flippers or a vestigial tail is a complete mystery! You two are the LAST BLOODY PEOPLE ON EARTH to judge anyone for anything, particularly without a shred of proof."

With a preternatural calm, Dad says, "Go to bed, Simone."

Mum and I are both taken aback at the notion of Dad doling out discipline and the use of my Christian name, but as I'm ready to end this conversation, I do as I'm told.

"Gladly," I reply. I stomp up the stairs without bidding either of them goodnight...for the first time ever.

26

—

STEPHEN

"HOW DO YOU want to be remembered after high school, Mr. Cho?"

"Mom, please, can I have one second? I need a timeout. Lemme get my head together, okay?"

My phone's been blowing up the whole ride down the expressway but I haven't even been able to glance at my texts because my mom's too intent on quizzing me until the very last moment. I finally unblocked Kent and Simone, largely because I didn't want to get into why I'd cut them out in the first place. Doesn't even matter.

My mother's been peppering me nonstop for the past week with potential questions that the alum might ask at today's MIT interview. She doesn't reply to my request for a respite and I see her narrowing her eyes at me in the rearview mirror.

Oh, did I not mention that despite being eighteen years old, I'm still *forced to sit in the back seat*? Her rationale is I'm safer back there. Didn't Ralph Nader himself conclude that shame was the best airbag?

Kent always says I should play it off like she's my chauffeur. Works in theory, but I ask you, what Uber driver rolls down the window upon drop-off, insisting I make the family proud? Some days it's like I want to contact NASA to calculate exactly how embarrassed I am, because the humiliation can't be measured on the tools I possess.

I'm so anxious about my interview right now I want to puke. I feel my guts churning and I'm all lightheaded. I can taste bile in the back of my throat and I swallow again and again to keep it down. Perspiration is pouring out of my palms and my feet are so sweaty that my socks are slipping around inside my stiff dress shoes.

What would make me feel better *isn't* more prep; I desperately need amnesty from this rolling quiz bowl. This morning she was shouting questions at me through the closed bathroom door; I can't even take a shit in private. If I could have a few minutes to listen to my tunes and center myself, I'd come back to this refreshed. I unzip the case and pull out my headphones so I'll be ready to plug them in the minute the warden releases me for yard time.

With every question my mom throws at me, the invisible band around my chest constricts harder, practically choking the life out of me. Thank God Caitlyn needs her for a day of wedding planning after she drops me off, so I'm taking the train home by myself. At least I'll be spared from the play-by-play recap until dinner.

Headphones in hand, I say, "I'll do a better job if I go in there relaxed. Take five?"

My mom doesn't look away from the road as she answers, generating oceans of bad karma as she cruises down the expressway at her usual forty-seven miles per hour in the center lane. "Oh, yeah, you think MIT wants students who'd rather relax? This is the homestretch, pal. Quit stalling."

I place my headphones in the seat pocket. My iPhone

chimes again and it's all I can do to not rip it out of my blazer, but the price for noncompliance is just too high.

As I've prepped for the interview, I've thought a lot about the question of my high school legacy. Do I have specific achievements? Sure, by anyone's standards, I'm having a decent run. But in fifty years, who's gonna give a low-flying fuck about the minutia around my Physics Olympics wins or my GPA down to the tenth of a percentage point? High school's the beginning of the beginning. What will be important is that I worked hard enough during my time at NSHS to put myself up for consideration at a place like MIT, that I sacrificed so much fun (so much freedom) to cultivate and maximize every opportunity for growth and success. *That's* what speaks to my character, right?

"Here's what I'm planning to say: the notion of a high school legacy is shortsighted. I'm not concerned with creating a narrative about my 'glory days' or garnering a full-page spread in the yearbook. Have I had significant wins? Definitely. I could rattle off an impressive list. But the details of the wins aren't pivotal, it's the aptitude and drive I've demonstrated in winning that's important. If no one remembers me when I leave NSHS, so be it, because I'm confident that I've pushed myself harder than I ever thought possible to set myself up for the next step. To me? That's enough."

My mother grimaces as she grips the steering wheel. "Ugh. Horrible. Try again, but with *specific* achievements. I'm thinking start with your GPA, then highlight competition wins. Talk about how your robot's arms are articulated. They need tangible evidence, not flowery, philosophical bullcrap."

I grit my teeth before parroting back everything she wants to hear.

We've only been in the car for twenty minutes, yet the ride feels never-ending.

★ ★ ★

"This is it," my mother says, pulling up to the curb in front of an intimidating expanse of steel and glass. The sun reflecting off the fifty stories of skyscraper windows is practically blinding. Dozens of pedestrians squint, not because it's so bright, but because they're glaring at my mother, as she's half-parked in the crosswalk. She pays them no attention. They make a wide berth around our SUV, scowling as they clutch paper bags full of burgers and fries and sad desk salads from various fast food restaurants.

Of course we've arrived in the middle of the lunch rush, making ourselves an obstacle, a target of impotent rage. Story of my life.

"Bye, Mom," I say. I grab my backpack and slide across the seat to exit at the curb. "Wish me luck." I try to open the door, but she has the child-safety locks depressed.

"You're prepared, you don't need luck. One more thing—before you go, what are you going to say when the alum asks you about your favorite music?"

"What? Mom, unlock the door," I say, trying the handle again.

She is resolute. "Listen, it's a common question and you should be ready for it."

Behind me, impatient motorists begin to sound their horns as she's blocking the right turn onto State Street. "I gotta *go,* Mom."

"Okay. *After* you answer the question."

Honk, honk.

"People are waiting," I plead.

She shakes her head. "*They* are not my problem. *You* are my problem. And your answer is…"

"Um, I…" I'm so rattled that I can't even think of a reply

264

that she'll deem acceptable, so I end up saying, "I'll tell him the truth, that I love old-school rap because even though my experience is wildly different, I connect with—"

My mom pounds the steering wheel hard enough to add to the cacophony of horns sounding all around us, a veritable Khrushchev in lululemon yoga pants, banging that shoe at the United Nations. "Absolutely not."

Hoooonk.

My blood pressure skyrockets with every beep, with each dirty look. I feel the flop-sweat start to roll down my face, dampening the collar of my overstarched oxford. "Mom, this question's about personal preference, an insight to who I really am. It's about my passion. They're not going to deny me a spot in the freshman class because Tupac—"

The horns sound with more and more insistence. The Yellow Cab driver directly behind us mashes his palm long and hard into his steering wheel, while the lady in the Audi taps out a staccato beat with hers.

"Please, you're going to tell them you love a man who shot *himself* in the jujubes? You know my friend from grad school worked in the Bellevue ER? She said everyone kept quiet that he shot *himself* because of the careless way he was carrying his gun. Do you want to tell MIT you emulate the guy who shot himself in the balls? No! Talk about *Swan Lake*! Or *Peter and the Wolf*! Talk about classical pieces featuring the oboe so you can bring the conversation back to your accomplishments in orchestra. Bach! Not Tupac! Or, let's be honest, One-pac! Understood?"

I nod mutely, feeling overwhelmingly defeated, finished before I even start.

Satisfied, she replies, "Okay, kiddo, I'll see you at home. Good luck. Now hurry up, these cars are waiting." She unlocks the door and I practically dive out of the vehicle. Pedestrians and motorists alike curse at me and flip me the bird as I get myself together.

"I *hate* the oboe," I spits at her tailgate as she pulls away. Long after I dropped out of symphonic band, she made me keep up with my lessons. Said she wanted me to be well-rounded. Oh, yeah, I'm *plenty* well-rounded. Between the oboe, the bowling, and the Physics Olympics, I've hit the Dork Trifecta.

I reach in my bag for my headphones so that I can listen to a song or two before my interview but I realize I left them in the car. Damn it. I head over to the concrete bench in front of the office building and sit on the opposite end from a woman reading a book with a busty heroine on the cover, who appears to be clinging to some oiled dude who looks like Fabio. I pull up my iTunes library and turn down the speaker, selecting the happiest song of the bunch—"California Love."

Before Dr. Dre can even welcome everybody to the Wild, Wild West, the lady with the book huffs, "Really? Think you're the only person out here, kid?"

Chastened, I mumble an apology and head inside to the lobby to read my texts. Simone's wished me luck and so has Kent. Of course, he's followed his good tidings with fifteen additional texts about that girl Noell. I don't know what voodoo he worked on her at Homecoming, but she seems to legit like him now and they spend all their time together.

Awesome.

Because I didn't feel alone enough already.

He's been making noise about hooking me up with Spencer, the four of us going out together, but the idea of a pity date feels worse than no date at all.

You know what? I half hope he doesn't get into MIT. I

hope he tanks his interview. I hope Noell throws him off his game. If he's just going to toss his social success in my face, then I don't even want to be around him. He's already got a foot out the door away from me anyhow. Like he was just biding his time before something or someone better came along.

Another good luck text comes in, this one from my Quantum Mechanics instructor.

Cool. Texts from my teacher friend. Could I *be* more pathetic?

I throw my phone back into my bag without replying to anyone.

I'm in the elevator up to the thirty-seventh floor, after showing my ID to Security. I'm heading to Burkholder Fitz Gamble, which is a law firm. The alumnus who's supposed to interview me works here. I guess this Alex Gamble guy went to MIT to study biomechanical engineering before Harvard for his JD and now he's a patent attorney who defends pharmaceutical companies.

The receptionist at the firm tells me to have a seat on one of the big padded benches and that someone from Alex Gamble's office will be out in a few minutes. Last night, I Googled Mr. Gamble to find out his background. I had a hard time finding much. He must be busy climbing the corporate ladder because he has, like, *zero* social media profiles. I did run across one thing, though. He races sailboats on his off-time, which is badass. Got a little distracted looking at the blurry shot of him on his boat next to a hot lady in a snug tank top. *Nice.* Wife? Girlfriend? He looks like a bit of a tool, so my assumption is that maybe girls are into smart guys once they get out of high school?

God, I hope so, because right now they look at me like I'm a walking petri dish full of HPV or something.

As I sit here, my leg starts to bounce. I can't keep it still. I just want this thing to start so it can be over. Let me get through this unscathed. Let this Alex dude be cool. Everyone says the interview is more of a formality than anything else, but what if it's not? What if my whole future rests on my having a satisfactory answer to what three adjectives others would use to describe me? (Note to self: don't say *loser, coward, reject*, no matter how true it may be.)

I bow my head and try to center myself. In my peripheral vision, I see a pair of shapely legs in red-soled, high heel shoes approaching me. I instinctively follow the legs up, past the curvy hips and narrow waist, over her considerable assets, only partially obscured by a conservative blouse, and up to the face, which absolutely fulfills the promise of the tight bod. The woman realizes I'm checking her out and I can feel myself blush.

Nice move, Cho, I say to myself. *Very suave. Let's put a pin in this so you can continue to sexually harass Mr. Gamble's assistant even more* after *your interview.*

"Stephen Cho, I presume?" she asks, holding out her hand so I can shake it.

I want to die. I seriously want to die right now. I could not be more embarrassed.

I jump up from my seat to take her hand so quickly that I spill the contents of my backpack. Every item in the bag spews out all over the floor. The hot lady bends over and helps me retrieve everything. "Here you go." She hands me my scientific calculator and a handful of pencils covered in bite marks because I tend to chew them while thinking.

Scratch that, I can *always* be more embarrassed.

"Thanks," I say, practically whispering this into my chest.

"Please don't worry about it," she laughs. "The alumnae

interview is nerve-racking, right? Borderline torture? Cruel and unusual punishment."

"Oh, my God, so much!" I exclaim.

"Trust me, you're not the first MIT hopeful who's been in here feeling anxious. You'll be fine, I promise. Take a couple of deep breaths. You'll feel the difference and I'm in no rush. I know how stressed you must be. Been there myself."

I comply and after a few lungsful, my heart stops trying to pummel its way clean out of my ribcage.

"So, now that you're together, why don't you follow me?" she says with a smile and a swish of her shiny hair. I like how her pale pink lipstick contrasts with her dark skin and the deep brown of her shoulder-length bob. She's giving off Gabrielle Union–realness. (Dwayne Wade is the luckiest man on earth. Fact.)

I wonder if this lady distracts Mr. Gamble when he's trying to, like, *jurisprudence* or whatever. Do they race boats together? Was she the woman in the picture? Pretty sure she was.

I plod along behind her while she glances back at me to see if I'm still with her, scrunching up her eyes each time, all friendly. This lady's making me feel better and I truly appreciate that. I bet she's an awesome assistant. If Kent were here, he'd be all, *Yeah, baby, Mr. Gamble* does *want you to take a letter.*

You know what? I probably owe Kent an apology. Suspect he was being helpful and cool in trying to set me up with Spencer.

We head down a long hall and finally arrive at the door of a large, glassed-in office in the corner of the building. The leather rolling chair in front of the formidable oak desk is presently unoccupied. She enters while I stand in the doorway, waiting for my interviewer to arrive.

"Wow, I'm glad I didn't screw up like that in front of Mr. Gamble, right? Whew." I sweep a hand over my brow.

"Um…" Her smile falters and she clears her throat. "Actually it's Ms."

I don't follow.

I say, "I'm sorry, it's *mis*-what?" I figure she's nice enough that I can be honest. "I didn't catch the end of what you said."

She sits at the desk and points to her engraved nameplate. "Gamble. Ms. *Alexandra* Gamble. Hi, Stephen, I apologize for not properly introducing myself back there, I thought you knew. Please, have a seat." She gestures to the open chair.

Fuck. My. Life.

I've crashed.

I've burned.

I've blown this interview in a way that interviews have never been blown before. I've invented entirely new ways to fail. Someday people are going to describe disasters as "That was a total Cho-show," instead of inserting the words *Hindenburg* or *Titanic* or *Chernobyl*.

Loser.

Coward.

Reject.

How am I gonna face my family after this? How will I say that I messed it up *again*, *like always*, despite their best efforts? That I lost everything I've been trying to achieve my whole life in less than an hour?

I feel like I'm drowning, like this glass office has turned into an aquarium and my mouth, my stupid mouth that keeps betraying me, is a set of weighted lead boots. The water's rising all around me and I can't fight, I can't swim, I can't pull myself to the surface no matter how hard I kick.

Do I even want to kick? I am a tsunami of suck. Maybe I deserve to sink. Maybe it's better if I don't try to save myself.

Clearly this Ms. Gamble is a sadist, making me sit here and answer her questions, like I still have a shot, like I don't appall her, like she's not going to stamp my interview form with the word NO, NO, NO, NO over and over in red ink.

Loser.

Coward.

Reject.

First I lost my chance at valedictorian and now this. When I saw the names on that damn sailing photo, I was too distracted by the tank top to notice which person was actually Alex. How do I always do this, how do I always miss the whole fucking point of everything?

Useless.

Useless.

USELESS.

I can't recover from this. There's no coming back.

For a minute, I thought I'd dodged the black cloud that perpetually follows me, the all-encompassing darkness that threatens to pull me under. Why have I been fighting it when it would be easier, so much easier, to just give in?

I told myself that things would improve once high school was over, that I could be a new me at college, a different me, a better me, but that's bullshit.

I want to make it stop hurting.

I want to quiet the voices inside my head.

I want to feel nothing.

I want the pain of being me, of being a loser, a coward, a reject, to go away.

"So, Stephen, tell me…" she begins, leaning across her desk, pretending like she's not disgusted with me, like she cares about my response. "How do you want to be remembered after high school?"

I give her my original honest answer, only in a more succinct form.

I say, "I don't want to be remembered."

27

———

KENT

FINE, DON'T TEXT me back.

To myself, I'm all, *this is not how a friend acts.* He should be happy, not just for me, but for both of us. This thing with Noell is the culmination of everything either of us ever wanted and now there's potential for him, too.

After she and I got together at the Homecoming game (thank you, Fireball Cinnamon Whiskey), he was like, "What about Mallory?" While I didn't say it, I was thinking, *sure, Noell's no Mallory, but she's also not my right hand and that counts for a lot.*

So much. The difference between virtual reality and *actual* reality? No comparison.

Does he not understand that Noell's friend Spencer is a real girl, who's right here, right now? Sure, he and I had plans to fabricate a female robot, but it was gonna take years to create a fully functioning prototype. While I still totally see the upside of a sex robot, there's much to be said about having a flesh-and-blood girlfriend right-freaking-now.

(With our luck, we'd program our robot with the kind of

artificial intelligence that would eventually want to destroy mankind, anyway.)

That's why I went over to his house last night—to talk to him about Spencer. Mrs. Cho had a fit because she was running interview questions with him at the dining room table, but I told her we had to discuss a school project and she gave him a quick break. Seemed like he needed it, too, dude was wiped out, eyes all dark-circled and skin sallow. Even his perma-spiked hair was lethargic, practically flattened to his skull.

We headed upstairs to his room, which is kind of a carbon copy of mine, except I don't have a signed photo of Steve Jobs. Lucky bastard.

"Before I forget," I said, reaching into my backpack, "here's your shirt. I ironed it and everything. Sorry it took so long to get it back to you. I used those little beads in the wash that make your stuff smell extragood to say sorry for the delay. Check it out, April-fresh!"

"Keep it," he said, waving the shirt away.

"Dude, this is, like, your favorite."

He said, "Nah, my mom shrunk it. I don't want it. You're small, you have it."

Typical Stephen, giving with one hand and taking away with the other.

What's ironic is the shirt did feel kind of small on me; I'd hoped it was because I'd grown. I feel slightly taller, but maybe that's just because Noell digs me and that makes me stand up straighter.

(Bonus points to me for not saying anything about "erect." Heh.)

I refused to let him bait me, though, so I said, "*Imma* pretend you didn't insult me and just enjoy my badass new shirt."

Stephen flopped onto his bed, belly-side down, and lay there all splayed out like a starfish.

"Yo, little tired there, bro?" I laughed.

"You have no idea," he replied, dragging out each word, like even the idea of saying he was exhausted was too exhausting.

"Well, I won't keep you, I just wanted to give you the 411 about Spencer."

He didn't reply so I continued.

"Spencer? Hot girl who hangs out with Noell? Field hockey player? Wears skirts so short you can see the crease where her ass meets her thigh when she bends over?" Shameful story, but once last year he and I dropped a handful of dollar bills on the ground by Spencer so we could watch her pick them up. Basically was all our lunch money that day, but being hungry was worth the show. "I *know* you know who I mean."

Listlessly, he replied, "Uh-huh."

Why did I go out of my way for him when this was how he reacted to my outstanding news?

"ANYWAY, Jasper was hooking up with Spencer but he dumped her and now she's on a major rebound. She agreed to do a double date." I waited for him to rally, but again, nothing. "Clarification, a double date with me and *you*."

Nada.

I said, "So, lemme sum this up for you, 'cause clearly you're not processing this. Smokeshow Spencer wants to hang with *you*. You familiar with the concept of low-hanging fruit? What's the downside here?"

He shrugged. "I'd just screw it up, like always. Pass."

I was exasperated. "Hold up, 'Pass'? Pass, like she's a bread basket in a restaurant and you're gluten-free? What in the actual fuck? Do you even *get* what I went through to make this happen? I had to go for a pedicure with Noell. I don't mean driving her to the nail salon, no, I mean *getting a pedicure with her.* And I'm not talking just soaking my feet and having them scrape off the rough skin and massage them and shit. Although, no lie, bro, I enjoyed that part. The deal is, Noell agreed to the fix-up, but only if I had my toenails polished because she thought that'd be hilarious. I have ten hot pink little piggies for *you.* There's a fuckin' *daisy* painted on my big toe." I pointed to my foot. "I got your friendship right here."

Into his covers, Stephen said, "Sorry to be such a burden. Maybe your life would be better if I weren't in it."

I said, "Brother, please. I cannot fucking wait until your interview's over tomorrow. Gotta tell you, you're being a total pill right now. Are you even excited for that? This is the last hurdle between you and a one-way ticket to Boston."

He let out a slow, steady stream of breath, which sounded like a balloon deflating. "I'm sure it's hopeless. Why would MIT want me?"

Okay, that was it.

I'd had my fill of his nonsense.

I was not about to talk him through everything he had going for him, listing off every achievement, particularly when I knew that if MIT could only choose one of us from NSHS, it'd be him over me a million times. He could show up to that interview in his freaking boxer shorts and they'd still toss scholarships at him, begging him to be part of their freshman class. Hell, no one had even confirmed *my* alum interview yet.

I told him, "Word of advice? Don't take this bullshit attitude into your interview tomorrow."

And then I went home, because I was *done.*

I didn't see him this morning; he left for school without

277

us. Simone was a couple minutes late getting to my house, so we were running behind when we knocked on the Chos' door. In his typical fashion, he'd already gone stomping off without us instead of waiting five minutes. We don't have any AM classes together and his mom was coming to get him before lunch so I didn't have a chance to see him before he left.

I felt bad about how we left it last night, even though I technically didn't do anything wrong. I've been pinging him all day about stuff to take his mind off being nervous, trying to get him fired up, trying to ignite that spark in him. He hasn't responded. Truth is, it's starting to hurt my feelings.

I glance at the clock on my phone. Okay, his interview *has* to be over by now. I try him again, this time not sugar-coating anything.

I finally text what in the actual fuck, dude?

My phone chimes and I glance down to see Stephen's message i'm so sorry. u were right, kent.

Okay, Cho, *that's* more like it.

28

MALLORY

I NEED TO get out of my own head.

I figured helping other kids with their probs will take my mind off mine. So, I signed up for an extra peer counseling shift because I could use some perspective.

With the whole Liam thing, I can't figure out if I'm sad or worried or just plain pissed off because he's *already* so tight with Simone.

I'm all, *her*? Really? And that's not rumor, either; it's fact. First, Elise saw them riding to school together the Monday after Homecoming a couple of weeks ago. I started hearing about *LiMone* (their couple portmanteau) a few days after that.

Please. *LiMone* sounds like a Walmart-brand soda.

I hear they've gotten very close, very fast, but I was so wrapped up in ending the field hockey season that I didn't pay attention until after we took the state title. (Told you so.) Didn't see for myself until I walked past them making out by his locker yesterday. Witnessed them with my own two eyes.

Tongue! *School* tongue!

Who *does* that?

When classmates asked about our breakup, and, of course, they did ask, I told them an abbreviated version of reality— that we'd grown apart, that senior year was too much of a grind. I didn't mention our (unrequited) love triangle, that there was a third person in the relationship who kept me from being present for Liam. To explain the full truth would be a complex answer to what should be a simple question.

Most people hate to hear about unwarranted emotional complications. They don't like *messy*. They want succinct, breezy, something that makes sense so they can move on. For example, look at the question, "How are you?" In casual conversation, folks expect us to reply with a "fine" or "good."

No one wants a dissertation on how my mom is a total bitch who plays favorites and how the two of us are locked in a power struggle that's only escalated since Braden died.

"How are you, Mallory?"

"Good, thanks. And you?"

That's how I play it, every day.

What's satisfying about peer counseling is that I can get past the surface with my counselees. I'm not afraid of the messy. I welcome the emotionally complicated. I engage so that I can help resolve. I want kids to know it's okay if they aren't "fine" or "good," that I'm here regardless.

Mr. Gorton's all, "I only want you to *listen* to them—what they're looking for is a chance to be heard. Then you give them the appropriate literature and point them in the right direction."

We're not supposed to, but I know I can do more than just emotional triage. I'm not just gonna hand out related pamphlets when I can offer solutions. He expects me to sit here and nod, like I'm a human bobblehead doll; that's just not me.

Would you not toss a drowning man a life preserver, especially if you have so many extras on your boat? Doesn't make sense. I just wish I'd been better at it when it mattered most.

Ultimately, people confide in me because I'm trustworthy. I've never once squealed about what anyone's told me. Literally, I'll take their secrets to the grave. I mean, I didn't even blab when I heard how Jasper cries after sex. Seriously. Sobbing. I'm saying boo-hoo-like-a-baby-with-a-bowl-of-Spaghettios-on-his-head tears. Every time. And I've heard this from multiple sources because *boyfriend gets around*.

How easy would it have been for me to be all, "What are you gonna do, JasHole, *cry* about it?" whenever he'd give me shit at the lunch table? I'm talking heroic self-restraint on my part. Yet I never have told. Never will, either.

At least I'm not forced to sit with Jasper anymore. That's a definite upside to the breakup.

If my mom weren't so relentless about my doing the whole Wall Street thing, I'd want to be a therapist. The one time I mentioned an interest, she said, "No kid of mine is going to be one of those Prius-driving deadbeats, getting paid in Kleenex and going home to all the cats in her studio apartment."

Another argument I lost. Why do I even try?

Maybe I wouldn't have been good professionally. If being there for Braden was my first test of being a mental health professional, then I failed. Profoundly.

I will always wish he'd said something to me, that I had a clue things had gotten so bad for him. If he'd opened up, if I'd truly let him in, could I have made a difference?

Maybe he kept those parts of him hidden because we were so tentative about our feelings for each other, both too proud to make the first move. What if one of us had relented? Seemed like any time we would touch on something real, the other would make a joke or redirect the conversation. I can think of a million examples where he and I did this dance, but the last time is the most profound.

It happened at my family's lake house, in late summer. Braden was always coming up north with us. Said he liked not feeling like an only child.

Anyway, Braden and I were outside that night, the only ones not yet asleep. We were lying down at the end of the dock, watching the meteor shower. The stars were whizzing across the clear Wisconsin sky, exploding like the fireworks grand finale on the Fourth of July. The beauty of it all left me breathless and I was glad he was there to witness it with me.

As we watched, he said, "We're seeing shrapnel from a supernova that exploded a billion years ago. This is that dying star's last hurrah, burning up in our atmosphere after traveling so many light years. Doesn't it make you feel small and insignificant, like nothing you do ultimately matters? Do you ever question why we're even here if we're so unimportant in the scheme of things?"

"Well, no, because it's all a matter of perspective," I replied. "Who's to say what's small or insignificant? I mean, who's the arbiter of that? Are we two tiny beings in an infinite universe? Sure, yeah. But when you look at what's finite in our lives—our families, teams, friends, activities, *that's* where we take on meaning. *That's* where we're significant. A grain of sand on a beach is nothing, an anonymous, infinitesimal portion of billions of grains that are all the same. They're interchangeable. Take away one grain and no one would ever notice. Place the same grain of sand in someone's eye? Then it's a big deal. Until it's out, that grain becomes that person's entire focus, it's all they can consider until it's gone. Context is everything. Our meaning comes from our context."

"I *heart* your huge brain, Mallory," he said.

"Shut up," I replied, and we both laughed and watched the sky for a few minutes.

"Seriously, Mal? I wish I could see it your way," he replied, his voice as wistful as I'd ever heard. "I don't share your confidence about my place in the universe. I've got to wonder what I have to offer. I need to figure out how to come across as the single, all-important grain and not just one of the trillions across the Sahara, you know?"

I rolled over onto my side, propped up on my elbow, concerned by the tenor of what he said. "Hey, what's going on with you? Everything cool?" I asked, placing a hand on his chest, feeling his heartbeat quicken along with my own.

He looked up at me for a long time, not saying anything in response, our faces closer than they'd ever been before. As I hovered over him, a hank of my hair slid out of my ponytail and spilled down, tangling in his thick eyelashes. For a couple of seconds, the whole universe was him and me. My defenses disappeared.

Suddenly, being with Braden seemed the only logical choice and I knew he felt it, too.

Maybe witnessing me soften proved too overwhelming, because the next thing he'd said was, "Shit, I got a grain of Mallory in my eye! Get it out!" and he brushed away my hair and then grabbed me, lifting me up and tossing me in the water. I started splashing him and we were so loud, we woke up my mother who sent Theo out after us. Then he jumped in, too.

We never had another chance to continue the conversation that night, to recapture that moment. Just like that, exactly like the meteors above us, we'd burned brilliantly and profoundly, lighting up the heavens for a couple of glorious seconds before ultimately flaming out.

In retrospect, I realize his whole good-humor, larger-than-life thing was a mask, a role he played, the way he hid his true self and his true intentions to the world.

He was nothing but smiles for everyone until he decided he was done smiling.

See? My job here gives me perspective. There I was feeling bad about the Liam situation and then I remembered Braden, remembered what could have been if I'd been brave. If I'd been able to relinquish control. I should have let Liam go long before I did. We'd have both been happier. Instead, I kept stringing him along out of self-interest.

Thinking of Braden causes a physical ache. I don't feel whole, like there's a part of me missing. Braden's a phantom limb. The pain of missing him overwhelms me. I carry my despair with me, like my movement is hindered, like I'm hauling around a fifty-pound pack on my back that I can never put down.

Thoughts of Braden consume my dreams. And even when those dreams morph into nightmares, I'm still so glad to be in his presence that I don't care if we're somewhere scary, as long as we're together.

There's a moment when my alarm goes off and I'm in the gray area between asleep and awake and I don't yet remember that Braden's gone. As I come to my senses, I recall the loss and everything comes rushing back and I feel like I'm pinned to the bed, so weighted down with grief that I can't move.

I'm not the only one who's struggling.

Theo's having just as much trouble, so I'm making the effort to be there for him. Lately, he and I have taken to sitting on the sectional in the media room for hours, looking at pictures of Braden on the iPad. We have a million stories between us. In remembering him fondly, we feel like a tiny part of him remains alive.

Theo still clings to the belief that Braden was killed by accident, despite Owen bearing witness. He argues that because there was no note, his death was unintentional.

Considering how quiet Braden kept his problems, would he have committed his final thoughts to the page? That's why I'm so desperate to get into his email.

Also, what if the impulse to end everything had truly been spur of the moment, completely unplanned? The train was running late that day due to a switching problem down the line. Normally, he'd have already been across the tracks and on campus by the time the Metra was due at the North Shore stop. What if the late train was too attractive a nuisance to ignore, a permanent solution to a fleeting thought?

But I don't say any of this to Theo; he's not ready to hear it.

Sometimes I wonder which of us is more heartsick. I figured one day the three of us would all be grown-ups together, with the nonsense and hierarchies of high school behind us, and then Braden and I might finally happen. We'd be older then, and Theo would be less likely to resent our getting together. I mean, maybe. Regardless of what might or might not eventually happen with him and me, I assumed Braden would be someone who was in my life permanently.

How could I know that permanence was so ephemeral, that forever could end at seventeen?

My fingers itch to pick up my phone, to look at his email log-in, but I have only a single chance left. One more password and that's it. I don't want to sever the possible connection between us, to eliminate the ability to ever find an answer as to *why*.

If I think about all that, I'll lose it, so I'll concentrate on being ready for my appointment instead.

As I wait, I reposition myself so I'm sitting like a lady in this stupid beanbag chair, but that's near impossible. Super glad I didn't opt for a skirt today. No matter how I plant, whoever sits across from me would have had a straight shot all the way to Panty City. Mr. Gorton should change the manual to include my suggestion that counselors wear leggings. I volunteered to do it for him, but he said the binder was fine like it was.

Thus says the man who's never had his thong ogled.

For a school like NSHS, you'd think they'd have a couple of bucks to pretty up the peer counseling room, but nope. The sum total of our resources includes said rules binder, a few beanbag chairs, handfuls of pamphlets, a macramé plant holder that's surely a castoff from some art project, circa 1972 and containing one dusty plastic fern, and a Hang In There Kitty poster that absolutely predates the invention of the LOL Cat phenomenon. How is it the alumni saw fit to fund a seven hundred and fifty thousand dollar Jumbotron for the football stadium, and I can't even counsel kids in a seat with legs?

Mental health merits real furniture, is all I'm saying.

I hear a soft tap on the door and I invite in my peer counselee.

"Hi, are you ready for me?" says a soft-spoken, heavy-set girl with amazing brows and ridiculously gorgeous chestnut brown hair. I'm serious, she's got the full Lovato going on up there. Like a thoroughbred's mane, or maybe Kate Middleton. Really, it's fabulous.

"I'm Farrah." Instead of shaking my hand, she gives me a meek little wave with her fingertips. She's holding a steamy cup of something that smells like a mocha. I can feel my mouth begin to water, so I swallow hard and smile.

"Hi, Farrah, I'm Mallory, come on in and have a seat."

I gesture toward the empty beanbag. "Sorry we don't have real furniture."

Farrah offers a quick, shy grin, but doesn't look me in the eye. "That's okay, anything's got to be better than those awful chairs in the hallway. It's like they're *trying* to make you uncomfortable or something."

"Right? Here, lemme hold your drink while you settle in." I take a surreptitious sniff. Yep, definitely a mocha. Liam used to be all over me for trying to smell everyone's food, said it was weird and I should just eat if I were hungry.

Won't miss that.

Besides, if I were to consume everything I wanted, (a) they'd have to roll me onto campus every day, and (b) I'd be disowned. So ironic because I've seen pics of mom at my age. She easily wore a twelve, if not a fourteen. Back then, the styles were all baggy sweatshirts and billowy T-shirts tucked into Bermuda shorts, so I guess size didn't matter so much. (Except for everyone's hair, which, GIGANTOR.) Of course, thanks to Dr. Baylor, my mom can cram herself into my skinnies now, but there's no way she'd have carried them off back then.

After Farrah's seated, I return her cup. She's forced to place it on the floor. Seriously, *no one* will throw us a couple of bucks so we can spring for a coffee table? I lean forward in my beanbag and say, "Welcome to peer counseling! Is there anything specific you'd like for us to cover? Or would you be more comfortable if we chatted a bit and saw where that took us?"

She looks down at her feet. "I don't know. I've never done this before."

I'm quick to reassure her. "That's totally cool, let's just get acquainted. What grade are you in, Farrah?"

"I'm a freshman."

"Ah, a freshman! I'm so old! I swear, my freshman year feels like it happened decades ago! I was SO overwhelmed when I got here," I say, trying to give her something to agree with or latch on to so that I know how to proceed.

She doesn't reply. Mostly she just looks at her feet.

I press on. "I was lost here for, what? The whole first month? I'm seriously lucky that my older brother, Holden, is an alum, so I had the lay of the land, you know?"

Holden lives in Costa Rica now, where he teaches English to village children. He started with the Peace Corps after graduating summa cum laude from Brown a couple of years ago. (Ask me how happy our mother was about *that* decision.) He's in the middle of a twenty-seven-month stint and has yet to come home. He says he can't get away, but it's more like he doesn't want to. The Peace Corps isn't prison camp, you know? They can't hold him there against his will. Truth is, he *hates* North Shore and couldn't wait to leave. I wouldn't be surprised if he never comes back.

I ask, "Do you have any brothers or sisters who came here?"

"Only child."

"Bummer," I say. "Holden was super helpful, telling me which clubs to join and which teachers were his favorites. He urged me to take a class with Mr. Conroy in the music department. I remember walking into the class and seeing this frumpy old guy who looked like he stepped out of a Harry Potter book, and I thought, ''Bout to get our Vivaldi on.' But Holden was right and Mr. Conroy knew everything about music from Chuck Berry to Macklemore. No lie, Kendrick Lamar thanked Mr. Conroy at some award ceremony last year. How random is that, right? Anyway, Mr. Conroy's History of Rock and Roll is amazing. Keep it in mind if you need an elective."

Farrah bobs her head in lieu of responding. She's pretty closed off, isn't she? I need to get her to talk, which means I should ask something she can't answer with a yes, no, or nod.

"Tell me, Farrah, how do *you* like NSHS so far?"

"'S'okay." Again, she says this more to her shoes than to me. Girlfriend is committed to those one-word answers. I try to read her expression, but it's hard as I'm mostly seeing her part and not her eyes. Wow, though, her hair is seriously bouncy. Glossy, too. I really want to ask her what shampoo she uses, but that would be unprofessional, at least at this juncture.

"Only okay for you? Are you having trouble in any of your classes? They're tough, but they'll totally prep us for college. Our classes are why *everyone* gets into a top college here. Like, this school is so good that it's sent real estate prices through the roof. Still, if you start feeling like you can't keep your head above water, I can arrange tutors. The Peer Tutors have actual desks in their room. Whiteboards and computers, too." I try to keep the envy out of my voice. I hear they even have access to office supplies.

She glances up. "No, I'm doing really well there. I aced my midterms."

"Awesome!"

I'm trying to assess her by what might appear to be random questions. But I know where I'm trying to go and so far, I've learned that academics aren't a problem.

"Yeah… I guess it's awesome," she mumbles, head down again.

Okay, social aspect, *go.* I ask, "Are you making new friends?"

"Definitely. I've met lots of cool kids in my classes. Our squad gets together to do homework. Everyone's really nice."

If she were being bullied, she'd lead off with who wasn't nice.

"Have you joined any clubs or activities?"

"Um… I'm in the web design and coding club, the gamers club, and I do Quiz Bowl, too. That's so fun!"

"The Quiz Bowl team's killing it this year, right?" I don't know this for sure, but it's an educated guess.

Her face lights up. "We're undefeated—we've crushed *everyone.*"

"Up here!" I say, holding up my hand for a high-five. We smack our palms together. I add another check to my mental list. Home life, *go.*

"And your parents? Do they, say, come to your competitions?"

This evokes an actual laugh. "Ohmigod, yes, and it's sooooo embarrassing! My mom and dad sit in the front row. They make banners and everything! They cheer louder than anyone. I sort of wish I had a sibling so they could spread out their enthusiasm and not just concentrate it all on me."

"Ever wish they wouldn't come?"

She shakes her head, which showcases her glorious mane. "No, totally not. I feel…safe with them there. Like, if I mess up, it doesn't matter, they love me regardless."

I keep my face neutral when I say, "You're lucky to have that." I don't explain how my situation differs, because this session is not about me.

Uh-oh, we're back to staring at feet again.

"I know and I feel kinda bad. I have friends on the team and their folks can't even be bothered to show up."

Been there.

I tab through my mental checklist—academics aren't a problem, nor is involvement/friends, and she has a supportive family. I have a feeling about where this is going, but I need her to tell me so that I can help her. If I bring it up, she'll feel attacked.

290

"Sounds like you have *a lot* going for you," I say.

She nods, but doesn't seem convinced. Time to switch tactics.

"Okay," I say, "I *have* to know something and this is totally off script and I'm sure Mr. Gorton would be mad, so please don't tell him I asked." I can see Farrah's shoulders tense. I'm about to lob a softball directly into her waiting glove, but she doesn't realize it. "Your hair is freaking *gorge*—what do you use on it?"

Again, another genuine smile. "Moroccan oil and Frederic Fekkai products. It's dumb, but I started buying his stuff because I'm Farrah Fakhoury and I liked the double Fs."

"Um, no, that's the opposite of dumb. That's a perfectly legit reason and look at your results! I'd die for your hair, I really would. Like, I just want to pet it, you know? You've got the whole My Pretty Pony thing going on and those? Favorite toy ever. I would brush their hair for hours. They were the best."

She presses her lips together and seems to be struggling over what she's about to say. After a pause, she tells me, "You could have my hair, if that meant I could wear your jeans."

Bingo. Problem, meet solution.

Totally conversationally, I say, "You know, when I was in seventh grade, I had to shop in the women's section with my mom, because none of the teen sizes fit me."

Farrah glances up at me through a lush fringe of bangs. "Really? You didn't always look like this?"

"Nope. I was a skinny kid, but I didn't realize that my metabolism had changed from when I was a little kid and I was eating too much. In fact," I say, "in junior high, my mom used to call me 'Calorie Mallory.'"

She gasps. "That's awful!"

I wave her off. "She meant well."

No, she didn't.

I continue, "I realized I didn't like having to buy mom-jeans, you know? I wanted to wear what everyone else had on. So I made changes. Took up field hockey, which is a ton of running. Also, I recorded everything I ate on an app so I'd be more accountable to myself. I could not *believe* how much hidden fat was in my favorite stuff. For example, I used to get mochas all the time and then I learned they're five hundred calories apiece! That's, like, a third of my daily allowance."

Two thirds.

Farrah glances at her cup in horror. "Holy crap, I drink three of those *a day*. What did you do?"

I shrug. "I decided to make them a treat instead, a once-in-a-while thing so they're more special now."

I don't mention that I eventually became obsessive, and, let's be honest, a tad exercise bulimic as I'm not in the Pro-ana business. I wouldn't wish how I feel on anyone. No one should be thin-spired by me. I preach moderation, even if I can't seem to practice it.

"Here's the thing," I say, offering up advice I wish I could take myself. "What you weigh is not who you are. Listen, you've got so much going for you—you're smart, you have phenomenal hair, you have nice friends, your parents rock. *You are already awesome*, just as you are. Don't let anyone tell you differently. If they do, you tell me, okay? However, if your pants size bugs you, if you feel like that's a burden you can't bear, make small changes, *if you feel like it and only if you feel like it*. I want you to go out into the world feeling like you're your best *you*, whatever size that entails."

Farrah is now sitting upright in her beanbag, looking me in the eye, with her shoulders squared. "It's that easy?"

"At first, maybe it won't feel like it, but the truth is, it can be simple if you want it to be."

"Should I pick a different track in gym class?"

Illinois has a mandatory physical education element, so no one's exempt from taking gym. However, NSHS tracks the levels of classes, so some people go super easy and pick sports like golf or Concepts in Fitness, which is basically for kids who would rather study about exercise than participate in it.

"Are you in Concepts of Fitness?" I ask.

She nods.

"I bet you'd adore the strength training class."

"A couple of my friends take that and they kind of love it," she admits.

"If you were to sign up for that, you'd get in more activity and you'd get to be with your squad more. Hashtag *workout-buddies*. Plus, you'd feel great from all the endorphins. That's what's called a positive fulfillment loop. The more you do it, the better you feel and the more you want to do it."

I believe my job here, especially with the underclassmen, is to make other kids as resilient and confident as possible because once their junior and senior years roll around, the pressure is going to be almost unbearable. If they don't go in strong, well, we've seen what can happen.

"Would you be into helping me figure out a way to be healthier? Like, go over my choices with me? Guide me in the right direction?"

"Totally. Figuring it all out with a friend makes it more fun."

"The buddy system, I like that." She sits there for a minute and finally shrugs. "I don't really have a lot more to tell you right now."

"We can always hang out again in another session. Let me give you my number so you can text me with a question between appointments." I hand her a card with my deets and digits on it.

"That would be great." Farrah takes the card and tucks it in her shirt pocket and then extricates herself from the beanbag. I rise, too, to walk her to the door. She scoops up her half-full cup and deposits it in the trashcan next to the door.

"Um, Mallory?"

"Yeah?"

She begins to fidget with her cuff. "I... I might owe you an apology. I thought you were one thing coming in here today, but it turns out, you're totally another. I think I heart you."

I look over my shoulder and press a finger to my lips. "*Shh.* Keep that to yourself. I have an image to uphold."

Quick like a ninja, she grabs me for a hug. I watch her head down the hall and I feel like my heart is smiling. I'd like to think I helped Farrah. I hope I did. She left the office with an awful lot more spring in her step than when she came in.

I'm rooting for her, but that doesn't matter because I believe *she's* rooting for her.

She turns around once before she exits and makes a heart symbol with her hands.

I laugh. "I heart you, too, Farrah."

While I wait for my next counselee, I find myself staring at Braden's email log-in again. I have to stop this constant obsessing, it's consuming my life.

What would I tell someone who came in here with this problem?

Hmm.

I'd probably suggest they do one more log-in attempt and if it's wrong, that's the universe telling them to stop, to move on, to let go.

Then again, I'm not one to take my own good advice.

I glance at the time. Huh. I thought I had a three thirty. He or she should be out here waiting. I peek into the hallway, wondering if I maybe missed a knock, but all the chairs are empty.

When no one's here by three forty-five, I collect my stuff. I'm about to walk out the door when I realize I should let Mr. Gorton know I'm cruising early due to my no-show.

I pop my head into his office, expecting to see him lining up his paperclips or straightening his Post-Its with a T square. (He's a little anal-retentive, is what I'm saying.)

Instead, he's weeping into handkerchief. His body is racked by deep, guttural sobs. He doesn't notice me in the doorway. I mean to back away quickly, before I'm noticed, because this is a private moment, then I realize he's not alone.

The other guidance counselors are inside as well. A couple of them are holding each other up while the third lets out a string of profanity not meant for my ears. Principal Gottfried is pale and silent and gripping her cell phone, fist pressed against her mouth as she nods.

I don't have to ask what's going on; I know what it looks like when we lose another of our own.

This is two kids in two months.

Two.

For a total of *four* since this summer.

That's it.

I'm done.

29

===

SIMONE

IS IT WRONG to be this happy?

Does this euphoria come from rebelling?

Is that why every teenager in the world eventually sneaks around behind his or her parents' backs?

I never disregarded Mum and Dad's wishes before this. But their opinion of Liam was ridiculous and they refused to listen to reason. No matter what I said, they were convinced he's a "user" and forbade me to see him. I told Liam what they thought and he laughed. He was all, "So anti-inflammatories are the new heroin?"

Too stupid for words, right?

Liam said his prescription made him tired and dopey at first, but now he's got plenty of energy, so they're absolutely improving his health. Now that soccer season's over, his knee should stop bothering him without the daily grind of training. Another week or so of rest and he'll be right as rain and done with the pills. However, instead of arguing any of this, I told Mum and Dad, "I won't see him, if that's what you want."

What I meant was, *you* won't see me see him. Worked like a charm for the past few weeks, too.

Liam and I have lots of time to spend together, due to my "pressing schedule at the newspaper" and "all the studying I'm doing with Stephen and Kent." Technically, I *am* studying with Liam…most of the time. The best part is they won't verify my whereabouts. Seventeen years of being as trustworthy/dependable as a prized hunting spaniel has given me some wiggle room.

Actually, I would spend more time with the boys, but Stephen's being impossible and Kent managed to charm Noell somehow at the Homecoming dance. Suspect there was schnapps involved. They're an actual couple now, which is beyond adorable. (They're called *KeNo*, which seems gamble-y; not a fan of the handle.) We sit with them at lunch sometimes. Stephen rarely joins us, says he feels like a fifth wheel, which is ludicrous.

The three of us were supposed to celebrate Stephen's birthday a couple of weeks back but Stephen bailed at the last minute due to a sore throat. His hat turned out brilliantly, and I so want him to have the amulet, but I've neither the time nor motivation to chase him as he's been beyond crabby.

While Kent and I have tried to cheer him up, Stephen perpetually shoots us down. He's been a bit of a vapor trail lately, never responding to texts. Is this another instance where we stop trying?

Every time we express our concern to Stephen, he rolls his eyes or mutters about how *we've* changed. That's not pleasant for any of us. Kent and I speculate if maybe we ignore him, he'll come around, the way a cat will cozy up as soon as you turn your back on it.

So maybe things aren't entirely perfect, but I fly out of bed every morning, excited to meet the day.

Walking the halls as *LiMone* is surreal—Liam's North

Shore's own personal Ryan Gosling. Everyone wants to stop and chat with him. They're always soliciting his opinion or trying to garner his approval, all, "Liam, Liam—can you give us a quote for the *Round Table* about your winning season?" or "Heard Duke's dying to recruit you—badass!"

For example, right now, all we're trying to do is get to his Jeep in the student parking lot and it's taking us forever. On our way, he's been stopped by two teachers, three guys on the JV soccer team, and a handful of underclassmen. I'm surprised no one's begged for an autograph. Ironic that his only detractors are my parents, the two people I desperately wish *would* like him.

"You need Secret Service agents," I say, after Liam's extricated himself from yet another admirer, having said goodbye with a complicated set of hand slaps and a half bro-hug. "Someone has to deflect all this love off you."

He ducks his head like he's embarrassed. "You're exaggerating."

"Not really. I thought that freshman was going to have you autograph her chest."

He laughs. "Didn't take you for the jealous type."

I squeeze his hand. "I'm just glad to be part of your fan club."

He spins around to look at me in the eye. "Come on, Simone, I don't have a *fan club*. I've just grown up in this town, so I kinda know everyone. No one's shouting about how they love me or anything. I'm not, like, I don't know, Zayn Malik."

A carload of cheerleaders passes us. One of them rolls down her window and shouts, "We love you, Liam! Wooo!"

"You were saying?"

While I suspect Liam's always been popular, his leading the soccer team to win the Division I state title brought his local

299

celebrity to a whole new level. He'd been hurting badly and benched himself partway through the game and that's when the other team came from behind. In the final two minutes, he insisted on finishing out the game. He scored the winning goal with less than a second left on the clock, causing the crowd to lose their collective minds. Too bad he's not interested in playing in college because he could go anywhere after that.

Although Princeton doesn't give athletic scholarships, his prowess on the pitch would give him a distinct advantage in admissions. Still, lots of other schools *do* grant scholarships. Last year, Duke University brought him down for a weekend and treated him like a rock star, as did Wake Forest and Georgetown. University of Florida told him he could write his own ticket and he has a guaranteed full ride waiting.

Unfortunately, Liam's dad has his sights set on Princeton for him, period, which is going to be an issue.

"I am *done* living by my father's dictates," he told me after he picked me up from my ACTs the day after Homecoming. The test took only three hours, but my parents assumed I'd be tied up all day. That's why I had no problem taking off with him for the afternoon in my premiere act of defiance. I felt guilty but ten seconds in his presence and I was game for anything. Drive to Mexico? Rob a convenience store? I was *in*.

"What does that mean, exactly?" I asked. "What does being 'done' look like?" I kept taking little glances to my left to admire his profile as he drove us down to the lakefront. He'd packed a couple of blankets so we could wrap up and he'd bought two huge mochas. So thoughtful!

"Means I'm not going to Princeton. Period. That's *my* early decision."

While I admired his conviction, I wondered if he'd still

feel that way once admitted. Why reject that kind of opportunity? "What happens when you're accepted? How do you
walk away from the Ivy League?"

The longer I'm in North Shore, the more I understand the
draw of a "good school." I mean, what if making jewelry isn't
my path? I don't want to limit my options so I've stepped up
my studies. Now I devote four to five hours a night to homework. I don't love all the work and there's a million things
I'd enjoy more, but I'd be remiss to squander the prospect.

He gave me a sly look as he navigated down the steep,
winding drive that divided the heavily wooded bluffs. The
trees on either side were so dense that they blocked out the
sky. Felt like we were traveling through a tunnel.

He pulled into the empty parking area, a small expanse of
blacktop that overlooked a rocky shoreline. The water was
gray and tipped with whitecaps, beating against the sand. Had
he told me we were looking at the Channel coast in England
and not this lake, I'd have believed him.

He said, "I figure the one sure way to not be admitted is
to not apply. Life's too short to do what you hate."

"Do your folks believe you're still applying?" I asked.

"Yes. My dad keeps asking how the process is going and I
tell him it's going exactly as planned, which technically isn't
a lie."

He put the car into Park and turned off the ignition.

I had to laugh. "Is it just me, or is this lying business sort
of hot?"

He pulled me to him. "So hot."

Of course, now every day, his father is all, "Did you hear
anything yet?" and Liam must say he hasn't. At some point
he'll be found out and he anticipates a shitstorm. He told me
his dad used to knock him around when he was younger, but

that tapered off once Liam grew taller than him. While his dad's still a tyrant, the physical abuse has been at bay, thanks to all of Liam's achievements.

For now, he's happily living in denial so we don't discuss it much.

We arrive at his Jeep and he opens my door for me, like the well-raised gentleman he is. For everything everyone says about Brits being polite, I can't recall a single boy showing me such respect back in London. Liam's car has very tall wheels, and no spoilers for a foothold, so he always gives me a boost to get inside. Don't need help, but I take it anyway.

See, Cordy? I'm developing some game.

"Where to?" he asks as he settles into the driver's seat. "You hungry? You want some pizza or a burrito?"

The first few times we went out, Liam was amazed I'd consume actual calories on our dates. He was shocked when I asked for my own box of Milk Duds at the movies. I didn't understand his reaction, so I offered to pay for them myself, which made him laugh. I suspect Mallory wasn't the easiest girl to date. He's never complained about her after that first night, but sometimes his reactions speak volumes.

"Hmm," I say, acting like I'm thinking hard. "I'm...in the mood for something sweet."

"Frozen yogurt? Dreamsicle cupcakes at Deerfield Bakery?"

I've been musing about the two of us a lot—so much, really, Liam is kind of all-consuming in my thoughts—and I've decided it's time for us to take our relationship to the next level.

Yes. I mean *that*.

"You ready to shag him, eh?" Cordy asked, via our Skype session last night. I was prepping for bed and she was getting up for an early class.

Ha! Kidding!

She was actually rolling home from her night, having just completed the Walk of Shame, hair a mess, dress askew, bra in her backpack, and eyeliner smeared for days.

"Yes? Maybe? I think so?" I replied.

"So long as you're sure." In a more serious tone, she said, "Listen up, Moni, you can only lose it once. 'Course, you can tell guys every time it's your first and they'll believe you because they're stupid and horny and naïve and that's what they want to hear. By my counts I've lost my maidenhood six times this term. Still, it's official just the once, so make it count with someone who's kind and amenable. You love him?"

"We've only been together a couple of weeks. Can't say that I'm 'in love.' But I could be easily and soon, though. I mean, I'm consumed with thoughts of him. Like, obsessed."

Whether it's first thing in the morning when he picks me up at the corner or when I randomly spy him in the halls, I feel like my heart's going to burst wide open, spraying showers of confetti everywhere like on the *X Factor* finale. He makes my pulse quicken whenever I think about him.

I took a breath and continued. "One touch ignites a fire inside me that feels like it could heat the whole world for all of eternity. To me, Liam's, like, a sip from a cool spring of water after a lifetime of thirst. Or like taking a leap off a blind cliff and soaring and then landing in a huge pile of marshmallow fluff. Is that love? I can't say, but it's certainly something."

"Meh, sounds close enough. You should go for it."

"Really?"

"Absolutely. But I've gotta warn you, babe, the real thing might not stand up against your fantasies. You probably believe you'll feel the flap of angel wings against your tender nethers or the songs of a thousand voices singing a perfect C note together or some Shakespearian crap like that. Not accurate. First time, there's grunting and rutting and sweating and pounding—actually, no, no pounding, you *wish* there were some pounding—for about thirty seconds and then it's over. Honestly? Kind of a hot mess. Gets better, though. Has to. God, I'd join a nunnery if every time were as bad as my first."

"*You* a *nun?*" I snorted. "You're not even Catholic."

She replied, "I'd convert if it were always so dreadful. Remember Niles the Night Terror from my first time two years ago? After we did it, he says to me, 'Can I borrow a couple of pence?' and I said, '*What for?*' and he replied, 'Want to buy a packet of Malteasers to get the taste of you out of my mouth.'"

Yikes. "Can't see that happening with Liam, though."

"Good, because you said you can't find Malteasers anywhere. I'm tired of having to mail you decent tooth polish and proper chocolate. Bloody savage country."

"I only wish…" I started.

She peered at me. "Finish your thought."

"Wish I could talk to Mum about this. Seems almost criminal to hide this info from her," I replied.

Cordy shook her head vehemently and raised her pointer finger at me on the other side of the screen. "No, no, *no.* Wrong. No one talks to their mum about sex. It's not done because it's *twisted.* After your parents are done changing your dirty nappies, they never want to think about your vag again, that's a fact. Your relationship with them is not the norm. I'm glad you're close and Fi and Angus are loads of fun, but, no. Hell to the no. Sex is not meant to be the topic of a family meal. You can't say to them, 'Please pass the jacket potatoes and PS, had my first orgasm, tremendous fan,' because it defies the natural code. You have to trust me here."

"You may be right," I said with more conviction than I felt.

"'Course I'm right. I'm right about everything! Who said to

you, don't buy the McQueen clogs, you'll sprain your ankle, but you did anyway and then you hobbled around like a lunatic for three months. I *know* things, you have to listen to me—it's the law."

"It's not the law."

"Well, then, it should be. Anyway, do it. *Doooo iiiiit.* Then tell me all about it. Now I have to sod off, I'm knackered. Text me about all the dirty bits when you're done. And lower your expectations!" With that, she disconnected the call.

After Cordy and I talked and I thought about everything I'd said, I decided that today is the day. D day. Or, more like V day.

"What else is sweet?" Liam muses. "You feel like a couple of Frappuccinos? We can get different flavors and trade halfway through. Or, if you want coffee and donuts, we can head over to Spunky Dunkers. Cake or yeast, glazed, powdered, sugared, your call. You tell me what's sweet."

I tell him, "You're sweet."

He grins up at me through his fringe of blond locks. "You're pretty sweet, too."

I'm emboldened, knowing what's to come, so I place my hand high up on his thigh.

"Liam, for a brilliant guy, you're just not that swift. When I said I wanted something sweet, I mean that I want you."

Liam drops me on the corner at 5:00 p.m., like he does every day, a spot just out of view of my house. He lingers as he kisses me goodbye. We're now tethered to each other in a way I could never before fathom.

I wanted to stay there with him, wrapped in his arms, all snug and drowsy in his soft bed. I liked being in his room, surrounded by All Things Liam, from his books arranged by color on his shelves to the framed and matted snaps of him coaching youth soccer.

However, we figured his mum would be back from the stable where she boards her horses soon. In this perfectly appointed home, a colder, far more tidy version of my own, it would be impossible for her to not notice the trail of clothing that began at his front door. So, reluctantly, oh-so-reluctantly, we extricated ourselves from one another.

That was...like nothing Cordy described. I had my expectations, but they were tempered after our Skype talk. She was so wrong about the angel wings and the chorus of one thousand voices united in harmony, because it's exactly how I felt.

Walking down my block, I'm giddy and euphoric and drunk on the sense of having been so close. Liam made it so it wasn't awkward, so that I wasn't nervous, so that I was comfortable in every way. He made me feel beautiful and precious and cherished.

Safe.

Desired.

The only sour note of the whole experience was when we were lying there afterward and he traced the tattoo on my shoulder blade. My mum, dad, and I have matching ink— Roman numerals of my birth year to commemorate when we became a real family. When I thought about that rainy London day we got them, I was overwhelmed with feelings of guilt. I hated the idea of doing something that would displease them, yet the draw of Liam was and is too powerful, too intoxicating.

I'm addicted.

I'd claim I could quit him if I wanted to, but that's a lie; I'd OD on him in a second.

When we were basking in the afterglow, before he touched

my ink, he told me he loved me. I tried to make a joke of it, saying, "You're supposed to say that *before* you get into my trousers," but this was no laughing matter to him.

He took my face in his hands and said, "I want to remember everything about this moment for the rest of my life. I want to file it away in deepest memory, for any time I'm upset or scared or angry. When I come back to this second, no matter what happens, I'll feel calm and happy and whole again."

What else could I do but tell him I loved him, too?

(Full disclosure, I also jumped on him again.)

I probably need to slap this grin off my mug before I go inside. One look and my parents will know that everything's different and then… I don't want to even imagine "and then." Would I even be in trouble? Can't say for sure what trouble looks like. Yet the idea of them being disappointed just guts me and I don't want that today, not after all that magic.

Maybe I should invent some good news so that my reaction seems appropriate. Yes, that's a fine idea. I'll mention one of my photographs will be featured on the front page of the *Round Table*. Wait, they'd want to see it, would frame the copy. They're proud like that. I'd have to con the editor into featuring what I'd shot, but I couldn't say why, not the real reason anyway, so I'd have to invent something else, too.

Damn it, lying is exhausting, as it's never just one fib. Each new falsehood builds on the last, like bricks in a wall, all pieced together with interlocking accuracy, and soon there's a whole fortress of fabrication, a temple of untruths, poised to come crashing down on a whole village of innocents at the most inopportune moment.

Why can't Mum and Dad just be reasonable?

What *could* I do, I wonder? How do I convince them Liam's not involved in anything untoward? Except for the untoward things he did today, *ba-dum-bum!* I tap out a rim shot on my imaginary drum set.

Christ on a bike, sex has turned me into Louis C.K.

I decide to pretend to be happy about an A on a pop quiz in my lit class. (If I said I'd written a theme, they'd want to read it.) This seems like the most innocuous lie I can concoct, the hardest to verify.

Clumps of neighbors are standing on their lawns as I approach my house, deep in conversation here and there. Lots of outdoorsy people in North Shore, always running around in shiny Arc'teryx jackets, but it's odd to see them standing in their yards when it's basically dark and drizzly. A bone-chilling wind whips everyone's hair around, but they don't seem to notice. The gas lights lining the block cast anemic circles of illumination, making the scene even more ominous.

I guess what's so bizarre is that no one typically gathers here; that's why I'm thrown. Our homes are spaced too far apart to encourage casual conversation. This scene is atypical and registers as wrong.

I let myself in the front door and the second I see the expression on my Mum's face, my heart drops.

She knows.

She knows and she's *devastated*. How is that possible? Am I truly that transparent?

Wait, has she been crying? Why is her face so splotchy? Come on, that's not fair. I'm almost eighteen. I'm not a little girl. She's the one who put me on the pill in the first place. They can't expect me to stay in a state of arrested development. The mature thing to do is to talk this out and tell her everything. If I'm not adult enough to discuss sex, then I shouldn't be having it. But I am and I have, so the horse has left the barn. I haven't been handling myself like an adult with all of the sneaking around.

Time for a serious discussion.

I say, "Mum, listen, I have to talk to you about—"

Before I can complete my sentence, she's swept me into her arms and she begins to sob.

"Simba, baby," she says into my hair. "Simba, I'm so sorry. Your friend…"

She struggles for a breath.

"Mum, what? My friend *what?*"

"He's gone. He's gone, Simba."

My blood turns to ice. "Oh, Owen, *no,*" I cry. I thought he was improving. We've yet to speak, but he did wave a few days ago. He even smiled. I thought he was rallying. I even saw him sitting at lunch with some other friends just today. That seemed like positive momentum.

Why, Owen? Why didn't you let me in? I wanted to be there for you. I tried, I really did.

I feel soul-sick.

My mum pulls back and looks at me with the most mournful expression in the world. "Honey, no. Not Owen. Your friend Stephen is gone."

Then my heart shatters into a million pieces.

30

====

KENT

"DON'T TELL ME it's going to be okay, Dad."

My father is huddled across from me up here in my old backyard tree fort. He looks ridiculous in this context, like a giant next to all my half-scale furniture. He climbed in to try to make me feel better.

But how can I feel better?

How can it be okay?

How can anything be okay ever again?

Stephen's *dead*.

He's gone because I wasn't there for him. I checked out on him as a friend. What kind of shitty person does that? I should have been more on guard. I should have seen the signs, been more invested. I should have looked out for him. I should have made the connection after getting his final text. I've read it hundreds of times since that day, trying to parse out his meaning. Had he already made his decision when he sent it? If I'd responded differently, would we have a different outcome?

All I know for sure is that my Spidey senses should have tingled.

Should, should, *should.*

I'm drowning in *should*s.

Why was I so short-tempered with him? Why did I want to punish him for being a jerk? Why did I delight in him admitting I was right? Those were his final words, literally. *u were right, kent.*

What a fucking microphone drop that was.

I didn't understand how dark it was for him and now it's too late to be his light.

I SUCK.

I've been in the tree fort for hours, ever since we heard. I had to get away. I had to get out of that house. I thought my mother was going to suffocate me with her grief, like *she* was his best friend for the past fifteen years. Like *she* was the one who failed to protect him from himself. She collapsed, crumpled to the ground. And then wouldn't get off the floor, she was wailing too hard.

I couldn't deal.

I couldn't make her feel better *because there is no better.*

So I ran out the back door, no coat, no shoes, no idea of where to go, except away. Then I spotted the old clapboard fort in the cradle of the old oak in the corner of the yard, with its shingled roof and tiny balcony, the place where Stephen and I spent so many hours as kids.

Dad had the tree house built when Stephen and I were deep in our *Lord of the Rings* phase, so we named it Rivendell. We were such nerds, we even conducted an official christening ceremony, breaking a bottle of sparkling apple cider on the balcony's railing before we stepped inside for the first time. Mom had a Rivendell sign made. We hung it next to the front door, where it remained until a big storm blew it away a few years back.

Stephen and I used to sit up here for hours, hanging out and debating everything, like whether Wolverine should have traveled back in time instead of Kitty Pryde or what could devastate a city more—Godzilla or hordes of zombies. As we grew older, our conversations started to include girls and college and the future. This fort was our special place; this was sacred ground.

I remember how mad Stephen was when he found out Braden and I had hung out in here without him after we finished camp in sixth grade. (Braden had gone on and on about how he "hearted" the view of the lake from here.) We came up here only a few times on our own when Stephen wasn't around, but that didn't matter to him. Pitched a real fit, was downright hysterical. He couldn't believe I'd take someone to *our* place, like he was my jilted wife or something. That pissed me off. I was all, "Pretty sure what's in *my* yard is *my* place, dude." Didn't talk to him for two weeks after that.

What I wouldn't give for those two weeks now. Like gold in my hand. To be in here again with him.

Instead, I'm with my dad. He's still wearing his fancy business suit, which is now covered in leaves and a few cobwebs. He doesn't seem to be affected by the dirt or decay. He left his consulting assignment in Minneapolis as soon as he heard, hopped the next plane and came directly home.

Our dads were another thing Stephen and I had in common, both management consultants, both gone all week long, both leaving us to be tended to—and over-tended to—by our moms.

Dad picks up one of my old camping lanterns and looks surprised that it still works when he switches it on. Not exactly a coincidence. I inserted fresh batteries last week when I snuck up here with Noell. Mom wouldn't let me borrow the car because it looked like rain and she doesn't like me driving on wet roads. Everyone was home at Noell's place so we came here for some privacy.

You know what makes zero sense?

I felt *guilty* about bringing her up here, like I was somehow disrespecting Stephen, like I should have asked his permission.

A wan glow flickers in the space between my father and me, casting ominous shadows behind us.

He says, "Kent, I never lost my best friend, but I understand loss. I've been so burdened with sorrow before that I couldn't get out of bed in the morning. I sympathize and I'm so sorry."

I already know what he means, but I ask anyway. "The babies?"

He nods mechanically.

My parents tried to have more kids for a long time after I was born. They wanted a big family, a house full of children. That's why we moved to North Shore—because we'd have plenty of room here. They were planning ahead. They wanted a huge fireplace mantel, large enough to accommodate half a dozen Christmas stockings. They loved the idea of tall ceilings with lots of wall space, so they could take and hang a million family photos of us, all smiling in terrible matching sweaters. Maybe Dad could even finally talk Mom into a dog and we'd put him in a sweater, too. Dad told me that, when they first got married, their running joke was about forming their own Mathers family basketball team.

Didn't happen.

Something went wrong after I was born and then my mom couldn't carry a pregnancy to term. She lost five babies in seven years. Four sisters and a brother. After the first two didn't take, my folks didn't tell anyone until they were beyond positive the fetus was viable. After me and until my brother, Mom had never made it past the first trimester. By the end of my Mom's eighth month, my parents finally exhaled, thought they'd reached the home stretch. They had a baby shower. They decorated a nursery in a jungle theme, with hand-drawn lions and elephants and giraffes dancing through an African veldt. They picked a name.

Hayes.

My brother was going to be called Hayes after my mom's grandpa. I feel like Hayes would have been a cool kid, with our mom's looks and smarts and our dad's equanimity. (Sometimes I call him Father Dad, as he can sound more like a pastor than a consultant.)

Or maybe Hayes would have been a mini-me. I was so excited to be an older brother, psyched to teach him how to play chess, how to use the Big Dipper to spot the North Star so he'd always be able to navigate and find his way home, so he'd never be lost. I planned to educate him on why Grandmaster Flash and the Furious Five's "The Message" is the greatest rap song of all time.

I'd help shape him in any way he chose to be shaped.

If Hayes had been my polar-opposite, that would've been awesome, too. Maybe he'd be tall and athletic, confident in every new situation. He'd be the leader and I'd be his follower. He could teach me.

I'd have been happy however he'd turned out.

After Hayes, the doctor said my mom had to stop, trying again was too dangerous. While my folks kept a lot of the specifics from me, especially the first few times, I was old enough to understand what it meant to lose Hayes. The doctor said his heart had forgotten to beat a couple of weeks before he was due.

I was really sad back then, but I figured if I couldn't have Hayes, then Stephen would be my brother. So he was.

Now I've lost my brother all over again.

Now I feel like my heart has forgotten to beat.

Each miscarriage changed my mom. She used to be relaxed and even kind of funny. With every loss, she turned more serious, more regimented, more focused on me, to the point that my life became her singular obsession.

That's why I don't fight her when her comingled love and concern pull me under like a riptide. I get why she smothers me. I deal with it. I try to tell her what she wants to hear because I know it's been hard. She's a great mom and I owe her that respect.

But today, I just couldn't.

I'm kind of glad to be up here, simultaneously freezing and starving, because my physical aching gives me something to focus on other than my conscience. I want discomfort.

"You won't make sense of this right now, Kent," my dad says. He grips my shoulders and looks me in the eye. "You want to, but it's impossible. I know it's your nature to reason things out—it's mine, too. Sometimes you just can't understand and you have to accept that."

I want to let my dad take over and make it all better, like he's done countless times before. But that's what a child does. Today I need to man the fuck up. I have to face this head on, accept responsibility for my part.

I can't push away my culpability.

I tell him why I deserve to wear the thorny crown of guilt. "We discussed suicide in my psych class last year. We talked about the warning signs. I knew how to recognize them. But I didn't see them and that's my fault."

315

"No, Kent, this is *not* your fault. Do you hear me? You didn't do this."

"Yes, I did. I was a shitty friend. I turned my back on him."

My dad is vehement. "No. That's hindsight bias. You know the outcome now and you think that because you have this information, you could have changed the outcome. You couldn't have. Doesn't work that way."

"I needed to try harder."

"You *did*. I know that Stephen wasn't always easy to be around, but you accepted that. You stuck by him when no one else did. You and him against the world. Even if you weren't perfect, you *were* a friend to him, a good friend. The best friend. You are not responsible. Do you hear me? *You are not responsible.* You can't control what happens in someone else's mind. You're not all-knowing and you're not all-powerful and you have to forgive yourself."

"What if there's something else I could have done, Dad?"

"Like not eat sushi, maybe?" he replies.

"I...don't understand."

"Your mom used to love sushi, did you know that?"

What is he even talking about?

"No, she *hates* it," I insist. She doesn't even want to be around us after we have it. Makes us brush our teeth before we can even talk to her afterward.

"You're wrong there, Kent. She used to eat it all the time— it was her favorite food. She was a real connoisseur. She lived for the weird stuff, like sea cucumbers and parts of the dorsal fin. The brinier the better. When we were trying to conceive, she knew the dangers of pregnant women consuming raw fish so she stopped eating it. Sushi never impacted the babies' health and development. But in her head, she's conflated sushi and loss, thinks it's her fault, like the bad stuff

316

lingered in her system, which is why she won't touch it now. She's still punishing herself, years later."

The temperature's been steadily dropping and I begin to shiver. I try to hide this from him, lest he force me inside. "I didn't know."

"Now you do. What I want to say is, you be sad for as long as you need to be sad. Or mad. You go wherever your grief takes you, provided it's safe. I'll be honest, it's going to be awful. The pain of loss will hit you in waves and can be all-encompassing, blocking out every other part of your life. I had to set reminders on my BlackBerry to brush my teeth, to put on pants, to go to work."

I have a hard time picturing my strong, capable dad ever not being on top of anything.

I tell him, "I'm never going to be happy again."

"No. You will. The worst thing is that you will eventually be happy again. You have a whole, big life ahead of you. One day you'll wake up and see the sun's shining and you'll think 'Thank God, the worst is over.' You'll think you're better, like you finally overcame it all. Then one small thing will set you off, something innocuous, like a margarine commercial. Believe me, a Country Crock ad destroyed me one day. *Destroyed*. Whatever it is reminds you of what could have been, and, bam! Salt in an open wound."

I close my eyes, trying to absorb his words. I want to believe him, to *hear* him, but I can't because my inner voice keeps shouting YOUR FAULT! YOUR FAULT! YOUR FAULT! over and over again.

"Listen to me Kent, the loss itself is bad enough, so don't make it worse by beating up on yourself. We can't always understand why things happen. You'll never find serenity until you accept that."

"Then how do I do that? How do I not beat up on myself?"

"Channel your energy into something else. Something positive. Throw yourself into it. You'll still be tempted to live in the 'what ifs' but by expending energy elsewhere, you won't have as much time. You have to feel your grief, but having a purpose elsewhere will keep your loss from becoming the sole focus of your existence."

We're both silent for a couple of minutes. The only sound is the patter of raindrops hitting the shingled roof a couple of feet above our heads.

"Dad, how long did it take you to completely get over Hayes?"

Sadly, he replies, "I'll never completely get over him. But I did get on with my life and that's the key here. Understand you're not going to feel better overnight. For now, your job will be to actively seek out the good moments and let them balance out the bad."

"I can't imagine ever having a good moment again."

My dad looks at me as though he's trying to see clean through to my soul. "Kent, is there any part of you that wonders if...you could just make the pain go away?"

His pupils are huge in the darkness of the fort and he's on the verge of tears.

"Are you asking if I'd ever consider suicide? Because, no. I wouldn't for a million reasons, but the biggest one is because I could never do that to you and mom. That's why I'm so messed up right now. I thought Stephen and I were the same. So when he'd say stuff like the world would be better off without him, I thought he was just being sarcastic or looking for attention. Because I'd never hurt myself, I couldn't fathom that he actually might, like it was a legitimate option."

My dad sits with this information. Finally, he says, "I be-

318

lieve you. But if that ever changes, even for a second, I need you to talk to me."

I say, "I will." And realize I mean it.

He rises, but can't stand to his full height unless he wants to get a lot of cobwebs in his hair. He brushes away the debris that's accumulated on his suit. "I should go check on your mother now. She's...not doing well. But that's not on you. You worry about you, sport, I'll be there for Mom. So...if you're not back inside in a little while, I'll bring you a coat and a sandwich, okay? Take all the time you need."

He touches his palm on my cheek and then he says, "Hey... think I just felt some stubble. Looks like your beard's finally coming in."

I'm sure it isn't, but I love him for telling me it is.

"I'll be in soon, Dad."

He exits and I hug my knees to my chest, huddling closer to the lantern for warmth, even though it doesn't emit heat.

I try to process what he's said. I need time to imagine what my life will be like without Stephen. Right now, I can't even get my mind around that. All I know is that I don't want anyone else to have to go through this.

I wish I understood *why*.

Not for Stephen; I am painfully aware of what went wrong there. But everyone before him, what were they going through? I think about Macey, Paul, Braden—they had entirely different problems than Stephen. And what about Ryan and Sarah two years ago? And Leif before that?

Why does this keep happening here?

What the fuck is wrong in North Shore? Can I do anything to help make it right? I think back to the suicide section in my psych class. At the time, it didn't register, but now I recall my teacher talking about protective factors. One of the big suicide prevention protective factors is identifying with other people of the same ethnic group, feeling like you're a part of something bigger than yourself.

How was Stephen supposed to do that up here?

North Shore's not real diverse. While there are other Asians in town, most are Chinese or Vietnamese or Japanese, which doesn't matter because the Chos didn't hang around with them anyway. The few Korean Americans our age have been away at boarding schools since junior high.

Until this second, it never occurred to me that being unique had to be yet another added stressor on Stephen. He was sensitive and he hated anything that made him stand out. All he ever wanted was to blend in, and he could never figure out how.

Stephen must have been looking to identify. I didn't realize that the ways I've changed this year must have impacted him. We were alike, two sides of the same coin, until we weren't.

I know my dad says this isn't my fault, but how do I not carry that guilt with me? He was my brother, for all intents and purposes. I had a responsibility to him. If I could have just stayed the same for a little while longer, he'd have made it to MIT and I know he'd have found so many more people like himself.

How can I not be at least partly to blame, regardless of what my dad says?

I wonder if Stephen's need to identify is why he gravitated to throwback hip hop? He was the one who introduced me to it all. The classic MCs were his heroes, with their overblown confidence and swagger, fronting all those qualities he wished he'd shared. He loved them so much. Stephen wouldn't give the new school artists a chance, considered their work blasphemy. When I tried to slip some 2 Chainz or Chance the Rapper to our playlists, he balked. He barely tolerated Lil Wayne.

Instead, he worshiped Tupac and Biggie and Eazy and Nate Dog and Jam Master Jay and Cowboy from Grandmaster Flash.

Wait.

I just realized that all of his heroes are dead.

All of them.

Nobody made it to forty. Most didn't make it to thirty.

No wonder his mom despised his music.

I guess it's possible that Stephen's death isn't entirely my fault. Maybe there were other factors at play, factors I don't understand.

Doesn't make the loss any easier.

31

——

MALLORY

"WHAT DO YOU think?"

My mother enters my room in a far-too-sexy-for-her-age, black body-con bandage dress, the tags still dangling from the gold zipper in the back.

"It's tight," I respond before pretending to concentrate on my Government homework. I can't concentrate on my work, though. Not now.

"Tight as in *good* tight or tight as in retaining water tight?" she prompts, turning back and forth in front of my mirror, assessing herself.

"Just tight. I mean, could you even eat in that thing?"

"No, but I'm not wearing it to dinner. Hey, how do the girls look? Do I need a better push-up bra?" She cups herself and begins to rearrange, hoisting higher and then lower. "Should I go more rounded or padded or maybe conical, kind of like a throwback to those bras in the '60s that made everyone's boobs look like missiles? Do I just do a bustier instead?"

Yes. Talking about my mom's breasts. That's the recipe for a great day.

I close my book. Any pretense of studying is now over. I need to manage this interaction. I'm particularly anxious about engaging with my mom when she gets into "girlfriend mode." I'm her *daughter*, not her pal. I'm not her confidante, especially because the second I'm no longer expedient, she'll launch back into attack mode. Like a viper that strikes out of nowhere. I learned long ago to not entrust anything to her, because she'll just throw it back up to me the second I displease her. She's like a mean friend, except one who lives in my house.

I deliberate before responding. "I don't know, Mom. Tell me where you're going so I have a better idea of what's appropriate."

"A funeral for one of my Pilates friends' kids. I forget his name. Something Cho. Somebody Cho."

"Stephen," I hiss. I feel my anger radiate to the tips of my fingers. My fists begin to clench. I ache to hit something, pounding it over and over until my skin cracks and knuckles bleed. "His name was *Stephen* Cho."

What I don't say is that I've cried myself to sleep every night this week thinking about him.

She snaps her fingers. "That's the one."

My entire body prepares itself for fight mode as the adrenaline courses through me, but I control myself. I don't have it in me to battle it out right now. I won't win, no matter how right I might be. The game is always rigged in her favor. I need to pick flight.

She holds up two different pairs of earrings, one that's a shoulder-grazing tangle of rose gold links, the other a pair of pearls dangling from bejeweled crossed Chanel Cs. "Chandelier or drop?"

Fight it is.

My voice dripping with saccharine, I say, "Is there a reason you're dressed like a Russian call girl to bury your friend's son?"

She whips around to look at me, unsure if I'm being bitchy or funny. Suspect she'd be scowling if her face could move. "Show a little respect, missy." She thinks *bitchy*, then. She fluffs her hair. "Besides, rumor has it a team from *Nightline* might be there and I *love* me some Dan Harris. I need to look good. Hey, you think he's single?"

I snort. "Are *you* suddenly single?"

I know she flirts when she's out but it never occurred to me that she might take it further than that. God. No wonder Dad's never home.

I can't with this.

I *can't*.

I have to get out of this house and out of my head.

I kick off my Uggs and slip on my running shoes and then I grab the closest jacket to me. Only after I pull it on and smell clean cotton and wintergreen do I realize it's Braden's hoodie. Too late now.

"Where are you going?" she asks.

"Does it matter?" I reply.

She simply shrugs, too taken by her own reflection to truly give a damn. She pulls her hair back into a French twist and then shakes it out, making duck lips at herself the entire time.

I don't care that it's cold and dark; I have never needed to run the stairs more than I do right now.

After a brutal session in the bleachers, I notice that there's light on in the counseling office. My body is spent. My legs are throbbing and my lungs burn from the effort, but I'm still way too amped up mentally. Guess I'd hoped I could outrun my thoughts. No dice. I can still practically taste the outrage. And I ache to wail on something.

Only someone as narcissistic as my mother could turn a crisis into an opportunity.

I'm too fired up to go home, so I start peeking in windows to see who's around. I could use a friend. People are always here after hours, whether it's a club meeting or a tutoring session or a late practice. In the Guidance wing, I spot Mr. Gorton.

He'll do.

I bang on his glass and he practically jumps out of his skin. I motion for him to open the side door.

As soon as I'm inside, he asks, "Mallory, are you okay?"

"Yes. Actually, no. No, I'm *not* okay because this needs to stop."

Mr. Gorton ushers me into his office and he takes a seat behind his desk. "Okay, Mallory, I'm listening."

"This can't happen anymore. Do you understand me? This *has to stop*. This is *out of hand*."

My lungs are in a vise being squeezed tighter and tighter. I feel the cords in my neck pull so taut that they might snap as I unleash.

I continue, steam practically pouring from my ears. "This is *an epidemic*. This is *ridiculous*. How is everyone in this community not completely up in arms? Why is there no action? How long does the list of names have to be? Just this year, we lost Paul, Macey, Braden, and now Stephen." I tick their names off on my fingers. "What's everyone waiting for? This many?" I splay my left palm to indicate five. "Or this many?" I splay my opposite hand. "What's gonna stop this? What if we're all, 'Maybe we actually try to prevent kids from throwing themselves in front of trains?' How about that?"

Mr. Gorton doesn't respond. I assume he's waiting for me to finish. He wields silence like a pro. Any counselor, peer or otherwise, knows that quiet compels the client to fill the silence. But I don't need his prompt, I have *plenty* to say.

"We have goddamned *satellite trucks* out there, okay? *Nightline* is sniffing around. There are reporters crawling all over this town, talking to everyone who's been affected. Well, guess what? *I'm affected.* But *my* reaction isn't to cry to a journalist. *My* reaction is that we find a way to fix ourselves, to help ourselves."

Nothing. He may as well be a statue. He's very good at this.

"The networks are still lurking around campus. It's been a week. When are they going to leave us alone? This story is, like, a perfect storm. Every media outlet in the country is salivating for details. I can't change the channel without hearing some empty suit blather on about 'suicide clusters,' explaining to those of us who aren't actually witnessing them first-hand, who aren't burying their friends, that they're 'multiple deaths in close succession and proximity.'"

I bristle over the faux concern so many on TV, radio, and the web have shown. America can't get enough of this story, of the poor little rich kids who can't hack it, like the One Percent are finally getting what's been long overdue. Like somehow karma came a-callin'.

"These anchors sit there with their pancake makeup and their shiny blazers and matter-of-fact expressions, all hair-sprayed and clinical and detached. Somehow they forget they're talking about kids from our swim classes, kids who rode the bus with us, or went to camp with us, or sat next to us in lunch. They're talking about the girl who handed me an extra pencil before a standardized test and the boy who'd skew the results because he was so smart. Macey was *real*. Paul

326

was *real*. Braden was *real*. Stephen was *real*. They were real people. Not statistics, not cautionary tales, but real kids who couldn't take all the pressure. They cracked. Paul wasn't the first, and it's real fucking unfortunate that Stephen probably won't be the last."

Mr. Gorton's totally mute right now, even though I just dropped an f-bomb. He's silent and motionless, eerily calm, like I'm not even here, completely losing my shit in front of him.

"Did you see Will O'Leary's show two days ago? He's *the worst*. He ran a feature where he interviewed some of our students and then was kind enough to 'mansplain' that the problem is we're a bunch of children who simply don't understand the consequences of our actions. That suicide is permanent. *This* is what passes for fair and balanced? Blaming the victims? How is that possibly supposed *to help*?"

No reaction. I'd stick a mirror under his mouth to check his breathing, except he just blinked.

"Some of us saw the clip in the student lounge yesterday. I'm sure you've already heard, but if you missed it, that's when Owen Foley-Feinstein walked up and punched a hole through the flat screen, right in O'Leary's smug face. I was there when it happened, you know. I found myself cheering for Owen, for his doing what I didn't have the guts to do."

Mr. Gorton's so motionless that if he were in a park right now, birds would land on him.

"With Braden? Who I loved? I was numb and I didn't know what to do, but I still blame myself for not being there for him. I am drowning in regret. I torment myself every hour of the day trying to figure out *why*. With Stephen? Someone who I couldn't even be bothered to give the time of day? A person who I'd refer to as a *random*? I've been bawling my head off.

327

I can't stop crying myself to sleep, his face in my mind. The bitch of it is, I can't even picture him clearly because I never bothered to look him in the eye. Yet I am haunted, okay? *Haunted.* He might have been the greatest guy in the world, and now I'll never know him. That's on me."

More blinking.

"Did you know that Asian American kids Stephen's age are the most at risk? Because I know it now. They have the highest rates of suicidal thoughts, of intent, and of attempts. Did you know that the suicide rate at MIT—the college Stephen wanted to attend—has quadruple the national average of suicides for Asian American students? I read that between 1996 and 2006, a Cornell task force found that thirteen out of twenty-one campus suicides involved Asian American students. *Thirteen out of twenty-one.* Did you know they're more likely than any other peer group to report anxiety or depression, but they're the least likely to seek help? What in the actual fuck? These are documented facts! What are they always saying in Econ class? *'If you can't measure it, you can't manage it. If you can't manage it, you can't improve it.'* We have the stats! We can measure it! SO WHY ISN'T ANYONE AROUND HERE MANAGING AND IMPROVING?"

I pace back and forth in front of his desk, my sneakers squeaking furiously each time I spin on my heels.

"So I'm mad. I'm mad at myself, but I'm madder at the circumstances that drove poor Stephen to that decision. I'm mad about the impossible standards here, the atmosphere that's been created, that made him think that he could never be good enough, that he may as well end the game, take his ball and go home. Why are we so all-or-nothing here? Why are we all about black-and-white with no shades of gray? Although, I guess I should be happy about all the news coverage on Stephen because, traditionally, the media's more likely to pro-file white students. At least there's a modicum of awareness. Hashtag *smallblessing*."

Mr. Gorton looks like he wants to say something and he parts his lips as if to speak, but something gets the better of him. His teeth clack together as he shuts his mouth.

"Personally, I've been living in mortal fear about not being accepted anywhere but the University of Iowa, when, in all actuality? Iowa's a damn good school. *Tennessee Williams* went to the University of Iowa. *Cat on a Hot Tin Roof? A Streetcar Named Desire?* What kind of messed up value system do I have to look at Tennessee Williams' alma mater like it's some kind of votech, a third-tier community college, like being a Hawkeye is a fate worse than death? Guess what? Seen death now. Not a fan. And Iowa City? It's Utopia in comparison."

Mr. Gorton has closed his eyes at this point, as though he can't even bear to look at me. Like he's pained.

The truth fucking *hurts*.

"You know how many kids I've been working with this week in peer counseling? *All of them*. They are lined up out the door and down the hall. The other peer counselors and I can't keep pace. What happens to the kids who can't get in with us? The grief therapists are gone, so we're the only line of defense. These suicides are all anyone wants to talk about and we're not even supposed to get in-depth. You want us to give them pamphlets and refer them back to you. I'm here on the front lines. And to be clear? I am a seventeen-year-old girl *who is afraid of bread*. I can't be the only thing potentially standing between life and death for our classmates! I can't do this alone. We need to look out for each other. We need *a system*. We need a *failsafe*."

"We need a gatekeeper."

329

"We need a—wait," I say, having forgotten that Mr. Gorton's even capable of speech. "What'd you say?"

He straightens up in his seat. "You're right, Mallory. I'm saying you're one hundred percent right. What we need is a gatekeeper."

"Like the song?" I ask, remembering that piece by Meg Hutchinson that I'd stumbled across.

He tells me, "The song is based on a real man."

"You're kidding."

How did I not know this?

"Yeah, 'Gatekeeper' is about this California Highway cop named Kevin Briggs who worked the Golden Gate Bridge for years. He was a former army officer, trained in crisis negotiation. In the course of his day, he'd patrol the bridge—called it 'walking the rail'—looking for people who seemed to be contemplating suicide. I guess he did it long enough and could recognize the signs. He'd stop the potential jumpers by talking to them, posing a couple of questions."

"You mean the lines about how they were feeling and what their plans were for tomorrow?"

"Right."

My pace in front of the desk begins to slow. "Nothing else? That's it? He'd know intentions by how they answered his questions?"

"Yes and no. You see, Briggs wasn't seeking specific answers. Instead, he wanted to break people out of their tunnel vision. He was dealing with people who saw death as the only way out. A lot of times those thoughts are temporary, fleeting."

I think about Braden that day, walking by the tracks, the delayed train rumbling along behind him. Was he a victim of his own tunnel vision? A temporary impulse? I feel sick about not being more cognizant. He needed a gatekeeper. What truly breaks my heart is that I now see the times he tried to gatekeep me.

Mr. Gorton continues. "What's deadly is when people have them at the wrong time in an expedient place. The officer being there shook them out of the fog. Because of what he did and how he did it, he earned the nickname the Gatekeeper. That's what we need here. A gatekeeper. Rather, we need to *become* gatekeepers. All of us."

I wasn't there to save Braden, but I could be there for others.

I finally sit down in the chair across from him and I pull up a blank to-do list on my phone.

I say, "Great. Let's get started."

NORTH SHORE HIGH SCHOOL
We breed excellence.

HOME | ABOUT | NSHS ACADEMICS | STUDENT SERVICES | STUDENT LIFE | PARENT ORGANIZATIONS

STUDENT BULLETIN

Students, please join us for the initial meeting of the Gatekeepers, a suicide awareness and prevention organization. First meeting is this Monday in the Liberal Arts Activity Center, 3:05 PM.

32

OWEN

"WE SHOULD CONSIDER modeling ourselves after Palo Alto's Project Safety Net."

Mr. Gorton is leading the Gatekeepers' first official meeting and I'm here because our family therapist thought it'd be a good idea. If there's anything I can do to fight what's been going on, I'm all over it. Dr. Kincaid said being a part of the Gatekeepers would help me heal. I don't even care about me now; I'm just real motivated to keep other people safe.

Mr. Gorton says we should roll out strategies to help safeguard classmates. 'Bout damn time. Looks like a lot of the peer counselors are here. The organization's open to the whole student body, though. For us seniors, there's only so much my class can do in the six months before graduation. Glad to see some freshmen in the mix because help for four years? Major impact.

Kent and Simone are here, and she brought Liam with her. I should be jelly, but I'm actually real glad about that. People follow him. If he's into a program, everyone'll follow suit. Even *Jasper* showed up because of Liam. If he misses me as a customer, he hasn't said anything. Maybe he's getting out of the game.

Hope so.

Mallory and Theo are sitting with me in the front row. He and I have matching casts on our right hands. When he asked me about mine, I told him that my only regret is hitting a screen and not O'Leary's actual smug face.

Mr. Gorton tells us, "Project Safety Net is a suicide prevention and youth well-being collaboration and they've done great work so far because they've garnered community support. Theirs is a multifaceted approach. They focus on a few different areas, such as decreasing the stigma around mental illness and improving mental health, reducing academic pressure, limiting access to means of self-harm, like rallying around efforts to fence in the Caltrain, all in conjunction with working to improve communication. It's *my* opinion we model ourselves after them. But what do *you* think?"

Everyone nods and I raise my good hand. "We gotta focus on drinking and drug use, too. I mean, that's a *thing*." I notice Jasper start to study his pants. Red-and-green plaid today, exceptionally festive. "My therapist was telling me about this study they did at Yale. He says that the number of kids who drink and take drugs and smoke and stuff at rich-kid schools is a lot higher than in poor ones. He says we also have higher rates of anxiety and depression."

"Do you have any idea why that might be? Would you like to elaborate?" Mr. Gorton probes. I get the feeling he already knows the answer, but wants us to come up with it.

"Maybe our houses are too big?" I suggest.

I like that Mr. Gorton doesn't laugh at me. Instead, he gives my idea consideration. He says, "Tell me more about that."

"Yeah, I guess I should explain what I mean 'cause that

sounds dumb, but hear me out. So, we live in these huge homes, right?" Everyone nods. "All of the, like, physical space is kind of a barrier to families spending time together. Live in an apartment house with one bathroom, you're gonna run into each other, you know? But kids here, on these estates and stuff, some of them have their own wings of the house. Whole days can go by where they don't see their parents."

I know of a couple of families in town who've built entire separate buildings for the teenagers, so they don't mess up the parts of the home where the parents entertain.

Mallory and Theo look at each other, like they're both just realizing something important.

"At Casa Foley-Feinstein? Both my parents work, all the time. We never had dinner together, didn't hang out and watch TV or anything. There was no, like, family suppers or group outings. Everyone had their own shit to do on the weekends. That's how it was for us. Real detached. 'Course, after Braden, everything changed for us."

Saying Braden's name makes Mallory catch her breath. She's on my right. Theo's on her other side. I notice his left hand clenching into a fist and Mallory wraps her arm around him.

I say, "For the first time, I feel like my folks are there for me. I'm not gonna lie, in the beginning, I was in a real dark place. I wasn't sure what was gonna happen and I pushed everyone away. I guess that was a wake-up call for my folks. Now, one of them always leaves the office early so I'm not alone. We're having meals as a family. Usually it's just something from Seamless, but that's, like, whatever. No one's gotta make a roast, it's just kinda nice to have a conversation over a box of breadsticks, you know? But the way it was for me before is still how it is for most kids. We were…disconnected. Not anchored."

"You were there," Theo says, his voice catching. "With Braden."

I nod. "That day changed my life. I live it over and over in my head."

"Can you tell us what happened?" Theo asks, in barely more than a whisper.

"Yeah, but I gotta tell you the whole story, that's what my therapist says. I can't keep pushing it down. But I gotta start at the very beginning, for context."

Mr. Gorton clears his throat. "Hold on. This story could be a trigger, so why don't we have those who weren't friends with him clear the room for a few minutes? Maybe get a soda, use the washroom?"

Almost everyone scatters, save for Mallory, Theo, Kent, and Jasper. I don't blame the others for leaving. Wish I could run from this story.

I look over at Theo before I start. "You cool?"

He nods and swallows real hard.

"I'd, um, just picked up some Chronic and wait… Is this, like, a safe space? Can I say stuff without being all incriminatory?"

"Absolutely," Mr. Gorton confirms. "Please. Go on."

"I'm chillin' in the little valley under the railroad trestle just down the street from the school."

I don't mention that I was meeting Jasper there—none of this is his fault.

"I figure, it's secluded and no one's gonna see me. I pack my bowl and I have a couple of hits. And *sheee-it*, the Chronic is intense. Like, my lungs are on fire, but with pleasure. The white trichomes are— Wait, you know what? Not important. Anyway, I'm down there and I'm rocked." I notice Mr. Gorton's expression so I add, "I mean, I'm not trying to make this sound so great, because I haven't touched anything since that day, not even a cough drop, and I never will again. You guys gotta learn to say no."

Jasper nods and that surprises me.

"Point is, I'm not in my right mind and my reactions aren't what they shoulda been. I'm having a hard time living with myself for being baked when everything went down. Like I wonder if there wasn't something I could have done, had circumstances been different. These doubts, these questions? I feel like they're gonna be with me for the rest of my life."

I watch Theo's jaw clench and unclench. To most people, he looks like a tough guy trying to keep his temper in check. But I know this is what he does when he's trying not to cry. He reacted the same way when his family had to put down Monster, their ancient golden doodle. He was an awesome dog, always catching tennis balls in the deep end of their pool. Monster was Theo's best friend until he met Braden.

I take a deep breath. "This is hard, but I think if I share what happened next with you guys, we can take something from it, we can maybe figure out some fixes. I don't want anyone else to go through this again, not someone like me, and definitely not someone like Braden. He was a good Joe."

I take a swig from my soda, clear my throat, and continue. The only sound in the room is that of warm air being pushed through the heating vents.

"So I see someone walking up and at first I panic, thinking whoever it is will bust me. As he gets closer, I realize it's Braden and he's cool. I knew he didn't partake, but he also didn't judge. I wave and say something like, 'S'up, stargazer?' 'cause we went to the same astronomy camp. But it was like he couldn't see or hear me and we're maybe twenty feet away. He looked exhausted, like he hadn't slept the night before."

"He'd been having insomnia," Theo said.

"There's a strong link between chronic insomnia and suicide," Mr. Gorton adds.

"I didn't know that," I said. "He was usually so, like, up, you know? Supercharged. Remember the thing with the forks?"

"Manic behavior's another red flag," Mr. Gorton says.

"Whoa," I say. "Maybe we all need to get better at spotting the signs?"

Everyone nods.

"Anyway, I thought that was weird he didn't say hey, but maybe he wanted to give me privacy, you know? Then, um, the tracks start to rumble a little bit because the train's on the way."

I stop and rest my face in my good hand. I hate reliving this. "I just wish I'd been more clearheaded. I wrestle with this a hundred times a day, no lie. We're working on it in my sessions, so now I'm down from thinking about it a thousand times a day. I'm trying to move on, but sometimes I find myself going back to the spot. Not just in my head, in real life. I do drills—I time myself running up the hill, to see if I'd been focusing, if I could have gotten to him before... I wonder if I'd have been better off learning how to recognize warning signs?"

I feel something warm and wet hit my arm and I realize that Mallory's crying. Didn't know she was capable of tears.

"Are you sure you want to hear this?" Mr. Gorton says, addressing her and Theo. They both nod.

"Go on," she says. "Please."

"I should have known what was going to happen when he put down his backpack. I should have and I didn't. I picture that goddamned backpack all day long, too—it was black and it had a couple of yellow eyes sewn on, like when you walked behind him, this evil bug would be staring back at you."

"The bag looked like a roach's face," Theo says in a choked voice.

I nod. "He was always doing stuff like that. Remember his Hello Kitty hat?"

Mallory smiles through her tears, just for a second, and wraps her big hoodie tighter around herself.

"He puts his backpack on the ground, and I guess I thought he was gonna pull something out of it? But he doesn't, he just sits it down all neatly and careful-like. Then the tracks start really humming because the train's close. The spot we're in isn't close enough to the station to slow down yet, so it's rolling right along, probably forty-five miles an hour. The conductor obviously sees Braden, so he begins to pull the horn. The sound is just, like, overwhelming. I can feel it in my bones and the pit of my stomach, it's that intense. I try to climb the hill, but it's real wet and I'm slipping all over the place and my reaction time is for shit. The engineer guy's just honking and honking and honking and the wail of the air horn's getting more and more desperate and Braden's standing there, right next to the tracks. I start yelling, 'Train! Train!' but he's in a daze, like, mesmerized by the sound of the wheels on the track. Then, calm as anyone doing something they do every day, like climbing into the shower or walking out the door, he takes a big step and stands in front of the train. At the last minute, he raises his arms in front of his chest, like he's suddenly trying to protect himself. And, honest to God, I think I'm hallucinating, I think *this can't be real*. But it was."

Mallory is openly weeping now and Mr. Gorton dabs at his eyes with a handkerchief. Kent is curled up with his feet on the chair, clutching his knees and quietly sobbing into his jeans. Jasper has his arm around him, trying to give him some comfort. Poor Kent's gotta be thinking Stephen's last moments were probably like this, too. Theo begins to quake, but makes no sound.

"Thought that'd be the worst part. No. He doesn't die. He isn't killed on impact, just thrown real far."

I don't share what happened next. They don't need to hear that he was still alive. I ran to him, I fucking dug in and made it up the hill. I held his hand while I dialed 911. I'll never forget the worst part—the worst part is that he still looked like *him*. He wasn't all disfigured. He was just there, regular old handsome Braden, only spread out real weird by the road, like a broken doll. People aren't supposed to bend that way.

I need a second, so I take another sip of my Coke and I struggle to get it down.

"We weren't tight but I was there in the last minute when he needed a friend the most. I just wish I'd been sooner. I can't forgive myself for not being there sooner. Working on it but not there yet."

Theo's tears have come. Mallory pulls him into her arms and he weeps like a little boy. He looks and sounds and acts like a man, but as he cries, I realize he's still just a kid.

We're all still just kids.

"I ride in the ambulance with him and I'm still at the hospital an hour later when his mom finally shows up. He was already gone by then. She said she was having coffee with a friend and didn't hear her phone at first. She's in shock. She starts babbling, saying that Braden had been depressed because she and his father are having marital problems. They want the big D but neither one of them is willing to move out of the big house, so they're just there, fighting all the time, like the *War of the Roses.*"

340

"I had no idea," Mallory says, more to herself than to anyone else. "I've been out of my head about the why. Why couldn't he have told us? Why didn't we figure it out?"

I look around and say to Mr. Gorton. "I think I know why. And I'm glad you cleared the room. People don't need to know about the DeRochers' private business."

"What was happening?" Mallory demands.

"She said his dad had a girlfriend. She told me Braden had been depressed about everything and withdrawn at home, but she figured it would pass. Assumed it was a phase and eventually he'd get used to the new reality of his parents dating other people in this fucked-up arrangement at the house, where everyone wanted to make sure they got every penny coming to them. She told me she and Mr. DeRocher were having affairs and that they'd been horrible to each other."

Thinking about this now, I'm pissed off. You don't want to be married anymore? Then don't be married. But, like, excuse yourself first before you begin this whole new life. Live under a different roof. Don't drag your kids into your bullshit.

A torrent of tears roll down Mallory's face, but it's like she doesn't even notice them. Some splash onto my pants.

Theo looks devastated. "I can't believe it wasn't an accident."

Mallory hugs him harder. "I'm so sorry, Theo."

I say, "I keep going back to that day in the ER, wondering if I should have reacted differently with his mom. I didn't want to hear whatever else she had to say, but I couldn't stop her from talking because she seemed like she needed to confess or whatever. I just sat there and listened. Like, maybe that was my penance for not being quicker. She kept saying again and again, 'We thought it would pass. We thought he'd be okay.'"

I take another long breath. "It didn't pass. He wasn't okay.

That's why I'm here. That's why I want to be a Gatekeeper. I failed 'cause I wasn't there for Braden."

"No, you didn't fail," Mallory insists. "Those of us in his life failed. The signs were there and we didn't see them."

I say, "Then I think you're with me when I say I'm not about failing again."

It's dark by the time we finish our meeting. We covered so much and I'm completely wiped, but hopeful. I feel like it's possible for us to make a difference, not just here, but everywhere. I've been looking for a documentary subject but didn't have enough passion about any topic before. I do now. I feel real strongly about this, about being a Gatekeeper.

We're putting a bunch of strategies in place to help everyone manage and deal. Not just monitoring for red flags, but fun stuff, too. Mr. Gorton gave us these suggestions from this Dr. Sonja Lyubomirsky lady on how to be happy, like keeping gratitude journals and savoring positive experiences and connecting with friends.

What's most important is that Mr. Gorton's talking to the school board this week to see about reducing the academic pressures, maybe decreasing our workloads, cutting down on homework. We can't keep up this pace. It's not possible. We've gotta relax the standards. Lessen everyone's burdens, help us all chill a little bit. If we lower the bar across the board, we all benefit. The group feels like if everyone has less of a boot on our necks, the whole student body would change for the better.

We figure maybe we can tell everyone they can stop trying to be so excellent.

Maybe we can settle for just being real good.

I exit the building via the door to the student parking lot, which is ringed in halogen lights. There's only a couple of cars left in this massive parking area. Theo and Mallory are a few paces behind me.

"Hey, this might be weird," I say, trotting back to them. "I feel like we're not done talking to each other, you know? Do you guys wanna, I don't know, come to my house for dinner? Tonight's pizza night, nothing fancy, but we're getting Lou Malnati's. We could order a salad for you, Mallory."

"Um, no," she replies.

"Cool. I'll just see you guys at the next meeting."

I thought maybe we could all try being friends again despite our parents' feud, but I guess not.

Mallory stops me by tugging my sleeve. "Wait, I'm so sorry, Owen, please. I meant, no, you don't have to order a salad for me. Theo and I absolutely want to come. I'd love to see your folks and pizza sounds freaking *amazing*."

Theo stands there with his mouth hanging open.

To him, she says, "What? I'm starving. Let's roll."

33

SIMONE

"YO, CHASTAIN IN the Membrane, we need to talk."

I'm sorting through the books in my locker when Jasper sidles up to me. Huh, that's odd. While he and I often chat in study hall, it's always breezy. Sometimes we compare notes on favorite places or bands, but we've never covered anything that might cause him to say *We need to talk*, as though we're confidantes, as though this is our norm.

What would we even discuss?

His ability to bend his arms while wearing four shirts concurrently, each one with its collar flipped just so?

Sure, I've attended his parties and he's driven Liam and me home in his Navigator a couple of times, but that's hardly the basis for a private convo.

"Um, okay. What's the story?" I ask.

He looks first over his left shoulder and then his right. "Not here. Follow me." He pulls me into an empty chemistry lab. "We gotta talk about L-Money."

I'm suddenly regretting my curiosity.

"What *about* Liam?" I ask.

"I'm worried."

"Worried how? Worried in what respect?"

"Worried about all the pills he's taking," Jasper says.

I let out a whoosh of breath that turns into an inadvertent laugh. "You? *You're* worried about Liam and medicinal anti-inflammatories? Jasper, I watched you carve *a bong out of a butternut squash* last month."

"And?"

"Are you serious? You're like the Stephen Hawking of getting high. You have a PhD in being shithoused. I can name five different illegal substances I've watched you ingest. You're hardly one to judge, Jasper, no offense."

Why is it that everything about Jasper smacks of an '80s film? From his smarmy, ironic bow ties to his stupid nicknames to his penchant for loud pants. I'm half expecting this conversation to be a ruse because he's secretly crushing on me, like how James Spader's character was actually into Molly Ringwald in *Pretty in Pink*. Cordy says this kind of thing happens all the time. Nobody fancies you and then you get a boyfriend, and, wham! Suddenly you're a hot property because you're off the market. She suspects it's the sex pheromones.

While I'm flattered by Jasper's attention, I'm not interested. I'm delighted to be *LiMone*. Liam's everything I could ever want and then some.

"Okay, number one, big difference between a couple of disco biscuits at a party and what our boy's doing." When he points at me, I notice his enormous gold signet ring that looks to be an antique. I'd tell him that was perfect for him, except I don't like his attitude.

He continues, "Number two, this is not about me—this is about L-Money. Number three, I'm telling you, he's in deep. He's in so deep that I had to cut him off a few weeks ago. His

345

usage is *seriously* out of hand. Here's the thing—I know him. I know him way better than you, in fact."

This comment rubs me entirely the wrong way. "Jealous much?"

He scoffs at that. "Um, hardly. I've known him all my life and this isn't who he is. The *in too deep* part is legit. If we're all about being Gatekeepers, we're supposed to be hypervigilant. This is me, going the full Batman and looking out for him."

Pfft. Batman. More like *Bateman*, as in Patrick Bateman, the preppy murderer from *American Psycho*.

"Jasper, I need to go to class. Pardon me." I try to ease myself out the door, but he steps in the way, putting up his arm to stop me.

"Chastity Belt, you gotta listen to me."

"*Chastity Belt?* How about *Simone?*"

"Whatever, I mean, *Simone*. He's not taking his own script, *Simone*. You know that, right, *Simone*? When he tweaked his ACL this fall, I gave him some Vicodin. I deal mostly in herb and Adderall, but I have other sources. Okay, full disclosure, I mean my mom's medicine cabinet. So, he and I talked about it and we figured if he went to the athletic trainers with his injury, he'd be benched. Didn't want to risk it in case he ends up needing that soccer scholarship at University of Florida. They have a kick-ass program and he'd rock it down there."

I interrupt, "He says he's not playing next year. Why would he even need a soccer scholarship?"

"'Cause his dad's a frigging psychopath who could pull his financial support at any time. On a scholarship, he can be his own man. Anyway, I figured he'd eventually see a doctor. When he didn't, I scored some more, enough to get him through State. That was like, six or seven weeks ago. After the season ended, I stopped supplying him and he snuck into my parents' room and cleaned out my mom's whole stash."

First my parents and now Jasper? This is too much. I do not have time for this nonsense. "Please. You have parties *all the time.* How do you know it was him? There's a hundred kids at your place on any given weekend. Could have been anyone."

"Because Storey-time Harper said after Liam was at his house last week, his dad's script went missing. Same thing happened when he showed up at Finn Stapleton's place on Thursday. Liam took all the hydrocodone the Stapler had left over when he had his wisdom teeth removed. Our boy has a problem, *Simone.* He has a problem and we need to help. I mean, his whole personality has changed and that is *no bueno.* We've got to, like, gatekeep him."

I truly don't want to be in the middle of this, especially when it's such a nonissue. Liam is fine. I know he's fine. He's fantastic, in fact. He's not some bum, staggering around skid row, aching for a fix. My God, he's a tenth of a grade point away from being the valedictorian! I wish everyone could just see that any changes in his personality or behavior are because he says he's so much happier since we're together, now that he has the dual burdens of Mallory and Princeton off his back.

I don't want to encourage Jasper, but I hate to argue, so I say, "Then maybe you should talk to him."

"Yeah, I did and now he's not speaking to me. A couple of us held a mini-intervention with him over the weekend and he's icing us all out." Could that be true? We haven't been sitting with that squad at lunch. "He's ignoring Storey-time, he's blowing off the Stapler, he's off the grid for all of Wild, Wild Weston's texts. No, wait, he replied to one of them, all *User Not Found.* C'mon man, oldest trick in the book."

347

"I'm sure he's just busy—we've been spending loads of time together."

Jasper won't be dissuaded. "At the Gatekeepers dealio last week, the Gorton Fisherman kept saying how drug use and suicidal behaviors were, like, interconnected. That doesn't worry you?"

Jasper's stretching now. I counter, "You *sell drugs*, for Christ's sake! If you cared so much, you'd stop dealing."

"I did. I've retired."

I roll my eyes. "Congratulations, did you get your gold watch?"

"What's that supposed to mean?" He glances down at his Rolex. "I wear a Submariner. Gold is, like, *no*."

"When a person retires after so many years on the job, they receive a—never mind. My point is, if he had a problem, he'd talk to me." I mean, we're practically enmeshed. We're *LiMone*. We're one, in every sense. "And why is everyone up poor Liam's arse anyway? Christ on a bike, he's been in agony. Cut him a small break! Do you realize how hard it's been for him to accomplish everything he's done this year while in constant, throbbing pain? He says he's managing his medicine and I believe him. He wouldn't lie to me. Not now."

Jasper snorts. "No offense, *Simone*, but it sounds like you're the only one who *isn't* trying to help him."

I duck under his arm and scoot out the door before he can grab me.

"Good bye, Jasper. This conversation is over."

"No, *Simone*," he replies as I retreat. "It's really not."

Owen

1:17 PM

yo, kent, w e still on for ltr? 👍👎

34

KENT

"WE'RE ROLLING IN five, four, three, two…"

Owen's been counting down, and on the one, he points to me. I open my mouth to say something, but I'm not sure what. From his spot behind the lens, he nods encouragingly. Nice, but not particularly useful as I'm still at a loss for words.

"Sorry, Owen, I don't know where to start," I explain.

"No worries, it's not like we're wasting tape, right?" He gestures toward his new Panasonic DVX 200 camera and grins at me. "Digital."

"Can you remind me of some of the questions again? Wait, is it okay for me to ask you stuff or will that ruin your take?"

"That's what editing's for, bro. We're cool."

I'm at Owen's house, being interviewed for his documentary about us forming the Gatekeepers. Or, I would be giving an interview if I could wrap my mind around something to say. "This is harder than I thought," I explain.

"I hear that, totally feel you. With me, after Braden? I shut down hardcore. Had trouble getting out more than a word or two. I could not deal. The idea of having a whole conversation would just knock the wind out of me, so I retreated into myself. I was an island. Like, I know Simone wanted to talk, but I just couldn't so I pushed her away. Pushed everyone away. I wanted to be inside my head where it was quiet. Wasn't until the folks brought me to therapy that I even started having conversations again."

While Owen didn't lose his best friend, we've both experienced a high level of trauma, so I ask him, "Does the guilt go away? Will it get better?"

He considers my question and answers, "Yes and no. Mostly, it'll get different. For now, you hold on to that, okay?"

I nod. Because I feel like I should be saying *something*, I tell him, "Your room isn't what I remember. Like, your books are alphabetized and sorted by type. Don't remember you being Mr. Dewey Decimal system. Didn't we used to joke about using hip-waders to plow through all your mess?"

I was shocked to see how neat and precise everything in here is, with each of his old medals and trophies arranged just so, and different quadrants of the room earmarked for every hobby/interest. We're sitting in the filmmaking portion, but there are also separate areas for playing music, for doing homework, for reading, and for gaming. I somehow remember him living like a bear, with empty pizza boxes for end tables and stacks upon stacks of dirty clothes, but that's not the case at all.

"'A place for everything and everything in its place.' Or, 'For every minute spent organizing, an hour is earned,'" he replies. "That's some Ben Franklin realness for you. I wasn't always tidy like this. Sorta used to live like a bear."

I laugh. "That's what I thought."

"Yeah, it was full-blown chaos up in here. But after Braden, I needed to feel like I had some measure of control, like I could look at one thing in my life and go, 'Uh-huh, that's exactly how it should be,' so I started with my room. Felt like if I could get my surroundings straightened out, then maybe there was hope the rest of my life would follow suit. Honestly? I kinda let this place be a wreck for so long because I wanted my folks to pay attention."

I'm awed by Owen's ability to be so open, so free about how he feels. I envy him. I now understand why Stephen used to fume about him in his speech class, not because Owen did anything wrong, but because I bet he showed the kind of confidence in his convictions that we lacked.

I make a tentative stab at opening up. "Opposite problem over here. If you recall, mine are real focused on me, especially my mom. That's where Stephen and I bonded. He and I used to tell these jokes..." I trail off, suddenly feeling like I've taken a cannonball to the gut when I realize this is one more thing he and I will never do together again. Dad was right. Here I was, feeling okay, and now I'm overtaken with another tsunami of grief.

"You used to do what?" Owen prompts.

"Nah, it's dumb."

"I doubt that, but you do you."

We sit in silence for a minute before it occurs to me that the best way to memorialize Stephen is to verbalize why he was my brother.

"In junior high, we used to spend hours coming up with 'yo mama' jokes. They were sorta stupid but we'd crack ourselves up. Stephen's were always hilarious. My favorite one was, 'Yo mama so mean that Taylor Swift wrote a song about her.'"

Owen laughs appreciatively. "That's awesome."

"You know what sucks? I came up with one he'd have

loved when my mom was following me around, stressing about what I should wear to his funeral."

When I got dressed that morning, I noticed the drycleaner had shrunk my suit pants. They were a good two inches too short, so I wanted to wear khakis and a sports coat, but my mother wasn't having it. She made me put on the suit anyway because she said I couldn't show up to the service all Casual Friday.

I'm reliving every emotion from that day. I was furious at my mom, but angrier at myself, for worrying about trivial stuff like my outfit. More than anything, I was afraid. Afraid to go to the service because I wasn't sure I could handle it.

"There I was, getting ready so we could go bury my best friend and all I could think of was 'Yo mama so stupid that when I told her pi-r-squared, she replied, no, they're round.' Kept thinking, the only person who'd love this is gone."

"I'm real sorry for your loss. Stephen was pretty fly."

I nod and swallow hard, keeping myself from busting out the waterworks. Again. Swear to God, it's like I've turned into a Very Special episode of *Keeping Up with the Kardashians* lately.

Owen suggests, "How 'bout I make you a deal? How 'bout the next time you come up with a joke, text it to me. That'll be, like, your mini-tribute to him, letting your tradition live on."

"Thank you."

"De nada mi amigo, sería un honor."

"Wait, you took Spanish?" I ask. "Weren't you in my Mandarin class?"

Owen shrugs. "Taught myself. Figured I'm more likely to bartend in Costa Rica than Beijing."

"The fact that you're doing stuff like making movies and

353

teaching yourself languages tells me that your future entails more than just opening cervezas for people."

When he nods, the beads on the end of his hair bang together. "You make a good point."

We're both quiet for a minute, but it's a comfortable silence.

"Hey, Owen?"

"Yo."

"I'm ready to do my interview."

"Cool...except I never actually stopped filming. Digital, bro. Got a ton of footage already."

"Oh," I say. "Can you still ask me a question, though?"

"You got it. How 'bout...how are you?"

I reply, "That seems like too easy a question."

"Is it? You could always answer, 'fine,' or 'good,' and then we could move on to something else. Or you could let it sit for a minute, let it marinate, and then tell me if that's how you *really* are. Take your time, it's digital. 'It does not matter how slowly you go as long as you do not stop.' That's Confucius, by the way."

I sit quietly, pondering the question. "Okay... How am I? Um...you know what? Not fine. I keep telling everyone I'm fine but that's a lie," I reply.

"What makes it a lie?"

I can't look at the camera. Instead I concentrate on the hangnail on my thumb. Isn't this how dogs behave when they're caught doing something bad, like napping on the bed or digging up the yard? They don't make eye contact with their masters because if they do, that makes the situation real?

This enormous pressure builds and builds in my chest. I'm afraid if I don't let some of it out, I'll puff up like that purple girl in *Willy Wonka* and Owen will be forced to roll me back home.

Finally, I say, "Mostly, it's a lie because I'm conflicted. Stephen was my best friend but that's not the whole story. He also made me furious sometimes. And I'm a horrible person because I was trying to find a way to not room with him next year. I blamed him for dragging me down. I felt like he held me back and I was not about having that follow me to college. I hate myself for feeling this. I'm sad and mad and full-up on self-loathing. I am anything but fine."

"Sounds like you're still in the anger stage of grief. Spoiler alert—it'll pass. But the shit that comes after is no great shakes, either. What was the big problem with you guys?"

"I was tired of being his cheerleader, tired of always trying to smooth things out for him, to talk him off ledges."

"Tired of being his gatekeeper?"

"In a lot of ways, that's exactly what I was, but I didn't realize it. I'll never stop wishing I'd taken the job more seriously. He'd have done the same for me, if I were depressed. He probably would have been great at it, too, because that kid loved to beat me at everything." I let out a bitter laugh.

Owen nods, saying nothing.

I continue, "That's the thing, I'm pretty sure he was suffering from depression, with manic phases thrown in. In retrospect, I see it now, all the signs, clear as a goddamned bell. The fatigue, the hopelessness, the way he withdrew, lost interest in everything? He may as well have painted a sign, you know? And on some level, I *knew*, I had to know, and I can't forgive myself for not taking action."

"What kind of action should you have taken?"

"Maybe I could have just put aside my frustration and really been there for him?"

"How do you know you weren't? Stop blaming yourself, man. That won't get you anywhere. Blame prevents healing."

My eyes fixed to the ragged skin around my thumb, I say, "He used to frustrate me so much because he was all talk—he was the king of not following through on everything he'd fantasize about, from talking to girls to jumping off the high dive. What's that expression, 'all hat and no saddle'? I realize now he had suicidal ideation—he'd say stuff like the world would be better off without him and that no one would even miss him if he were gone."

My chin begins to quiver and my eyes well. Before the Gatekeepers, I'd never let anyone see me cry. Now I don't care. Good thing, because I'm like a fucking water fountain.

"I never took him seriously. I'm a dick because I never took him seriously. I figured, *please, like he'd actually do anything.* I dismissed so much because he was incapable of following through. I feel like this was my fault. I wake up with the guilt practically suffocating me every day because I didn't understand what he was trying to tell me. I was wrapped up in my own world and I'm a shitty friend and because of that, he's gone."

"No. You did as much as you could with the tools and knowledge you had. You have to tell yourself that. I repeat these words to myself every day, like a mantra."

I look long and hard at him. "When did you start to really believe these words?"

He gives me a tired shrug. "I'll let you know when it happens."

Two hours, and half a box of Kleenex later, we finish our interview. For the first time, I feel a tiny glimmer of hope, like I won't be sad forever, like I have a future after Stephen.

Yeah, fine, about fifty times I wanted him to stop filming so that I could run away, but I felt like I owed it to Stephen

356

to be brave and soldier on, so that's what I did. I thought the easiest part would be sharing all the positive stuff about Stephen, all the good times, but it turns out, that was the hardest.

I will miss him every day for the rest of my life. But I also understand that I have to get on with my life, that living well is my obligation. It's on me to fulfill his promise for both of us now.

(Mental note: Owen says I should continue work on the sex robot in his honor, whenever I get back in that headspace.)

"You did great, Kent. Thanks, bro. I hope this film helps people. I feel like the more we discuss the impact of suicide within the Gatekeepers, the more safeguards we put in place, the better we'll be going forward," Owen says.

I wonder what Stephen would think about Owen being the one to memorialize his life.

That he'd probably hate it brings a wry smile to my face.

"I'm glad we've reconnected. You grew up to be a really good guy."

"Hey, man, thanks. You, too." Owen begins to busy himself disassembling his camera rigging.

"Would it be weird to say that I wish you and Simone would have worked out?" I ask, gathering up the used tissues.

He shrugs. "Not weird. I really vibed with her and I thought she might feel the same, but then, I was a vapor trail. I don't blame her, I was in a bad place. In terms of choosing between us, let's see…fucked-up stoner or Mr. Class President? Hell, *I'd* pick him. Dude's a catch."

"You're selling yourself short," I say. "Plus, I'm starting to get a weird feeling about Liam."

"Yeah? How's that?"

"Eh, can't put my finger on it. I mean, he's nice and all, but there's something off. Like in an old Japanese horror movie where the dialogue doesn't quite line up with how the actor moves his mouth?" I say.

"You talkin' *Mothra vs. Godzilla*?" Owen asks.

"Or *Godzilla vs. Mechagodzilla*."

"Which, in my opinion was the best of the Godzillas," Owen says.

"Right?" I exclaim. "I forgot you were a fan. Jesus, it's been too long. Have you ever seen *Terror of Mechagodzilla*?"

"Seen it? I got a download of it right here," he says, pointing to his laptop. "I am super into Japanese horror movies right now, particularly the directors. Tell me you've seen Shimizu's *The Grudge*."

"Yeah, only about ten times."

We smack our palms together in a high five. After the gut-wrenching dialogue over the past two hours, it's a little surreal to suddenly shift into being two regular bros hanging out, talking about old monster flicks.

While it's not yet getting better, per se, Owen's right, I can see the very beginning of it getting different.

For now, that'll do.

35

SIMONE

"HE SAID *WHAT*?"

"It's madness, right?" I say, after recounting the whole Jasper conversation with Liam.

"You think you know who your friends are and then they pull something like this? With your girlfriend? That's such bullshit. You've been through enough with Stephen, Jasper shooting off his mouth is the last thing you need."

How can I be so sure that Liam is fine, despite what I hear from the naysayers?

Because he was an absolute angel when he found out about Stephen. He snuck over and scaled the wall to my room that night. Then he held me while I cried my heart out. The next day, he cut class with me and drove me down to the city so I could place Stephen's North Shore hat at the base of the Bean in memoriam. Liam could not have been more loving or attentive or thoughtful, none of which would have been possible if he were all, I don't know, *tripped out* or whatever.

Right now, Liam's particularly agitated and has yet to sit down. He paces around his bedroom while we talk. I keep gesturing for him to come sit beside me, but he's too keyed up.

"Could Jasper *be* any more of a hypocrite?" he says.

"I made that exact point," I reply. I feel like a coach watching a boxing match, anxious to towel and water Liam, to patch up his cuts the second the round is over. I pat the spot on the bed next to me, encouraging him to join me. He ignores my invitation.

"This kid was sneaking 40s into the movies when we were in junior high! He was drinking in eighth grade! He's, like, a waste of a human being. He's a *garbage* person."

"That's a bit harsh," I say, shifting positions. I don't want to defend Jasper but don't want to excoriate him in that manner, either. Had he not invited me to his party back in October, I might have never connected with Liam. And for both of us, that night was a game-changer.

"*Pfft*, if you knew half the stunts that kid's pulled, you wouldn't be saying anything nice," he replies. "Case in point? Baby Jesus. Each year, he thinks it's hilarious to swipe every single Christ child out of every single manger on display at the holidays. They talk about him on the news—they call him the Grinch. He has hundreds of them in his closet. *Hundreds*. You know, he vandalized the stop signs, too."

About a month ago, every sign within a two-mile radius had been altered in the night. Some read Don't Stop, Can't Stop; some Stop, Collaborate, and Listen. There were a few Don't Stop Believin's, a handful of Stop, Hammer-Times, and the one that made me laugh out loud was Stop Defacing Signs. My dad went mad; he made me ride around with him to find all of them, like a vandalism Easter egg hunt. Said they were the best thing he'd seen in this country so far.

"Those were funny," I admit.

"Seriously?" Liam says, looking a tad disgusted.

"What? Clever is clever. Dad got a huge kick out of them."

Then I clarify, "Still, yes, he's a juvenile delinquent, which makes his accusations even more vile."

"Thank you," he replies, mollified. I reach out for him and he takes my hand, finally allowing himself a seat. I lean into him but he doesn't lean back.

I muse, "What did he mean by saying the conversation wasn't over?"

Liam pushes his fingers through his hair. "Who knows with that one? Given his track record, probably nothing. He's all talk."

Jasper is not all talk.

He spoke with Liam's parents. Squealed on him is more like it. Suffice it to say, the conversation did not go well...for Liam.

Thanks to Jasper's interfering, Liam's lost his car, cell phone, and computer privileges. He's essentially under house arrest, permitted to leave for school and student government meetings, where his mother picks him up and drops him off. The only time I can see him is at school.

The whole thing is so awful.

If these Draconian measures weren't bad enough, I'm in a world of trouble, too.

We'd just sat down to dinner—wings again, Dad's become a tremendous fan of buffalo chicken wings, largely because he can't get enough of anything served with ranch dressing—when there was a knock at our front door.

The sound was less of a *knock* and more the noise of someone trying to break the damn thing down with bare hands. Warhol immediately hid, hero that he's not, but Dad marched into the foyer, armed with a broomstick and false bravado.

"What are you planning to do, Angus? Housekeep them into submission?" my mum asked, chasing behind him.

"Stay back, Fi," he warned. Without a peek through the spyhole, he swung the door open, expecting to come face to face with some variety of criminal, but instead found a bony woman in equestrian gear and a man who looked less like a thug and more like the president of a real estate investment trust.

Liam's parents.

"We need to talk about your daughter," said Liam's dad, forcing his way past my father and into our foyer. His dad is built like a former college athlete who's now stuck riding a desk all day long, so he brushed past my dad without any difficulty.

Everything about Liam's dad is the antithesis of mine—where Mr. Avery's hair is short and neatly barbered, my dad's is chin-length and perpetually swept up in a man-bun. Mr. Avery is tall and solidly muscular, while my dad trends pasty with an odd confluence of flabby pectorals and skinny limbs. Where Mr. Avery seems to live in a blue pinstripe business suit, forever looking like he's just stepped out of a board meeting, my dad favors long jumpers, paint-splattered track pants, and flip-flops, perhaps more like the man who might ask Mr. Avery for a quarter on the street outside his office in the Loop.

Mr. Avery was pleasant the couple of times I've been around him, but I realized that was for appearance's sake. The real measure of a man is how he treats others when no one's looking. He's been perpetually cruel to Liam, physically, when he was younger, and now, verbally. In eighth grade, Liam had to fib and say he'd fallen to explain the wrist his father broke when Liam accidentally smashed his mother's Waterford vase while roughhousing with Jasper. Jasper's folks sent over five new ones to replace the one that broke, but it didn't matter.

I suspect that Liam has had a harder time dealing with the

mental aspect—with physical, the wounds heal eventually. If Liam brings home an A, his dad will grill him on why it wasn't an A+. When Liam made the varsity team as a sophomore, his dad was all over him about why he wasn't a starting player. No matter how good Liam is and has been, it's never enough for his father.

Our two dads stood there for a moment, sizing one another up. Liam's father looked like a rogue bull elephant, ready to begin stomping at any moment. Dad had his chest all puffed up, trying to be tough, but ultimately failing and defaulting to being British instead.

"Name's Angus Chastain, and you are?" Dad asked. He reached out to shake Mr. Avery's hand, but he was still holding the broomstick. Mr. Avery wasn't interested in taking the eventually empty hand Dad proffered.

"We're Liam's parents. We're here to talk about her." Mr. Avery glowered at me, his emphasis on the word *her*, like the word was particularly bitter in his mouth.

"Her name is *Simone*. What about Simone?" Mum said with a preternatural calm. She positioned me behind her, a lioness shielding her cub.

"She's had a terrible influence on our Liam," Mr. Avery replied. "And now he's in the shitter, which is clearly *her* doing."

That's when Dad laughed, sure that this was all a case of mistaken identity. The look the Averys gave him in response was downright murderous.

"I don't understand. Simone isn't permitted to see your son," Mum replied. She straightened her back while she spoke, as though someone suddenly stuck a steel rod in her spine. When completely upright, Mum's almost six feet tall and quite imposing, far more than Dad. "No. You must be mistaken. That's impossible. Right, Simba?"

I've started to sweat. Rivulets of liquid panic roll down my back. I try to speak but my throat is too dry, too constricted to form proper words, particularly under the Averys' hostile gazes.

"Impossible?" Liam's mom snorted. "She's at our house every day. If you were the kind of people who kept track of their kid, you'd know."

Both my parents turned to look at me and I found myself wishing the ground would split open and swallow me whole. I'd wondered if my lies wouldn't eventually catch up to me, but I never envisioned this.

"Simba," Mum asked, her normally firm voice taking on a pleading edge. "That's impossible, yes? You've been at the newspaper."

I shook my head, not able to look in her eyes, incapable of making a sound.

"Oh, Sim," Dad said, sounding more hurt and disappointed than angry.

Mr. Avery gestured toward me. "You keep her *away* from Liam, understand? She stays away from our son or there will be consequences."

"Beg your pardon, but it almost sounds as though you're threatening our daughter," Mum said, attempting to clarify a situation that I'd later describe as surreal, even though Dad despises my perpetual misuse of the term *surreal*. Makes me put a dollar in a biscuit tin when he catches me saying it. He says surreal is not being lectured by bullies in a foyer, surreal is Magritte's bowler-hatted, bespoke men raining down on row houses.

"That's not a threat," Liam's mother said, jaw set and arms firmly crossed, clutching her own elbows. For all the muffins she bakes and the good morning hugs and darling Homecoming posters, I suddenly saw the ice queen Mrs. Avery was back in her advertising agency days. "That's a *promise*."

"Your Liam has problems," Mum said, her own frosty calm turning into something else. "Problems he had before he ever met Simone. I'll thank you not to come into my home and make baseless accusations."

"Let's do the math here," Liam's dad responded, his lip curled into a sneer. "Liam was the perfect kid, an ideal student, and a dedicated athlete a couple of months ago. But now that he's hooked up with this one—" he thrust his chin in my direction "—I'm hearing that he's taking drugs and lying about college applications. Hmm, let me think about that...before meeting Simone, Liam was headed to Princeton. After meeting Simone, he's on the path to heading to, I don't know, *prison*? You claim she's innocent, but she lives here, with you...two *bohemians*. Read about you on the internet. Real nice example you've set." He let out a cruel laugh. "Yeah, sure sounds like *Liam's* the problem. Let me tell you this, he will be fine again the second she's out of his life. This isn't him, this is *her*."

"Let me tell you this," Mum hissed, her patience spent. "Your 'golden child' was high the first night we met him. Get your house in order before making accusations in mine."

I ached to talk to Liam, to hear what had happened to him before all of this, to offer some sort of comfort. As impossible as his father was when he'd done well, but not well enough, I was terrified of how Mr. Avery might have reacted to hearing anything negative about Liam—anything that could somehow reflect badly on himself. I wouldn't sleep a wink that night, agonizing over Liam's state of mind.

"Let *me* tell *you* this," Liam's dad countered, inching closer to my mum. I was holding my breath, waiting for someone to throw a punch, and I feared it would be my mum who struck the first blow. "If I see her around my kid again, then I—"

"Wait," my dad said, inserting himself between them, always opting to be peacemaker over the antagonist. Dad rarely fought; he was much more likely to work out his emotions through his art. I half suspected he'd whip out some colored pencils and paper, instructing us all to sketch our feelings. "Let me stop you all right there. So, you don't want your son to see our daughter, yeah? And we don't fancy having our daughter around your son. Looks to me that we're on the same page. We want the same thing. I'd say we've accomplished our mission here and there's nothing left to discuss. We'll call it a night before this gets even more ugly, right?"

That seemed to take the wind out of Mr. Avery's sails, yet he was determined to have the last word. "You make sure she stays away."

"We will," Mum said, nodding. "We will do that because we're her parents and we love her and even as virtual strangers, we can see your son is on a collision course with trouble. We'll gladly keep close watch on our daughter because wherever your son is headed, we'd prefer he not drag her down with him."

Mrs. Avery began to protest, but Mum shut her down, adding, "If you don't see that, if you can't comprehend that your Liam might have issues, despite every advantage you've given him, despite being exemplary parents, whatever happens next is your fault and your responsibility."

In a softer voice, Mum continues. "I've seen what drug use can do to the most talented among us, so I'm begging you to find him help. Regard this as a serious threat. With our daughter removed from the equation, you might assume your problem's solved. Simone's not the issue, despite your beliefs.

Your son is wrestling his own demons. Get him to treatment. Now. Please. This isn't the time to punish him, this isn't the time to rend your garments or cast blame. Reach out because it's not too late. Too many tragic things have already happened in this community this year. *Help* him. Don't let your child become another statistic. I beg of you, don't ignore what's going on under your own roof."

"Uh-huh," Mr. Avery replied, dismissing everything my mum had just said. "Follow your own advice. Get *your* house in order before you go looking for trouble in mine."

With that, the Averys left. I wanted to warn Liam, to tell him what to expect, but I had a feeling reaching him would be impossible. And I was right.

Dad closed the door behind them and collapsed a little bit as he leaned against it. The whole interchange had zapped him of his spirit. I hated that they had to witness anything unpleasant and that I was the cause of their unhappiness.

Mum turned to me. I braced myself for yelling or accusations or for the firm hand of justice. Instead, with the saddest eyes in the world, Mum simply asked, "Why did you lie, Sim? I'm not angry, I'm confused. Please tell us why."

I had to tell them the truth.

"I lied because I love him."

"Oy, Simba that's not enough reason," my dad said, squeezing me tight so that I was mashed against his scratchy cardigan. "That's never enough reason."

"Sim, sweetie, the boy is in danger, and by association, he's endangering you. We can't let that happen. We exist to keep you safe. I've always trusted your judgment before, but now? Now I'm not sure what to think."

"It's just a few pain pills," I argued. "Prescription stuff. No big deal. Liam is ridiculously smart and he knows what he's doing. He can stop any time he'd like."

Dad sighed. "Never in the history of ever has that phrase proven true, Sim." He pulled me in closer and planted a kiss on my forehead.

Mum said, "Love, I hope you won't mind excusing us. Your father and I should talk."

"Don't you want me to be part of the conversation? We always talk as a family," I said.

"We speak as a family when we function as a family," she replied. "Off you go."

My feet felt like those heavy boots the old-timey scuba divers used to wear to keep themselves pinned to the ocean's floor, but I made myself climb the stairs to my room anyway. I couldn't bear to be around my folks right then, even if they had wanted to be with me.

I stripped off my sweat-soaked shirt as I reached the top of the stairs, anxious to shed at least one item that was weighing me down. The air meeting my bare, damp skin gave me goose bumps. I found Warhol camped out on my bed, vibrating with nervous energy, tail thumping a million miles an hour, sitting next to my phone. In a panic, I grabbed it and texted, u there?

I never received a response.

I learned the next morning that Liam has lost use of any way to communicate with me because his parents are serious about punishing him.

How he's being disciplined pales in comparison to what mine have decided to do to me.

We're moving back to London at the end of the term.

36

===

MALLORY

"HEY, STRANGER, WHERE have you been hiding?"

Liam brushes past, not even turning to look at me. Did he not hear? I try again, louder this time. "Liam, hi! Didn't see you at the last couple of Gatekeeper meetings. Will you be there this afternoon? This is the big day!"

Mr. Gorton lobbied for and won approval from the school board to approach the Parents' Association. He spoke to the PA last night in a closed-door meeting to discuss imposing limits on our workload. With their approval, the teachers will have a finite amount of homework they can assign, which should lessen the burden on each student, hence allowing us more time to decompress. Mr. Gorton's going to brief us on the specifics of the agreement at Gatekeepers today.

The whole Association meeting has been such a big deal, it even pinged my mother's radar.

"Assignment limits? Never going to happen," she told me yesterday, after she'd skimmed a couple of emails about the Gatekeeper's proposal. She had her iPad in one hand, balanced on her knees, and her third (fourth?) glass of wine in the other.

"Of course it will," I said. "The Association would be foolish to deny our request for relief."

"Foolish or not, never going to happen," she replied, tabbing from her email back over to ShopBop.com.

"Disagree. It's the only logical course of action," I argued.

I resented the way she was smirking at me, like she knew something I didn't. Sometimes I think she gets off on taking the counterpoint, no matter what it is. I could be all, "Here's why it's important we protect the environment," and she'd go off on a tangent about how convenient non-recyclable plastic bags are and why everyone's better off using disposable diapers.

"We're not asking for a three-day school week or anything. Just some guidelines on amounts of homework assigned and test frequency. We had teachers and guidance counselors help us phrase our request. They're on board. What's to object? We're trying to save lives."

As my mother perused ShopBop's shoe section, she explained, "Mallory, the objection is pure economics. Decrease competition by limiting workload and test scores go down. When test scores go down, property values decrease. Property values go down, the tax base decreases. High net worth individuals flee because their properties' values are diminishing, and then the town loses even more revenue from its tax base. Less tax base negatively impacts the school. Then the quality of education suffers and the school can't hire the best teachers and then the whole thing is a vicious downward spiral. Schools are the linchpin of the community. No one's going to mess with a good thing. North Shore has a vested interest in maintaining the status quo. So, sorry, never going to happen."

That is *ridiculous*.

I said, "No one would be so callous when lives are at stake."

370

She shrugged. "Facts are facts. Take Arizona, for example. They estimate how many prison beds they'll need based on standardized testing of third grade reading scores."

I snorted. "So, what, you're saying if we have one hour less of Trig homework a night, we're all going to turn into criminals? That's a stretch. I mean, with the rash of suicides here, we have to do something. Do people not love their kids?"

She sipped her wine and put a pair of suede Rag and Bone booties in her shopping cart. "People love their children. They also love their status. While I wish you luck with your little proposal, don't be surprised when the Association votes no."

As there's no one in North Shore as narcissistic as my mother (save, possibly, for Mr. Avery) I chose not to believe her skewed worldview. I'm confident the Parents' Association will do the right thing.

"Remember?" I prompt, trotting up to Liam. "The big meeting was last night?"

"Uh-huh," he replies, accelerating his pace down the hall. What's up with that? I thought he and I were cool. I didn't make him being with Simone into a thing. I let it all go graciously. I'm even nice to Simone because she seems to be into the Gatekeepers. We're on the same team.

Now that I'm out of Liam's orbit, I see how we weren't good together. Not enough contrast between us. He probably relates better to Simone's lack of intensity. Or maybe he's just into hideous trousers.

(Sorry, it had to be said. Harem pants will never be the new black.)

"You won't be there?" I press, breaking into a slight jog to keep up with him. "Today's meeting's too important for us not to show up in full force."

Being involved with the Gatekeepers is exactly what I've

needed. Without them, I would spend all day staring at Braden's email log-in and I can't do that. I have to get on with my life. I have so much untapped energy now that the field hockey season is over, it feels good to pour it into something with an actual purpose and not just debating fonts for the Italian Club mixer invite.

Being with this group makes me realize that we're all going through something and the best way to get through it is to rely on each other. I mean, who'd have guessed that Owen Freaking Foley-Feinstein would end up back in my and Theo's life, and that we'd both be thankful every day for him? If Braden felt like he could have leaned on a collective group of us, like he had more of a formal support system, maybe everything would have been different. Maybe we could have helped Paulie and Macey. Maybe Stephen would still be here, ruining the curve for everyone.

I so wish we'd come together sooner. I wish we hadn't each been battling everything on our own. But we're here now, collectively strong, and that's the best we can do.

Liam stares straight ahead while I scurry alongside. "Can't make it, sorry."

Perspiration streams down from his hairline, soaking his shirt collar. "Hey, are you okay?" I ask.

"I'm fine."

"You don't look fine. You're sweating even though it's so cold and—"

He grabs my wrist. "What is it that you need right now, Mallory?"

I extricate myself from his grip and shake out my hand. Not cool. "Whoa, Liam, manhandle much? I better not have a bruise. Ow. Seriously, *ouch*. I just wanted to see how you were doing."

"Whatever."

Liam is practically running away from me now.

"*Whatever*? I think the words you're looking for are '*I'm sorry, Mallory.*'"

He turns around to flip me the bird and I notice the black eye and split lip right before he turns the corner and vanishes from sight.

Oh, no, Liam.

Jasper comes up behind me. "You okay, Malady?" he asks, genuinely concerned.

If someone had told me at the beginning of the semester that not only would I be BFFs with Owen, but that Liam would regard me as the enemy and Jasper would be my ally, I'd have laughed. Yet here we are.

Jasper and I made peace with the advent of the Gatekeepers. He's as concerned as the rest of us with helping the kids in our school, so I've stopped being so hard on him. I promised I'd stop calling him the JasHole and he pledged to stop being one.

So far, we're both keeping our word.

I mean, yes, his first inclination was to throw a huge party for the Gatekeepers, but he was reasonable when I objected.

"Um, Jasper? Is free and easy access to unlimited liquor the *best* idea right now?" I'd asked. Our group had just been discussing the link between the increase in adolescent alcohol use and suicidal ideation.

"Valid point, Mallomar," he'd replied. He's finally taken to making plays on my name, after all these years. I'm shocked to find this endearing. (It's an entirely different universe around here now, I'm telling you.) "We need to do something, though."

As an alternative, his dad rented a whole bowling alley and chartered buses so that we could have an all-school outing. The event ended up being awesome. Everyone agreed it was so refreshing to participate in a sport where our futures didn't depend on the final score. Most of the student body attended and it was hilarious to see some our elite athletes tossing gutter balls, while people like Kent completely slayed.

The night felt like we were all part of something bigger than ourselves.

Jasper and I were paired up at the outing. Despite initial trepidations, we were high-fiving and performing victory dances by the end of the night. I may even have admitted I didn't hate his look—grass-green cords with tiny candy canes embroidered on them. We bonded and we're firmly on the same side now.

"You have any clue what's going on with Liam?" I asked. "He practically just ripped my head off. I thought he and I were cool."

Jasper shrugs. "Can't tell ya what's up. He's stopped talking to me."

"You're kidding!" I stop in my tracks. "Since when? You *luff* him." I make a little heart with my hands to demonstrate my point. "You guys are BFFs."

A flash of something—sadness? regret?—crosses his normally implacable face. "*Were*, past tense. I talked to his parents about his new drug habit. I even implicated myself, saying I'd supplied him in the beginning. I thought that might afford him some protection, given how his folks are always sucking up to mine. But you saw his face." He gestures toward his eye and lip. "That'd be a *no*."

Before we can discuss this further, the warning bell rings and we have to go to class.

"I'm legit worried," he says. "We need to do something. I'm gonna rally the troops for lunch to discuss a strategy. You in, Maladjusted?"

I nod. "Count on it."

★ ★ ★

Owen, Theo, Kent, Jasper, and I are meeting to download what happened with Liam. We're an odd fivesome; not a group you'd ever imagine together, sort of like our own Breakfast Club, Generation Z–style.

"He's all agitated now? As in aggro?" Owen asks. "I saw him barf in the sink in the men's room yesterday. Said he'd had some bad fish. That makes no sense. I was, like, 'On Sloppy Joe Day? Who eats fish on Sloppy Joe Day?'"

"He couldn't sit still in class this morning," Jasper adds. "His knee was bouncing so hard, Mr. Lawless had to say something."

"Withdrawals," Kent says, his lips forming a thin, grim line.

Kent still doesn't talk much when we're together as a group. Yet when he does speak, his thoughts always add value and I'm grateful for his input. He'd have been an excellent peer counselor. For everything bad that's happened this semester, I'm finding a few silver linings. Having the collective wisdom of the Gatekeepers behind me is at the top of that list.

"Withdrawals? That sucks," Owen says.

"Wouldn't withdrawals mean the drugs are leaving his system? Seems like that's *good* news," I say.

Kent replies, "Yeah, jury's still out on that. Simone says his parents went batshit, really cracking the whip."

To himself, Jasper mutters, "Literally and figuratively."

I chose not to elaborate for the group to help Liam keep some semblance of dignity.

Kent says, "From what I've pieced together, doesn't sound like he's getting help. His mom and dad are just sweeping the whole thing under the rug."

"They aren't putting him in treatment?" I ask. "Even outpatient?"

Kent shakes his head.

"That's a *bad* idea. You've got to figure the pills were just the symptom—there's something bigger going on there, right?" Theo says.

We all nod. Jasper clenches and unclenches his fists, as though he wouldn't mind punching something, or, rather, someone. When they were kids, Liam spent every waking moment at Jasper's place to avoid his dad's wrath.

Theo adds, "If his family doesn't figure out the root of his problem, then how's he ever going to get past it? Denial works...until it doesn't." The Gatekeepers has brought a hidden depth out of my brother. I'm so proud of him. He's a lot more like Holden than I ever realized.

Kent explains, "Simone's only allowed to see Liam at school and now they're moving back to England way early. Her folks say it's because her dad can't seem to work here, but I bet it's because of Liam. She can't stay away."

Theo picks at a rough part of his cast. "What a clusterfuck."

"Her leaving is going to be really bad for Liam," I say.

Kent says, "She's the only person he's even talking to."

Jasper says, "You know, he's not been without a girlfriend since, like, the fourth grade. He's not so great on his own."

"What can we do for him?" I ask. "How do we go about, I don't know, gatekeeping him?"

Owen says, "Dude's a freaking powder keg right now."

Jasper adds, "Seeing him yelling at you in the hallway, Malcontent? That's not the L–Money I know. I remember him microwaving hot cocoa to give to the mailman on snow days. I'd be like, 'What are you doing?' He'd say it wasn't fair for the mailman to have to work when the weather was bad, so he wanted to do what he could to make the day easier for him. Who does that?"

"We need to keep an eye on him," Kent says.

Owen replies, "For sure. Mr. Gorton says that someone else's suicide suddenly puts the option on the table for others. We've gotta be vigilant."

"Agreed, but how do we help someone who wants nothing to do with us?" I ask.

Owen sighs. "That's, like, the million-dollar question."

All of us Gatekeepers are gathered, waiting for Mr. Gorton to begin the meeting. People are starting to glance at the time on their phones; he's never late. Simone has just shown up and I'm surprised to see her here without Liam. She peers anxiously around the room for a minute before she picks the seat next to me, and when she does sit, she barely inhabits the chair. She looks ready to spring up and run away at any moment, a kitten spooked by loud noises and quick movements.

"Mallory, hey, have you, um...seen Liam? You have an afternoon class together, right?" she asks. She sounds tentative, like she's afraid to even speak to me. Her (clueless) bravado from the day I met her is long gone. She seems diminished somehow, as though no longer firing on all pistons. Like she's traveling at half speed.

"Haven't run into him since this morning," I reply. I noticed he wasn't in our AP Statistics class sixth period and I wondered if he'd cut in order to avoid me, but I don't say that. I don't say anything about his terrible behavior. She seems so breakable right now, all hollowed out and made of glass, and I feel protective. So I offer, "Maybe he went home sick?"

"Yeah, maybe," she echoes, but doesn't seem convinced. She toys with her Cheerios bracelet, talking to me from behind her curtain of hair. The blue has long since washed away. "Does...he seem 'off' to you?"

I don't want to sound like a jealous ex-girlfriend but I do want to express concern, so I tread lightly here. "We don't talk now, so this isn't firsthand knowledge. From what I hear, he's not been himself."

The poor girl looks so glum, so bereft of her (annoying) joie de vivre, which has faded much like her indigo bangs. I add, "The semester's been really hard on all of us."

The door to the lecture hall swings open and Vice Principal Torres enters. Following him is Principal Gottfried, who strides in on her tottering heels and power suit. She used to teach second grade reading at my elementary school, so it's still weird to see her here, all professionally dressed and blown-dry. I still picture her in her fuzzy cardigans and pretty, flowered skirts, untamed curls spilling halfway down her back. She'd hug us when we'd sound out particularly big words and she always smelled like chocolate chip cookies.

Principal Gottfried was involved in some big brouhaha when I was in fifth grade. Something about teachers coaching students on their standardized tests? I guess the superintendent was having an affair with the elementary school's principal and they were working together to inflate our scores so that the principal would be granted a raise. Principal Gottfried, who was Miss Gottfried back then, was the whistleblower on the whole thing.

I was young at the time, so I was never quite clear on all the details of the scandal. But it was so bad that half the town stopped talking to the other half. One group of parents was outraged that their kids were essentially cheating/ being cheated and the other half was outraged to hear their kids weren't as gifted as the tests results indicated. My mom stopped doing yoga with a whole group of her girlfriends. While I'd like to believe she was one of the people outraged about the cheating, my gut says she was actually Team Special Snowflake.

Principal Gottfried clears her throat and approaches the lectern with a piece of paper in her hands. She dons a pair of bifocals and reads, "Students, I regret to inform you that your club is not officially recognized by North Shore High School. As unrecognized clubs are not covered by the district's insurance policy, they are forbidden to assemble anywhere on the NSHS grounds for liability reasons. Further, they are barred from use of any and all school resources, both material goods as well as intellectual property, which includes the North Shore Knights website and all other forms of social media."

We all look at each other in wild confusion.

"What does that even mean?" Jasper demands.

Principal Gottfried glances down at the sheet of paper. Dolefully, she says, "That means the Gatekeepers can't exist here on campus, Mr. Gates."

The entire room begins to buzz and dozens of hands shoot up in the air.

"The Gatekeepers are important," Owen protests, not even waiting for her to call on him. "What are we supposed to do? There's, like, at least fifty of us in every meeting. Are we supposed to all cram into a Starbucks or something? I feel like you're playing lawyer-ball right now."

"I'm sorry you feel that way. I'm afraid my hands are tied. The school can't condone any unofficial activities."

Owen persists, "Then how do we become all North Shore-official?"

Without meeting his eye, she says, "To be recognized, your organization will need to pursue a charter."

"Why didn't you say so?" Owen says. "Let's do that."

Principal Gottfried grasps the sides of the lectern and gazes

379

out at us with the same kind of expression she'd wear when classmates would stumble over words when reading aloud. "Unfortunately, Mr. Foley-Feinstein, we can't accept new charters this far into the academic year. We encourage you to submit in the fall."

"That's too late! Half of us will have graduated by then!" Kent exclaims, in the loudest voice I've ever heard him use. He flies up from his seat, his cheeks flushed with rage. The fire in his eyes takes me by surprise. "Just admit that the school board doesn't want us to exist. I mean, if you guys were behind us, then you'd have to accept responsibility for overworking us."

She says, "Mr. Mathers, Counselor Gorton presented your ideas to the Parents' Association last night *with the school board's blessing.* However, there was a vote and…" She exhales and glances down at her paper again, as though it might somehow help her. "I'm afraid the majority of your parents did not agree that the standards should be lowered or workloads decreased. And, unfortunately, these same parents insisted your group be formally recognized with a charter, which is why you have to disband."

We sit in stunned silence.

She removes her glasses and rubs her eyes, her tone decidedly gentle, reminiscent of the days when she was still Miss Gottfried. "I'm so sorry. We support you, but our hands are tied. Ultimately, we have to answer to your parents."

I can't believe my mother was right.

Jasper stands. "Where's Mr. Gorton?"

The principal's expression morphs from apologetic to downright pained. "Counselor Gorton is taking some personal time. Now, students, I have to ask you to please vacate this room."

37

SIMONE

"I'M TAKING WARHOL out for a little jog around the neighborhood."

My parents installed tracking software on my phone, so walking the dog is the only way I can leave without suspicion. I'm worried sick about Liam—he disappeared without a word after lunch. I waited for him at his locker and he never showed. I'd hoped he'd attend the Gatekeepers meeting, but there was no sign of him. I can't try his house, obviously, but I have a feeling he's not there anyway. Mallory suggested he might be at the bluff, so checking there seems to be the best plan.

"Can't hear you, be out in a sec," Mum says from her darkroom. Because we're leaving so much sooner than we'd planned, she's been working 'round the clock to get all her photos in line. She said she can do the actual writing back in London, where it's safer for me. I pointed out the irony of them assuming I'd be more secure in one of the largest cities in the world, currently plagued by the threat of global terror, but no one thought I was clever.

I fought the decision, but ultimately I was outvoted.

I'm heartsick.

Liam believes we can still make it work, him and me. He's decided to take the University of Florida scholarship. He's not thrilled about playing soccer, but he says he'd rather be a Gator than be beholden to his father for one more minute.

Even though I'm going back to England now, I hope to return in the fall for college. I'll apply to U of Florida the minute my ACT scores are in. Wouldn't that be lovely, to be somewhere balmy with Liam, palm trees gently swaying in the breeze, finally away from all forces trying to keep us apart?

I realize this all sounds vaguely Capulets and Montagues, yet I feel our plan is feasible. And at some point, his parents will relent, once they realize this addiction nonsense is just that—nonsense. Overblown fantasies from watching too many episodes of *Dateline*, which is Dad's newest obsession.

Once Dad's away from the telly and home in an environment that inspires him, I'll stop bearing the brunt of his artistic block.

Mum emerges from her darkroom and glances out the window. "What were you saying, Sim?"

"I'm taking Warhol for a walk."

"Bloody freezing out there, isn't it? You really want to walk him?"

"He's restless," I say. "Plus, look at his bottom, see how fat he's become? He's porky from all the training treats. Tubby could use a bit of exercise."

"Okay, but take your phone," she says.

"Naturally," I reply.

I bundle Warhol into a bright yellow sweater and clip on his leash. I take my time going outdoors, so I don't appear too anxious. I don't start jogging until I'm down the block, then beelining due east to the bluff Mallory described.

Warhol and I are in a full-on run when I spot a bit of Liam's navy-and-silver North Shore letterman's jacket from the stone path that borders the bluff. He's here, with his legs curled into himself, looking out at the lake from under all the branches. Thank God.

Relief washes over me. I loosen my death grip on Warhol's leash, shaking out my hand so the circulation returns. Warhol, delighted to be out adventuring, yanks me along, causing me to go even faster. He's not supposed to pull, but I'm too distracted to worry about proper training.

Liam glances up at us as we make our way down to him. "Hey," he slurs. "I know you."

My reprieve from panic is short-lived.

This is wrong. The feeling of dread begins to creep in, quietly nipping at my heels, wrapping its cold fingers around my neck.

"Liam, what happened to you this afternoon?" I ask, trying to keep the dismay out of my voice. "Where'd you go?"

"Hello, doggie!" He tries to scoop Warhol up in a sloppy embrace. The dog isn't used to such an effusive return of affection and slips out of his arms. Warhol looks at me as if to say, *What's all this, then?*

Liam crawls out from under the pine canopy and struggles to his feet. He's disjointed and rubbery as he tries to give me a hug. He's moving as though he's trying to walk through water. His pupils are tiny pinpoints, even though it's dusk.

"Are you okay?" I ask, searching his face. I want him to say yes, even though in my gut, I know he's not. I can hear my dad's voice in my head saying that this is not what okay looks like.

Something is profoundly off.

His lips curl into a grin. "I am out-freaking-standing. I am A-okay. I am Liam!" He throws his arms in the air like that cheerleader at Jasper's party whenever they played her jam. The motion causes him to stagger before he catches himself.

Something here is very, very off.

"What's wrong with your voice? You're raspy."

"Raaaaaahhhhspy. That? That is a fun word. Raaaaaahhhhspy."

"Liam, talk to me," I say. I sound like I'm pleading and Warhol picks up on the stress in my voice, the sharp quick notes. The dog loved Liam when they met the first time, but now seems anxious to move along. "What's going on?"

"We just went ahead and fixed the glitch," he says, quoting the Bobs from *Office Space*, the first movie we ever watched together. I'd not heard of it, but he promised me it was a cult classic in this country and I couldn't consider myself truly American until I'd seen it. Didn't care for the film, actually. Made me question why everyone in the school is working so hard to get into a good college so they can get a degree, only to land a job that's nothing but useless TPS reports and eleven bosses.

With the leash looped on my wrist, I grip Liam's arms, shaking him to get his attention. "What'd you mean by that? Where'd you go?"

"Met my friend."

"What friend?"

"Harry Jones." Then he giggles, but the sound that comes out isn't like his regular laugh. It's all high-pitched and shriek-y. Warhol tugs the leash, as though he wants to leave. "Harry Jones. Jarry Hones. Harry Jonesing."

Harry Jones…according to *Dateline*, that's slang for heroin. My knees buckle beneath me and I brace myself with a tree limb to stay upright. It's as though someone sucked all the air from my lungs and I'm gasping for breath through a cocktail straw. I feel like I'm looking at Liam through an entirely different pair of eyes. He's become a photonegative where the dark spots are light and the light dark. This is him in front of me, yet entirely different, terribly skewed and disturbing.

Oh, how stupid am I?

How could I buy the lies he's been selling me?

How did I not see this coming?

Was I blind by choice? By love? By my own innocence?

Ultimately, the reasons don't matter. I'm a right fool because Liam is high. Liam's not just high, but he's *chasing the goddamned dragon*. *Dateline's* Lester Holt was right—Liam's moved on from opioids to opiates, exactly like the show predicted. *Dateline* even had a flowchart and he's following it perfectly. Local rumor is the illegal stuff is even easier to score than its prescription cousin and Liam's now living proof.

Goddamn it again.

I wrestle him off the ground and up the bluff. I seat him on a bench and he squirms around like a toddler who refuses to have his shoes tied. I practically pull teeth to get the barest idea of his afternoon. I glean he was in such a bad way from withdrawals that a quick trip to the rough areas north of town seemed a far better idea than white-knuckling his way through AP Government.

My parents were right.

My parents were right and I'm an idiot and Liam is in too deep. I thought that whatever it was with him and the pills, I could love him past it, but I was kidding myself. Liam's self-destructing, regardless of who cares for him.

Liam is in danger.

"Let's get you home, get you sorted," I say, trying to drag him up by his sleeve.

He remains planted. "Nope. Home is *no bueno.*"

"Liam, please. You can't stay here, you're not safe. Come along, let's go."

He offers me what I assume he believes to be his sweet, slow smile, the one that makes me weak in the knees, but it comes across as rather menacing, particularly with how his tooth catches the split of his lip. I feel a small stab of fear, just a tiny prick, but enough to register.

"Negative."

Warhol's growing more and more tense right alongside me. The fur on the back of his neck rises and he flattens his ears. He lets out a low, guttural growl. "Warhol, behave." I flick the braided leash to quiet him down. "Time to go home."

"Time to stay here."

How messed up is he right now? I can't leave him; what if he takes more? Is he smoking it? Or snorting? I can't imagine him using a needle, but then I never envisioned him doing anything even remotely related to this. We're in uncharted territory. I'm desperately afraid for him.

I look around to see if there's someone I can call for help, but the area's deserted. I'm on my own. This is my problem and mine alone.

He slumps down on the bench and then suddenly he's clawing his legs, as though they're covered with biting insects. Who is he right now? I don't know this man at all. He's almost completely nonsensical and I'm terrified at what might happen next if he's left alone.

I'm starting to fear for my own safety. Yet if I show agitation, I worry the situation will worsen.

Projecting fake serenity, I pretend to keep calm. To carry

on. To channel Queen Elizabeth II when she woke up to find a psychiatric patient had broken into her chambers and was sitting on the edge of her bed. Did she scream or throw punches? No. She kept her head. She was the quintessential Brit, engaging the intruder in polite conversation about his family until a footman woke up and seized him.

As patiently as I'm able, I say, "Do you have anything left from what you bought? You need to give it to me."

He swings his head side to side, as if it were a pendulum, and finally replies, "That does not sound like something I would like to do."

I bend over and bring my face down close to his. My resolve seems icy, but my heart may well fly out of my chest. In my sweetest voice, I tell him, "Listen, Liam. I will fight for you. We didn't come this far for me to not fight for you. I love you, okay? But you've a problem, that's clear now. I'm sorry I didn't see it sooner. I'm sorry I was in denial. Thing is, I will stand beside you. I just need you to get up and give me the drugs."

His eyes, which have always been so soulful and intense, turn cold and hard. He's a stranger to me now, a zombie inhabiting what once was Liam's shell. The outside hasn't changed but the inside's all different.

"Don't think so."

My anger supplants my fear. While I care desperately for Liam, I have no love for this alien in front of me. Fury infuses me with a burst of strength and my muscles feel taut, primed for action. I've always opted for flight, but today I choose fight.

"Damn it, Liam, let's go!" I hook my hand in the space under his arm and pull him up. We're both surprised when I succeed in lifting him off the bench. I pat at his jacket, searching for something, maybe a Ziploc bag or plastic bottle. I locate a small square of folded aluminum foil in his pocket and I take it from him.

I half-expect him to be grateful, to be reticent, to recognize that I love him enough to try to save him from himself.

"NOT YOURS."

With that, he pitches forward, lunging for the packet. Warhol, my sweet little fatty, my loving boy, dives at Liam to protect me, but he's stopped short by the leash. Once Liam reclaims his great prize, he sweeps me aside with his forearm and sends me toppling down onto the rocky path. I land hard, skinning my hands and knees as I stop myself from rolling right off the edge of the ravine. Sharp stones and twigs pierce my skin but the pain of my broken skin has nothing on my breaking heart.

Liam takes off down the path at a slow jog, which is likely faster than my most balls-out sprint, and disappears into the gathering darkness. I'm in such shock that I don't try to follow him.

I don't know what else to do, so I text Kent.

Now that my aggressor is gone, Warhol concentrates on administering first aid via kisses, licking away my tears almost as quickly as they fall.

Almost.

38

KENT

"THIS IS SOME BULLSHIT."

The five of us from lunch head over to the Goodmans' house. I'm so mad about the school board nonsense that I don't even *want* to go exploring in the hopes of finding a stray pair of Mallory's underwear.

(Clarification: I'm not saying I wouldn't be interested to see a thong, I'm just saying that's not my purpose.)

"Is Simone coming?" I ask.

"Nope," Mallory tells me. "Said she had homework. I don't buy it. I feel like she wanted to search for Liam. She told me she was concerned because she spotted his mom's car circling the school. She thought Mrs. Avery was looking for him, too. I'm worried, Kent. What should we do?"

I never thought there'd be a time in my life when Mallory deferred to me. The great irony of this whole situation is that she and I are becoming friends. Like, she's *nice* to me, has been hugging me and stuff and sending me texts to see how I am. I've smelled her hair and everything.

(Very flowery, five stars, would recommend.)

All I want to do is tell Stephen every detail...and then I remember. The most fucked-up part is that she and I wouldn't even be buddies if he were still here.

Believe me, I would trade a lifetime with her for five more minutes with him.

"Specifically, *why* are you worried?" I ask.

"Liam taking off without saying anything is out of character. He's Mr. Can't Be Alone Ever. So I told Simone, if she could, to check out the bluff at the end of Mayflower Road. There's a huge pine tree a couple of steps off the path. I used to sit with him in the open space under the branches. He and I would meet up so he could decompress whenever his dad hurt him."

Owen winces. "Was that, like, a usual thing at his house?"

Jasper and Mallory glance at each other, feeling out what the other person knows.

Jasper says, "The old man stopped knocking Liam around on the reg a couple of years ago. Probably because he got taller than his dad. But the man's still a flaming dickbag to him, which is almost as bad."

"That sucks," I say. "I had no clue. You never really know, do you?"

Mallory nods. "The few times his father lost it when we were together would send Liam reeling. He'd go mute, like, all fragile, forgetting that he was a huge athlete and could punch back ten times harder. I think when you're walked on for so long, you forget you have any power."

Jasper runs a palm over his slicked-back hair. "Everyone deals with something. Some of us are just better at hiding it."

No one comments. We're all surprised to hear any sort of disclosure coming from the guy who embodies "perfect," who's the epitome of "lucky."

Jasper claps his hands together, uncomfortable at our attention. "So, if Simone's handling Liam, what do we do? Malibu,
Kent State, what's the plan?"

"We figure out our next steps for the Gatekeepers," I say,
taking control of the group. "We have to exist, you know?
It's imperative. If we can't work *within* the system, we find a
way around it."

Owen pumps his fist. "*Yaaas*. We owe that to our friends."

I say, "Mallory, you look up how other clubs in schools get
around the no-charter thing. Owen, check out any spaces
in North Shore where we could gather. Could be a church
or a rec center. Jasper, see if you can ballpark costs for us to
open and run our own Gatekeepers center. Theo, find out
who's in the parents' organization. You said your mom's on
the email, maybe everyone's carbon-copied. Let's appeal to
each parent individually, see if we can change their decision.
As for me, I'll try to get in touch with Mr. Gorton."

We each pull out our various electronics. As we work, I
catch Mallory sneaking glances at me. What's that about?
Uh-oh. She can't read my mind about the underpants, right?

"I have his Facebook profile up," I say a few minutes later.
"Gorton posted 'On Administrative Leave, FML.'"

The fuck-my-life abbreviation makes Owen laugh. "FML,
Mr. Gorton? You never consider our teachers or counselors
existing anywhere but in the school, do you? In my head,
it's like they just climb into lockers at the end of the day and
wait for first period the next morning, like putting a ventril-
oquist's dummy back into the case. You don't assume they
have a regular life, and, like, eat dinner at the Olive Garden
or buy socks at Target."

"Right?" Mallory says. "Sometimes I forget that we're just
their jobs."

I tell them, "One time we ran into my fourth grade teacher at the grocery store and it blew my mind. I looked in her cart and was all, 'Why would she need toilet paper?'" and everyone laughs.

"I'd really like to hear what Mr. Gorton thinks. Can you send him a direct message?" Mallory asks me.

"On it," I reply, head bent over my laptop, fingers flying across the keyboard.

"Check this out," Theo says, holding up his Android. "I Googled 'North Shore' and 'Parents' Association.' Here's a Facebook post by Stephen's mom."

That catches my attention.

Theo scans the text. "Let's see… She's talking about the meeting last night. Says decreasing the workload will 'make us less competitive going forward.' Says 'holding students to a lower standard will just spit in the face of Stephen's legacy.' Also, 'lower test scores impact property values.'"

"Are you fucking kidding me?" I say, springing out of my seat. "You know she's been texting me, saying she wants to talk? I've ignored her because I'm sure she's going to lay a huge guilt trip on me, and, let's be honest, I am chickenshit. But, now? Boom, the gloves are OFF."

Owen puts his good hand on my forearm. "Bro, it's okay. Settle. Stephen's mom's hurting and she's doing the only thing she can think of right now, which is pushing forward. Do not hold her responsible for anything when emotions are so raw. She gets a pass today, okay? I don't forgive anyone else for not wanting to ease up on us, but she gets a pass."

He does make sense. I fall back onto the banquette, defused.

"You cool?" he asks.

I say, "I think so. Honestly? I don't even know that Mrs. Cho was Stephen's problem. Was she super strict? Hell, yeah.

My own mom's a lot like her and sometimes her micro-management's a lot. But I can handle it because I understand why. That was Stephen's problem. He never understood why. He just figured he was destined to do everything wrong, which is why she was always bitching at him."

More to herself than us, Mallory says, "Trying to figure out why will drive you mad."

I nod. "With Stephen, he held himself to a higher standard than Mrs. Cho ever could. Shoulda seen him before our Physics meets. He'd practically slip into a trance, he was so intense. He'd stay up all night for a week to prep. And for what? To win some stupid trophy to be sold for a quarter at a yard sale in ten years?"

My eyes begin to water and my voice breaks, but I don't fight the tears. If I cry, I don't care. I'm learning it's okay to show you're vulnerable. "I heard from him coming home on the train that day. I think he was so convinced that he'd screwed up his alum interview that his life wasn't even worth living."

The guilt returns. The feeling of not having done enough surrounds me like one of those impossible-to-remove plastic clamshells. Remorse clings to me like spilled honey. I try to talk past the lump in my throat, but it's hard. "I fucked up. I had no idea he meant to harm himself. I was... annoyed. Thought he was being all Johnny Drama and then I was smug when he admitted he was wrong and I was right. I gloated to myself. Now I want to pull a Superman and fly backward around the planet to reverse time that day. I want to go back and be different. Be supportive and maybe keep him from—"

"Kent, it's not your fault," Mallory says. I am full on crying now. She gestures for Jasper to bring me a bottle of water, which he sets down beside me.

"He did it on the way home from his alumni interview. I'd bet you anything he thought he'd fucked it up. How did he not know that no matter what happened with MIT, he'd be okay? Even if they said no, every other college in the country would fight over him? How did he not see how great he was?"

The group is quiet, intently listening.

"How did it not occur to him that every other eighteen-year-old kid might be nervous, too, might stammer a little over his answers? He's not the White House press secretary, you know? He wasn't someone who had to answer questions professionally, he was allowed to stumble and be thought-ful. He held himself to such a high standard that there was nowhere to go but down. I see that now. Everyone in this goddamned school is like that, too. Like the world is gonna end if we aren't one hundred percent perfect all the time."

I wipe a stray tear away with the cuff of my shirt. In the past, I'd have been mortified to break down in front of the popular kids. But having feelings doesn't mean you're weak. I finally realize they aren't looking at me like I'm a loser, like I don't belong.

Because I do belong. We all belong. We're in this together.

Mallory grabs me and hugs me close and tight, her face pressed against my neck.

Then Owen, Theo, and Jasper join in the hug. They all hold me for so long that it gets a little weird.

I say, "You guys trying to have a five-way here?"

Jasper tells me, "There is something *deeply* wrong with you, K-Pop. I like it."

And that breaks the tension.

Owen looks thoughtful as he returns to his seat. "This is

395

why we have to be here for each other. We gotta keep the Gatekeepers intact. Like, assure everyone we have options. I mean, our futures are a huge deal, but right now is important, too. We can't be miserable every day in the hopes of building something great ten years down the road. That's a shitty way to live."

"Amen," Jasper says, toasting us with his Diet Coke.

Something dings in my pocket and I pull out my phone. "Goddamn it."

"What?" Mallory asks.

I give them the condensed version of Simone's 911 text.

"Aw, Jesus, Liam, why?" Theo asks, cupping his face in his left hand.

"We have to find him. Now," Jasper says, standing and heading towards the door. "He's a danger to himself."

I grab my coat. "Listen, I'm more worried about her than him," I say, pulling a coat on over my hoodie and winding my scarf around my neck. "Simone's become an entirely different person, you know? Like in a real short amount of time. She was all world-wise and chill when she got here. She was confident and sure of herself."

"That's why I vibed with her," Owen offers. "She's totally different now."

"Yes, *exactly*," I say. "She didn't grow up in all this, she doesn't know how to handle it. North Shore has her twisted and Liam's got her all… I don't even know how to describe the changes, except, well, she's a fucking mess. I don't trust her judgment right now. She shouldn't be alone."

"Kent's right," Mallory said. "She was relaxed to the point of comatose at first, just so stoked to be a citizen of the world. The girl I sat next to today is an entirely different entity."

"Let's split up and go looking, that way we cover more ground," Owen suggests.

Mallory organizes us. "How about… Theo, you take Owen in your car. Kent, you don't have a car and you know Simone best, so you're with me. Jasper, can you strike out on your own? You'd be most tuned in to other places Liam would go."

Jasper gives her a curt nod. "10–4, Malamute."

She adds, "Okay, Gatekeepers, let's do this."

39

MALLORY

"WAIT, WHERE DID Simone say she was going?"

After I peel out of my garage, I realize I have no idea where to head.

"She didn't. Let me text her to see." Kent furiously presses numbers and keys. His phone's silence overwhelms us. There's a thin sheen of sweat on his forehead. "C'mon, Simone, hit me back."

"Maybe she went home? Call her house," I instruct. "Or do they not have a landline?"

They do, and her mom tells him she's out with the dog.

"Do we try the bluff or somewhere else first, like her house?" I ask, more to myself than to Kent. We sit in my driveway for what seems like a lifetime, but in all actuality, it's about thirty seconds. "Screw it, we'll head to the bluff."

I gun the car and arrive at the scenic overlook in minutes, but there's no sign of either of them. I didn't think she'd stick around, but I'd hoped. "Where does she live?" I ask. "Maybe we can retrace her steps if she's on her way home?"

"Cottonwood Avenue. Spruce Street seems like it would be the most direct route to Cottonwood, let's try that," he says.

"On it."

I take the corner at Lake Ave so fast that I can feel one of the LR4's wheels leave the ground and we tilt dangerously to the side. Kent grasps the *Oh, Jesus* bar over his head, all the blood having rushed from his face. He doesn't complain, possibly because he's too terrified to speak. His knuckles are white as he braces himself between the dashboard and the passenger side door, stomping hard on the imaginary brake pedal.

We career around town like this for another fifteen minutes until Kent finally suggests, "We might have a better chance of spotting her if we don't go Mach 10. Like, what if we *don't* drive your car like we stole it?"

He makes a valid point, especially since the sun's gone down. Simone's been all about dark colors lately, so she might be lost in the shadows if we zip by too quickly.

"How fast is Mach 10?" I ask.

"About seventy-six hundred miles per hour. I mean, Mach 6 or 7, sure, that'd be great for our purposes, but I feel like Mach 10 is pushing it."

I shoot him some side-eye. "How do you feel about me driving twenty miles an hour, Miss Daisy?"

He nods vigorously. "I feel real good about it."

After I slow down, Kent releases his kung-fu grip. I glance at his profile and realize there's something extrafamiliar about him. He reminds me of someone.

"Hey, Kent, has anyone ever told you that you look like—"

He interrupts me, his tone terse. "Like Farmer Ted, the kid in the oxford from *Sixteen Candles*? Um, yeah, a million times. And no, I'm not going to scream JAAAAAKE for you, so don't ask."

I was going to say the nerdy kid in *The Breakfast Club*, but same diff. But I feel like Kent could use a win today, so I say,

"Actually, no. You look like a younger version of the guy who plays Owen Hunt on *Grey's Anatomy*. Kevin McKidd?"

Kent visibly straightens up in his seat and the corners of his mouth twitch up into the grin he's trying to suppress. "Oh. Yeah, I like him. He's kind of a badass. He was great in *Trainspotting*."

I say, "Never seen it. What's it about?"

"A bunch of guys on heroin."

"Oh. Then it's apropos for today."

Now Kent gives me the side-eye. "You have a twisted sense of humor, Mallory."

I wasn't trying to be funny.

I slow to fifteen miles an hour and we cruise up and down the quiet streets of North Shore. Everyone's already decorated for the holidays and it's like a winter wonderland up here, with all the giant lights and the urns full of decorative pine branches. The moment it snows, the whole town will be transformed into a Currier & Ives greeting card. I can't wrap my mind around how anything bad can happen in a place so besotted with beauty and perfection, yet here we are.

"So...how's Noell?" I ask, crawling along, eyes peeled for Simone. My anxiety level is ratcheting up higher and higher the longer it takes us to find her. This whole situation is as fucked-up as a soup sandwich. How did we even get here? How did Liam go so off the rails? He should be going through, like, *fraternity rush*, not withdrawals.

"I'm sorry, *what*?" Kent says, looking at me as though I've just sprouted a supplemental head.

I explain, "I'm a nervous talker. I need frivolous conversation right now. I need banal stories about how high school should be, you know, with sock hops and soda fountains."

"*Sock hops?* Did you drive so fast we broke the space-time

400

continuum and it's suddenly the 1950s? Have we gone back to the future?"

"Fine, sock hops are a bad example." I clutch the wheel. "I just need to escape reality for a minute. In an alternate universe, you and I? We're in a movie montage, decorating the gym for the Christmas formal. We're caroling dressed like people in a Dickens novel. Or we're having a flour fight while we ice sugar cookies. Maybe there's frosting on my nose. *That's* where we should be. We're not supposed to be tracking down a girl who's been abused by her smacked-out boyfriend. Who may or may not be so triggered by the event, who may be so upset, so fragile that she reflects on her good friend's suicide and suddenly sees it as a viable option. So I need you to distract me because I am freaking right the fuck out."

"Oh, if you're gonna put it like that, then Noell's the best. She's awesome. We're totally in luff." He folds his hands over his heart and sighs, his face wreathed in smiles.

I glance toward him. "Aw, happy endings give me life."

"No," he says, scowling and dropping his hands to his lap. "I was being facetious. I didn't get a happy ending. She dumped me when I needed her most after Stephen. You didn't notice she was never at a Gatekeepers meeting? Said she couldn't handle it. Said it was 'too real,' whatever that means. She's banging Weston now."

I cluck my tongue. "Typical. She's perpetually trading up."

Kent mumbles, "Love life advice from Mallory. And I thought today couldn't get any better."

"Listen, I'm not trying to hurt your feelings, just pouring the tea," I explain. "Noell falls out of love as quick and easy as she falls into it. Sorry you didn't know that. I feel like the relationships you don't have to work to establish aren't worth having. Plus, I always say the secret to love is less about who you meet, and more about when you meet."

Kent's expression is stony. "Please share more of your clichéd wisdom, it's really boosting my self-esteem."

"My point is, you can do better. Set your sights on someone less attainable. Ultimately, you'll be more satisfied."

He snorts audibly, but offers no explanation.

We drive on in silence, heads on a swivel, cruising up and down the streets we think Simone may have taken.

"You mind if I turn on the radio?" Kent asks. "I can hear myself think and I need that to stop."

"Knock yourself out. Wait, do you know how to work the controls? Lemme show you."

I reach for the radio, but he waves my hand away.

"Um, Mallory, I just got early decision to Princeton. For Physics? I can explain derivations within String Theory. Pretty sure I can figure out your stereo." He smirks.

I inadvertently kick the brakes and we both lurch forward. "Whoa, hold up, you already heard from Princeton? You're *in*?"

"Yeah, but it's my safety school."

Princeton is his *safety*? FML.

I say, "I thought Princeton only lets you apply for early decision if you're sure you want to go there."

"The Ivies are all different, but with Princeton, you're allowed to apply anywhere with nonbinding admission. I'd planned on MIT, but now without Stephen… Eh, I don't know, I'm not into it anymore. I mean, Princeton was good enough for Richard Feynman, right?"

"Did he go to North Shore?"

Kent snorts. "That'd be a *no*. He won the Nobel Prize for his work in subatomic particles. Yeah, he did his undergrad

402

at MIT, but a lot of Nobel Prize winners were Tigers first. You know, their mascot? There's Stephen Weinberg, John Bardeen, Arthur Compton, Clinton Davisson... I'm sure I'm forgetting some. Anyway, you're hoping for Princeton? Majoring in? I'm assuming physics is off the table, what with your nonexistent knowledge about Feynman."

"Definitely. I'm looking at finance or economics."

"Cool. What would you do with that degree?"

"Investment banking."

"Huh."

"What *huh*? What do you mean by *huh*?" I demand.

"I dunno. Feels like you'd be better working with people, like as a psychologist or therapist or something."

Hearing the truth spoken from such an unexpected source gives me pause. While it's not at all the same, this reminds me of the time Braden, Theo, and I were at the mall. I told them I'd seen a dress in a magazine and I wanted to try it on. I didn't say where I was going; I'd just planned to text them when I was done. But when I came out of the fitting room, Braden was sitting right there waiting for me. I was all, 'How'd you know where I'd be?' He pointed to the mannequin in the window and said, 'That dress has lemons on it. You love anything with a lemon print. Knew this was the place.'

I steal a glance at Kent. Have I been missing something here?

Kent begins to fiddle with the dashboard, first activating the seat heaters and then the hazard lights.

"Earn yourself a scholarship to Princeton, didya?" I ask, stifling a laugh. "You know, I'm happy to help you, the sound system's more complex than it appears."

"I'll figure it out," he says.

He turns another knob.

"And now we're in four-wheel drive," I say, pulling over briefly to put the car back into two-wheel drive. As I ease onto the road, he touches a few more controls.

"You hot there, pal? You just flipped on the AC."

Kent exhales heavily out of his nose. "Mallory, will you please turn on the radio for me?"

I hit the switch and music begins to play. "I have satellite radio. You scan up or down using these buttons," I say, and then I give him a quick tutorial on the various functionalities, concluding with, "...and this one controls the volume."

He monkeys around with the stereo, jumping from station to station until he finds what he's looking for. Suddenly, the car's reverberating with the sounds of old, terrible gangster rap.

"All of that effort for *this*?" I ask, wrinkling my nose in distaste.

"What have you got against classic hip-hop?" he asks.

"What do you have *for* it?" I counter.

"Let's see...um, *everything*?"

"It's just *noise*. Everyone swearing and throwing around the n-word."

"Oh, you could not be more wrong, Mallory," he says, so disgusted that he curls his lip. Curls his lip! At *me*! I invented the lip curl. *I* made the lip curl happen, not him.

"Then educate me."

"Okay, take this band, for example? Public Enemy is arguably one of the most important musical acts of all time. Chuck D., the lead singer? He's not swearing and 'throwing the n-word around.'" His expression is that of total disdain. I think I've offended him and, for some reason, that kind of bothers me.

He continues his explanation. "He's as much a philosopher

as he is an artist. His music spoke to a generation and a group of people who'd never had their struggles represented before. His words brought the disenfranchised together, let 'em know their stories deserved to be heard. And he encouraged activism—not through violence, but through social change."

"Huh." I'm unsure how to respond to that, less because I can't negate his point, and more because I can't recall the last time someone challenged me. "What's this song called?"

"'Fight the Power.'"

I snicker. "'Fight the Power'? Um, I hate to break it to you, pal, but you're a white male from North Shore on his way to the Ivy League. You *are* the power."

"You think I don't know that?" he replies. "Like that thought never occurred to me?"

"Seems pretty hypocritical is all."

He clucks his tongue at me. "That's where you're wrong."

"Okay, present your argument, like we learned in Mr. Canterbury's debate class. Hit me with your best case for why you're not all hypocritical for listening to this music, I would really like to know."

His expression is…smug?

He says, "Easy. What I connect with, what I understand, what moves me so much about this particular song is Chuck D.'s anger. He is *pissed off* at how the world is. But he's not all enraged and unfocused. He channels his feelings into a message. That's why it's so powerful. See, it's his intention to educate everyone about what's going wrong and what's unfair and unjust to make positive change."

"I don't know his music, but I'm guessing *you're* not the one being targeted by what's unfair. You do watch the news on occasion, yes? Catch the *Daily Show*? Do you even read Twitter hashtags?"

405

"Listen, Mallory, I can't claim to know what it's like to be hassled for the 'crime' of walking down the street in a hoodie." He plucks at his own hoodie beneath his jacket for emphasis. "For those who are hassled? That's bullshit. *Their lives matter.* And, yeah, I *do* watch the news and it's enraging. The comments sections everywhere are even worse, makes you wanna weep for humanity sometimes. I'm not trying to co-opt what Chuck D's audience is going through, to be something I'm not, acting all, 'Me, too, my brother,' from the comfort of my parent's six-bedroom, three-car-garage home."

I reply, "Then I give you an A-plus for checking your privilege. Still, don't you feel like kind of a poseur, hearing these guys rap about how hard life is on the streets? When you live *here*?"

I point out the ten thousand-square-foot Georgian manor we're driving past, where fifteen landscapers in cherry pickers are putting the finishing touches on the tall trees' holiday lighting scheme.

I add, "How do you relate to all that old Bloods and Crips stuff when the biggest beef up here is Brooks Brothers versus Vineyard Vines? Where the neighborhood planning associations send out letters stating *No coloreds*, meaning white holiday lights only, without any clue exactly how offensive, like, how *tone-deaf* this directive comes across?"

"Then strip away the specific actions and words—just examine the feelings."

I look over at him. "I don't follow."

"Break down not *what* Chuck D.'s saying, but *why* he's saying it and *what's* behind it. Like, I understand the *feeling* of being trapped by circumstances. Granted, my circumstances are way different up here in North Shore, but *feeling* like I don't control my own destiny rings true. Look at how we

406

live right now, all the bullshit hoops we jump through daily —how much of that's by choice? Have you ever been mad about how things are? Felt desperate? Needed to escape to a place where things are different? Wanted to make the world better? I get it. Don't you? Aren't these feelings what ultimately consumed our friends? Aren't we in the Gatekeepers to address them?"

I nod and he continues. "When things are bad, when it's all too much—and it's been *way* too fucking much lately—I put on my headphones and I listen to my music so loud that it makes my teeth vibrate. I'm talking about a baseline that rattles my vertebrae. And then I feel better. Like a little bit of that pressure escapes and my lid's not gonna blow anymore. Because someone else has been here before. Not *here* here," he points to another mansion, "but metaphorical here." He points to his chest.

Okay, so I get it now. I fight the urge to not ruffle Kent's hair, so instead I say, "You just won your debate."

"Not surprised. I'm a really smart guy. Got in to Princeton, you know."

All conversation stops when we think we've spotted Simone going down Arbor Cove Lane, but it's a false alarm.

"Stairs," I say.

He cocks his head. "What? Stairs? Is this a word game? Am I supposed to say something random? How about—potato. Index card. Juicy Fruit. Galoshes."

"When it's too much for me, I run the stairs in the stadium. Over and over, until I'm ready to drop."

"Do you *like* doing that?"

No one's ever asked me that before. So I answer him honestly. "Not particularly."

Kent sits with this information for a moment. "Tom Skil-

407

ling's predicting snow later this week. You can't run the stairs in the snow. I'll put a playlist for you on Spotify, if you want to try something different, something that won't give you shin splints. Who knows? Ice Cube may work better for you than cardio."

I can feel my lips curve into a smile. "I'd like that."

He smiles back.

I tell him, "Fingers crossed Princeton takes me, too. If we're there together, we should hang out."

Kent's whole face lights up before he catches himself and tries to play it off. "It's a date. See you in September."

"Easy there, it's not a *date* date," I caution him. "Don't get the wrong idea. You're just a worthy adversary…and a decent friend."

"Okay," he replies affably. After a long pause, he adds, "Yet by your logic, you're exactly who I should aspire to be with, right? Did you not ten minutes ago tell me to set my sights on someone unattainable? Yes or no?"

"Is *shut up* an option?" I ask.

He laughs. "No, it's not. All I'm saying is, who's less attainable than you? Don't flatter yourself, I'm not saying you're what *I* want. I'm only going *by your own logic*, which points to you being the right person for me, the highest-hanging apple on the tree. Way I see it, you have to either agree that we'd be perfect together or admit that your theory on dating is wrong. I'm comfortable with both eventualities, although I'd prefer to have been right."

I glance over at him again. Between the play of shadow and light, he sort of looks his age in here, which surprises me. Is it possible he's not going to get carded for PG-13 movies his whole life?

If so, how would I feel about that? I've gone the perfect-guy route and it did not work out. What if I opened myself up to interesting, to quality? The last time I had my chance to do just that I didn't and I'll forever regret it.

I ask him, "Are you flirting with me, Kent?"

His reticent grin is heartbreakingly sincere. "I don't have that kind of confidence, Mallory. But thank you for thinking I have game."

Hold on, what if his saying he has no game is actually the *ultimate* amount of game? Did he somehow just Tom Sawyer–me into painting his fence?

Before I can ponder further, Kent strains to look out the window as we hit the intersection on Elkpath Road. "Wait. Here. Pull over here, I see something."

I'm not even parked when he flies out of the passenger seat, practically tucking and rolling. I take off after him, in the direction of the railroad crossing.

Simone is here, I see her now, too.

Oh, no.

fuck fuck fuck fuck fuck.

Simone is standing by the tracks, a smallish, fattish dog at her side, facing the north. There's a train about a mile away that should be here within the next minute or two. Her head's down and the slope of her shoulders reads as despondent. She emanates sadness, radiates hopelessness.

My mind races with the possibilities of her intentions, all of them grim. Kent's already running toward her, but he's slower than I am. I sprint alongside and quickly overpass him.

I reach Simone first.

In one fell swoop, I grab Simone and wrestle her down the embankment, away from the clear and present danger of the oncoming train. Her tubby dog is rolling along behind us on

409

the other end of his leash, profoundly confused as to what's just happened, yet utterly delighted.

When we reach the bottom of the hill, I throw my whole self on top of her to make sure she can't move and Kent leaps on top of both of us. He knocks the wind out of me. Somehow I assumed he'd be light as balsawood, but he has a surprising amount of ballast, like there might be some actual muscle under his jacket. He grips both of us firmly, pressing our bodies into the grass. Adrenaline courses through my system and my face is streaked with terror sweat, but something in me causes me to turn to Kent and say, "Worst threesome ever."

My God, he's right. I *do* have a twisted sense of humor.

When he laughs, he loses his grip on Simone and she struggles free partway, so I lunge and grab her legs, bringing her down again as the Metra continues to hurtle toward us.

"What in the bloody hell are you lunatics doing?" she sputters loudly, over the clatter of the oncoming train.

"We're gatekeeping you," I reply, putting her in a headlock and practically dragging her up the embankment in the direction of my car.

Kent grabs the leash and he and the dog trot along behind us, as we place valuable space between us and the tracks. He tells her, "You're not jumping today."

Simone wriggles out of my clutches and begins to pick stray leaves off herself before brushing at the dog's sweater. "Christ on a bike, what's wrong with both of you? I wasn't going to leap."

"Sure looked like it," Kent replies. He's bent in half, leash looped over his wrist, with both hands on his knees, panting hard. I should probably have him run stairs with me some time. I feel like that would benefit his cardiovascular system, and as his new friend, I'm obligated to look out for him, to gatekeep him in some respect.

"I wasn't jumping," she insists.

"Sure seemed like it," Kent says, still gasping for air.

Yes. Cardio. Definitely.

"He's right," I agree.

She says, "No, no, I heard the train coming, so I figured I'd just wait for it to pass, be better safe than sorry."

"Uh-huh, then what were you doing right by the tracks?" I ask, still completely dubious.

She looks back at the spot where she'd been moments before. "I was reflecting."

"Reflecting?" Kent asks.

"I was standing here thinking about Stephen, wondering what must have been going through his head that afternoon." She fishes a twig out of her hair and looks at it for a couple of seconds before letting it drop to the ground. "How much pain he must have been in to feel that taking his life was his only option. That there was no joy, no tomorrow to look forward to, no eventual happy ending. I hate that he felt he had nothing worth living for. I hate that he wanted it all to stop. I hate that I'll never see his huge grin again."

Her words are like a kick in the stomach.

"I miss him all day, every day," Kent says. "You know how many times I pick up my phone and start to text him before I remember, nope, not an option anymore. Then I get mad at him, like, 'Why'd you leave me here to deal with all this shit on my own?' We always figured everything out as a pair, you know? We were a team, better together, like Eric B. and Rakim on *Paid in Full* or Kanye and anyone. I can't do MIT without him. Like, I really don't even know how I'll do any

411

college without him. And then I get mad at myself for being pissed at him. It's this whole shame spiral."

My thoughts bounce back and forth between Braden and Stephen. The only difference is I actually did text Braden after he was gone. And then I'd sit there, waiting for those ellipses to appear, but they never did.

Braden was kind of a throwback, though, the only person I knew who preferred email over text. People who expressed themselves with slices of pizza and taxi emojis made him seethe. That's why he used to say "heart" this and "heart" that; he was mocking the reliance on emojis. Used to say that one day, our generation would speak entirely in hieroglyphics.

That's why I can't stop stalking his log-in.

Had he any final words, I feel like he would have emailed Theo or me. Or maybe he had his own version of corresponding with those who'd passed, perhaps confessing in an email Macey would never read.

"Do you wonder if Stephen's somewhere on the other side, looking down on us, saying, 'What if my life wasn't so bad after all?' Like he regrets his actions? Like if he had another shot, he'd make a different choice?" Kent asks.

"Kent, no. Don't go there. You'll never get passed it if you let your mind go there," I tell him.

Trust me, I know.

"We can't change what's happened," I say. "Our only choice is to be cognizant and present and alert. Our choice is to be there for each other. And if that means I accidentally wrestle someone down a hill while trying to help, so be it."

Simone says, "Standing there in that daze, I realized exactly how much I appreciate the gift of life. How it's far too precious to ever squander. I finally accept why my parents were so insistent on keeping me safe, on keeping Liam away. They already knew what I've just now figured out."

"So you're okay," Kent confirms. He makes tentative patting motions up and down her arms and shoulders, like he's conducting a half-assed security line search at the airport. "You're telling me that you can deal, that you are okay."

"*Okay* is a relative term, but, yes, I'm okay," she replies.

"All is well, you're not going to snap?" he says.

"Yes, I'm well, Kent."

"You're sure about that?" he demands.

"Profoundly sure."

He shouts, *"Then why the fuck did you not return my texts?"*

She replies, "Because it's dangerous to text and walk."

Which isn't funny.

Nothing about this day or week or month or semester is funny, but for some reason, this response makes Kent laugh. Then I join in. Then Simone starts in, too, and our laughter is like a burning ember touching down in a field of dry brush; it just ignites everything.

I guess we all have twisted senses of humor.

We stand here hooting and cackling until we practically lose our breath. The train rushing by is what finally sobers us up. We watch in sudden silence as all the cars fly past, each window a cozily lit vignette of a suburban mom or dad coming home to their green oasis, their little slice of paradise by the lake after a long day of work in the city.

"We have to talk to Liam's parents, though," Simone says. "They have to know what he's doing now."

We return to the warmth of my car, with Kent and me in the front and Simone and her dog in the back. We sit here on the side of the road, hazard lights blinking out a steady beat, as she tells us everything.

413

"They won't listen to you," I say. "Mr. and Mrs. Avery—they're not going to believe you. They don't know you and it sounds like they definitely don't trust and/or like you. Jasper tried to talk to them, too, but I'm not sure how credible he is—they probably just assumed he was trying to deflect some of the trouble off himself. You'd be wasting your time going over to see his folks, setting yourself up for failure."

"If we're Gatekeepers, don't we have to try?" Kent asks.

"Yes, absolutely," I say. "Not Simone, though, it has to be me. Let's get you both home and then I'll take care of this."

"No, I'm coming with you," Kent insists. "No arguments."

Before we can go anywhere, my phone rings and Theo's picture flashes across my screen. "I should answer. They might have found Liam."

By the time I hang up, I feel like someone's taken a baseball bat to my soul. Despite the heated seat and steering wheel, and the thermostat being set on seventy-eight degrees, my entire body has turned to ice.

I didn't put the conversation on speaker, so Simone and Kent only catch half the conversation. They hear "Liam" and "car accident" and "ambulance" but they've wildly misinterpreted the information.

Simone is sobbing in the backseat, her head in her hands. Her chubby dog keeps trying to comfort her, nudging her and placing his paws on her shoulders, but to no avail. "No, no, no, not Liam," she cries.

"Liam is okay," I say, turning to face her, my heart a stone in my chest. "Simone, do you copy? *Liam is okay.* Jasper found him by the bluff. Then he wrestled him into the car because he was going to take him back to Liam's house. They were arguing and Jasper lost control of his Navigator out on Plymouth Rock Road. They…went over the guardrail into the ravine. Liam was thrown out of the car but he walked away. Simone, he was able to *walk away*."

"Oh, thank God," Simone exhales. "He was so lucky."

"What about Jasper?" Kent says. "Mallory, *what about Jasper?*"

I grab Kent, clinging to him and whispering into his coat, "Not so lucky."

parenting and

...interpretation...

SOCIALITE AND PHILANTHROPIST VANESSA GATES STUNS IN HER VALENTINO ORIGINAL AT THE MET GALA

All eyes were on Vanessa Gates last night when she arrived at the Met Gala. In an astoundingly beautiful micro-pleated gown made of silk and jersey, Gate was reminiscent of a Greek goddess, her star neatly eclipsing every celebrity in the room.

5

Th
hel
31
int
foll
Men
Qua
the
donat
be m
Men
Shore

News

40

OWEN

THE DOCTORS SAY it will take a miracle for Jasper to survive.

Good thing I believe in miracles.

Right now, his team of physicians are pulling him out of a medically induced coma. We're told this was the last resort to decrease cranial pressure. He's been under for three days. After the docs bring him out of it, they'll have a better idea about the extent of brain damage.

Jasper *can't* have brain damage. He can't. That's not fair. He was doing the right thing; he shouldn't have been the one to get hurt. He wasn't always the best dude, but he's come around. He fixed his own karma; he doesn't need the universe doing it for him.

The Gatekeepers have taken shifts holding vigil in the hospital's waiting area after school ever since the accident. But today's real important, so we're here in full force. Mr. Gorton's joined us, too.

Well, we're all here except for Simone, who's at home packing, and Liam. His parents admitted him to a rehab facility the night of the accident. Mallory's worried that his folks put him there less because they admit he has a problem and more to cover their own asses, as he's still a minor and they're liable.

I say his family's reasons don't matter, as long as he's getting some help. On top of the addiction, he's going to have to deal with almost killing his best friend. If the car hadn't landed exactly where it did in relation to that old oak, it would have kept tumbling all the way down. Jasper would have died on impact.

I'm just real grateful that the accident happened when his folks were home. They were supposed to leave the next morning for Bali. If Jasper has any semblance of a normal life after this, it's because his family brought in rock-star type physicians from around the world.

I'd never met his mom, but I've seen her in tons of magazines. She's usually, like, covered in diamonds, hanging out on yachts with dukes and princesses and sheiks when she's not doing her charity stuff. But right now, she's here in the same NSHS sweatshirt someone handed her at the accident scene three days ago, insisting everyone call her by her first name. She hasn't left the hospital at all, not even to shower or brush her teeth. Asked us all to call her Vanessa, too, not Mrs. Gates, and keeps telling us she's real touched that so many of us care.

I told her what Euripides once said—"Friends show their love in times of trouble, not happiness."

Because Jasper's in the ICU, his family can only visit with him for a few minutes every hour. She seems to want people to talk to her, so I've been telling her about my Gatekeepers documentary. She suggested I interview the other kids while we wait, said no matter what happened, I'd want a record of this.

That was very cool of her. Who even thinks about others at a time like this?

Yesterday, I shot footage of different Gatekeepers telling me what nickname Jasper had given then. I cut them all together last night to show his mom when I got here today. She liked it a lot, even showed a hint of a smile.

Mr. Gates (who does not share his wife's love of informality) has been here the whole time, too. He's mostly been on the phone. Lemme just say this—from the sounds of these calls, I would not want to be an Avery right now. Suspect Jasper's dad did not amass his impossible fortune by being Mr. Nice Guy.

Regardless of their individual approaches, his parents are rallying around him. If anything good comes of this, it's that. I know that more than anyone.

Jasper's mom and dad are in with him now, watching the doctors bring him out of the coma. We're told that even if his brain recovers, he has a long road to recovery, lots of surgeries ahead, between the broken bones and internal injuries.

So, we're all sitting here, real nervous.

Mallory's friend Elise approaches me. I met her a few times back when my parents hung out with Mal's. (I think their moms were in college together or something.) I never really talked to her before the Gatekeepers, though. Honestly, didn't even recognize her at first. She used to look like every other girl up here, like Mallory's clone, but now she's more interesting. She's sort of Goth now, with her hair dyed dark, a few piercings, and some ink. She strikes me as the kind of person who wouldn't be personally invested in Gigi Hadid's dating life.

"Hey, Owen, I heard you wanted to interview me? Can we do it now? Otherwise we're just going to be sitting here freaking out as we wait."

Sounds like as good a plan as any.

I say, "Do you wanna grab your coat? I've been doing most of the interviews outside. Unless it's too cold for you?"

"Actually, that sounds perfect. I'm so ready to get away from all this recirculated air," she says. "Makes me feel suffocated."

Huh. "Hey, do the fluorescent lights, like…zap all your energy?" I ask.

"Ugh. So much."

Thought I was the only person who felt that way.

"Sorry it's not nicer out. Yesterday was better, a lot sunnier," I say, gathering up my filming gear. "Today I'll definitely need my 5-in-1 reflector to get rid of shadows."

Without even asking, she grabs one of my cases so I don't have to hump it all out myself. "I like the gray skies. Being able to see my breath while we talk all seriously will add an interesting element. Good visual. Whatever I say would have less gravity on a warm, sunny day, right?"

"Actually, yes."

"Today kind of makes me think of this one scene in Michael Moore's documentary *Roger and Me*. You familiar with the bunny lady?"

I shake my head. I sort of miss the beads on the ends of my dreads, but they pulled on my scalp and eventually gave me too much of a headache. I took 'em out last month. "No. And Moore's a great filmmaker, how'd I miss that?"

"Probably because you weren't born. That was his first. Find it on Netflix. Anyway, Moore's interviewing this ex-auto worker about her life now that the GM plant's closed. For most of the interview, we see the lady tending to these fluffy rabbits. She's real upbeat and the bunnies are super cute, with their fuzzy ears and twitchy noses. Then we cut to a scene where it's colder and darker and her hopes haven't materialized. With weather alone, you get the feeling that her life's devolved. The scene ends with her butchering a rabbit on a weathered old picnic table because that's what's for dinner now that the assembly plant is gone. I mean, she's eating her pets. She doesn't have to *say* her life is a shit sandwich because of GM. Instead, Moore shows it."

"I hate it. But I also kinda love it," I say.

"Right?" Elise dons her jacket. "Shall we roll?"

After we're set up on a bench outside, I give Elise my first prompt. "Describe North Shore for me."

She scrunches up her forehead as she considers. "Hmm. I guess I'd say that North Shore is a beautiful façade, held together with duct tape and Crazy Glue."

Dark. But accurate. I nod, encouraging her to elaborate. I like how quickly she gets real.

"What do you mean by façade?" I ask.

She answers, "Seems like most North Shore parents want to believe their kid is a star, you know? What's that quote about not everyone being able to march in the parade, because someone's gotta sit on the sidewalk and watch it pass by? The problem is, everyone up here expects their kids to be in the parade, like there's no honor in being a spectator. Parents do their kids a disservice when they perpetrate the narrative."

"Can you explain why you mean by 'the narrative'?"

Elise is supposed to be talking to the camera, but instead, she's speaking directly to me, like we're having a real conversation. "The narrative of our fairy-tale lives, where everything looks perfect, where appearances are more important than reality. On top of that, we're, like, wreathed in commendations from a young age, celebrated and congratulated for everything. That's not the real world. I mean, our bosses

421

won't give us trophies for showing up to our jobs someday. That's a baseline expectation."

I stop the interview. "You sound like Mallory's brother Holden."

She smiles. "I love Holden. I'll take that as a high compliment."

"Good. That's how I meant it."

Her cheeks flush pink and I start filming again.

She tells me, "Seems like nobody strays from the prescribed text to deliver the real story. *That's* why we have problems. When everything's not perfect in our lives, we assume *we're* defective, that there's something wrong with *us*. But that's bullshit. Life is inherently imperfect. We're imperfect. We should embrace that. The messy parts are what make it interesting."

Why have I never hung out with this girl?

"Bottom line?" she says. "People around here like to put on this big front that nothing goes wrong in North Shore, but they do go wrong, terribly wrong. Again and again. Until everyone's ready to talk about what it's really like here for us, until people are willing to shine a light on the problems, not just on the drinking and the drug use, but the parents who give *things*, not time, then it won't change. In fact, everything's gonna get worse if nothing changes. And, I don't know about you, but I'm *done* burying my friends."

"Amen, sister."

Before I can figure out if this is a conversation or *a conversation*, Mallory and Kent come bursting out the hospital's sliding glass doors.

"He's awake!" Mallory cries, while wrapping her arms around Elise and jumping up and down. "He's awake and alert and he sounds like himself."

422

"Wait, how do you know? Were you allowed to see him?" I ask. Elise is already blinking away tears.

The news makes me feel like I'm a helium balloon, ready to fly up into the sky the second someone lets go of my string.

"No, not yet," Kent says. "But it's *what* he said that makes us think Jasper's back."

"What'd he say?" Elise insists.

"First, he wanted a mirror to check his hair. Then, he asked for some gel. And then…" Mallory is giggling, her hand over her mouth. "Then he asked his 'Mama Llama' for 'a dirty martini and a clean blonde.'"

"*Definitely* a miracle," Kent confirms.

Elise looks thoughtful. "You know, Albert Einstein said that there are two ways to go through life. The first way is as though nothing's a miracle and the other is as though everything is."

I think we all know the way I go.

41

KENT

MIRACLES MAKE YOU do stupid things.

If I hadn't gotten another text from Stephen's mom right after we learned that Jasper would be okay, I'd have never agreed to meet up with her.

But it did, so here I am.

Shit.

I so don't want to be here. I've been standing at the Cho's front door for the past ten minutes, motionless, like I'm rooted to the spot. This is the same place I've stood in a million times, the same door that I've banged on a million times. Yet I can't seem to bring myself to knock for the million-and-first time.

I don't want to step inside. I haven't been in this house since before Stephen died. His family didn't have a reception or anything after the funeral service. The service was just over and we left.

The great irony is that Stephen would have loved his own funeral—*everyone* showed up. Everyone. He never wanted to have a party, joint or on his own, because he worried no one would come. The turnout would have thrilled him. If he'd been there, he'd have made me talk about it for days afterward, too. *So even the cute red-haired girl from New Trier's Physics Olympics team was there, can you believe it?* he'd have crowed. *How would you assess her tear flow? Would you say she bawled (a) hard, (b) the Kim Kardashian why-would-you-say-that Vine degree of hard, or (c) Crying Guy from A & E's* Intervention *hard?*

I miss him.

I miss my best friend, my wingman, my cheerleader. At this point, I can't even recall what annoyed me about him, because I miss him annoying me. I miss him getting under my skin. I miss him challenging me. I miss him being diffi-cult. I miss him giving me shit.

"Do...do we knock or do we just live out here now?" Mal-lory asks, shivering in her thick Canada Down jacket, its coy-ote hood tied tight around her face. "Do we just camp out in this portico forever? If so, we should have brought snacks."

When I told her I'd agreed to talk to Stephen's mom, she insisted on coming with me. Said I shouldn't have to do this on my own. Guess she thought I needed gatekeeping.

So I knock. Mrs. Cho answers the door.

There's something different about her today and it takes me a minute to figure out what it is. She's a mess. I've never seen her with a hair out of place or unglossed lips. But now she looks like she just crawled out of a can of potato chips. I'm used to seeing her in coordinated yoga gear when she's not in her dressy showing-houses outfits, all starched blouses and trim skirts. I've definitely never known her to wear sloppy sweatpants and...Stephen's *All Eyez on Me* Tupac T-shirt?

She glances down at herself with a shrug. "Laundry day. Come on in."

"I hope you don't mind that I brought my friend, Mal-lory," I say.

425

"Not at all." Previously, Mrs. Cho would have grilled everyone for ten minutes on what we were doing with Mallory. Then she'd have been all over Mal about her GPA, afraid she might somehow be a threat. But today she simply says, "Tell your mom I'm sorry I haven't joined her at Pilates in a while."

She invites us in and we follow her through the house and back to the kitchen. While everything in here is the same, it's all different, too, like we're seeing the Bizzaro World version. The air, which always smelled fresh, like lavender and cut herbs, is heavy and stale. The normally pristine hardwood floors are streaked and overrun with dust bunnies. A profusion of fingerprints dot the stainless steel fridge. Mrs. Cho used to be so anal about keeping that door spotless that Stephen and I would wrap dishtowels around our hands when we wanted to grab juice boxes.

We get to the farmhouse table in the breakfast room and Mrs. Cho has to shoo a cat—a cat!—off my seat so that I can sit. "Kent, Mallory, thanks for coming by."

I nod, unsure of what to say, but Mallory jumps right in. "How are you, Mrs. Cho? Mom says she misses you."

"Oh, I'm good, I'm fine," she replies, even though she's clearly neither. For some reason, this causes Mallory to poke me under the table, and she catches me right between the ribs with her pointy digit.

"That's great," I say. My face feels strained as I try to arrange it from a grimace into a smile.

This is awkward.

This is awkward and terrible, and I keep straining to hear Stephen's feet pounding down the staircase. My body physically anticipates jumping up when he arrives, giving him the half-hug-bro-slap that we used to do.

426

I've never been here without Stephen. The house feels so big without him, so empty, so familiar and yet so unfamiliar.

"You look different, Kent," she says.

"Stress," I reply. "Rough semester."

"No, not that," she replies. "Older, maybe. More mature."

"Again, stress," I tell her. Pretty sure I look haggard after these past few weeks, like I'm suddenly smoking two packs a day and slugging down pints of Jim Beam instead of cans of Coke.

"Where are my manners?" she asks. "Can I get you something to drink?"

Mal and I glance into the kitchen, which is overrun with dirty dishes.

"Nothing for me," I say.

"I just had a mocha," Mallory tells her. "I'm good for now."

"Okay."

So awkward.

I can hear myself swallow. When I shift in the chair, the cushion makes a farting noise.

So very awkward.

I don't know why I'm here today, what we possibly have to cover. Everything about being in this room is confusing and foreign, even though I've been seated at this table for hundreds of breakfasts, lunches, and dinners. For thousands of study sessions and Physics Olympics preps and class projects. For dozens of platters of chocolate chip pancakes and freshly squeezed orange juice, served in those short glasses adorned with red cherries.

Every visit to this table has been some version of the same, with Mrs. Cho steamrolling over us about one thing or another. Nipping at us like she was a sheepdog and we were the little lambs who kept trying to escape the pasture. We

427

could set our clocks to Mrs. Cho's monologues. Stephen and I would smile and nod while we'd kick each other under the table and roll our eyes.

But today? This feels like the first time I've ever been here.

Largely because I have no clue as to what's going to happen next.

Mrs. Cho finally says, "I got a letter. Well, no. Stephen got a letter. He was admitted." She unfolds a dog-eared envelope emblazoned with the MIT crest. She passes it to me, gesturing for me to see the letter inside. The heavy paper stock has been softened by frequent handling. The edges are smudged.

I take and scan his acceptance letter, unsure of what to do.

I don't know how to respond.

No, that's a lie. I feel like I want to ball up the letter. Like I want to throw it. Like I want to stand on this table and shout, *What a waste, what a fucking waste!* I feel rage, my blood hot and angry, making my face burn. I feel like I want to throw open the cabinets and find those stupid cherry-print juice glasses, smash them against the wall, tell her no, terrible things actually *wouldn't* happen if we ever drank OJ from concentrate.

Before I can open my mouth, I feel Mallory wrap her fingers firmly around my wrist. I imagine this is her way of restraining me, of keeping me from springing up. Instead of channeling my pain and loss at Mrs. Cho, I concentrate on the warmth of Mallory's palm. I like her hands better when she's not using them to poke me with her bony fingers.

"Kent is glad you emailed," Mallory says, ever the politician. "He's really been missing Stephen. He talks about him so much. I wish I'd known him better."

She's trying to prompt Mrs. Cho to talk, to move this thing along, and I couldn't be more grateful.

Mrs. Cho wraps her arms around herself and rocks back

and forth. Dude...who *is* this person wearing a Mrs. Cho suit? This woman that's all calm and nice and gentle? And where was she for eighteen years? What happened to the Tiger Mom who had an opinion about anything and everything, up to and including what's an appropriate amount of toilet paper to use?

"I just wanted him to be safe," she says, more to herself than us.

Mallory squeezes my wrist.

Mrs. Cho's voice goes soft. "That's all I wanted. Him to be safe. That's why we moved here from Los Angeles. We thought, 'We should raise our family in this wonderful place. This is where our children will be safe.' And I kept him safe from every element. Every element but himself."

I start to say something but Mallory gives my wrist a yank. I glance at her and she shakes her head, almost imperceptibly. *"Shh,"* she says, too quiet for Mrs. Cho to hear.

"You've heard about the LA riots. I don't know if Stephen ever told you, but I was there."

Mallory raises an eyebrow as if to verify with me. I nod my head to indicate *yes.*

Stephen always speculated that his mom's family was targeted because they were immigrants. He thought that this experience was why his parents had essentially rejected all the Asian parts of themselves, why there were so few nods to anything South Korean in his life. Being different made them stand out and standing out was dangerous.

She explains, "Los Angeles was a powder keg, primed for a spark back then. Relations were terrible between Koreans and African Americans after shopkeeper Soon Ja Du received no jail time for killing a fifteen-year-old girl named Latasha Harlins. Soon Ja Du thought the girl was stealing orange juice, but video showed she had money, wanted to pay."

Mallory and I glance at each other, puzzled as to why she's telling us this.

"My parents owned a small grocery store. I worked for them, helped them keep their books. Rioting began in our neighborhood when white police officers were found not guilty for beating a man, even though everyone had seen the videotape."

"Rodney King?" Mallory asks.

Mrs. Cho nods. "Our store was burned to the ground. Stephen knew that. I almost never spoke of the experience, so there are details he never knew. Important details. I was waiting until he was old enough to understand." She squeezes her eyes shut for a moment. "I waited too long."

Then she begins to fold and unfold Stephen's letter, likely for something to do with her hands. The new cat jumps up on the table and settles in next to her, but she doesn't notice.

"Sixty-two people died during the riots. My brother Seutibeun was one of them."

Mallory and I exchange glances. She has no idea that this is new information to me.

"My brother wanted to be called by the American version of his name—Stephen. He loved this country and everyone in it. He was friends with our customers, went to school with them, played basketball with them, listened to their music. The African Americans in the community hated us, though. They thought we Koreans were colluding against them, thought we were exploiting their communities. In turn, my parents distrusted the locals, assumed they were all gang members. Believed they were always trying to steal from us. Stephen wasn't swayed. He was the common ground between the two worlds. He'd explain himself by saying he liked who he liked and every color was the same to him. After the riots started, we all had to protect our businesses. Owners stood on the roof with rifles to prevent looters. Stephen was furious, said no matter what happened, we could rebuild. Said inventory wasn't more valuable than life."

Mrs. Cho stops to dab at her eyes with the sleeve of her son Stephen's T-shirt.

"The gangs left us alone at first because Stephen treated them with respect. But on the third night of the riots, he was speaking to a friend out front. Another shopkeeper thought he was a looter because he wore American clothes—he dressed just like everyone in the neighborhood. He and his friend were gunned down right there on the sidewalk. Our store was blamed for his friend's death. We were targeted and that's when the looters retaliated."

"Did Stephen know any of this?" I ask. I can't imagine that he did.

She shakes her head. "I kept it from him. I didn't want him to know how ugly the world could be. I wanted him to be safe."

In this context, all of Mrs. Cho's actions as a mother make sense—all the micromanagement, her hypervigilance, every bit of pressure and guidance that we'd interpreted as bossiness.

The one thing she never did was to explain *why*, and that might have been the one thing that changed the outcome.

Yet I don't offer Mrs. Cho this opinion because it's just speculation on my part. It's possible Stephen would have been even more anxious, knowing that he was someone's namesake, that it was on him to honor the other Stephen who never got to grow up.

There are no easy answers because Stephen was complicated. Likely the other Stephen was, too.

All I can do, all any of us can do, is to be here for his mom now.

I'm compelled to give her some measure of solace.

"Stephen was exceptional," I say. "Better than everyone else because you cared so much for him. That's why he got in to MIT and I didn't."

I actually have no idea whether or not I've been admitted.

Yet I tell her this lie because it suddenly feels like it should be truth.

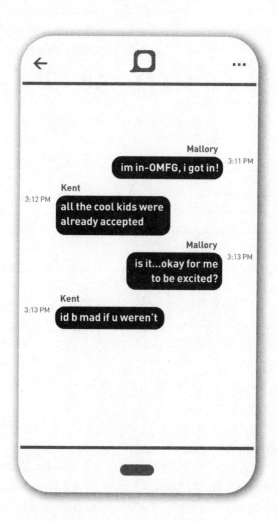

42

MALLORY

"THAT WAS INTENSE."

Kent gives me the oddest look from his seat on the passenger's side. "Ya think?"

"Wait, you *didn't* find that whole scene with Mrs. Cho intense?" I ask.

"*Ring, ring, ring.* Hello? Oh, okay, hang on," Kent says. He holds out a pretend phone. "Captain Obvious is calling for you."

"Shut up."

"How were you never on the debate team with snappy rejoinders like that in your arsenal?" he asks.

"Okay," I say, coming to a stop. "This is your house. Get out of my car, now, bye."

His smile fades as he becomes more serious. "Sorry, Mallory. That was...hard. I don't know that I could have gotten through the whole conversation without you. Thank you for being there."

"That's what Gatekeepers do," I tell him, adding, "and that's what friends do."

He says, "If you need anything, if there's anything hard

that you can't do on your own, you tell me, okay? I'll be there for you."

I dismiss his offer with an, "I'm fine, I'm good."

And then I realize what I'm saying.

"Actually, I'm not fine. I'm still far from good. Do you mind coming back to my house with me? There's something I have to do and I could really use a friend."

"Is this weird?" I ask. I have Braden's North Shore email log-in pulled up on my laptop. Kent is sitting next to me on my bed for moral support.

"Obsessing about hacking into your dead friend's email? No, what could be weird about that?" Kent replies.

I stiffen next to him. This was a mistake.

He sees that I'm upset and quickly changes his tune. "Mallory, no, bad joke. Sorry. I totally understand you. I do. You feel like this is your last chance for answers, like there's some kind of golden ticket in his email."

"Basically, yes. And if I screw up his password one more time, I'll never get in. I'll never know if there was something else, one last thought, one final word. He said he was going to email me, but I never got it. Not knowing if that letter's stuck in Draft will haunt me."

Kent's leaning against my headboard, but I'm completely rigid, so tense right now, so tightly wound that I might snap in two.

He says, "From Owen we know that there was a lot of shit in Braden's life that he never talked about. It's really sad, but we do have a better understanding of why he might have felt bereft. Still…you're hoping to find a new clue, right? A breadcrumb of sorts?"

I nod.

435

He asks me, "In a perfect world, what would you wanna know?"

I tell him, "In a perfect world, I'd like confirmation that he felt the same way about me that I did about him. Because he never told me. Why couldn't he ever tell me?"

"Um, *duh*."

"What do you mean, *'duh'*? And who says *'duh'*? What are you, nine?"

"No, *'duh'* is reserved for when someone says something that's a mile past dumb and a tenth of a mile before moronic. So lemme break it down for you—you are Hot Mallory and until he grew into his looks the summer after eighth grade, Braden was a big tool. Like, *huge* tool. You didn't know him, he went to a different junior high than us. But I met him in grade school. We were buds. We went to astronomy camp together, and trust me, we tools? We can smell our own."

"He was *never* a tool," I seethe, anxious to defend his honor.

"Girl, *please*. The puns, Mallory? Only someone handsome like Braden could get away with puns. Save for limericks, puns are the lowest form of humor. And speaking in emojis? The girls' hats? The weird cartoon backpacks? All that stuff comes across super cool when you look like Channing Tatum. When you don't? Not so much."

"I never thought of it that way," I admit.

"Lemme ask you something—if you cared about him and he was into you, what's with all the Romeo and Juliet business? Like, *hook up* already. What was the problem? It's not like you were going anywhere permanent with Liam."

"Oh, poor Liam. Has Simone heard from him?" I ask. "Does she even want to?"

"Nope, he's still in lockdown in rehab, and she won't admit it, but I'm sure she does want to, because she's a mile past

436

dumb and veering close to Moron City Limits, too. PS, you changed the subject."

"Guilty."

"Then what is it you want me to do?" he asks.

"Do you know any password hacking programs?"

"I'm sure I could find one on the dark web. Do you have any bitcoin?"

"I'm sorry, could you repeat that? I don't speak geek."

He rolls his eyes. "Before we go to that kind of trouble, why don't you tell me the passwords you tried? Maybe we can figure it out if we put our heads together."

I show him my list of all the combinations, mostly pets' names and combinations of football numbers.

"You're missing the most obvious one," he says. "I can't believe this wasn't your first inclination. Here, gimme this."

I pass him my laptop and he taps in a phrase. "Wait! No! Don't press enter yet! What if it's wrong? What if we're locked out forever?"

"Then we find out if Schrödinger's cat is dead and we move on with our lives. Mallory, I'm being serious here, do you trust me?"

I hold my breath until I'm sure of my answer.

With a whoosh and more than a little head-rush, I exhale. "I do."

"Then here we go."

He presses enter and the screen suddenly populates with all of Braden's email.

"Oh, my God! Oh, my God, Kent! You did it! You actually *are* a genius! I can't believe you did it! Holy shit, how did you know? What did you do? What black magic did you work?" I have flown off the bed and I'm jumping all around my room.

I can't believe it. I *cannot* believe he figured it out so quickly.

He shrugs. "Braden was a simple man with simple tastes. He felt how he felt, with very little pretense. So, what's the most basic phrase? What's simple to the point of obvious? What kind of thing would he say to himself over and over in the course of a day when he'd log in? What's the one thing he'd never forget?"

"If I knew, we wouldn't be having this conversation. What was it?"

"His password was...*iheartmallory.*"

His password renders me incapable of speech. I needed a sign, a clue, a golden ticket.

And now I'll have it, always and forever.

My initial moment of elation comes crashing to the ground as I realize what this means. I finally understand why Owen is always quoting Thomas Hobbes. He's right; Hell really is the truth found out too late.

Braden and I missed our chance. We both felt the same way and we missed our chance to see where it could have gone. We blew what might have been the greatest opportunity of our lives, and for what?

What did we gain by not talking to each other, by not admitting everything? What did we win by sacrificing a future together? What if Theo actually supported our being together? We wanted to protect Theo... but what if he didn't require our protection?

Would having shared our feelings for each other have been enough to save him? To keep his demons at bay? To bring him around?

Or would losing him have been so much worse if we'd been together?

I can't say.

I wanted to know how he felt and now I do.

438

Yet nothing has changed.

I wonder, though, if I could change. Maybe that was the point of this whole exercise.

Maybe this was Braden's way of reaching out and gate-keeping me one last time, telling me not to let anything get in the way of whomever it is I should love.

Kent asks, "So, what do we do here? Go through sent mails? You want to try the drafts folder first? How do we proceed?"

I take my laptop from him and click it shut. "We don't."

He scratches his head. "Wait, what? *Why?* That's it? You're done? What was the whole point of this exercise then?"

I don't know how to explain my epiphany to Kent, so instead I say, "The point was confirmation. Braden hearted me, Kent. He *hearted* me. And that's enough."

"Who was *that?*" my mother asks after she sees me saying goodnight to Kent at the door.

"That was my friend Kent. We're in Gatekeepers together? You've met him, like, three times already. And you saw him two days ago. You don't remember?"

"There's nothing exceptional about him so it didn't register. And I've never heard of his parents. Wait, why is he here so much? Jesus, Mallory, you're not *seeing* him, right? He's not your rebound after Liam, yes? Please tell me you can do better than *him.*"

Oh, my God.

I get it now.

I get why I was so reticent with Braden, the biggest reason why I was afraid to show him how I felt.

It wasn't Theo. It wasn't Liam. It was my mother.

439

My mom didn't think he was good enough for me, didn't think he'd help my star rise like Liam would.

She didn't care about my being with Liam because he was best for me. She wanted me to be with Liam because that was best for *her*.

And I was the one who wasted everyone's time trying to argue, trying to fight a battle I was destined to lose.

The only way to win against her is not to play.

Well, I'm done playing.

43

SIMONE

Eight months later

"WELCOME BACK."

Mallory's waiting for me in the arrivals area of Terminal Five at O'Hare, grinning like a lunatic as she holds up a sign that reads *SIMONE AND WARHOL CHASTAIN.*

She sweeps me into a hug, practically crushing me. The ten pounds she's groused about gaining must be all muscle because her arms feel like a couple of boa constrictors squeezing the air out of me.

"I can't breathe!" I protest.

"You're fine," she admonishes. "Are you exhausted? What is it, eight hours on the way back or nine? I always forget. I still don't understand why the flights are different amounts of time going and coming."

"Jet streams," I explain.

"Not a fan," she replies.

I peer at her neck. "You're wearing it!"

She touches the simple pearl strung onto the gold box chain

that I designed for her. "Oh, honey, *always*. This is only my favorite thing ever."

"I'm so glad."

"My God, he's a moose now," she remarks, taking Warhol's leash. "Much bigger than when I saw you at Spring Break."

My family returned to London not long after Jasper's accident. But because of what we'd been through together, Mallory and I began to talk and discovered common ground. We quickly, inexplicably became tight and now she's one of my dearest friends.

I'll admit it, I never saw that coming.

What's worse is that she and Cordy ADORE one another. Were thick as thieves when they met during Mal's Spring Break. They're going to team up on me, and soon. My shoe and trouser wardrobe will never be the same. I'm so afraid of what will happen when we're all together at my mum's book release party next spring.

As we head to baggage claim, she asks, "On a scale of one to ten, exactly how full of shit are you, passing Porky off as an emotional support dog?"

"Please," I reply. "No higher than a seven. Eight tops. He's a perfect gentleman, beautifully trained, a little prince, really. He's not riding in the cargo hold like he's a bit of luggage. The service dog route is the only way since he can't exactly fit under the seat, can he? Of course, the larger lie is passing him off as a bulldog of the English variety and not the pit kind."

To bring Warhol to Britain, we had to lie regarding his pedigree. While I'm a huge proponent of honesty, there was no way on heaven or earth we were leaving him behind. Wasn't happening. Fortunately, with his coloring and his underbite—and everyone's willingness to not examine his papers too closely if it meant a Suri/Chastain homecoming—our ruse worked.

Plus, Warhol's a very lazy sort and he much prefers his short jaunts in the city than the wilds of suburbia, so it's all worked out brilliantly.

"You realize you finally sound British? I like it. Makes you sound smarter."

"Should make me sound politer, then, when I tell you to piss off, Mallory."

"It really does!" Mallory beams and gathers me in another crushing hug with her mighty pythons.

"Are we swinging by the Center before tonight?" I ask. We're meant to meet up with a group of Gatekeepers for dinner tonight, with the screening of Owen's film tomorrow. My parents are coming for it, too, but not until the morning. The three of us are staying at the North Shore house, which has since been turned into an Airbnb.

Mrs. Cho is less than pleased at this development.

Oh, well.

"Would you like to hit the Center now and not wait until tomorrow?" she asks.

"Yes, so much! I'm dying to see it in person, plus I made a little something for Mr. Gorton."

I created small gold filigree pendants shaped liked gates specially for my friends in the Gatekeepers. Normally, I work less with precious metals and more with beads and stones and wood and sometimes even old bones, as my aesthetic trends toward big, bold statement pieces. But I'm learning every aspect of jewelry making during my new apprenticeship, so I'm becoming capable of intricate metalwork, too.

Mallory laughs at me. "You're allowed to call him *Dave* now. Everyone else does."

"Can't. Too informal."

We climb into Mallory's LR4 and half an hour later, we

arrive in North Shore for a tour of the spanking new Gates Community Center.

"This is a marvel," I say.

"Right?" Mallory replies. "Amazing what you can do when you match unlimited funds with steadfast purpose."

I'd seen only plans for the Center before now; the drawings didn't do the place justice. While the structure itself is impressive, a smaller-scale model of North Shore High School fabricated to blend seamlessly into the surrounding neighborhood, what leaves me breathless is what the Center does.

When NSHS banned the Gatekeepers from meeting on campus, I assumed the organization was finished, especially when Mr. Gorton quit his job in protest. All of that went down around the time we were returning to London. But due to the generosity of Jasper's family, the Gatekeepers were able to continue to meet at an off-campus location Mr. and Mrs. Gates had leased, with Mr. Gorton hired on as the director.

Jasper's dad gave zero damns as to what the community/ the other parents wanted and he funded and built the Center himself in record time.

I guess he finally decided that charity needed to start at home.

The Center opened last month and serves as a hangout spot for students to gather all day now, and once classes begin, after school and on weekends. They can engage in social activities and service initiatives, with unlimited access to counseling and mentoring. The Center will be offering outings and field trips and talent shows, all in a safe place that encourages collaboration, not competition, to honor the memory of everyone we lost and strengthen those still here.

Mallory and I stroll the grounds with Warhol and Mr. Gorton...whom I still can't call Dave. He's not nearly as buttoned-up and slicked-back as he used to be, as evidenced by his cargo shorts and Tevas. He's far younger than I recall.

I spot Theo on the vast expanse of lawn, wearing a pinny, playing a game of touch football with a bunch of junior high–aged kids. He loses his concentration when he spots me and the opposing team captures his flag. He just shrugs and waves.

"I'm sorry you won't see Owen today," Mr. Gorton says. "He's usually volunteering at this time, but he's been busy doing interviews."

What started off as a piece about the Gatekeepers morphed into a critical look at what it's like to grow up here. The movie's not only been accepted to a number of upcoming festivals, but also nabbed him a spot in University of California, Los Angeles's freshman class for film studies.

Owen used to say he had no clue what he wanted to do with his life until he began to make this movie, and now he says he can't imagine ever doing anything else. I'm thrilled for him. He deserves every happiness. Mallory tells me he's gotten very tight with her friend Elise, who's off to University of Southern California. Even better.

"Would you like to see the memory gardens?" Mr. Gorton asks. We walk through a lushly landscaped area and he points out which specific trees in the distance were planted in honor of Braden and Stephen.

"We haven't labeled them, but every tree on the other side of the fence represents a young life lost in North Shore in the past three decades," he explains.

"There're so many," I comment, looking at a veritable forest. "Far, far too many."

"The good news is that there are no new trees since we formed the Gatekeepers," he says. "Listen, why don't we give

445

you a minute of privacy out here? People like this area for silent reflection. Just come back when you're done."

Mallory and Mr. Gorton head inside the Center and I find
myself alone in the garden. I'm conflicted by the beauty of
this spot—the trees are so gorgeous, yet every leaf represents
heartbreak. But there's something so powerful about the trees;
they represent rebirths, new beginnings. When it's winter
and the branches are bare and barren and buried under snow,
we'll still have a promise of spring, of what's to come if we
have faith and patience.

I linger by a golden pear tree outside of the garden's entrance. I decide this one is Liam's tree, even though he's not
gone forever.

I think about Liam a lot.

The pain of everything has lessened—it's not the gaping
hole in my soul anymore. Rather, it's morphed into a bittersweet ache, brought on by the most random of circumstances,
like when I hear The Weeknd or I see wafts of steam coming
off warm water on a cool evening and I'm suddenly trans-
ported to the lawn chairs at Jasper's house. Whenever that
happens, I swear I can smell the chlorine and the pine trees.
If I close my eyes, I'm still there with him.

No one ever forgets her first love, especially when it comes
to such an abrupt end.

We emailed for a bit after I went home, Liam and I. With
me back across the pond, he was given access to his electronics
again. Plus, his family is essentially being sued into oblivion by
Mr. Gates's team, so they have bigger problems now. They had
to sell their house, leaving North Shore in shame.

I had such hopes for him after his first trip to the rehabil-
itation facility. His notes from that time were upbeat and I
thought he was going to get back on track, right his course.

I allowed myself to fantasize that, maybe, just maybe… I even applied to American colleges.

After a while, the correspondence stopped. He relapsed and had to be sent away again for treatment. The guilt over what happened with Jasper proved to be too much to handle without self-medication. While it was an accident, Liam will always blame himself.

He's on his third stint in rehab, this time in Florida. He lost his University of Florida scholarship right quick, but he hopes to take some community college classes down there once he's out of the facility and into the halfway house. I'm happy that he's getting a tiny portion of what he'd wanted for his future.

He says he still loves me, but I'm no longer naïve.

I told him he needed a year of sobriety before I'd even consider a face-to-face meeting.

Love is not enough.

Oh, who am I kidding?

I'm still naïve enough to be hopeful about someday.

I find the cherry tree planted for Braden. I offer an apology for not understanding exactly how impactful his life and death would be when I took those awful photographs for the newspaper. Mallory still grieves for him and my heart aches for her.

Warhol and I walk some more and we come to Stephen's tree. The leafy magnolia brings tears to my eyes and I can barely stand to look at it. Such promise. Such loss. Warhol gives the tree a respectful sniff and lies down underneath it. He did love Stephen so. We all did. I pledge to come back in the spring to see the tree in full flower.

After visiting each tree, I pull myself away and head back to the Center. I hate that there's a whole damn forest out there. When Warhol and I leave the garden and return to where

Mallory's waiting for me, she simply gathers me in a hug, because there's nothing left to say.

Mallory picks me up for the screening since my folks are driving separately a little later. They're wiped out from their flight and need to nap. We're under strict orders to save them prime seats, just in case Owen forgot to reserve them. I feel a spark of excitement as we approach the reception before the film. I wasn't at NSHS long, but I feel an unbreakable bond with so many of the students, an undeniable closeness that can't be tempered by distance or time.

I hear the throbbing beat of classic rap music emanating from the room where the reception's being held and I have to laugh.

"Sounds like Kent's already here," I say.

It's been eight months since we've been in the same place together as he couldn't make it to dinner last night. We've spoken scads of times and have written a million emails and texts but we keep missing each other. He came to London in April for Easter on a family trip but I was in Tokyo for my dad's latest exhibition, a McMansion built from rolls of paper towels and gallon jugs of Windex, called *Disturbia* and inspired by our time in North Shore.

At the mention of Kent's name, Mallory shrugs noncommittally, looking away from me. I thought they were pals. They worked so hard to bring the Gatekeepers to fruition. Plus, they'll be at Princeton together in a few weeks. I'd hoped they might hang out more.

"By the way, Mal, when are you telling your mum you're not majoring in finance?" I ask. "You're opting for psychology, right?"

"Yes, and I plan to tell her...when I receive my Princeton diploma."

We both laugh. I knew she'd figure out a strategy for dealing with her mother eventually.

Owen runs up to me and practically hug-tackles me. I forgot what it's like to be in the country of aggressive hugging. I didn't realize how much I missed it.

"I am so very proud of you, my friend," I exclaim. "You found your purpose."

"'Your purpose in life is to find your purpose and give your whole heart and soul to it.' That's a Gautama Buddha quote but I feel like I'm livin' it." His face is wreathed in smiles as we talk. We catch up briefly but there are so many people vying for his attention that he's whisked away after a few minutes.

I can't even get near Jasper. The media covering the event have swarmed him and it's one flashbulb going off after the other. After financing Owen's film, he figured out what he wanted to do for a living. He (and his dad) started a production company and he's well on his way to becoming a movie mogul. He's recently started splitting his time between here and Hollywood. His pants are covered with tiny embroidered film reels and the ladies are lined up a mile deep to talk to him. He spots me and gives me a small salute, calling, "Hey, Simian!"

Only Jasper can make a walking cane look sexy.

I'm on my way over to say hello to Owen's parents when I'm swept off my feet and spun in a circle by some random tall guy who reminds me of the gent from *Grey's Anatomy*.

Yet he's a complete stranger, so I'm none too happy about the manhandling.

"What in the bloody hell?" I sputter.

Who does this person think he is?

"I can't believe you're here!" he exclaims, bouncing up and down. The voice is so familiar, but it takes me a second to connect the voice to body.

Holy shit.

I say, "Well, I guess I know who's getting the Most Changed award at the class reunion, Kent. Christ on a bike, did you manipulate genetics as part of your senior project?"

"Growth spurt," he explains. "I grew nine inches and gained sixty pounds since last summer. Mom always said I'd be a late bloomer."

"Yet you didn't say *anything* to me? Not a word?"

"Dude, you see me every week on FaceTime. You didn't notice?"

"I thought the screen was distorted." I turn to Mallory. "Are you *totally* blown away, too? Or have you two even seen each other since graduation?"

"You didn't tell her yet," Kent says. When he grins, I detect traces of the boy I met a year ago. I'm gob-smacked looking up at him now, instead of looking down, seeing a man instead of a child.

"I wanted that to be a surprise," she replies all coquettishly, taking his hand.

The slowest horse to cross the finish line is…me.

"Whoa. *Kent.* Oh, my God! This is the guy you've been all squidgy and secretive about for the past few months."

"Didn't want to jinx it," she says. "Was waiting to see if it was the real deal."

"And?" I prod.

Kent shrugs. "Eh, we'll see what happens in college."

Mallory smacks him. "You tell her it's the real deal."

Kent says, "No," while nodding his head yes.

We all circulate and catch up, yet I'm drawn to the interaction between Kent and Mallory. In so many ways, this pairing makes perfect sense. I wonder if they'll make it after they leave North Shore?

And then I wonder what making it would even look like.

Because they're together and happy in the present; the future really doesn't matter; right now is enough.

A bit later, we're called into the theater and we sit. Mallory's in the middle between Kent and me. Theo's on my left and Owen's to Kent's right. Mum blows me a kiss from the seats Owen reserved for them and my dad puts his arm around her. Returning to England was the right call and we've sorted ourselves out again as a family, which is such a relief.

I'm not meant to be a rebel.

The lights dim and the curtain rises. I take Theo's hand as Mallory reaches for mine. Glancing back and forth, I see our whole row is connected, all of us holding on to each other, grasping hands or linking arms, not because we have to, but because we can.

The film begins with a long shot of the school, with white text scrolling over the green of the lawn and ivy-covered walls. I laugh when I realize that *of course* Owen would go for a *Star Wars IV* crawl-opening.

Of course he would.

The print on the screen reads:

To Whom It May Concern:

When you grow up in North Shore, there's a sentiment that you're not allowed to have problems, that you can't be sad. That nothing can go wrong.

From the outside, you'd swear we lived charmed lives.

451

But just because we look like we have it all doesn't mean that we feel like it. There's a degree of pressure on us in North Shore that outsiders would never suspect.

Our parents grew up watching John Hughes's movie **The Breakfast Club.** *When our folks were young, it was enough just to be Brian the brain or Claire the homecoming queen or Andy the jock, but now they expect us to embody all those traits concurrently.*

That's a lot to ask.

And for some of us? Sometimes?

It's just too much.

Sincerely yours,

The scrolling text ends with the movie's title coming up on screen:

THE
GATEKEEPERS

★ ★ ★ ★ ★

AUTHOR'S NOTE

IN 2012, THREE promising Lake Forest High School students ended their lives by stepping in front of commuter trains. The losses came in rapid succession, first in January, then February, then April. My hometown of Lake Forest, Illinois, became the focus of national news as the media attempted to make sense of the story.

But how could anyone make sense of the senseless, especially as my town was a microcosm of the rest of the country?

How could anyone find a way to explain the more than five thousand *daily* teen suicide attempts in this nation?

And how could anyone rationalize that which takes more young adult lives than cancer, heart disease, AIDS, birth defects, stroke, pneumonia, influenza, and chronic lung disease, collectively?

To be honest, I avoided much of the 2012 coverage. I didn't seek out answers. I wasn't looking for clarity. I didn't need to learn everything to protect my own teens because I don't have children.

All I wanted was to bury my head in the sand and pretend

none of this had happened. The events were simply too sad to contemplate.

By trade, I'm a humor writer so I tend to eschew that which isn't uplifting or funny or lends itself to a punch line. I perpetually aim for the Hollywood happy ending, impossible given the circumstances. And, selfishly, I didn't want to think of my pretty little town as anything less than perfect. In my head, Lake Forest was the bucolic gem I'd fallen in love with watching all those John Hughes movies so many years ago. I didn't want to imagine something unseemly roiling under the surface of its pristine exterior.

Unlike the fictional town of North Shore, the city of Lake Forest has been incredibly proactive in attempting to prevent teen suicide and the community wholeheartedly supports these efforts. After thirty-three teen suicides in an eighteen-month period back in the early 1980s, the city established a youth center called CROYA (Committee Representing Our Young Adults) to safeguard our most precious commodities. The Gates Community Center in this book is based on the real-life good work done by CROYA.

And yet we've still lost some of our best and brightest here in Lake Forest.

Senseless.

That's why for me, denial was the easiest way to deal with every heartbreaking article, each tear-jerking story. There are those who run toward the burning building of raw emotion, but I'm not that person. In that respect, Mallory is a part of me, as we both trend toward action over sentiment.

Because I'm not good with processing sorrow, I knew that if I dwelled in the stories, if I really dug in and tried to understand them, my sadness would morph to anger. I didn't want to be the jerk speculating about people I'd never met and situations that didn't involve me, so I detached, opting not to use my platform to inform or educate or enlighten.

Not long after the tragedies, I was invited to Purdue, my alma mater, to lecture freshmen classes for a day. After spending ten minutes with the students, I realized the speech I'd prepared was absolutely irrelevant. My message had been drawn from my checkered academic career, titled *Cs Get Degrees.* I'd gone down there with the intention of making students feel better about slacking in college, as my life/career were living proof that how you start the race is irrelevant; what matters is how you finish.

Instead, I learned that no one was having fun on campus, no one dared slack, not even for a minute. Cs might get degrees but they sure as hell wouldn't get a job come graduation.

I met students from all over the country that day (even some from my sleepy Indiana hometown) and every one of them had the same story—that campus was a pressure cooker and the competition they'd all faced in high school had simply intensified in college.

I returned home with two thoughts: (a) that I'd never be admitted to Purdue today, and (b) that it's so much less fun to be eighteen than it was in 1985.

The visit entirely changed my perspective on what it's like to grow up now, particularly on Chicago's North Shore. Here I'd been envious of the kids who'd been raised with so much opportunity, only to discover that the opportunity came at a cost.

A couple of years later, while working on a deadline for another light memoir with a happy ending, I learned that a college friend's son had committed suicide.

Her boy was smart and handsome and athletic, the star player on his football team. He had tons of friends and came from a loving, supportive family, with a pack of younger brothers who thought he hung the moon.

Yet even with everything going for him, even with his family's support, even with what he'd achieved and a limitless future stretching before him, he couldn't outrun the depression that lied to him, that told him the only way through was out.

More than seven hundred people showed up for his funeral.

Despite being surrounded by all that love in his life, my friend's son still felt alone.

Even though I'd never met her son, his life and death left an indelible impression on me. I couldn't remain in denial about the pressures his peers are facing.

I couldn't stand by and do nothing.

I couldn't remain detached.

I had to do something. To say something.

I chose to live in Lake Forest because this was John Hughes's hometown. His movies were a love letter to my generation. Through his films, he told us that he understood what we were going through, that our feelings were real and valid and important. He didn't always have solutions, but that didn't matter; what mattered is that he listened.

He made sure we knew that we were not alone.

Because of his inspiration, this book is my love letter to *your* generation.

What you're going through is real.

What you're feeling is important.

You are heard.

And you deserve your Hollywood happy ending.

RESOURCES

Suicide Prevention Lifeline:
(800) 273-8255
https://suicidepreventionlifeline.org/

Society for the Prevention of Teen Suicide:
http://www.sptsusa.org/you-are-not-alone/

American Association for Suicidology:
http://www.suicidology.org
American Foundation for Suicide Prevention:
https://afsp.org

Grant Halliburton Foundation:
http://www.granthalliburton.org

The Jason Foundation:
http://jasonfoundation.com

The Dave Nee Foundation:
http://www.daveneefoundation.org

Depression and Bipolar Support Alliance:
http://www.dbsalliance.org

Teen Mental Health:
http://teenmentalhealth.org

ACKNOWLEDGMENTS

WHO GETS TOP billing here? Which person do I praise first? Do I express my undying gratitude to my agent Jess Regel of Foundry Literary + Media for persuading me to give voice to Kent, Owen, and Stephen? Or, do I offer my boundless thanks to editor Natashya Wilson of Harlequin Teen—my very own Rick Rubin—and the person who pushed me so far beyond my boundaries as a writer? The Gatekeepers exists in this form, thanks to the ministrations of these two brilliant women, and the words "thank you" can't properly express my level of appreciation. I wish I could send both of you miniature ponies or baby goats or whatever is the most cute and awesome thing one could ship via UPS.

I want to send out big love to the entire team at Harlequin Teen, from sales to marketing to art to copyediting. You all made publishing a pleasure again, every one of you, first winning me over with a PowerPoint and then impressing me every step of the way. Your systems, your attitudes, your dedication, and your attention to detail are second to none. Your support has been invaluable and I feel so lucky to be working with each one of you. Particular thanks go to Siena Koncsol in publicity—your enthusiasm is contagious!

I'm so grateful to for the feedback from my first readers, Quinn and Anneke. Spot-freaking-on. And a million thanks for beta testers Joanna Schiferl, Alyson Ray, Laurie Dolan, Tracey Stone, Rebecca Goodman, and Lisa and Becca Lappi. You are the best! For Gina Barge, thanks in perpetuity, especially for allowing me the surreal opportunity to bring cupcakes to Chuck D and to make him laugh. (If you don't know, now you know...kitten.)

I've been blessed by the support of other authors, in particular Amy Hatvany, Stephanie Elliott, Lisa Steinke, and Liz Fenton. You all make "girl power" a thing and I'm so lucky to know you. (And even luckier to read you!)

Over the course of this book, I've had the honor of spending time with a number of Lake Forest police officers. Tremendous credit goes to Chief Waldorf for assembling such a dream team and to Sgt. Brett Marquette for his outstanding community outreach. Great thanks to everything the LFPD does to keep this town safe. You've been there on the front lines when life has gone awry for our most vulnerable and I'm perpetually impressed by your care and compassion. I can only hope that what I've learned from you in the course of writing this book will in some small way make your jobs easier.

Finally, and for always and forever, for Fletch.